THE GENERATION KILLER

ADAM SIMCOX

This edition first published in 2023 by Gollancz
First published in Great Britain in 2022 by Gollancz
an imprint of The Orion Publishing Group Ltd
Carmelite House, 50 Victoria Embankment
London EC4Y 0DZ

An Hachette UK Company

1 3 5 7 9 10 8 6 4 2

A CIP catalogue record for this book is
available from the British Library.

ISBN (Mass Market Paperback) 978 1 473 23080 4
ISBN (eBook) 978 1 473 23081 1

Typeset by Input Data Services Ltd, Somerset

Printed in Great Britain by Clays Ltd, Elcograf S.p.A

www.gollancz.co.uk

To Kirsty, Alife and Oscar – the original squad.

Prologue

Summer had judged Manchester, and had found it wanting.

It bloated its concrete and scorched its roads, constipating its buildings with sweat and fury. Storm clouds squatted overhead, refusing Mancunian pleas to break or leave. Rain was as familiar to Manchester as a kissing cousin, but it had become timorous, reluctant to shower the city in its sopping wet smooches.

On the sixth day, God created MANchester; that was what the locals claimed. Such was the pent-up charge in the city, those locals were beginning to wonder why He had bothered.

Most were, anyway. Others were like Megan, who used the long days and bijou nights as a passport to delve into the city's nooks and crannies, to document every last cobbled stone and neglected alley. She worked alone and celebrated that fact. Her art didn't invite collaboration; in fact, it actively discouraged it.

There were exceptions, of course. From time to time, a wandering soul would catch her eye and jolt her muse. That was what had happened on her latest project.

It promised to be her most exceptional yet.

The last of the day's sunshine barged its way into Megan's flat, but she left the light on anyway. It was always on. Her ragtag collection of foster parents had always chastised her for it, but they'd never had to endure the screaming night terrors that she had. The light stayed on. Always.

She trudged into her bedroom, flopping down onto the bed and letting her eyes wander over the dozens of photographs pinned to the walls. The Lads Club in Salford. The Victoria Baths. Granada Studios. Manchester Town Hall. The frame of them all *just so*, an ongoing series that was missing one final location.

'I can hear you, you know,' she said.

'How?' replied a boy's voice.

'I can hear you breathing.'

'I'm not breathing.'

'Everyone breathes.'

'Not me.'

'Come out then,' she said, 'and stop *not breathing* in the shadows.'

A dead boy emerged from next to the wardrobe.

Thirteen or thereabouts, he wore an old-fashioned green blazer, grey shorts, a mucky white shirt and a stained black tie. A buzz cut of ginger hair completed the picture.

'We talked about this, George. You can't just keep breaking into my flat.'

'This is important, though.'

'So are boundaries. You hiding in my bedroom is breaking them.'

'I was going to wait outside, like you said,' George replied, 'but then I found it, and I got too excited.'

'You found what?'

'The arches, Megs. I've found the arches.'

Megan subconsciously gripped the camera that bounced against her chest, suspended by a leather strap around the back of her neck. She checked the camera's shutter count. It read zero, as it should; she'd thrown in a new roll of film just before she'd left the house. Still, if George really had found the arches, it paid to be sure. She didn't work digitally. Her work relied on a special sort of film that only one developer in the world made. No second chances; you got the shot, or you didn't.

'It's just up here,' said George, pointing to the canal footpath ahead of them.

The arches were an urban myth, a bauble offered up to hunters of lost Mancunian legends. A few smudgy photos of them nestled on urban explorer websites, most looking as much like derelict toilets as a town hidden beneath a city. That, ultimately, was what the arches were: a suburb of long-abandoned shops, built deep within Manchester's bowels to service the city's inhabitants as they hid from Hitler's bombs in World War II.

Certainly if anyone was capable of finding them it was George. It was one of the unsaid things between them; his ability to get anywhere and everywhere was one Megan gently exploited. She consoled herself with the fact that he seemed to love it. It gave him purpose.

'Keep up,' he called as he reached the pathway, beckoning her with an insistent hand.

Night had settled but had neglected to tell the temperature, which sweltered stubbornly, licking Megan's back like you would a stamp. There was something in the air that she didn't like. It felt spiteful, like it was laughing at her.

She was close, though. She could feel it.

She scratched at the birthmark on the back of her hand, picking off the fresh scab. She knew she shouldn't, but it calmed her when nothing else would.

'It's through here,' said George.

She saw a circular pipe. Mulch was smeared on its lips,

darkness draped around its mouth. It didn't look to be much more than four foot high.

'You've been down there?' she said.

'Course. How'd I know it was down there otherwise?'

Megan frowned. 'You never said anything about a pipe. There's no other way?'

George shook his head. 'This is it.'

She nodded, reluctantly shifting on her feet, moving closer to the pipe. A faint red glow came from some undetermined point in its depths. She could fit. She'd need to duck, then crawl, but she'd fit.

'*Hello?*'

Her voice was snatched by the tunnel, passed from side to side, losing strength with each hand-off.

'What are you doing?' said George.

'Trying to judge how deep that thing goes.'

Very, by the sound of it.

She took another couple of steps closer, steeling herself, wavering.

'I'll go first,' said George. 'Follow me.'

He pulled himself up, grunting with the effort, then turned back to her. 'You coming?'

Megan gripped the pipe's upper lip and swung herself upwards. A blast of cold, dank air greeted her. Normally it would have been a relief from the heat outside, but there was nothing normal about this situation, and certainly no relief. This was what you had to do, though, to get the shot. Any artist of any worth had to suffer for their art at some point.

George stopped, turning around, his head grazing the top of the tunnel. 'I can't wait for you to see it.'

Megan nodded, squashed down her fear and began to shuffle into the guts of the pipe.

★

4

'How much further?' said Megan.

George didn't reply. Instead he stopped, rising to his full height and putting his hands on his hips. As she reached him, Megan did the same.

The pipe had spat them out into an alcove that looked down upon a cathedral of tiles. It reminded her of a pantomime she'd been taken to as a girl; she'd been treated to a box seat, and she was afforded a similar vantage point here. Instead of a stage, though, there was a metal gurney in the centre of the room. A large hypodermic needle hovered over it. Mucus-infested tiles stretched off in every direction. Water roared in the distance.

He's behind you; that was what she'd screamed along with the other pantomime-goers.

He's behind you.

She turned.

He wasn't. No one was. Only the pipe and its selfish darkness.

She frowned. A few feet to her left was some sort of desk. Or control desk, to have it right; it looked ancient, like something out of a comic book. Rust bubbled from its surface, and pools of dank water lay around it.

There was an insignia on it. Megan leaned in to take a closer look.

A cross had been emblazoned on the desk's base.

A swastika. What the hell is a piece of Nazi machinery doing in a Manchester dungeon?

'Come over here a second, George.'

'This isn't even the best bit,' said George.

'I'm sure,' said Megan, 'but I want to get a picture of this desk. You've been in all the other shots. Can't break the tradition now.'

George looked over his shoulder, sighed, then reluctantly obeyed, perching himself against the control desk.

'Smile.'

He didn't, but Megan took the picture anyway.

George led her down a flight of stone steps, across the centre of the room (Megan was careful to skirt around the table and the needle that sat above it) and into a clammy, low-ceilinged corridor. Water spewed all around them, like a sprinkler vomiting mould. Small dishes leaked light from the ceiling. The outlines of door frames were etched into the sides of the tunnel. An ancient-looking telephone was bolted to the opposite wall, a prop from civilisation that looked utterly out of place here.

Megan's finger pushed down on the camera's button, firing off a machine gun's worth of shots.

I could do an exhibition on just this place, she thought. It's incredible.

'Really good stuff's through here,' said George, pointing at a rusty steel door ahead of them.

Although it wasn't really a door, Megan thought, more an impression of one. Its imprint could be seen in the tiles, like someone had drawn a pencil outline on a planning sketch. The door stood half open, a strange staccato light seeping out.

'What is that?' said Megan.

'Hard to explain,' said George. 'Easier just to show you.'

He slipped through the doorway, disappearing from sight.

I don't like this, thought Megan. Something's off. Maybe it's the Nazi desk in the other room: big-arse red flag right there. That, and the serial killer's operating theatre.

Plus, there's the light coming from the room in front of me. How?

I should get out of here.

She stayed where she was, though, her toes tipped for flight, her camera clutched tightly in her hands, her palms sweaty.

I *should* get out of here, but then I'll never know what's in that room. And what's in that room could be the defining shot of my career, the truth that we're all seeking.

A muffled sound behind the door. Tinny. Insistent. Familiar somehow.

Taking a deep breath, Megan opened it.

It was as if someone had set up a home cinema room in a sewer.

George sat quietly, cross-legged, facing a wall. Next to him was an old projector. It whirred noisily as it passed reams of film through its innards, throwing a smeary image onto the wall in front of it.

The image showed a boy sitting on a chair in a pure white room. He was dressed in a surgical smock, and his legs were so short his feet didn't touch the floor. They swung to and fro above it. The balloon he held in his hand seemed absurd, its redness a cut lip against the room's white backdrop.

'What is this, George?' said Megan. 'What is this place?'

He turned to her, placing a finger against his lips. 'Shush. It's about to start.'

A woman's voice began speaking.

'Day three, test subject Walter Truman. How are you feeling today, Walter?'

The boy — Walter, Megan assumed — stared directly at the camera. 'I didn't sleep too good.'

What the hell is this? Some sort of live theatre shit? Is someone playing a joke on me here?

'You didn't sleep too *well*,' said the woman's voice, off-screen, 'not *too good*. The correct sentence would have been *I didn't sleep too well*.'

The boy nodded, clutching the balloon a little tighter to him.

'Why is it that you didn't sleep well?'

'Saw them again. When the lights went out.'

'You saw who?'

'The man and woman.'

'Describe what the man and woman looked like, Walter.'

Walter scratched at his arm, an action that released the balloon. It drifted away from him, floating towards the ceiling. He reached for it.

'Leave the balloon, Walter,' said the woman. 'Tell us about the man and woman.'

Walter pouted. 'Don't want to.'

'Why not?'

''Cos I don't like thinking about them. They're scary.'

'What's scary about them, Walter?'

'Don't like their faces.'

'Why don't you like their faces?'

'They look like trees.'

'How so?'

'Got leaves on them.'

'What do they say to you, these people?'

'Weird things.'

'Weird things?'

'Like they're confused. They don't know who they are. They can't remember.'

'That *is* weird,' said the woman off-screen. 'Can you see them now?'

The boy shook his head. 'Wears off by the morning.'

'I see.'

The sound of a door opening could be heard. A man in a surgical gown and mask walked into frame. He held a syringe in his hand.

The boy drew up his feet, wrapping his arms around his legs, trying, it seemed to Megan, to make himself smaller.

'Now, Walter,' said the woman. 'You know it only hurts for a moment.'

'Always hurts,' said Walter, his voice only just audible. 'And it makes me see the tree people.'

'They won't hurt you,' said the woman's voice, her on-screen colleague reaching out and taking Walter's arm.

He inserted the needle quickly, his thumb pressing down on the plunger, then swiftly withdrawing it.

Walter put his head between his knees and began to cry.

'Are they in there with you now, Walter?' came the voice off-screen. 'Do you see them? Describe them to us.'

'No,' Walter mumbled, his arms still wrapped around his head.

The balloon floating above him popped, making the gowned man flinch.

'They're here, aren't they, Walter?' There was a hint of excitement in the woman's voice. 'Describe them to me.'

The man in the surgical gown grabbed Walter's head and forced open his eyes.

Walter looked into the distance. He began to scream.

The projector clunked to a stop, and the image warped.

Megan realised she hadn't taken a breath.

George turned to her. 'He wanted you to see that.'

A chill massaged Megan's back. 'Who did?'

'I'm sorry,' said George.

'You're sorry for what?

He's behind you, screamed a voice in her head, just as though she was back at the pantomime.

He's behind you.

Megan swallowed.

She turned.

He was.

Part One

The dead won't bother you, it's the living you have to worry about.

John Wayne Gacy

Serial killers suck.

Daisy-May Braithwaite

Chapter One

'Move,' said Daisy-May. 'Just fucking *move*, would you?'

The stuffed pink bear in the chair opposite didn't, mainly because it was a stuffed pink bear. Daisy-May could have believed there was a mocking look in its beady plastic eyes, though, one that said *I'll move when I'm ready, and maybe not even then.*

'Bastard bear. Don't you know who I am? I'm the Warden of the Pen, the queen of fucking purgatory, and when I say move, you move.'

She waved a hand at the bear. The bear didn't wave back.

'Is it 'cos I'm young? You think just 'cos I'm a teenage sensation, that gives you the right to blank me? No, mate, I'm not having that. The Duchess didn't care about my age. She thought I had the right stuff, so who are you to say otherwise?'

The bear stared implacably back at her.

What was she doing wrong? The Duchess had been able to move things with her mind (had, she'd told Daisy-May, on one occasion broken the mythical Xylophone Man's neck with the merest flick of a finger), because that sort of power came with the job. The Duchess had assured Daisy-May it would be the same for her.

But then she'd assured her of many things. Lied to her about many more.

13

Like how Daisy-May had been murdered up above — on the soil — and who'd done the murdering.

Focus, you silly cow, she told herself. Stop picking at the scabs of the past, and focus.

She leaned forward, her face inches from the bear, her arm stretched towards it, then closed her eyes, visualising the bear hovering out of its seat, just as the Duchess had taught her.

'Move,' said Daisy-May. '*Move.*'

She opened her eyes and yelped in triumph as the bear hovered in the air, its furry body tilting slightly to the left, as if tipsy and making its way home.

She beckoned to it with her outstretched hand and it began to inch forward, before picking up pace and sailing straight past her.

She turned to see an elderly man standing at the entrance to her office. He was holding the bear, a small smile on his face, like he was sharing a joke with the stuffed toy.

'That was you controlling it, Remus?' asked Daisy-May.

Remus chuckled. 'I picked up the odd trick from the Duchess over the years.'

'Ma'am. You picked up the odd trick from the Duchess, *ma'am.*'

The man bowed his head, his thinning greased-back hair doing a poor job of hiding the crown of scabs on the top of his head. 'Quite right, ma'am. It's easy to forget one's manners when you get to my ripe old age. Not something you're burdened with, of course.'

Daisy-May glowered. 'Pretty dark over here, Remus, with all that shade you're throwing.'

'I'm sure I don't know what you mean,' said Remus, nibbling at his bloodied lower lip.

Course you don't, thought Daisy-May. You're just a lost little lamb. The sort that's got wolf's teeth you won't hesitate to use.

Remus was a fixture of the Pen, the prize or punishment for those unfortunate enough to be tasked with ruling the realm. He'd been the number two to the Warden since whatever came before time immemorial, and Daisy-May knew she should value his counsel and take advantage of the thousands of years of experience he possessed.

Something about him bothered her, though.

It's 'cos he's a straight-up snob. Always looks at me like I'm going to pinch the silver.

Take the uniform change. One of Daisy-May's first orders of business had been to dispose of the starched, fascist-lite uniform of the Pen. 'Always reminds me of the SS,' she'd explained to Remus. 'If this regime's going to be kinder, the uniform's going to be kinder too.' Remus had flinched like she'd slapped his ancient cheeks (face *and* arse) when he'd seen the punk stylings she had in mind. It was under the Duchess's regime that existence itself had almost ended, the millions of Dispossessed (a nice word for a purgatorial subclass of people who had been abused and looked down upon over the centuries) in the Pen rising up in revolt. If a skinny tie and drainpipe jeans were part of that never happening again, then so be it.

It wasn't just the uniform change Remus held in disdain, though; it seemed to Daisy-May that he reserved his ire for everything she did. It wasn't in what he said, but what he didn't: a raised eyebrow at one new policy suggestion, a weak smile and a strong shake of the head at another.

He didn't so much kill her with kindness as drive-by-shoot her with understated disapproval.

And he could move things with his mind. He was every inch Warden material, and what was she? A shit-kicker girl from a shit-kicker family, from a shit-kicker council estate. Someone who'd never chased power, but had caught up with it anyway.

That's why I chose you, the Duchess would have said. *It's because you didn't chase it, and you weren't born into it. There'll always be a hundred Remuses in any organisation, and you're worth a thousand of them. Don't you forget it.*

She'd try not to. Her imposter syndrome had other plans.

'What can I do for you, Remus?'

'There's something you need to see.'

Daisy-May didn't doubt it. When you were the boss, there was always something you needed to see, and usually something even more important that you needed to do.

'Is it Hanna? Has she found her?'

Remus shook his head. 'There is no word from the Duchess, and when it comes to Hanna, no news is good news.'

'Never realised you were so glass-half-full, Remus.'

Remus smiled. 'If you'd let me send more of our operatives to the soil, we'd have a greater chance of finding her. That girl has already almost toppled existence once; the damage she could do on the soil, unchecked, isn't worth thinking about.'

'It's my job to think about it,' said Daisy-May, 'and there's no badder bitch than the Duchess. She'll find her, and when she does, she'll take her down.'

'If you say so. Ma'am.'

'I do,' said Daisy-May. 'If it's not Hanna, what do you want?'

Remus led her out onto the main gantry. A dozen or so video screens glowed with crime scenes from around the world, ones that her Dying Squad of paranormal investigators should have been en route to, and would have been if the tunnel separating the living and the dead hadn't been so mortally poisoned. Her team below, stuffed into the bowels of the command centre, noted the details of the crimes then sat on their frustrated hands, the sense of inertia growing all the time.

Daisy-May balled her fists up, trying to knead out the uncertainty. 'What am I looking at?'

Remus pointed at the top right-hand screen. It showed a gaggle of men and women in yellow jumpsuits encircling a body on the floor.

'Are they police?' asked Daisy-May.

'Soil police, yes,' Remus replied. 'They're not who made the request for us, though.'

Daisy-May whistled. 'We have a pickup?'

'We have a pickup. And that's not all.'

Remus told Daisy-May what *that's not all* entailed.

She nodded along.

When he stopped talking, she started thinking.

'Where's Joe Lazarus?' she said, finally.

It had been a while since Joe had been involved in an old-school stake-out.

He couldn't say he'd missed them much.

The last one had involved a Lincolnshire farmhouse and a string of dead bodies that included his own; he hoped this one would be easier, in the *surprise, you're dead* stakes.

At least it didn't involve squatting in a ditch.

What it did involve was a craggy clump of rocks overlooking one of the newly developed Dispossessed townships.

They'd changed, the Dispossessed. Whether that was for better or for worse was a matter of debate as far as Joe was concerned, but one thing was undeniable: they'd evolved from the confused, brain-muted half-souls he'd first encountered in the Pen. Since they'd risen up against the Duchess – and since Daisy-May had managed to talk them down, and sell a more inclusive afterlife for them – their intelligence had developed at a frightening pace.

Why that was was a matter of some debate amongst the Dying Squad intelligentsia, but Joe thought he knew: it was because of the kindness shown by Daisy-May. That intelligence had always been there; it had just needed someone like the Pen's new Warden to recognise it, then bring it out.

'Time's fucking dragging, man. How long do we have to stay here for?'

Of course, intelligent didn't always mean polite.

Joe shifted on his stomach, levering himself with his elbow. His new partner was to his left, having adopted a similar on-the-belly position. Tall and lean like a crash-diet whippet, Bits (a nickname Joe had objected then eventually succumbed to) twitched sporadically, animated by a dozen different ghost drugs in his system.

'That really depends on you, doesn't it?' said Joe. 'This is your lead we're following.'

'Not my anything,' said Bits. 'Heard tell of the bloke, that's all. Know this is his patch, and know sooner or later that he'll be along.'

'Well, that's three things more than I know,' said Joe, turning back, raising the binoculars once more, 'and that means we stake out this patch until we get a glimpse of him.'

'Could be hours,' said Bits.

'Could be days,' said Joe. 'That's the job, and you're lucky to have it.'

'Feel lucky,' said Bits, 'lying next to you, with rocks sneaking up my arse.'

'There's a chain of command here,' said Joe, 'and I'd ask you to remember that.'

'Fuck-all chance of forgetting it,' mumbled Bits.

Joe grimaced, biting his tongue. He tried to remind himself that there were worse things than a dawn raid with an insubordinate colleague. Not that dawn (or any other time of day) really existed in the Pen. *Night* simply meant black and red volcano clouds, *day* grey and red. The light never changed – it was watery, like it couldn't get up the courage to be one thing or the other – and dawn? Well, that was just a squelchy mishmash of the two. Still, it was better than the Pit, a hell Daisy-May had been good enough to release him from.

It was better than that.

'That's him.'

Joe looked to where Bits was pointing. A male member of the Dispossessed, head down and hands scrunched into the pockets of his black trench coat, was walking amongst the smattering of cabins and huts below them, looking around him as if he suspected some sort of imminent attack. He stopped at the last building on the right, a spooned-out dollop of concrete at the end of the street, knocked on the door and waited.

'You're sure?' said Joe.

Bits nodded. 'That's Zed.'

'And you're sure that's his name? Because it sounds more like a cleaning brand.'

'We catch him, you can ask him for a birth certificate,' said Bits.

Joe took a breath. 'All right then. Are you ready for this?'

Bits said that he was.

Joe doubted that – your first dawn raid was never something you were really ready for, particularly if you were a newbie (and a Dispossessed newbie at that), but he supposed he'd have to take Bits's word for it.

Joe slowly withdrew a gun he had no intention of using and stood listening at the concrete hut's shabby, flimsy door. There was a murmur of clicks and whirls, a sure sign that Dispossessed were inside. He had submitted to a crash course in the language over the last few months (it was pretty difficult to train a Dispossessed task force if you couldn't understand them) but he struggled to make out any specific words. He'd let his knowledge of the language slide because of Bits's fluent

English – it was one of the reasons he had been chosen for the task force in the first place.

He counted down to Bits with his fingers.

Three.

Two.

One.

Now.

His foot connected with the door, splintering through it easily.

'Dying Squad,' he yelled. 'Everyone on the floor, *now*.'

It was several seconds before he could truly appreciate the horror of what he was seeing.

The room was like some sort of Victorian back-street abortion clinic. Blood, dried black, stained the walls, crusting it like wallpaper. Zed, the male member of the Dispossessed they'd been tailing, stood with a female counterpart next to a crude metal gurney that rested in the middle of the room. Both were covered in blood fresher than that which decorated the walls, and both carried crude metal instruments that could have passed for torture devices if Joe hadn't known what they were really intended for.

The true horror was saved for the woman on the gurney, though. She lay unconscious, her insides splayed open with a rusty metal clamp.

Like a bear trap, thought Joe.

Zed and the woman turned towards him, their shimmer betraying their Dispossessed status. Zed froze, but his colleague didn't. She shoved the metal gurney towards Joe, spilling the opened-up woman from it; it slammed into Joe's knees and knocked him backwards.

'Go!' she yelled to Zed, a click and whistle Joe could have understood even without his recent language lessons. Just as he began to lever himself up, the woman landed, knee first, on his stomach. She reached for the gun, but he was too quick for her; he swung it upwards, driving the handle into her forehead. Her head snapped back and then Bits was there, hauling her off, pinning her arm behind her shoulder.

The woman unleashed a string of high-pitched screams at Joe's new partner.

'What's she saying?' said Joe.

'She says I'm scum,' said Bits. 'Says I'm a traitor to my kin.'

The woman spat in Bits's face.

Joe glowered at her, then reached over, wiping away the spit with the cuff of his sleeve as the woman continued to struggle.

'This bloke here's a credit to his kin, not a traitor to it,' he said to her. 'Bits, you, me, we're all the same. The Warden wants us to be equal; that means paying the price when you fuck up, as well as reaping the rewards when you don't.'

He turned to his partner. 'Cuff her. I'm going after Zed.'

As Joe raced through the back door into a vista of sprawling half-soul humanity, he knew that *going after Zed* was a lot easier to say than to actually do.

The Pen was a teeming anthill of souls – millions of them – and although there was more structure to it than when he'd first arrived, with settlements, houses and cabins like the one he'd just stormed into, it was still the Wild West. And like the Wild West, losing yourself was the easiest thing in the world to do. That was why he'd brought the gun.

He held it out in front of him, his left hand steadying his right arm, one eye squeezed shut, the fleeing Zed still in range, if only just. His finger tensed on the trigger.

He fired, ready for the kickback, his left hand gripping his right.

If that misses, he's gone, thought Joe. No way will I find him in amongst all those bodies.

He squinted as the bullet – although in truth it was more of a homing pigeon – arced towards its prey, then found its target. There was an explosion of colour, and a mushroom cloud of pink erupted into the sky.

He allowed himself a smile. *Try hiding from us with that shit following you around. It's like the conscience you didn't know you had.*

He began sprinting towards the cloud. It would follow Zed wherever he went for the next hour, and although he would have preferred something more definitive (such as the gun he'd used the last time he'd ventured to the living, breathing world of the soil), he believed Daisy-May had it right. She'd decreed that non-lethal force be used against the Dispossessed, knowing that the temporary peace she'd brokered wouldn't last too long if the authorities started shooting the underclass.

Dead bodies weren't great at offering up leads or confessions, either.

The cloud moved left and right over the throng of Dispossessed, and Joe dived into them, his eyes flicking upwards to follow the trail. They'd been after Zed for days, lifting stones and kicking over woodpiles, and he'd be damned if they were going to lose him now. It felt good to be chasing down leads and the miscreants at the end of them. It felt good to be making a difference again – he hoped.

The cloud pitched right and Joe squeezed past a woman and her child in response, colliding with an old man as a result. He would have liked to stop and pick him up, to explain why catching this scumbag was so important, why his carelessness wasn't just another example of brutality against the Dispossessed. It was vital he follow the fleeing Zed, though, because he was the only lead he had, on a case that had consistently confounded him.

It was two months to the day since the first mutilated Dispossessed body had turned up.

If it had just been one, maybe no one would have noticed. But it was a string of them, shredded to pieces, spread across townships in the Downs. As horrific as the killings were, Joe had argued that it wasn't the purview of the Dying Squad; they were needed on the soil, solving crimes the living police couldn't. Daisy-May had shot back that as their route to the soil was currently impossible, due to the poisoned Gloop, they needed to get their arses in gear and find out who was behind the killings.

She'd been right. It was a way to blood his new Dispossessed partner, and it was a problem to solve; he'd got the mystery in his nostrils and he wouldn't rest until he caught the killer. It was the nature of the killings that intrigued; the Dispossessed's bodies had been taken apart in an almost surgical manner. Not skilled, admittedly – Joe doubted whether the killer was going to be co-opted into surgical private practice any time soon – but it went beyond a regular frenzied killing. The first body they'd found had reminded him of a ripped-apart motor in a back-street chop shop; the male Dispossessed's chest had been torn open, the steel clamp still affixed. His instincts had told him that this wasn't a regular killing. His eyes did a good job of telling him that, too.

They hadn't worked out where the actual killings were taking place, though: all they had was the aftermath. That was, until Bits had come through. His Dispossessed status meant he heard tittle-tattle Joe and Daisy-May were deaf to. He'd got a lead that a man called Zed was involved, which had led them to stake out his homestead. The scene they'd come across – and the fact that Zed had run a mile when they'd raided the place – suggested the lead had been solid.

Joe supposed they shouldn't be surprised by this fucked-up state of affairs. Freedom and the Dispossessed's burgeoning intelligence meant they had the potential to become as depraved and corrupt as everybody else.

It could be they had the first Dispossessed serial killer on their hands.

It could be something else, though. Something bigger, that he couldn't see yet. The woman at the kill sight spoke to that. Any time there was a gang of fucked-up people, there was usually a scumbag at the top orchestrating them.

He should know.

He'd been that scumbag.

The crowd parted when they saw who he was, then reacted accordingly.

An elbow flung into the side of Joe's head felled him, the gun tumbling out of his hand and instantly spirited away.

A kick connected with his back, slamming him to the ground.

He felt a hundred eyes on him, the crowd's energy quickening, like they were sharks in the water and he was trailing blood. If this turned any nastier, it would be over quickly for him. The crowd stayed where they were, barely restraining themselves, the whole thing on a precipice.

He climbed carefully to his feet. He saw the pink cloud getting ever further away, then, in a puff of smoke, it disappeared altogether.

An hour? he thought. That thing barely lasted five minutes.

He held his arms up, a sign of peace he hoped would translate, and began backing away, smiling a smile he didn't feel.

The crowd watched him go, insolence and anger on their faces.

This wasn't going to end well.

For anyone.

Joe looked at the pulped, bloodied body of the woman he'd asked Bits to cuff. His partner stood in the corner, leaning against the wall, flexing his fists. 'She went for my keys. Swear down, she left me no choice.'

'Cuffed, and she left you no choice?'

'I know her type. You don't. Give her an opening, she'd have sliced me up. Look at the body on the floor.'

Joe crouched down next to the woman they'd found in the makeshift operating theatre. The metal clamp on her chest had been ripped away, making it seem like something had eaten its way out of there. He looked back to their unconscious, bloodied prisoner. 'You've just beaten a suspect senseless. One who was in our custody.'

Bits laughed, a parched, croaking yelp. 'Custody? What do you think this world is?'

Joe got to his feet and took a step towards him. 'I think this world is one I know, and you don't.'

'Know where Zed is, then, do you?'

He squeezed his fists together, trying to work out the anger. 'Do you?'

'Happens that I do. Happens that the cuffed girl gave him up, with a bit of persuasion.'

'We don't use that kind of persuasion here.' Joe hated himself, but asked his next question anyway. 'So? Where's Zed? Where will he run to?'

Bits smirked. 'Tell you in a minute. Got something to show you first.'

'We don't have time for this,' said Joe.

'Don't have time not to.'

Bits led him to a room behind the primitive operating theatre. It was sparsely furnished; all there was, in fact, were two hulking metal suits in the centre of the room.

'What the hell are they?' said Joe, placing a hand carefully on one of the rusty metal surfaces.

'Thought you'd know,' said Bits, 'seeing as you're such a brainbox.'

'Looks like a deep-sea diving suit,' said Joe, running his hand across the flaking outer layer. 'An old, beat-to-shit one.'

'Might be old, but they've been using it for something, these Dispossessed. I'd say that means they ain't simple killers. Means there's something at play here that we can't see yet.'

'I'd say you're right,' said Joe. 'We need to catch Zed and ask him. Where's he going to be?'

'Where all Dispossessed run when people like you chase them.'

The Downs represented what the Dispossessed used to be before they realised there was more to existence than a light in the sky that would carry them to heaven.

If the reason for this acceleration of intelligence and sophistication was still something of a mystery (though Joe was sticking to his Daisy-May-showing-them-the-light theory), one thing was sure: it hadn't caught on in here. There were none of the trappings of the new settlements that had sprung up over the last couple of months; indeed, no signs of settlements at all. The Downs was essentially a rabbit warren of filth, desperation and hopelessness, and indicative of how the Dispossessed had begun to fracture into a hierarchy based on their intelligence. The more intellectually developed – the Zeds of this world – took advantage of those who were less so, but these victims still had enough intelligence to remember the life they'd left behind.

The Dispossessed here were at the very bottom of the food chain. The growing consciousness that their brethren had experienced hadn't taken with them, for some reason, and so they were content to wander from day to day, speaking a dialect so sharply native Joe couldn't begin to grasp it.

'Stinks here,' said Bits, scratching at his arm and looking around disdainfully as they walked unnoticed through the throng. 'Pure lobots, man.'

'Lobots?' said Joe.

'Lobotomised. Retards. Look at 'em. Don't know what fucking day it is. Don't know who they are, or what they were.'

'That was you not so long ago,' said Joe. 'Try using some of that humanity that's been gifted to you.' He looked at a woman and child, hand in hand, as they passed. 'Besides, you see anyone unhappy here? Seems to me you people were better off before. No one fucking each other over then. No one carrying out butcher-shop operations. I'd take simple and happy over smart and miserable any day of the week.'

Bits snorted. 'Course you would. Luxury of never having to choose either way. Tell you what, I'll crack you on the back of the head and you can slum it here for a while. See how it goes for you. These people are nothing but pigs in a sty, man.'

Joe stopped, causing Bits to follow suit.

He supposed his new partner had a point. Ignorance hadn't exactly been bliss for him when he'd first joined the Dying Squad; he'd thought himself a good man when in fact he'd been the epitome of bad. Maybe he should cut Bits a break.

'You and I have got off to a bad start,' he said.

Bits scowled at him. 'What's a good one look like?'

'We don't have to like each other, but we have to work with each other,' said Joe. 'It's what the Warden wants, so it's what's going to happen. I'm the ranking officer, and what I say goes. Do you have a problem with that?'

Bits dug his hands into his pockets and considered Joe insolently. 'Know what I was? On the soil?'

'How would I?'

'A fucking gangster, mate, a fucking wrong'un. No sniff in Manchester that I wasn't involved in on some level, no pill I didn't slip my fingers round. What do you think of that? Want a dealer as your new partner, do you? You being the ranking fucking officer?'

Joe took a step closer. 'While we're playing *tell me your truth*, what do you think I did on the soil, while I was still drawing breath as well as a cushy pension?'

Bits sniffed him like he smelled of every policeman who had ever booked him. 'Dolphin trainer?'

Joe smiled, despite himself. 'A copper, and that should make me better than you, but as bent as I was, it makes me worse. I took bungs, I nicked drugs from people like you then sold them on, and I planted evidence because it suited me to. I also happened to run one of the largest county lines gangs the country had ever seen. Oh, and I helped murder the girl you now call "guv". So by all means keep the gangster shtick going, but know this: however bad-ass you were on the soil, my soul was tar black. The only way to change that is by catching the Zeds of this world. Giving something back, even if there's no one around to take it.'

Bits frowned, looking Joe over. 'Bent copper? Surprised I couldn't smell it on you.'

'Yeah, well, I've been trying to wash the stink off.' Joe held a hand out. 'I'm a fuck-up. Like you.'

Bits looked at the offered hand, then finally shook it. 'Some of my best friends are fuck-ups.'

'Let's not get ahead of ourselves,' said Joe. 'Where do we find Zed?'

They found him in an underground pit that was a loft extension of hell.

Joe had never been there before, because no member of the Dying Squad (no member of anything but the most primitive Dispossessed collective) would have thought to look there.

It was home to a thriving community of mole-people who had never seen what passed for daylight in the Pen. The floor stretched away in endless concentric circles, hemmed in by walls that enclosed it like a beehive, the torches attached to them throwing light and shadow at anything it touched, each level crowned by a low, crumbling ceiling. The scene reminded Joe of a painting he'd seen once by some ancient Dutch painter, a surrealist nightmare grown in a lab.

Maybe he visited here. Maybe he drew it from memory. Unlikely the living could ever venture here, let alone return back to the soil, but what isn't here?

And now that I really look at it, it's not a beehive it reminds me of. It's an anthill.

A really, really fucked-up anthill.

What was a hive of identical patterns to Joe clearly meant something to Bits, as he feinted left and right, both of them stooped, the low dirt ceiling crumbling ominously onto their heads.

'What is this place?' asked Joe.

'Place where the Dispossessed first arrive in the Pen. Basic place for basic bastards. Some of them never leave. Like rabbits, right? Cosy warren. Dark, cramped, but safe from whatever's out there. People who never took a risk in the outside world, they don't start now.'

Joe shook his head. 'Never really thought about how the Dispossessed got to the Pen before.'

Bits shrugged. 'Why would you?'

'How can they stand it?' asked Joe, as his head caught the ceiling, sending another flurry of dirt onto his shoulders.

'People are people, man. What they don't know's a lot scarier than what they do. They're already dead. Enough of a shock on its own.'

'I suppose,' said Joe.

Bits held his hand up, bringing them to a stop.

Joe tried to see past his partner into the gloomy, barely lit corridor. His hand instinctively went to the backup gun he'd concealed in his ankle holster. He drew it out.

Bits beckoned him on, and Joe started shuffling forward again, trying not to let his suffocating claustrophobia overwhelm him.

Then they were out of the tunnel, falling upon a scene so vast, Joe struggled to comprehend it. Below them was a monumental cavern teeming with thousands of the Dispossessed. As the seconds went by, their numbers increased, hundreds of souls pouring through a blazing white portal. Each was covered in a slimy white substance, like foals making their way out of their mothers' womb, bumping into each other as they stumbled into their new existence.

'How are we going to find Zed in all this?' he said.

Bits smiled, hunkering down and taking in the spectacle below. 'Last time I was in the nick, before I died? Shared a cell with this Chinese lad. Smart. Spoke better English than me. We had a laugh. Anyway, night before I'm released, he tells me why he got banged up. Hasn't told no one at this point, and there's a book running on it. Most lads reckoned murder, but not me. Know a killer, me, and that wasn't Sonny. I had it down as gambling gone bad, which was as right as it was wrong.

'See, Sonny worked as a bank vault manager at the Municipal Bank of China, and he gets this idea. He'll nick two hundred thousand yuan from the vault he's supposed to be managing – 'bout fifteen grand to you and me – and buy lottery tickets with it. When he wins, he just replaces the money. Genius, right?'

'Moronic,' said Joe. 'The odds of winning the lottery in a country as large as China? Stratospheric.'

'If that means big, I'm with ya. Chinese, they buy hundreds of billions of tickets every year. Flat-out mental to think you have a chance. But get on this: Sonny fucking *wins*. He won't tell me how much, but it's Ferrari and high-class hookers big. The perfect crime, right? All he needs to do is replace the money, quit his job, then sail off into the sunset on his private yacht.

'So *obviously* he steals more money. He's clear, and more importantly rich, but the dumb bastard can't quit. And he doesn't nick some pissy fifteen grand this time – the mad bastard steals four point three million quid and blows it all on lottery tickets. That's when the luck, probability, whatever the fuck, bends him over, because he doesn't win another dollar. So, like every bad gambler in history, he doubles down. Steals another six million quid and spunks it on more tickets.

'Know how much he was left with, including the amount he originally won? Ten grand. Biggest bank robbery in Chinese history, and he had just about enough to buy a second-hand Skoda. Lucky fucker manages to get out of the country, on account of his parents living in England, but that's where the luck ends. He got banged up – hence bunking in with me – then, the way I hear it, he got shivved when he was waiting for trial. Dead within seconds. Kept tabs on him, 'cos whoever heard a story like it? Them Chinese, man. They don't forget. Get you in the end, always.'

'Probably not all of them,' said Joe. 'Seeing as it's a country of a billion and a half people.' He shifted on his feet. 'How does that relate to our runaway?'

'Zed's just like my Chinese mate: he won't take the money and quit. Couldn't if he wanted to. He'll come here, because this is where the fresh meat is. Dispossessed get funnelled here from fuck knows where, and people like Zed, they're jackals. Like to get them fresh off the boat. Most'll be too dumb and too dazed to resist.'

31

'To what end, though?' said Joe. 'Why is he snatching Dispossessed from here? Why is he cutting them up?'

Bits shrugged. 'Who knows, man. Because he can?'

Joe shook his unconvinced head. 'Even if your theory's right, how are we going to spot him amongst all this?'

Bits smirked, jabbing a finger at the crowd below. 'By opening your eyes and using them.'

Joe followed Bits's finger and saw him. Zed, standing slightly to the left of the surge, eyes open, looking for something.

And he wasn't alone.

There was a woman next to him. Blonde, short, but with a bearing that made her seem tall. As she paced back and forth beside Zed, there was something odd about her movements: they were laboured, as if she were an astronaut on the moon, fighting the lack of gravity.

There was something else strange, too.

She didn't glimmer.

Everyone in the Pen glimmered, because everyone in the Pen was dead. This woman didn't. Not that she seemed entirely three-dimensional either; her form was blurry, indistinct, as if she were a hologram beamed from another time and place.

If that had been it, Joe would still have struggled to comprehend everything he was seeing. It wasn't.

There were five members of the Dispossessed down there with Zed and the woman. All of them were clambering into bulky metal diving suits, like the ones they'd found at the chop shop. They were heading back through the white doorway of light, whereas everyone else was walking forwards, into the Pen.

That was impossible, though, because it would mean they were going back to the soil.

The woman stopped pacing, and looked up, directly at them. Joe's eyes locked with hers.

Neither flinched. Seconds felt like hours.

The woman nodded, almost to herself, then reached out for Zed and yanked him towards her. Even from this distance, Joe could see the glint of a knife in her hand.

She drew it across Zed's throat.

Zed's hands grabbed at the wound as he sank to his knees on the floor.

The woman took one final look at Joe, then backed into the blinding tunnel of light, following the last diving-suit-clad Dispossessed.

It almost looked like she was smiling.

Chapter Two

'That's impossible.'

'And yet it happened.'

'You can't go back through the tunnel, Joey. That's a one-way trip.'

'It's *Joe*, and you should tell that to this woman. She pretty much moonwalked back through it.'

'You didn't see what you thought you saw,' said Daisy-May. 'It'd be like a baby going back into the womb 'cos they didn't like how the world looked.'

'And she didn't glimmer.'

Daisy-May threw her hands up. 'It gets better. Next you'll be telling me she changed into Elvis for an encore.'

'If you love that, then you're going to love the fact that she didn't go back alone.'

Daisy-May closed her eyes. 'What?'

'She followed two of the Dispossessed down the tunnel. They were wearing these weird metal suits. Like something a deep-sea diver would have used in the 1930s or something. We found a couple of them at the crime scene.'

'I know,' said Daisy-May. 'The clean-up crew confirmed about the suits. Didn't think for a minute Dispossessed would be using them to get to the soil.'

'Maybe the woman in that room can give us some answers,' said Joe.

They were standing outside a makeshift interview room, looking through the one-way glass at Bits, who was slouched against the wall, scratching at his arms, eyeing the cuffed suspect they'd brought in. She sat in a chair opposite him, grumbling at the medics tending to her wounds.

Joe eyed Bits eyeing the woman eyeing Bits. The last time he'd left them alone, his partner had beaten information out of her; he was going to make sure that didn't happen again.

'She killed him, the woman who didn't glimmer,' he said. 'Cut his throat, just like that, in a *you're dead in the afterlife* type way.'

'Dispossessed in those parts wouldn't have the wit.'

'I agree,' said Joe. 'Which suggests she isn't Dispossessed.' He turned to look at Daisy-May. 'She was with Zed. Looked to be helping him. It was only when she saw us that she turned nasty. For whatever reason, she didn't want us to arrest him. That raises all sorts of questions.' He nodded at Bits. 'He can back me up. For what that's worth.'

'I believe you,' she said.

They let the silence settle.

Daisy-May turned back to the glass and the twitching Bits. 'What happened with the suspect? She's banged up bad, mate.'

Joe gritted his teeth. 'I take full responsibility.'

'That tells me fuck all.'

'I didn't make my orders to Bits clear enough.'

'Pretty sure you'd have told him not to beat the suspect.'

'Actually, I didn't.'

'You shouldn't have to,' said Daisy-May. 'That's the point.'

'He's full of anger,' said Joe. 'Fucked off at the afterlife for a dozen reasons, and at the soil for a dozen more. Once he's ironed out his seventies copper flaws – and drops the casual

35

racism – he might be all right. He was useful finding and tracking Zed. Had a hunch that played out well, even if he had to beat a suspect to get it. That's half the battle, no matter what facts-whores like me say. Can't teach that. Can't fake it, either.'

Daisy-May placed her hands behind her back.

Joe flinched a little under her judgemental gaze. It was as if she were trying to read his soul.

'Can he bottle his temper?' she said eventually.

'I can help him try,' said Joe.

'The big man loves 'em, apparently. Triers.'

'Just like I love a challenge,' said Joe. 'Bits'll be all right. I was, wasn't I, and who's a bigger challenge than me? Who tried harder than you?'

'Glad I've got something right, then,' said Daisy-May. 'Plenty would say I haven't.'

'Who's plenty?'

She looked down, scuffing her toe against the floor. 'The second in command that I've been lumbered with? Remus? Proper lippy, man. Got no respect for me, and fuck, who can blame him? I'm a teenager running an afterlife realm. If you and me didn't have the history we do, would you respect me? Really?'

Joe thought on that a moment. It was a surreal question to be asked, and one he knew he was fortunate to be able to hear. Their history – at least when they'd been alive, soil-side – had involved Daisy-May acting as a drug mule to Joe's bent copper kingpin. When the deal went wrong, he might not have killed her himself, but he did little to prevent it happening. That she'd later freed him from hell was a debt he knew he could never repay. That didn't mean he wasn't going to keep trying.

He'd start with a few home truths.

'I wouldn't respect you if you felt sorry for yourself, but then that's not the Daisy-May – the Warden – I know. She's a bad-ass, smart-as-shit warrior.'

Daisy-May looked away, the self-doubt crawling all over her. 'Trying to get on speaking terms with that girl again. I like her. She's ducking me at the moment.'

'I get that,' said Joe, 'and for what it's worth, I think you've had a bum deal. But this is the situation, and you've just got to run with it. The Duchess is no fool. She knew what she was doing when she made you Warden.'

Daisy-May grunted non-committally.

'Any word from her?' said Joe.

She shook her head. 'Last I heard she was in Tibet. We've got contacts all over the world, and not a single one has been able to land a glove on Hanna, let alone seen her.'

'The Duchess will find her.'

'Dunno, mate. The world's a big place. Lots of crannies and nooks to hide yourself in.'

'Hiding's not the problem. It's when Hanna makes herself known we should be worried.'

'No disagreement from me there,' said Daisy-May. 'Can't say I like an unexploded bomb like her wandering around. Won't end well for the living, or the dead. Good job the Duchess is hard as fuck and twice as wily.'

They watched the prisoner in silence for a few seconds.

'You think I did the right thing with the Dispossessed? Bringing them into the fold? Trying to include them?' said Daisy-May, finally.

'I don't see you had much of a choice. It was that, or the end of everything.'

She picked at the weave of scars around her wrist. 'Thought it'd help. Seems to have made things worse.'

'You showed them there was another path,' said Joe. 'There was never any guarantee they'd walk down it nicely.'

Daisy-May nodded uncertainly.

'And you're acting like this was something you had a choice in,' he continued. 'Whatever kick-started the evolution of their intelligence – if anything *did* kick-start it, if it wasn't actually there all along – it's done now. They wanted a seat at the table, and you've given them one. Can't be a shock they've got shitty manners.'

Daisy-May looked away. 'The way they're butchering each other, though, like this Zed fucker and that woman in there have been doing. I'm responsible for that.'

'Bollocks,' said Joe. 'Human beings, souls, whatever you want to call them, they've been fucking each other since time immemorial. Free will and all that. You've got enough worries to take on; why don't you let being responsible for human nature slide?'

He looked at her quizzically. 'This isn't just about the Dispossessed, though, is it? This is about something else.'

Daisy-May smirked at him. 'Good police work that, mate.'

They'd decamped to the control room. Daisy-May had changed the general vibe of the place: garage rock played in the background (unthinkable in the Duchess's day) and posters of gone-too-young music icons adorned the walls. *Kind of my fantasy Dying Squad team*, Daisy-May had said when Joe had asked her about them. *Cobain would be a shoe-in. Don't know about Winehouse, though; she's too much of a wild card even for me.*

Dozens of crime scenes filled the glowing screens. It was the one smack in the middle of the room that Joe's eyes were drawn to, though. It featured an unusually sun-blasted Manchester, and a posse of yellow-suited figures milling around a tent, tape encircling it like an unwanted VIP cordon.

A second image popped onto the corner of the screen. It showed, in a much tighter shot, a man. He was skeletal, his mouth open in a rictus cry. The same yellow-suited figures clustered around him, taking pains not to disturb the battalion of red balloons that encircled his body. It was as if his skin had melted onto the tarmac, a Mancunian wax-skin homage to the Turin Shroud.

'Christ,' said Joe.

'Not his style,' said Daisy-May.

'What am I looking at?'

'This footage was taken twenty-four hours ago. Only time we see footage like this is when we get a pickup.'

'A pickup?'

'You were a pickup,' said Daisy-May. 'Someone that gets killed on the soil and is then tagged as potential Dying Squad. Someone who needs to avenge their death, find the truth behind it.'

'By the looks of it, there's a whole squadron of people trying to do just that,' said Joe. 'What's with the yellow outfits?'

'They're radiation suits,' said Daisy-May. 'Dead body you're looking at belonged to a Stanley Veins. The old boy was found like this, in the middle of a Moss Side housing estate, glowing like fuckin' Chernobyl. Whoever killed him pumped him with an industrial amount of radiation.'

'Jesus.'

'Still not our prime suspect, mate.'

Clicker in hand, Daisy-May pointed at the other screens. A variety of locations appeared: rolling fields, a children's playground, a gloomily lit underpass, a car park, the inside of a church. Men and women, all pensioners like the first victim Joe had been shown, lay in the locations. All were emaciated. All were surrounded by a shroud of red balloons. All were dead.

'These bodies were discovered over the last twelve months. All in the UK, all irradiated,' said Daisy-May. 'Soil police

39

reckon it's the work of one person. Press have cooked up a trash-as-fuck name for him, obviously: the Generation Killer.'

Joe went to speak, and she held up a hand to stop him. 'You're going to ask what the connection is between the murder victims, and I'm going to answer *I don't know*. We don't get the case files for this sort of shit. Stanley boy here is why we have any connection at all – going to be up to you and Bits to piece how it all fits together.'

'Why the balloons?' said Joe. 'What's their relevance?'

'That's for you to find out.'

'Is it?' said Joe.

'What do you mean?' Daisy-May shot back.

'I'm knee-deep in a case already. One that just got a hell of a lot more complicated. That woman I've brought in is either responsible for cutting up her fellow Dispossessed or she's going to tell us who is. Chances are she's going to be able to give us intel about that woman who didn't glimmer, the one who was herding diving-suited Dispossessed back through to the soil. It's months of work that promises months more – I can't just abandon it.'

'You're not: I've got people here who can follow up the leads you've brought me. You know how many chances we get to actually save the living?'

'I didn't think that was the point of the Dying Squad.'

'Only because it never gets the chance to be the point,' said Daisy-May. 'The Duchess once told me that the dead helping the living used to be a thing. This ain't that – the soil police will never know we were there – but it's the next best thing.'

Joe nodded. 'Fair enough. And this is an actual, real-life *case*.'

'Yeah, and who knows, crack it and maybe there'll be more of 'em. Be nice to help the living for a change. It'll be a novelty for you, considering the type of copper you were on the soil.'

Joe smirked at her. 'Well, they say you should try everything once.'

'*They* are fucking idiots,' said Daisy-May, ''cos believe me, smack and drug muling are bucket list items to swerve.'

She jabbed the clicker at the screen and the bodies disappeared, trading places with boys, girls, men and women ranging from three to thirty-three. All looked pasty, pale and drawn.

Except that's not right, thought Joe. They look more than drawn, they look fucking ill. They look like they're dying.

And they're all holding a single red balloon.

'This is why the press on the soil have christened him – or her – the Generation Killer,' said Daisy-May, ''cos he kidnaps then kills the oldest and youngest members of the family. For the oldest, you've seen his handiwork. For the youngest . . . it gets a whole lot sicker. Three days after the body of grandad or grandma is discovered, junior gets released, holding a red fuckin' balloon. Even if junior is pushing thirty. To begin with, it seems like they're fine. They can't remember a fucking thing, let alone identify who took them, but other than a pinprick on their neck, they look A-OK.'

'I'm guessing by these photos they're not,' said Joe.

'Gold star for Sherlock. The kids are injected with radiation, just like their grandparents, but a much lower dose. It's not enough to kill them, at least not straight away, because whoever this fucker is, he wants them to suffer. Within weeks of being found, they die from radiation poisoning.'

Joe shook his head. 'That's so screwed up it makes me glad I'm dead.'

'It makes it sound like you're out of it, which you're not.'

Daisy-May brought back the image of Stanley's dead body, and then a photo of a young dark-haired woman. 'The latest victim, Stanley, his body was found the same day that Megan Veins went missing.'

'What do we know about her?' said Joe. 'How was she taken?'

'Like I said, we don't get a case file,' said Daisy-May. 'But if the killer's following the same pattern, it gives us a day to find her.'

'That's a big if,' said Joe.

'A desperate one too. She might already be poisoned. But it's the only one we've got. You and Bits need to collect Stanley and get him to work things back, make him remember where he was taken before he was killed. If he can, we have a fighting chance of saving Megan.'

'You want Bits in action again?' said Joe. 'After the shit he pulled today?'

'Manchester's his town,' said Daisy-May, 'and we need every advantage we can get.'

Joe tapped his foot, trying to jump-start his brain. Every time he was given an assignment like this, it was an opportunity to redeem himself. He didn't believe it would ever be possible to *completely* redeem himself – his crimes on the soil had been too brutal for that – but he'd settle for part of the way. Each case solved was a down payment on not going back to hell. He hadn't forgotten what the Pit was like.

He didn't deserve to.

'If it's two days since this bloke was killed, his spirit could be anywhere by now,' he said.

Daisy-May nodded. 'And would be, if it wasn't for Elias. You've met him, right?'

Joe had. Elias was a living, breathing emissary of the Pen on the soil, someone who had dedicated his life to caring for those undead souls stranded in the living world, those who'd lost their sense of self. He'd helped Joe when he'd been investigating his own murder, at a time when no one else could, or would.

'He's good people,' said Joe.

'Yep. He recently settled in Manchester and started up a mission there, which is lucky for us, and luckier still for the souls he helps,' said Daisy-May. 'He picked up Stanley just as soon as he could, and he's looking after him as we jaw away here. He's going to be a good point man for you to have on the ground.'

'No doubt.' Joe placed his hands on his hips, looking over the screens. 'There has to be some connection, this killing of the youngest and oldest generations. Something that motivates him to do it.'

'Or her,' said Daisy-May. 'But you're not here to provide a psych report, mate, you're here to save a girl's life. Important you keep that front and centre: all that matters is finding Megan Veins. You do that, maybe you'll have a happy accident and catch the killer too.'

'Agreed,' said Joe. 'One final question. The Gloop's poisoned – no one knows that better than you. How do Bits and I get through it without killing ourselves?'

Daisy-May allowed herself a smile. 'Thought you'd never ask.'

Joe and the Duchess's older sister had a solid hate–hate relationship. Joe often said that Mabel was as unforgiving as she was unlikeable, and Mabel preferred colonic irrigation to Joe. Just because he didn't like her very much, though, that didn't mean Joe didn't have grudging respect for her. Her role in the Pen was vital: supplying investigators like himself with the tools to catch those who needed to be caught. Sometimes that was by handing him a bad-ass gun, sometimes it was by arming him with a glorified magnifying glass.

And sometimes – this time – it was by sticking him in a huge, clod-hopping metal suit.

'You've got to be joking,' he said, as he stared at it warily.

43

Mabel scratched her backside. 'Think I last told a joke in 1912.'

Joe flicked a finger against the suit's brass hide. They were the ones he'd found at the crime scene, and looked like they'd been washed in acid, the patches of scorched metal giving them the appearance of jaundiced Dalmatians. Two copper pipes jutted from the back – their purpose wasn't immediately obvious – and the helmet was like that of a deep-sea diver. A circular glass faceplate was front and centre, the grime of God knew what smeared liberally over it.

'You're not expecting me to get in that, are you?' he said.

'I'm claustrophobic, man,' said Bits. 'Getting a panic attack just looking at it.'

'It's safe enough,' said Mabel, admiring the two suits with the pride of a new mother. 'Slow, yeah, but you're crossing the Gloop, not running the hundred bleeding metres.'

'It looks older than you,' said Joe, 'and twice as difficult to deal with.'

'You grab the rope, you pull yourself through, you get to the soil,' said Mabel. 'There's enough clean air in the tank to get you there and back.' She jammed her hands on her hips, studying Joe disdainfully. 'Or don't, makes no difference to me. Whack on an oxygen tank like last time and see how far ya get.'

'These suits are evidence,' said Joe, 'and we picked them up less than two hours ago. How can you possibly know they're safe?'

Mabel scowled at him. 'Because it's similar to something I've been working on: I didn't know better, I'd say they'd nicked my design. This'll get you through the Gloop. Lucky for you I'm a bleeding genius; managed to add on a couple of gadgets of my own.'

Joe circled the suit. It had been placed in front of the stall

Mabel had run for a century and a half, deep in the heart of the Pen but not so deep that access to the Gloop was impossible. As well as equipping her investigative foot soldiers like an afterlife Q, Mabel was supposed to act as the Duchess's eyes amongst the Dispossessed, feeding in reports from the trenches. Those reports hadn't always been what the Duchess wanted to hear, but that didn't mean she hadn't needed to.

'How do we walk in them?' Joe asked.

'You put one foot in front of the other,' said Mabel. 'Even you should be able to manage it.'

Bits ran a hand over his suit's scorched surface. 'We've seen these fuckers in action, man. We know they get the job done.'

Mabel nodded approvingly. 'You're the brains of the operation, clearly.'

'We don't know anything,' said Joe. 'We saw them walk into a doorway of light. We didn't see what happened to them afterwards.'

'What choice do we have,' said Bits, 'if we're going to save this Megan lass?'

And that was where Bits had him. What was the risk, compared to that? Joe's life had been one of selfish, slow-burn evil. If he was to atone for that (and he knew, deep down, he never could), then it was his duty to put his personal safety aside. You got in the shonky-as-fuck metal suit and you walked into hell. It was his job. It was what he'd been brought back to do.

'All right then,' he said. 'How does it work?'

Several crash landings later, Joe had pretty much cracked it. He wouldn't be giving any lessons, but he reckoned he knew enough to get through the Gloop. If he could do it in a respirator, he could do it in a big bastard of a diving suit. It even had a poison/pressure alarm to warn them if the limits of the suit protection were about to be breached. Factor in the compass on the steel arm that would guide them to the soil, and Joe had to concede it was a fancy bit of kit.

Mabel reached down under the stall, bringing up a leather satchel and slinging it around Joe's neck.

'What's this?' he said.

'Been some changes since the last time you flounced around on the soil. Gum you had was Nicorette; this is caviar you won't want to quit.'

She withdrew a clear plastic syringe from the bag and held it up. 'You inject this into your veins, and it'll keep you *you* for two hours. It's powerful as hell, and you've got enough to see you through. Stop taking it, though, and your memory will crash hard.'

'Not big on drugs any more,' said Bits. 'Dying's as hardcore as cold turkey gets. Don't want to relapse.'

'You'll want it more than the alternative,' said Mabel.

'You said we'll crash hard. How hard is hard?' asked Joe.

'You'll remember your name, but not much else. Certainly not the golden boy act you've been working so hard to maintain.'

Joe stared at her coldly. 'And the suicide pills?'

'In the pack. Feel free to test 'em out now.'

'Suicide pills?' said Bits.

'In case we get stranded on the soil with no way back,' said Joe. 'Some prefer to end it rather than become an amnesia victim.'

'Let's skip that bit, yeah?' said Bits. 'Died once, and it's fucking overrated.'

Joe looked at the suit like it had cheated on him. 'When we start to hear it go nuts, how long do we have to get through to the soil?'

'Minutes? Seconds? When that suit starts shrieking, you best start moving, and quickly, 'cos that shriek's either gonna mean

46

death by weaponised soil air, or somethin' that isn't as dead as we thought.'

'The Gloop's a graveyard,' said Joe.

'How'd you know?' said Mabel. 'You been into it?'

'Have you?'

'Met someone who has.'

'Bullshit,' said Joe. 'No one going in there could survive.'

'Neither did this fella,' said Mabel. 'Not for long. Lasted long enough to scream, though. Scream, and say a single word, over and over.'

'What word?' said Bits.

'*Diablos.*'

'We're a bit old for ghost stories,' said Joe.

'Especially as we're actual ghosts,' added Bits.

'Don't matter to me whether you two morons believe me or not,' said Mabel. 'I don't know whether the poor bastard was lying, or just mad with pain. I do know that the Gloop was always scary at the best of times. Now? Who knows what's in there?'

Joe stood surveying the sky-colonising wall in front of him and told himself it was going to be all right.

Mabel's scare stories about who – or what – might be waiting for them in the Gloop were just that. They had the suits, they had their wits and they had a plan, which was more than most in the Pen had.

It wasn't that that was troubling him, though, not really. It was going back to the soil, and the drip-feed amnesia it would bring. It was the fear that he'd relapse.

Because ultimately Joe knew that he was an addict, and it wasn't booze that was his demon, or drugs. It was weakness. It was evil. It was fear that the person he'd fought so hard to

47

become in the Pen – the good man, who did the right thing – would recede along with his memories, leaving in its place the man he'd been on the soil. Morally vapid, clinically corrupt, in it only for himself, a bent copper who turned a blind eye to murder and ran child drug gangs with impunity and relish. That man had been murdered, and who could say that wasn't an appropriate death?

Joe hated that man, and he wanted him to stay buried. He was afraid that with soil air in his nostrils, the grave he'd been buried in would turn out to be a shallow one.

'We doing this, or what?'

Joe turned to his new partner and his muffled voice. His beady, blazing eyes were just visible through the suit's helmet. 'If you knew what "this" was like, you might not be in such a hurry.'

'Don't believe that old cow's nonsense, do yer? She's straight-up senile.'

'Mabel's a pain in the arse but she's no mug,' said Joe. 'If she says there might be something dangerous in the Gloop, we best go on the basis that there is, and we should be ready for it.'

'With what?' said Bits. 'Harsh language and a slap round the chops?'

'If I know Mabel – and unfortunately, I do – I reckon these suits will have a few tricks up their sleeves.'

Joe reached down, his gloved hands clumsily prising open the chunky leather bag, then pawing a rusted metal spike and a length of rope from it.

'Something you need to know when we get to the other side,' he said, threading the rope through the eye of the spike, then hammering it into the ground. 'It's worse than you've heard with the amnesia. Those syringes will help stave off the worst of it, but we've got hours to find that girl, not days. The living person you were on the soil will want to get out, and he'll want to play nasty. Don't let him.'

'I like the living fella I was on the soil, though,' said Bits. 'He was a proper laugh. Better than this do-gooder I'm playing now, anyway. More real.'

'It was your realness that meant you ended up in the Pen,' said Joe, twanging the rope, checking its tautness. 'Authenticity's overrated. Better to be a fake good guy than a genuine villain.'

'Can't have been that much of a wrong'un, can I?' said Bits. 'Otherwise they'd have just tossed me in the Pit.'

'Think it was your potential that saved you from the Pit, rather than any good deeds,' Joe replied. 'It's up to you to live up to that potential.'

'If you say so,' said Bits. 'Remind me of a boxing coach I had once. He was full of bollocks motivational quotes, too.'

He grabbed hold of the rope. 'What am I supposed to do with this?'

'Keep hold of it,' said Joe, 'no matter what tries to make you let go.'

With that, he stepped forward, and the wall swallowed him whole.

Chapter Three

Nothing could have prepared Joe for this.

The Gloop as he knew it was a thing of pulsing, terrifying pink beauty. *A womb* was how the Duchess had described it to him. To Joe, it had been like stepping into a living brain, images carved onto every last surface, each one leading to places and people all over the world. Despite its terrifying strangeness, there was also a sort of reassuring peace.

Not any more. Now, there was only devastation and war.

The membranous surfaces were blank, bleached black and green, the colour and soul drained from them. It reminded Joe of pictures he'd seen of Hiroshima after the bomb had dropped: rubble and wreckage, the hope and wonder of the place scorched away by horror and the worst of humanity.

The silence, too, was almost painful. Before, the sounds of the Gloop had been muffled, almost as if they'd been fed through the speakers of an echo chamber. Now, there was only suffocating nothingness, their movements failing to make even the slightest of sounds. The gravity of the place was unchanged, though; it still fought you like it was a point of principle, making each movement slow and painful.

Mabel was wrong, thought Joe. There are no devils here. They've got better taste. This is what death looks like. The death of hope. The death of joy. The death of everything worth living for.

He looked behind him – Bits was a few feet away, fists gripping the rope, helmeted head snapping left and right. Joe felt a certain amount of pride that his partner was keeping it together; going into the Gloop for the first time was no joke. Going in when it had suffered an almost fatal trauma made that lack of comedy even more tangible.

The metal arrow fixed to his arm twitched right. Mabel had told him to think of it as a weathervane; when the pull of the door they were heading for got stronger, so would the divining rod's reaction. Right it was.

Ten minutes, that was what Daisy-May had said to him. *Ten minutes walking through a poisoned-to-fuck wasteland to get you back in the hero game. You can suck that up, right?*

There wasn't much he wouldn't suck up for that girl – he owed her – and it was good to be working a case again. Trying to bust the chop-shop gang had been important and it had been necessary, but it wasn't what he'd been brought back from the dead to do. He was Dying Squad, and they were meant to do good on the soil, not in the Pen.

After a few moments, the metal divining rod on his arm lurched to the left. Joe turned to Bits, pointing. His partner nodded, the signature from his suit thumping in Joe's. The idea was that if they became separated, that signature would act as a homing beacon, drawing them back together. It wasn't something Joe wanted to test; getting split up in this hellscape was as bad a scenario as he could imagine.

They continued to shuffle forward, the silence so crushing even the sound of their hands grasping the rope was swallowed, and Joe saw that they were being led to a trench. He held up a hand to slow Bits, then peered down into the darkness. The opposite side had to be almost a hundred feet away, but that wasn't where the divining rod was telling him to go.

It was demanding they go down; the closer Joe put his right arm towards the crevice, the more insistent the arrow became.

Of course, he thought. It was never going to be at the top, a couple of minutes' stroll from the Gloop's entrance, was it? The doorway back to the soil, back to Manchester, has to be at the bottom of the pitch-black death trench.

He felt a tap on his helmet and turned to look at Bits, whose face was just visible through his screen.

Where are the bodies? his partner mouthed.

Joe thought that was an excellent question, and one that he should have considered himself. The way the Duchess told it – Daisy-May too – there had been thousands of Dispossessed in the Gloop when it had been poisoned. There should have been tangles of bodies everywhere, consumed by vines and crumbling away. Some would have rotted more quickly than others, but there should still have been some sort of presence.

Instead, there was nothing. A cemetery without the corpses.

He shrugged, the universal language for *I've got no fucking clue*, and reached towards his helmet, adjusting the lamp on the top. A thick beam of light forced its way out, cutting through the black below. The trench was craggy, with uneven slabs of rock sticking out this way and that. Climbable, and Joe could now see that previous Dying Squad members had felt the same thing – the murky imprints of climbing poles could be made out on the rock face below.

I wonder what happened to them? he thought. He decided he didn't want to know.

They'd taken time to hammer another tent peg – Joe struggled to think of them as anything else – into the ground just above the trench, then threaded a sturdy length of rope through it.

He had no idea whether it would hold, or whether it could support two grown men in oversized metal diving suits, but he also knew they didn't have much of a choice. It was chance the rope, or try and find their way down without it.

He stood with his back to the trench, rope in hand, and took a breath.

We're nothing compared to the size of this place, he thought. We're fleas on a dog, specks of dust on a bed sheet.

He nodded to Bits, then took a step backwards, feeding the rope as he did so. His heels reached the lip of the trench. Giving a final thumbs-up, he stepped backwards into nothingness.

He went with the fall then began to swing the rope, aiming for the rock face a few feet away. A jolt went through his body as his boots crunched into it, the rope holding. Walking like a bruised spider, he manoeuvred himself closer to the climbing spike that had been hammered into the wall, then fed the rope through it. He looked up at Bits, his head torch cutting through the gloom, and gave him the signal to follow.

Bet he can't wait. Who wouldn't want to swing down into a dark death trench? Especially when we've got no idea how far down it goes, or what's at the bottom of it.

Kicking away from the face of the cliff, gravity fighting him, he let the rope slide through his fingers and eased himself lower into the darkness, swinging himself back against the rock face then rinse-and-repeating, his breath pinging and singing in the suit, the weighty bass growl signature telling him Bits was still above him, and hopefully progressing in the same manner.

Then, when he was a couple of hundred feet down, he heard something.

A whisper of a scratch, like a modem trying to find a connection, fading almost immediately. Going faster now, he swung down another few feet, a squall of poison static buzzing angrily as he did so. He thought back to Mabel's briefing, how she'd explained that when the weaponised soil air began to get too much for the suit's defences, its glorified Geiger counter would start shrieking. The noise the thing was making suggested (although it was more of an aggressive demand) that they were at that point.

That was when he saw it.

It began as a murky shape in the darkness, something making its way up from the depths of the trench, indistinct but unmistakably huge, swimming in the same way a meteorite flew when it was really falling. Joe felt a tug on the rope and saw Bits was just above him; he too had noticed the mass emerge from the poison dark.

And whatever it was, it was making Joe's suit shriek louder.

The shape closing on them was hundreds of feet high, and twice that again wide. Now Joe saw what it really was: thousands of Dispossessed bodies sutured together, limbs, teeth, eyes and hair welded into a cocktail of bodily horror. It moved like a jellyfish, surging left then right, all the time getting closer, the suit shrieking to match the fear Joe felt.

His stomach flipped as it became clear the Dispossessed were feeding on each other; mangled teeth chewed on fractured arms, eyeballs crunched in spasming jaws as mouths vomited up green-brown pus.

It can't die, he thought. It's trying to. The fucking thing is literally trying to eat itself to death, but it can't die. This is beyond anything I've ever trained for. I'm a Lincolnshire copper, not a monster hunter.

He looked up, past Bits, to the rocky outcrop they'd descended from. They could go back, turn tail and run from this abomination back to the Pen, but then what? That wouldn't get them any closer to Manchester, or the case he'd been tasked with. And it wasn't like this ball of death was going to shift out the way for them; it was making a mockery of the Gloop's gravity, hurtling towards them like a dead planet. The way he saw it, there was only one option open to them: they'd have to go around it.

He tugged on Bits's foot, then glanced down at the rope. He made a show of taking his left hand from the rope, then nodding downwards.

Bits shook his head, a *you must be fucking kidding* motion that needed no words.

This wasn't a negotiation. It might be suicide, but it was the only chance they had.

Looking his partner dead in the eye, Joe released his right hand from the rope and fell into the darkness.

Fusion. That was the word that came to him as he fell.

Hundreds of half-souls must have been fused together when the Duchess's bomb had gone off, this fusion sufficient to keep them alive, feeding and sustaining each other parasitically, in an almost living hell. They deserve better, Joe thought, as dozens of stitched-together faces screamed at the void. They deserve the peace that death will bring. He couldn't give them that, but he could try and make sure he didn't join them in hell.

He lowered his head, straightened his back and turned himself into an undead missile. He had to hope Bits followed his lead; hope too that if it didn't work, he was savvy enough to ignore that lead altogether.

Not yet, he thought.

Closer.

Closer.

Closer.

Now.

He squeezed his right fist, kicking his boots' boosters into life and directing the suit towards the base of the Dispossessed mass. He gasped, the pressure of the Gloop fighting against him, g-forces colliding with compressed air, the suit's restraints cutting into his shoulders as it screamed in Geiger-counter pain.

This worked in the Pen, he thought, as he flew ever closer to the mass in front of him. It has to work here.

He squeezed his left hand, activating the suit's braking system, lurching it to a dead stop. The unforgiving pressure of the Gloop meant it was like slamming into a brick wall. He tumbled backwards, control wrested from him, a twig plunging down a waterfall. His breathing chased the suit's alarm, the sight of the fused Dispossessed sporadic in the midst of his tumble, as he cartwheeled underneath them, inches away from grasping hands.

It was the first thing he'd been taught as a copper: leave the designer suit at home, because in this job you'll be puked on, shat on and bled on. He doubted his old sergeant had had mutant death balls in mind, but the principle held firm.

He squeezed his left fist again, applying the brakes; it slowed him, rather than stopping him, but that was all right, because he was passing under the terror ball. He'd take his chances with the trench floor over the hell mass any day.

Nausea racked his body as he squeezed his fist again and again, his descent slowing a little more each time, if not his racing, lurching stomach.

Squeeze.

Squeeze.

Squeeze.

Finally he wrestled back control of the suit. He was the right way up, if there was a right way up in the Gloop, and drifting slowly downwards. He moved his helmeted head left and right, the torch that had been fixed to it slashing through the gloom, revealing dozens of bodies, clumps of rotting vines growing from them, shooting past him overhead.

They were trying to get out, he realised, as the metal arrow on his arm pinged to the left and stayed there. They knew the way out was down here, and they were trying to reach it. The poor bastards never stood a chance.

His feet thudded into the ground.

He'd made it.

Had Bits?

Joe looked up into the darkness, searching for him. The suit's light gave him a range of around fifty feet, vision that revealed nothing but corpses.

He'll make it. If he survived in the Pen for all those years, he can survive here.

The suit's alarm had now quietened, reverting back to its gentle scratch of static. Alone, draped in darkness in a place so alien it almost redefined the word, he almost missed it.

Come on, Bits, he thought, staring upwards, straining for the telltale bass ping that would indicate he was in range. I haven't had the chance to learn to hate you yet.

He stood there for moments that seemed like hours, gazing up into the darkness, his breathing and his growing sense of fear his only companions.

Nothing.

Bits was gone.

Joe followed the arrow on his arm, because the only other option was staying here to die a drip-feed soil-air death, utterly alone. The going was slow – the pressure of the Gloop seemed to be greater here, at the bottom of the trench – but workable.

As he progressed, the trench on either side of him began to narrow, the sense of blackened claustrophobia becoming more acute with each footstep.

If this narrows much more, I'm not going to be able to get through, or get back, for that matter. I'm going to be wedged in, with soil-air sickness the only thing to show for my efforts. I thought being shot to death in a farmhouse was a bad way to go, but I reckon this'd be worse.

A minute and several dozen steps later, he found the doorway to the soil.

Close, its light was watery, like sunshine drowned in a puddle. No less stark for it, though, so ink-black was the darkness around him. When he'd crossed from the Gloop to the soil before, it had been hurried and frenzied; he'd been yanked through by Daisy-May, with a desperate member of the Dispossessed in pursuit. Now, with more time to study it, he could appreciate the almost Renaissance beauty of the doorway. It was like a skilled – if avant-garde – artist had painted a watercolour impression of a busy Manchester street onto a brain stem.

This is all that's left, he thought. *All this destruction, but Manchester's still standing. God bless it.*

He took a step towards it, then heard something that wasn't his own breathing, or the ubiquitous radiation static. It sounded like a heartbeat. Faint at first, but growing louder by the second.

He looked up and behind him, wondering what fresh hell was going to be inflicted upon him, then realised that it wasn't a heartbeat he was hearing, but Bits's suit. It was kicking out a baseline growl that indicated he was in range and getting closer by the second. A faint blob of light appeared in the distance, one that went high, then low.

Bits's torch light.

And it wasn't alone: the poison-warning crackle was back.

Jesus. That thing's chasing him.

Bits came into view, doing the same jump-land-jump motion they'd practised in the Pen, and it was the distance he got with those jumps that meant he was still dead-alive. Joe knew he wouldn't be for much longer: the creek was narrowing, allowing for little more than a sideways shuffle, and although that should have been a good thing, should have been sufficient to keep the fusion monster out, he had his doubts.

The mass of it? Even with the gravity of the Gloop, it looked like the beast could barrel straight through the trench. Or worse, bring it down on top of them.

He'd never been so close to it, and this proximity brought with it a fresh checklist of horrors: headless torsos stretched the papery membrane covering them, their grasping hands erupting boils of pus. Joe couldn't decide whether they were trying to escape the mass they'd been fused into, or whether they were trying to pull him into it.

Either way, it was bad news.

He turned to the doorway to the living world and began shuffling towards it, the trench suffocating, narrowing, both sides of it clawing at his suit, determined to keep him there for ever.

One–two, one–two, one–two he went, each step trickier than the last as he squeezed himself between the walls, the suit yelling, the sound of beast against rock indicating that the Dispossessed monster was trying to force its way to them, and was willing to pound against physics and the walls of the Gloop to do so.

He was a foot away from the doorway to the soil when he realised he was wedged. He was so close, he could feel the Mancunian night light on his hand.

The suit screamed.

He twisted his neck round to see Bits just a few yards away, shuffling towards him.

The beast was further back, its spindles of limbs slamming against the trench wall, trying to smash through.

I don't know what it wants, thought Joe, whether it just wants to escape this hellhole, but as long as we're in its way, that's no good for us.

I'm going to have to get out of the suit. It may kill me, but if I don't try, I'm as good as dead anyway.

The breathlessly tight trench would only allow him to point upwards in Bits's general direction. He hoped he understood the command, realising that it didn't matter, because in a minute he'd see Joe getting out of the suit, and he'd follow, or he wouldn't.

Fighting every survival instinct in his body, knowing he only had seconds left, Joe shuffled backwards, closer to the beast, because those inches would allow him to free himself. He slipped his arms out of the suit's sleeves, then reached inwards, undoing its restraints, swearing when the left one caught fast.

He felt something bind itself around the right leg of the suit. If the creature behind him had breath, Joe imagined he'd be feeling its sickness on his neck it was now so close.

Come on, he thought. Come on.

At last he yanked it loose then reached upwards, flicking the three latches at the base of the helmet.

Taking in a final lungful of the suit's filtered air, he pushed against the helmet.

Four seconds and six feet, that was all that separated Joe from the relative safety of the living world. They were the most excruciating four seconds and six feet of his afterlife.

When he'd finally wrestled the helmet open and launched himself out, the Gloop fighting him every last step of the way, he quickly saw that Bits had beaten him to it. He too had freed himself from his suit, and was swimming just over Joe's head, aiming for the shimmering portal. Joe kicked off from the suit, using its shoulders as a diving board. He was taken back to his first time in the Gloop; he could have believed it would have been the same for an astronaut ejected from an airlock without his spacesuit. The pressure was terrific, crushing down and around him as he dragged himself through the ever-tightening chasm towards the light.

Daisy-May swam through this for the best part of ten minutes, he thought. No wonder the Duchess chose her.

He felt his lungs expanding, begging to explode, a thousand silent screams behind him as the monster tried to force its way through the trench towards him.

A monstrous tentacle made of God knows what stretched out, snaking at his feet.

He closed his eyes, gave a final swimming push, and dived into the Mancunian night.

Chapter Four

The Duchess had always craved solitude in her retirement. She'd never imagined she'd actually get it.

All she'd ever known was noise. In her soil days, that had been the yell and scream of eighteenth-century New York, and in the afterlife, as Warden of the Pen, it had been the rumble and boom of the millions of Dispossessed souls under her watch. There was also, of course, the yelp and carry-on of the Dying Squad. All this time, she'd believed she'd wanted release from such a cacophony of noise and confusion, but now that she had it, she found she didn't much want it.

Certainly she could take or leave the Suicide Forest.

The Sea of Trees (to give the Japanese forest its statelier title) stretched out in front of her, still and soundless. Like her, it was as if the place was a ghost in the living world; she had never known anywhere so starkly devoid of life. She hoped she wasn't wasting her time, because if she knew her younger sister, it was time she didn't have to waste.

It wasn't unusual, she supposed, to disapprove of a younger sibling's life choices. Hanna hadn't coupled with an unsuitable boyfriend, though, or proved to be loose and unreliable with money. She'd escaped from hell, then fomented revolution amongst the Dispossessed so violent it had almost toppled existence. It was that revolt that had forced the Duchess to abdicate to Daisy-May.

If that had been it finished, the Duchess could have lived with it. She'd been coming to the end of her Wardenship anyway (her appointed successor pointedly having failed to show his face to relieve her), and Daisy-May was the worthiest of successors, unsullied by Pen politics and grasping ambition.

It wasn't finished, though. When it came to Hanna, it never was.

The rumours that her youngest sister had made it through the Gloop, despite the Duchess's best efforts to blow it – and her – up had proved to be correct. There had been sightings of her from the Pen's various soil-based informants, but many of those sightings had turned out to be as wild as they were inaccurate. When the Duchess received reports that Hanna had been spotted in Japan, though, close to Mount Fuji, her spirits had risen. She knew of this place, knew her sister knew of it, too.

All the Jankie girls knew about the Sea of Trees. Their grandmother had made sure of it.

There is a place, in the godless land of Japan, that has power you cannot conceive of, Oma Jankie had told them. *A sea of trees, where the living go to die and the dead go to live. The trees are packed tight, letting not a breath of wind into their sanctuary, and what a sanctuary it is, my dears. The dead have power there, amongst the knotted roots and blanket of leaves. Ancient, unknowable power. I will journey there one day, when I pass over. That is, if the devil doesn't take me first.*

She'd cackled at that, Oma Jankie, like it was an in-joke her silly granddaughters wouldn't get. The Duchess got it now, and her fear was that Hanna had got it too. Why else would she have travelled such a vast distance? Unknowable ancient power would be dangerous in the calmest of hands; in the hands of her unhinged sister, it would be terrifying.

Plenty of reason for her to be unhinged, though, isn't there, Rachel? screeched the voice of her long-dead grandmother. *Bitter, too. You took her title, and then when she asked to share it, you gave it away to the first waif who came your way.*

Hanna gave the title away when she took her own life, the Duchess replied. *I didn't want it then, and I don't want it now. Neither did Daisy-May, which is why she was so worthy of it. And it's not as if the next in line turned up, is it? Where is he, Oma? Where is the next Warden? Why didn't he come? Answer me that.*

She didn't.

The Duchess reached into her pocket, bringing out a slab of chewing gum. She broke it in two, popping the smaller half into her mouth. She hated it – hated this dependence on the drug – but knew it was necessary. Her power in the afterlife hadn't immediately waned when she'd abdicated her title, and her resistance to the soil's air was considerable, but not so considerable that it wouldn't fade with time. She could last on these daily half-rations in the way the Joe Lazaruses of this world never could, but there were limits even to her power.

She flicked the gum around her mouth, drawing out its Pen-radiation goodness, and walked soundlessly forward into the parched-of-noise forest. It was unknowably vast, but the rumble in her gut told her she'd been right to come.

Hanna was here. She could feel it.

After an hour of walking, the Duchess felt the air change.

If she'd still been a soil-breather, the hairs on the back of her neck would have prickled; as it was, it was like her body began to sing, some unseen conductor calling out the tune. She stopped, looking around her at a forest that seemed utterly devoid of earthly trifles such as daylight or oxygen, the canopy of trees so thick it was as unforgiving as the most brutal night-club bouncer.

Ahead, there seemed to be some sort of makeshift camp. The earth was blackened, as if souls had been chargrilled in the ground.

She was here, thought the Duchess. And recently. I can feel it. I can feel her.

The former Pen Warden reached into her backpack, bringing out a small metal pistol. The barrel was elongated, the body a stubby whirl of moving dials, a glass vial of green liquid jutting from it. It was useless against the living, but all too fatal when applied to the dead. She didn't want to kill her sister – there had been altogether too much killing in her two lifetimes – but she was also prepared to do what was necessary, if it was necessary.

She moved forward, the trees above allowing a scalpel sliver of light through, directly into the centre of the camp. There were no visible signs of life, and any soil breathers present would have seen nothing but knots of tree roots, gnarled bark, and earth that looked untouched for centuries. The Duchess knew her own dead body, though, and she knew too Oma Jankie's feelings on this place. This was where the Japanese came to die, fulfilling what they felt was their honourable duty. The suicides it had hosted over the centuries would have released a vast number of souls, ones that would not have been able to pass on, and it was exactly those sorts of individuals her younger sister had proved so adept at influencing in the Pen.

The Duchess stood amongst the silence, and realised she was not alone.

Her fist tightened slightly on the barrel of the gun, her finger finding the trigger.

She waited.

Let them come to me, she thought. Friend, or foe.

Laughter came from behind her, a honking giggle.

She turned.

Standing there was a woman.

A long mane of red hair flowed erratically from her head, almost like it was trying to jump from her scalp. A tatty white dress hung reluctantly from her slender frame. It was her face that made the starkest impression, though.

She didn't have one.

Where there should have been eyes, a nose and a mouth there was instead a perfectly flat pouch of featureless skin. It was like she'd been half finished by a lackadaisical devil.

It would have shocked any living soul who glimpsed it, but the Duchess hadn't been alive for the best part of a hundred and fifty years. She'd seen untold horrors in her reign as Pen Warden, and a Noppera-Bō spirit like this was small fry.

'She said you'd come.'

The Duchess understood the woman's Japanese tongue, because a mastery of languages was a requirement of being Warden of the Pen, and such mastery had been obtained through ritual beatings and habitual cruelty by her Oma.

Still, it was a neat trick, considering the woman didn't have a mouth.

'Who said I'd come?' the Duchess asked, the kindness in her voice offset by the fact that she was pointing a loaded weapon at the woman.

'Hanna.'

'And what did Hanna say I'd do when I came?'

'She said you'd try and stop her,' said the woman, 'but not to worry, because there's no stopping what she's started.' She took a step forward.

'Stay right there,' said the Duchess, raising the gun slightly. 'I have no desire to shoot you, but that doesn't mean I won't.'

'You cannot threaten me,' said the woman, 'because there is nothing you could do to me that I would not welcome, or that would not bring me eternal peace.'

She's insane, thought the Duchess. Or at least she's carrying

66

the insanity that Hanna's infected her with. It's what she does.

'I have a message for you,' said the woman, reaching under her tunic.

No, thought the Duchess, as she saw the bulge across the woman's chest and realised what she was about to do.

'Hanna says change is coming,' said the woman without a face, 'and there's nothing her big sister can do to stop it.'

A blinding green flash erupted, skittling the Duchess off her feet and throwing the gun from her hand, the shock wave knocking her backwards, clean through one of the trees behind her. Her ears whined in protest, her vision juddering. Fighting unconsciousness, she hauled herself to her feet, knowing an attack could come at any moment. Her gun would offer scant protection when it did; it lay in a mangled, melted heap on the floor.

The smouldering heap of clothes that constituted her sister's messenger meant she wouldn't need it anyway.

Shibuya was a future everyone wanted, paid for by a past everyone tried to forget.

A giddy tumble of commerce and tradition, the ward of Shibuya-ku hosted two of the busiest railway stations in the world, the epicentre of Japanese youth culture, cloaked-in-honour heritage, and a dilapidated, long since abandoned love hotel created in the early eighties to cover the huge demand for no-tell motels that amorous couples could hire by the hour.

The owners of the hotel, the name of which translated roughly as the Western Rodeo, had gone big on Western allure, theming the rooms accordingly. To them, love meant boxy rooms with wobbly, unconvincing sets depicting locales as varied as the Wild West, Hollywood, and swinging London Town. Unfortunately for the owners, the good people of Tokyo weren't too keen on paying premium prices to bump and grind in poorly turned-out am-dram sets, so the hotel went bust, then fell into ruin. No one had entered it in years.

Tonight, though, the Western Rodeo was open for business once more, although its guests had no intention of paying, and their intentions were anything but romantic.

No, Hanna Jankie's intentions were much grander than that.

Ten of her most loyal disciples sat in a circle, patiently waiting for their orders. The eleventh sat away from the main group, her left arm exposed, the twelfth etching a jagged spiralling tattoo onto it with a cannibalised Dying Squad pistol, filtered soil air burning into long-dead skin. It was a ritual all the group had undertaken, cementing the promise they had made to each other and, more importantly, to their leader.

Hanna closed her eyes and listened to rain on glass. It was the sort of downpour Tokyo raised itself to occasionally, when the old spirits screamed, demanding to be heard, offering to wash away the sins – and failures – of the past.

She knew how they felt.

She'd requested a similar hearing with her sister back in the Pen, but the Duchess had shot her down, both figuratively and literally. She'd live to regret that.

If tonight went as it should, they all would.

The Tokyo authorities prided themselves on the militaristic efficiency of their rail service; the 5.09 Shibuya to Osaki commuter train, for instance, had been late only once in its last five years of service. That occasion, when it had left a whole 135 seconds past its scheduled time, had brought a great deal of shame to the Razinski corporation.

This evening, with the time standing at precisely 5.07, Hanna Jankie aimed to bring a great deal more.

She and her followers waited on the platform, the sardine commuters shivering and twitching at something they couldn't see but could feel as Hanna and her team passed through their living bodies. Taking their assigned positions, they spaced themselves down the platform. One disciple for each carriage.

Each knew their role.

Each knew what was at stake.

Each knew the consequences of what they were about to do.

All great achievements are borne on the back of sacrifice, Hanna thought. These men and women know that better than anyone. It's the language of the dead that compels them to act, but I flatter myself they would do so without it. After all, it's not every day you get the chance to change the world.

She heard the juddering of the approaching train and swallowed. She wasn't used to being nervous. She liked it. It meant something here mattered. As one, the team looked up, searching each other for weakness or doubt.

No one found any.

In perfect harmony, they each popped a stick of green gum into their mouth. They chewed. They gave beaming smiles. Hanna was the only one who abstained, for she was to play a different role.

The train ground to a halt.

Hanna squeezed her fists together.

The doors opened. The commuters surged on in total silence. There was beauty in it, she decided. Grace.

One of her followers slipped through the driver's door. The others took a carriage each.

What I'm about to do is heresy, thought Hanna, but the old laws don't count any more. At least, they won't count after this. This is the start of the new order.

A station officer bellowed at the commuters, moving down the platform and using a glorified broom to pack them ever more tightly into the carriages.

They do so without a hint of complaint. And my sister called the Dispossessed dumb, cowed animals.

The doors shut.

The announcer announced.

The train juddered into life and eased away from the platform.

There was a two-minute window before it arrived at the next station.

Two minutes to change the history of everything. A wealth of time. An eternity.

The passengers sweated and fidgeted, trying to grasp an inch of personal space that wasn't there to grasp.

Hanna counted to twenty in her head.

Yuri, her faithful servant, a soul who had battled her way from the Pen to the living world alongside her, chewed her gum and smiled from the other end of the carriage.

'Thank you,' she mouthed.

Hanna nodded.

Yuri slammed her elbow into the train window. A crack appeared in it. The commuter next to the window jumped, Yuri invisible to her.

'Again,' said Hanna. 'Quickly.'

Yuri nodded and hammered her elbow into the glass again, and again, and again, until it shattered.

Wind sucked its way into the carriage. Yuri reached for the window, ripping out a jagged sliver of glass. She grasped the hair of the man in front of her and dragged him backwards, the passengers around him yelling in protest.

'Do it,' said Hanna.

Yuri nodded, smiled like she'd been singled out for special praise, then plunged the shard of glass into the commuter's throat.

Blood arced from it.

People screamed.

There was a rumble in the distance that was made by nothing earthly.

Hanna moved quickly through the carriages, watching a similar scene play out in each one, her disciples slashing at the closest commuters, screaming, packed in, panic spreading like a virus.

The train was getting faster. A swift glance into the driver's compartment showed that was because he'd been dispatched. That was good.

Come on, thought Hanna. Do what you do. Don't fight it. Come to us. Punish us.

The rumble in the distance became a sonic boom of fire and light.

She tensed, ignoring the human bloodshed and the moans of pain that went with it. He was here. She couldn't see him yet, but she could feel him. The hairs on her arms rose, tingling with anticipation.

Screams from her own team, to go with those of the commuters. The sound of teeth ripping into their flesh proof enough of his presence.

The train grew ever faster.

A yowl of terror came from the next carriage. He was close now.

A doubt slipped into Hanna's mind. She was about to kill something that was considered unkillable, a force of supernatural might whose very name instilled stone-cold fear. If she couldn't kill it – and many others had tried and failed over the centuries – her crusade would be over before it had truly begun.

You can *kill it, though, little Hanna*, her long-dead grandmother told her. *Your plan is a good one. Stay strong.*

I was born strong, Hanna thought. I died strong. I was

reborn stronger. And I'll need every last ounce of that strength against him.

Against the Xylophone Man.

A creature so mythical, one name was never enough.

Many knew him as the Infernal Serpent. Many more as the Culler of Wretches. Hanna knew him simply as a cruel, small man who had tortured her for decades in hell, who had used her for his own means in that realm, teaching her the language of the dead in order to foment revolution amongst the Dispossessed, just because it amused him. Or, more importantly, amused his master.

It was madness to draw his attention in the way she had. Spirits interacting with the real world always attracted the Xylophone Man like a moth to napalm, and the spirits under her command had done much worse than that: they'd committed cold-blooded murder.

Worse than madness. It was suicide.

Hanna smiled.

She and suicide were old pals.

The Xylophone Man walked through the carriage door opposite her, his elephant skull smeared with the entrails of her followers. Only one remained: Roshi, one of the souls she had commandeered from the Sea of Trees. He bowed to her as the Xylophone Man opened his jaws, displaying a helter-skelter of teeth.

Don't look at them, thought Hanna. That's what he wants you to do.

Roshi tried to fight, despite the fear Hanna knew he must feel, because she'd asked him to do so. The Xylophone Man locked eyes with her as he raised his hand. Roshi's back snapped rigid and he levitated in the air. The Xylophone Man's jaws pivoted, his teeth shredding Roshi's skin, devouring him in several snapping gulps.

The train began to shriek.

'It was a mistake to free you from the Pit,' said the Xylophone Man, wiping a gloved hand against a bloodied, crumbling tusk. 'One I will now rectify.'

'I've committed no crime,' said Hanna, swaying with the jerking train. 'I'm guilty of no transgression.'

'Your followers have,' replied the Xylophone Man, 'and they wouldn't jump without your say-so. That makes you guilty in my eyes.'

'Breaking the ancient laws on a technicality,' said Hanna, smirking. 'How pitiful.'

The Xylophone Man growled, reaching a hand out to her. 'You will come to me, and you will kneel, and your soul will be mine once more. Mine, and my master's.'

Hanna stayed where she was, totally still. Her body didn't snap rigid, or float in the air, robbed of its control and ambition. The Xylophone Man looked down at his arm like it had betrayed him.

'What have you done to me?'

She glanced over her shoulder. The driver's lifeless body was still slumped in its seat, the passengers who had seen this screaming the information to their fellow commuters. Through the window in front of him, she saw that a mass of people had gathered in the distance, grouped by the side of the tracks. Straddling the centre of those tracks was an eighteen-wheel juggernaut of a truck.

She turned back to the Xylophone Man and grinned. 'What have I done to you? I've set you free. This is where it ends.'

The world exploded like it had no choice but to agree with her.

Hanna and the Xylophone Man were thrown from their feet as the train collided with the truck. It flipped and tumbled, rolling again and again and again, the bodies in it crumbling

73

and snapping and breaking. It performed a final flip, then came to a stop in a shower of sparks and fire, its wheels still spinning, a decapitated chicken that didn't know it was dead yet.

Finally there was silence.

Hanna opened her eyes. She'd been flung free of the train; it lay spread-eagled and broken in front of her, a toy cast aside by a stropping toddler, surrounded by dozens of broken and bleeding bodies. The lucky ones had died instantly. She should feel something about that, she supposed.

She got to her feet, dusting herself down, then looked across at her followers, a hundred men and women, strong and true, souls who had all but rotted away in the moss of the Sea of Trees, but ones who now had a passion and a purpose, thanks to her. Soon, they would have much, much more.

She beckoned for them to come to her.

The Xylophone Man was lying on the floor, commuter corpses strewn all around him. The mask on his face was shattered and pulped, revealing the pale, drawn, pencil-like face of a simple man called Oliver Pipe.

'How?' he gasped. 'How have you done this?'

Hanna kneeled down next to him. 'With the help of friends. You wouldn't know much about friends, would you, Oliver? It's difficult to believe you ever had them, either in your soil days or in the afterlife.'

She placed a foot against his neck, yanking a gasp from him. 'As to the how, if you guzzle your food like that, well, occasionally you'll eat something that disagrees with you.'

She moved her foot away, causing the Xylophone Man to gargle blood, then crouched down next to him, triumph dancing in her eyes.

'You see, those poor souls you devoured had taken poison – the suicide pills, in fact, that the Dying Squad are equipped with – and that poison is now surging like acid in whatever passes for a bloodstream in your body. In an hour's time, the mighty Xylophone Man, the feared Culler of Wretches, the terrifying Infernal Serpent, will be nothing but a crumbling cluster of brown and green neurons.'

She looked around, then reached down and picked up a large piece of metal that had been ripped free of the train. 'Unfortunately for you, I don't have an hour.'

Her followers had gathered behind her, a blood pack waiting for its meal.

She scowled down at the Xylophone Man's shattered mask and the mangled face beneath it, stamping downwards, smashing it into pieces and causing him to scream in pain.

'How does it feel, Oliver? To be afraid? To be the hunted rather than the hunter?'

'I'm necessary,' gasped the Xylophone Man, trying and failing to get up. 'I keep order.'

She snorted. 'Like you did in the Pen? You wanted me to foment revolution there. Besides, order is what we've had since the dawn of time, and look where it's got us. War. Famine. Pain. I'm going to change all that. It's time for *disorder*. It's time for a new world.'

She raised the metal shard over her head. 'And your death will herald it.'

She plunged it into the Xylophone Man's chest, and it was as if the sky screamed in agony alongside him.

Black blood, congealed like swamp water, spilled from his mouth. Hanna kneeled down, dipping her fingers into it, holding it up to the light, the sound of sirens blaring in the distance. She turned to her followers and nodded.

They spilled forward, the hundred-strong group fighting to get at the Xylophone Man, to scratch and bite and rip and tear and rend.

Hanna laughed, dragging her bloodied fingers through her

hair, then smearing two dabs against her cheeks, the screams of a demigod being ripped limb from limb soundtracking it all.

There was no one left to stop her now.

It had begun.

Chapter Five

Daisy-May had always told herself that she wouldn't get an office. Private offices were the old, fusty regime of the Duchess, a regime the Duchess herself had helped raze to the ground. It turned out that telling yourself something was very different to actually doing it, though, and when it came down to it, she needed somewhere to regroup and think. Or hide, if you were being snide.

She'd kept it simple, with a single screen on the opposite wall, a rickety old desk, and a paucity of the Duchess's eclectic primness. It could have been a meeting room in Slough, which, when you thought about it, wasn't that hellishly different from the Pit. It did the job, though. Which is more than I'm doing, thought Daisy-May.

Still, she couldn't deny that the sight of Joe and his new partner, Bits, stumble-pogoing towards the Gloop walls had been an entertaining one. Considering their history, it was incredible how much she'd come to rely on Joe, and sending him back to the soil wasn't a decision she'd made lightly. When it came down to it, though, the Dying Squad was a ragtag collection of screw-ups and criminals, whose only real experience of the police was being arrested by them. If they'd been the cleanest of the clean and the best of the best, they'd have ended up in the Next Place, not here with the rest of the fuck-ups. Joe at least had a history of police work, even if it was corrupt, bent-as-they-come police work.

She winced as nausea churned in her stomach, growling at her, its claws exposed. Dots danced in front of her eyes and hot bile rose up her throat. She cried out in pain and vomited, clenching her fist as her body was racked with agony spasms.

This was happening more often. What had been a once-a-day occurrence was becoming a several-times-a-day treat. And it was a little worse each time.

It had begun soon after she'd returned to the Pen. She'd shrugged it off until she couldn't any more, the attacks, which stole upon her with the grace of a ninja and the force of a sledgehammer, getting progressively worse. They could be evidence of any number of things. Post-traumatic stress from the ordeal she'd endured under the Xylophone Man. The sheer suffocating responsibility of ruling an afterlife realm. The fact that she was a sixteen-year-old girl in a world of monsters and gods that hadn't asked for her and certainly didn't want her.

Or it could be none of those things, thought Daisy-May, because I know what it is, I just don't want to admit it. It was the Gloop. I swam through a sea of poison, and I shouldn't have survived. Someone agrees with me on that score, and they've come to collect the levy. Only so many times you can cheat death, even when you're dead.

She looked down at the pool of vomit by her feet. There were spindles of green intertwined with blackened chunks of God only knew what.

And old God won't tell, not that I really want him to, 'cos that shit looks like soil disease. It means that there's something wrong with me, something that maybe can't be cured, because who can cure the dead? Who even knows how?

'Is everything all right, ma'am?'

She looked up to see Remus standing in the doorway, smiling.

She reached under the table, steadying her shaking leg, trying to get the spasm of pain under control. 'Everything's always all right. I'm the Warden of the Pen. What could be better than that?'

Remus's nose twitched, taking in the smell she'd been responsible for.

'Help you with anything?' said Daisy-May.

'You asked me to report if I had any information on the Duchess.'

She sat up in her seat, her pain forgotten for a moment. 'She's been spotted?'

Remus nodded.

'Where?'

'In Japan.'

'What's in Japan?'

'The Japanese, mostly.'

'Funny fucker,' said Daisy-May.

Remus bowed his head in apology. 'It's a country riddled with the dead and their spirits.'

'Isn't every country?'

'Not like Japan. And if the Duchess is there, it's a good bet her younger sister is too.'

Daisy-May closed her eyes, wanting the room to stop spinning, wanting the world to slow down, even if it was just for a few moments. 'How much of a problem do you think Hanna's going to be?'

'I think the point is, she's the Duchess's problem,' Remus replied. 'More importantly, the soil's problem. Not ours.'

'Disagree with you there,' said Daisy-May, the room lurching. 'We allowed her to escape to the soil. That means she's absolutely our problem.'

'Which is precisely the reason the Duchess is tracking her. She's the most formidable Warden the Pen has ever known: Hanna doesn't stand a chance against her might.'

'The ol' Duchess is the benchmark, no question there,' said Daisy-May, 'but Hanna's proven to be tricksy as fuck. And until Rachel catches her, she's a danger to any living soul she comes in contact with.'

'You should refer to her as the Duchess, not Rachel,' said Remus. 'There's a certain protocol to these things.'

'You do love a protocol.' Daisy-May smiled weakly. 'God bless them, someone has to.'

'Protocols ensure things run smoothly,' said Remus, his tone starched. 'Perhaps if you were a little more respectful of them, things would be going better here.'

'*Ma'am.*'

'Ma'am,' he repeated, his eyes flashing.

'Sticking to protocol almost ended existence,' said Daisy-May. 'Sometimes you need to tear things to the ground to build them back better.'

'You're beginning to sound like Hanna,' said Remus. 'That was her belief, too.'

'Not crazy about your tone, mate.'

He bowed his head. 'My apologies.'

A spasm went through her, and it took everything she had to control it.

She inhaled deeply. 'Apology accepted. What else can I help you with?'

Remus shifted uneasily from foot to foot. 'It's less what you can help me with, more what you can help our prisoner with.'

Daisy-May looked up at him, intrigued.

'The woman Lazarus arrested has offered to make a full confession. She claims to run a gang that's been butchering their fellow Dispossessed. She also has information on the souls that were being ferried back to the soil.'

'She just offered that up?' said Daisy-May. 'Got to be a catch.'

'Of course,' said Remus. 'But it's one she'll only reveal to you.'

Joe always said she had the demeanour of a punk rock brat but the hardened instincts of grade-A murder police. Daisy-May had been quick to dismiss the compliment, while secretly storing it as a precious heirloom, an all too rare keepsake of praise in a life devoid of them. Those instincts were humming now, telling her that there was something wrong with the woman in the interview room.

'So, what's her story?'

'A remarkable one, and one best heard first-hand,' said Remus. 'I wouldn't do it justice.'

'You can understand her?'

'Perfectly,' said Remus. 'Her English is excellent.'

'It's better than her face. She's banged up to hell.'

'It was how Lazarus and his partner brought her in.'

Joe wasn't kidding about Bits roughing her up, thought Daisy-May. Which says all sorts of bad things about my judgement in recruiting him. Another fuck-up. Another black mark against my leadership.

She adjusted her leather jacket like it was a tie. 'All right then. Let's see what she has to say.'

Daisy-May had never really got a handle on the whole 'bad cop' thing. The 'good cop' thing either, truthfully; when she'd been an active member of the Dying Squad, all she'd cared about was the truth and a suspect's willingness to share it. Some hid it like it was a precious diamond, burrowing it away lest the daylight expose it and turn it to dust; others treated it like a hot coal they were throwing from hand to hand, desperate

81

to get rid of it. Within seconds of stepping into the interview room, Daisy-May knew this woman wouldn't hide the truth. On the contrary, the raw, frantic look in her eyes suggested she was searching for it.

'You're the boss girl?'

Daisy-May sat down opposite the woman, rolling her neck. 'I'm the Warden, yeah.'

The woman sniffed. 'You're young.'

'Rarely feel it.'

'My people speak well of you. Said you were kind when others weren't. You gave us things when others wouldn't.'

'Yeah, well I'm wondering if that was a good thing,' said Daisy-May, 'way crime's going in the Pen. Didn't used to be any, if you can believe that.'

'One goes with the other,' said the woman. 'Give people free will, not every choice they make will be one you like. Doesn't mean that choice didn't need to be made.'

'Speaking of which, apparently you have something to say to me.'

The woman placed her hands on the table. 'I am responsible for butchering the Dispossessed. I will make a full confession.'

'Sounds like you already have.'

'A confession is nothing. The gang I could give you is everything. Names. Locations.'

'I thought Zed was the main man,' said Daisy-May.

The woman snorted. 'Have you seen him? How could you imagine him to be the main anything?'

Daisy-May frowned. 'Why would you give us all this? We thought the murders were random; the work of a serial killer at best. You've made us look like mugs for months, and all of a sudden you're willing to give it up?'

'Because I want something in return,' said the woman.

'Which is what?'

'I want you to find my son.'

'He's missing?' said Daisy-May.

The woman nodded.

'When did you last see him?'

'I don't know time.'

'Yeah, it takes the piss in the Pen,' said Daisy-May. 'Friend of mine always told me it had no meaning here.' She leaned forward. 'What's your son's name?'

'Eric,' said the woman. 'My light and life, Eric.'

'Do you have any idea of who took him?'

'My boss lady.'

Daisy-May frowned, slumping back in her chair. 'I thought *you* were the boss lady.'

'I am,' said the woman. 'Everyone has a boss, though. Even me.'

'You know what I think, love? You're wasting my time. You're sending me on a wild-as-fuck goose chase, keeping me from where I need to be, which is rounding up your gang.'

'There is no gang without the woman.'

Daisy-May blinked. 'What woman?'

'You have never seen her like before. No one has. She is not one of us.'

'How do you mean, she's not one of us?'

'There is no shine to her,' said the woman.

'No glimmer? Is that what you mean? She has no glimmer?'

The woman nodded.

Fuck me, thought Daisy-May.

'She has taken Eric. Taken other Dispossessed's sons and daughters too. She steals our children so that we will work for her. Makes us do the operations on our kin.'

Maybe Joe was right, thought Daisy-May. Maybe he did see a blonde who didn't glimmer, herding two Dispossessed lambs down the tunnel. Maybe I should have listened to him rather than shutting him down. Sometimes there are things you need to hear, even if your ears disagree.

All of which means this case isn't finished, and I just sent my best man back to the soil.

Guess that means I'm up.

'Why is she making you cut up Dispossessed?'

'To begin with, she was there with us. Taught us how to do it. Once we could, she didn't come any more. We had to record the results. Once we have killed fifty, cut them up, she will come to collect results. Return Eric.'

Jesus.

'And how many have you killed so far?'

The woman swallowed, her tough facade crumbling slightly. 'Thirty-one.'

And we haven't found anywhere near that number of bodies. This is a killing spree the likes of which we can't imagine.

And I didn't notice.

'None of this tells me *why* she's having you do these dissections.'

'You think such a woman would tell me? I am a tool she uses. Knows she can use me, as long as she has my son. You find her, you must ask her yourself why she does these things.'

'Oh, I intend to,' said Daisy-May. 'Bet on that.'

The woman sagged in her chair. 'I worry for Eric now. The woman will be angry that the killing has stopped. I am happy for me. So much blood on my hands. Blood I will never get off. I had no choice.'

'You could have come to me,' said Daisy-May. 'I would have helped.'

'I come to you now.'

'When we'd already caught you. When you had no other option.'

Daisy-May turned away, thinking. 'Why is she taking Dispossessed back to the soil?'

'I never had anything to do with that,' said the woman. 'Zed neither. That's something else.'

When Daisy-May turned back to her, she could see that tears were pricking her eyes.

'Please, find my Eric. When she realises you have me here, she will kill him.'

Daisy-May nodded. 'Where can I find her?'

'If I knew that,' said the woman, her bruised face held proudly aloft, 'I wouldn't need *you*.'

'You're going out.'

'I am.'

'Out *there*,' said Remus.

'That's where out tends to be,' said Daisy-May. 'Otherwise it'd just be in.'

Remus tried to keep pace with her as she marched towards the compound's main entrance, their footsteps the only noise in the deathly white corridor. 'At least take a team with you.'

'Remus, old boy, if I can jump off a hot air balloon into a sea of rioting Dispossessed, I can walk the fucking grounds looking for a missing child and a woman who doesn't glimmer.'

Remus placed a hand on her arm. She stopped, turning to him. 'That's what the woman told you?'

'Amongst other things. Her boy has gone missing, and the kid ain't alone. Thirty kids in the last two months, all gone. Plus a massacre we've been ignorant of.'

'A massacre?'

'Don't have time to retell the sordid story,' said Daisy-May, 'but we find these kids, the killings stop. Trust that.'

Remus shook his head. 'Rumours and gossip are not the concern of the Warden.'

She jabbed a finger at him. '*I* decide what my concern is. Why did I not hear about these missing kids?'

'For the same reason that I'm only just hearing about it. It wasn't reported to us.'

'Thing like this, we shouldn't *need* it reported. Should have people on the ground, feeding us this sort of info.'

'How do you mean?' said Remus.

'Way this woman tells it, this mythical woman that doesn't glimmer is behind the Dispossessed getting cut up. Joe ID'd her herding Dispossessed out of the Pen, too.'

Remus shot her a look of unfiltered patronisation. 'Ma'am, you're a little too old for ghost stories.'

'I'm living in one,' said Daisy-May. 'Joe's had eyes on this woman and I didn't believe him. Didn't take it seriously. You best believe I am now.'

He placed his hands behind his back. 'Ma'am, the Soul Extraction Agency—'

Daisy-May shot him a look.

'The Dying Squad,' said Remus, correcting himself, 'consists of a skeleton crew that works mainly on the soil. We simply don't have the numbers to uphold law and order in the Pen.'

'That's why we're taking on members of the Dispossessed,' said Daisy-May. 'Up the numbers to keep the peace.'

'An admirable effort and stance, and one that will, in time, provide results, I'm sure. Time, though, is something we have little of. If we are to maintain order in the Pen, we need boots on the ground. Now.'

Daisy-May looked behind her at the main compound doors, impatient to leave. 'How do you suggest we get those boots, mate? And the undead feet that'll go in them?'

Remus licked his lips, wrestling with something. 'What do you know of the Gabriel Initiative?'

Daisy-May winced as a fist of nausea closed around her stomach. 'Fuck all.'

He looked at her, concerned. 'Are you all right, ma'am?'

'Fine.' She bit down on the inside of her cheek. 'What's the chat with this Initiative?'

'It's an ancient law,' said Remus, the look of concern still on his face. 'One that says that in times of crisis, special measures can be enacted to bring in outside help.'

'What sort of outside help?'

'A taskforce, made up of elite soldiers who would help keep the peace.'

'Sounds like a military dictatorship,' said Daisy–May. 'Where do these soldiers come from exactly?'

'The Initiative is unclear on that point,' Remus admitted. 'It merely states that they would be under the full command of the Warden of the Pen.'

Daisy–May closed her eyes, fighting the vomit bubbling in her stomach.

'You're clearly unwell,' said Remus, reaching out a hand to her, which she batted away without opening her eyes.

'I'm fine. Just been a long-arse day.' She stood up straight and smiled at him. 'No to the Gabriel Initiative, Remus. The fact that the Duchess didn't order it, even when the Dispossessed were rioting, tells me it's something we want no part of.'

He bowed his head. 'Of course. I merely offered it as a suggestion to ease your load.'

'And I appreciate it. Keep those suggestions coming, mate, I need all the help I can get.'

She hit a large brown button next to the door. It began to slowly ease open.

'When can I expect you back?' said Remus.

Daisy–May stood in the doorway, looking behind her for a

final time. 'When I find this lad Eric, the other missing kids, and the non-glimmering cow who took them.'

'Been a while,' said Mabel, hands on hips, a scowl on her face. 'Sweet Jesus, girl, you look terrible.'

'Bit blasphemous that, mate,' said Daisy-May, accepting the old woman's embrace.

'Think Jesus sweats the small stuff?' Mabel broke the hug, and ran her eyes over Daisy-May's gaunt frame. 'What they feeding you in that job? Arsenic?'

'I'm fine. Nothing that seeing your mug won't help cure.'

Mabel snorted. 'Not a prescription I'd fill out, that one.' She placed the back of her hand against Daisy-May's forehead. 'How long you been throwing up?'

'How'd you know?'

'Because you're the colour of a blood frog, and because you swam through a sea of poison. Should have killed you within seconds, the Gloop. That it didn't doesn't mean it hasn't left its mark. Question is, how deep does it go?'

'I'm fine,' said Daisy-May. 'Just a bit queasy sometimes. You're as bad as Remus.'

Mabel snorted. 'That old fart giving you stick?'

'More what he doesn't say than what he does.'

'Pay him no mind,' said Mabel. 'He's been giving Wardens shit since the day he died. Means well, and his voice is worth listening to now and again.'

She kneeled down, rummaging for something under the stall, then handed Daisy-May a small wooden box.

'What's this?'

'Radiation pills – not that you need 'em, of course. They'll help with the nausea. Amount of pure soil air you huffed, surprised you're not yakking every five minutes.'

Daisy-May looked down at the floor.

'If they don't cure it, got something more drastic in mind.'

She nodded, sliding the engraved cover partly off, and plucked out a pink slab of pill. 'You sure these aren't meant for horses?'

'If they've had a gut full of that poison, then yeah, they are.'

Mabel tilted her head. 'You didn't just come here for my pills.'

Daisy-May shook her head. 'You got any reports about children going missing in the Pen?'

Mabel looked from left to right, then leaned forward. 'Nothing that you'd call solid, but yeah, I've heard things. It was in my last report.'

Daisy-May frowned. 'It wasn't in any report I've seen.'

'That's got more to do with your eyes than my report.'

Another fuck-up, thought Daisy-May. Another thing I've missed. Add it to the pile.

She popped one of the pills into her mouth, gurning as she gulped it down. 'What'd it say, your report?'

'Why? Bit late now, ain't it?'

She grimaced, the pill's aftertaste bitter and tangy. 'Why don't you let me be the judge of that?'

Mabel smirked. 'That's my girl. You've got that look.'

'What look?'

'Like you're using your mind. What's on it?'

Daisy-May took a breath. 'I think it's connected to Joe's case. Way the Dispossessed are cutting each other up. Those suits you modified for me too. You tell me what's what, maybe I'll know for sure.'

Mabel grunted, leaning further forward. 'Started happening a couple of months ago. First one child a week would go missing, then two. Now if we get through a week without ten kids going missing, it jars. Always the same type. They're not like your lad Bits – these kids are old school Dispossessed, dumb, but happy with it. And they're always from the same place. The Downs.'

Daisy-May stared into the distance, lost in thought, or at least searching for a coherent one. 'This report say anything about a woman? One who doesn't glimmer?'

'Nope,' said Mabel, ''cos that'd make it a fairy tale and not a report. Only way you don't glimmer is if you're breathing on the soil.'

Daisy-May nodded without looking at her, hunting for answers in the distance.

'I know you're not thinking of going there to kick up a fuss,' said Mabel, ''cos you're the bloody Warden, and you've got staff to do that.'

'Being Warden seems to involve people that *haven't* been Warden telling me how to do my job,' said Daisy-May, indignation prickling on her skin.

'You've got responsibilities now. You can't just go gallivanting about righting wrongs.'

'Sound like the Duchess there, Mabel,' said Daisy-May. 'It was not caring about this shit that meant she had to hand over control to me. I'm not going to make the same mistake.'

Mabel shook her head. 'You've got a good heart, girl, I've always said it. Too good for this place, and too good for this job.'

She turned to the back of the stall, considering, then took what looked like a starter pistol from the canvas sheet and handed it to Daisy-May.

The girl held it up to the light, staring fascinated at the translucent body. A green slime-like substance moved backwards and forwards within it, like a living lava lamp.

'No guns, Mabel. Think I was clear on that.'

'That's no gun,' said Mabel. 'It's a distress beacon. You get in trouble, you shoot. Just make sure that trouble's big, 'cos when that gun calls for help, they'll know about it on the bleedin' soil.'

Daisy-May smiled her thanks, then tucked the pistol into the back of her belt.

Mabel sighed. 'If you're set on this, worse people to search out than the Judge. What he doesn't know in the Downs ain't worth knowing. Not when it comes to skulduggery.'

'Who was reborn and made this bloke a judge?' said Daisy-May. '*We're* supposed to be law and order in the Pen.'

'The Downs ain't the Pen,' said Mabel. 'Never has been and never will be. Soon as you get there, you'll remember that.'

The Downs may have been hell to newbie Dying Squad members, dazzled by its apparent squalor and all too real filth, but to Daisy-May it was like slipping on an old pair of broken-in Converse trainers. The place was all she really knew.

Before she'd taken on the role of Warden, she'd spent many hours here, learning the language and the intricacies of Dispossessed culture. She didn't mind the yelling, or the screaming, or the incessant chatter. Maybe it was because it reminded her of home so much, of the Nottingham council estate with her alcoholic mother and a father she'd never known. Noise and confusion, that was where she felt most content. It was one of the things that made the straitjacket job she'd been lumbered with so difficult: there was little room for chaos when you were the gaffer. You were supposed to bring control, not bathe in confusion.

Maybe I'll give myself a couple of hours off being Warden, she thought. What's the point of being the boss if you can't skive occasionally? Besides, I'm working a case. Been a while, and it'll be a while longer after I get done with this one. Might as well make the most of it.

She allowed herself a rueful smile at an afternoon off now consisting of finding a load of missing children and a woman who flouted the rules of the dead.

What was this mysterious woman's aim? Daisy-May knew why she was taking the kids (at least she thought she did); they were the ultimate form of leverage. Why use that leverage to get their parents to kill and maim, *that* was what she couldn't figure out. What was the purpose of the experiments? What was the woman getting out of it? And where was she hiding all the children?

Maybe she was just a sick fuck in it for the kicks, but that didn't ring true to Daisy-May. There was something else at play here.

Whatever. Find the kids, stop the killings, it was that simple.

Doubt gnawed at her. Had she made a mistake sending Joe back to the soil? There was no doubt he could make a differ-ence there, but he could have made a difference here, too. Was that the way it was going to be, having to drop everything when one of the living was threatened?

She couldn't say she much cared for that, no matter what she'd said to Joe.

Daisy-May stood on the lip of the hill overlooking the Downs, letting the energy of the place wash over her. Directly ahead was a hotchpotch of thirty or so shacks, and to the left of them what she could only describe as a barn, its roof corrugated, its windows squinting out at the charcoal sky. The front door swung open and two men stumbled out, scrapping and enjoy-ing every second of it.

'The Wild fucking West, man,' said Daisy-May warmly. 'God bless the Downs.'

She heard chatter from behind her and turned to see a gang of children making their way up the hill. She smiled at them, beckoning for them to come over. They slowed, looking at her warily.

'What you want?'

She was grateful that in terms of age, she didn't look so different to the boy who had just spoken to her. It was only on the inside that she felt ancient.

'You guys OK to be out here alone?' she said, in note-perfect Dispossessed tongue. 'Hear it's not safe nowadays.'

'Why we're in a group,' said the boy, who Daisy-May would have placed as ten years old. 'Always have to be five of us now. Five of us, we're safe.'

She crouched down. 'Safe from who?'

A girl who could have been no more than six pulled at the boy's sleeve. 'Not supposed to talk to strangers.'

'She's not a stranger,' said the boy, staring at Daisy-May. 'She's the Warden.'

'Definitely shouldn't be talking to her, then,' said a girl at the back, roughly Daisy-May's age when she'd died. 'What'd whole-souls ever do for us?'

'She did plenty,' said the boy. 'Didn't always used to be the Warden, did she? She'd come round. Talk to us. Help us.'

'I want to help you now,' said Daisy-May. 'Do you know any of the children who have gone missing? Lad called Eric, for instance?'

'I do.'

A tall, lanky boy raised his shimmering, translucent hand. The older girl kicked him. 'No words, yeah? We agreed.'

'I don't want many words,' said Daisy-May. 'Just ones about the missing kids.'

'My friend, he went missing,' said the tall boy. 'Said a lady had a job for him. He was excited. He went to meet her, but he never came back.'

'When was this?' asked Daisy-May.

'A week ago,' said the boy.

'He say where he was meeting this lady?'

'Nah. Didn't believe him, anyway. Not till he never came back.'

Daisy-May nodded. 'Thanks. Keep together, and don't stray out of the Downs, OK?'

The girl snorted. 'Downs is the least safe place in the Pen. That's where the kids are getting snatched from.'

'Even more reason to stay together and stay safe. And don't talk to strangers, unless they're the fucking Warden.'

Especially if you have parents who care about you.

The small girl looked delightedly shocked at Daisy-May's curse.

'One last question: you know a bloke called the Judge?'

The tall boy at the back nodded. 'Everyone in the Downs knows the Judge. He's the law around here.'

I'm the law around here, Daisy-May thought but didn't say. At least I'm supposed to be.

Dispossessed being smuggled into the Gloop, Dispossessed hacking each other apart, missing kids, all at the shitting behest of a woman who doesn't glimmer. What's the connection? What does she want?

I figure that out, maybe people will see me as the law.

Maybe I will myself.

Chapter Six

It was a full minute since he'd exited the Gloop, and every inch of Joe's skin still burned. Kneeling on the floor, shaking, he dry-heaved up whatever it was his body had absorbed. Hopefully not enough to poison him.

'Fucking . . . lightweight.'

He looked up, the alley they'd ended up in wavering and blurring in front of his eyes. Bits was a foot or so away, leaning next to a wall, supporting himself with his left hand.

'You made it,' gasped Joe, getting slowly to his feet.

'Had tougher piss-ups in Sunday school,' said Bits. 'Can't say I appreciate this hangover, though. Done nothing to earn it.'

'You outran a monster,' said Joe, wobbling but alive. 'Seems like you earned it to me.'

'What was it?' asked Bits. 'That ball of nightmare chasing us?'

'Who knows. If I had to guess, I'd say those poor fuckers were close when the poison blast happened. It fused them, mutated them. Just one of the afterlife's many ways of fucking you over, in the most horrific way imaginable.'

Joe took in his surroundings. He knew Manchester to be a place of rage and rain, but despite the night light, heat seemed to radiate off the alley's concrete edges. A shimmering road could be seen in the distance, dozens of cars yelling and honking at the night sky. The place felt clammy.

'What's it like to be home?' he asked.

Bits pushed himself away from the wall, taking in a lungful of soil air. 'Like it's the best thing that's ever happened to me, as well as the worst. What now? The cop shop?'

Joe shook his head. 'The living police here don't even know we exist; they certainly aren't expecting us. Besides, if they'd got anything on the Generation Killer that was worth knowing, we wouldn't be needed. No, now we track down Elias, who should be keeping our spirit witness warm for us. He's based in Ancoats. Do you know it?'

Bits nodded. 'You like your pills and your powders, you know Ancoats. Old warehouses, young dealers and fuck all besides.' He scratched at his arm distractedly. 'We got a cat's-piss chance of finding this missing girl?'

'We do our work, and we see where it takes us. Fingers crossed that place is somewhere we can save her,' said Joe.

Bits shoved his hands in his pocket, his eyes shifty and twitchy. 'You carrying?'

He talks like his words are fighting with each other, thought Joe. Like they carry a grudge.

He nodded, opening the leather satchel, which he'd taken from the suit, and bringing out a hypodermic needle. 'Guessing this isn't the first time you've shot up in an alley.'

'Twat,' said Bits, glaring at the syringe then reluctantly taking it, holding it like it was infected. 'Can't believe you're making me do this.'

'I'm not making you do anything,' said Joe. 'You do this, you get to help me do a good thing. You're not going to get addicted. This isn't like when you were alive.'

Bits snorted. 'Not what Mabel said. We'll crash hard if we

96

don't top this up every two hours. You think that's anything but addiction, you're high already.'

Joe looked at the needle in his own hand. 'I don't like it any more than you do, but I like the alternative a lot less.'

He rolled up his sleeve and eased the needle into the crook of his right arm, squeezing down the plunger then withdrawing it and tossing the syringe aside. It lay on the floor, the rats oblivious to it.

'You see?' he said. 'Nothing but a pinprick, then it's done.'

Bits blinked furiously as he replicated Joe's movements. Joe pretended not to see the tears in his partner's eyes.

Humidity slumped over Manchester as they walked down Market Street, a tram trilling, the city's inhabitants bathing in the heat of the night. Joe marvelled at the way they laughed and joked; their aura was almost visible. That was the thing about the living – they had an effervescence that was wasted on them, a force of nature they took for granted. It had taken being dead for him to truly appreciate that.

'How long is it since you were here?'

'What year is it now?' said Bits.

'Twenty twenty-two,' said Joe. 'I think.'

Bits whistled. 'Twenty-six years since I karked it.'

'Nineteen ninety-six, then,' said Joe. 'That year means something. Why?'

Bits nodded, looking upwards at the towering buildings, his home town's encroachment into the sky. 'Year Manchester got bombed, wasn't it? Levelled the whole city centre.'

Joe clicked his fingers. 'The IRA. They called it in, though, right? There were no fatalities. Well, unless you count the Arndale Centre.'

'There were fatalities, believe me, or one of them. Me.'

Joe looked at Bits in surprise. 'Bollocks.'

97

'Why'd I make it up?'

'They got everyone out,' said Joe. 'I was on the Nottingham force at the time, and they had us on standby to assist: no fatalities meant we weren't needed. I read the report afterwards; it was by-the-book good.'

Bits snorted, indicating they should take a left. 'Not for me.'

They'd come to Exchange Square, Corporation Street running alongside it like a proud uncle. Bits stared at it, wonderingly. 'This is all new, man. None of it was like this.'

'This was the epicentre of the blast, wasn't it?' asked Joe.

Bits nodded. 'Old as fuck and twice as broken down. Manchester was a dump, but it was our dump. This? This could be anywhere. Where's the soul? Where's the heart?'

'In the bin with the stabbings and the gang warfare,' said Joe. 'That's one of the upsides of gentrification – your chances of getting mugged go down.'

Bits's eyes wandered over the square. A tram stop had been cut into its belly, gleaming department stores and smaller shops jostling and crowding it, a shimmering edifice of capitalism penning it in from the rear. 'Arndale. Good times in there. Shit shops but good drugs.'

'Good drugs? It's a shopping centre, not a nightclub.'

'Everything's a nightclub if you try hard enough.' He sniffed, almost as if trying to ferret out an errant pill. 'It's where I died, over there. When the bomb went off.'

'Are you sure you're remembering it right?' said Joe.

'Good at remembering my own death, me. I'd shot up in the toilets. Wicked-strong gear, knocked me clean out. Next thing I know, I come to in a pile of rubble and I'm looking at bits of me splattered all over the place.'

'That's why you're called Bits?' said Joe.

Bits scowled at him. 'Nah, it's 'cos my head was always in bits. Drugs. Glue. Whatever. Anyway, I come to, and there's flames going straight through me. I'm fucking dead as dead. Then there's this blinding light, and I'm in the Pen.'

Joe looked at him curiously. 'When did you remember all this?'

'Never forgot it.'

'That's impossible. The Dispossessed only began to develop consciousness recently.'

Bits barked a joyless laugh. 'Typical whole-soul, full of assumptions about what you know and what we don't. We've always known who we were, man, we just couldn't communicate it. Didn't have the words, and you clowns didn't have the ears. Like calling the uneducated thick. Your girl Daisy-May was the first one to get that. Her and the other girl. One with the white hair. Hanna. Lass who almost ended existence.'

Joe nodded. 'Imagine having that on your CV. I never met her. I was on the soil when all that kicked off.'

'She had presence, know what I mean? Kind of person that spoke and made you want to listen. Told us we could be different, things could be different, if we kicked against it properly. And she was right. Things are changing, and not just this pretend-cop bollocks. Dispossessed have had enough of being dispossessed. That could play out lots of ways, you know?'

'I do,' said Joe, jamming his hands into his raincoat. 'A lot of those ways wouldn't be good for either of us.'

'Whatever happened to her?' said Bits. 'Hanna?'

'I don't know,' said Joe, 'and for all our sakes, I hope we never have reason to find out.'

In the early 2000s, Sankey's Soap modestly assumed the title of Greatest Nightclub in the World.

Housed in a long-dead soap factory, deep within grime-lashed Ancoats, the club's warren of rooms presented cutting-edge underground electronica and pharmaceutical isolation inside its four hedonistic walls. Joe had been here once, seconded from Nottingham on an undercover drug bust. It had been successful for him in that he'd caught the dealer; even more successful when he'd pinched the dealer's drugs to resell.

Time and tide wait for no disco ball, though, and the jack boot of capitalism meant the building was to be sold for flats. Scaffolding clung needily to Sankey's skeleton, wood tattooed onto its windows and doors.

'You remember this place?' asked Joe.

'Don't remember anything any more,' said Bits. 'Warehouses and smackheads, that's what Ancoats is to me. Now it's flats and posh-cunt pubs.' He nodded at the former nightclub. 'Clubbing here was before my time, too. Hacienda was my era.'

'Flats now, the Hac,' said Joe. 'Expensive ones, too.'

Bits looked at him, disgusted. 'Straight up?'

Joe nodded.

'That's savage, man.' Bits looked at the building in a disdainful new light. 'What are we doing here?'

'Follow me,' said Joe, walking down the gloomy alley that ran alongside the warehouse, 'and I'll show you.'

They passed through the wall closest to them, that always-present tingle humming in Joe's ghostly molecules as he did so, his inability to get used to walking through walls there, as always. Bits was more nonchalant, simian-strolling his way through.

They came out in a deserted, boxy space. Darkness invaded the room's crevices, chewing on shadows and hiding the street lights outside.

'Elias?' called out Joe. 'Are you there?'

When there was no reply, he reached into his pocket and drew out a small box. The box was agitated, whatever was in it rattling against its plastic walls.

'You ever seen these before?' asked Joe, holding the jiggling box up to Bits.

'Unless that's gear in there, no.'

'It's much better than gear. Though no less trippy.'

He slid the box open and two luminous scarab beetles flew out, lighting the room with a pale blue glow. They hugged the ceiling, criss-crossing each other like Day-Glo sparklers.

'Jesus,' said Joe, when he saw what they revealed.

'Not here,' said Bits, looking all around him. 'Not here, ever.'

The room contained dozens of souls. All were huddling together for comfort, each one staring fearfully at Joe and Bits. Green vines grew from almost every man, woman and child, indicating they'd been stranded on the soil for some time.

'They can see us,' said Bits, his eyes flicking from person to person.

'Of course,' said a voice from behind them. 'They're dead, just like you.'

The partners whirled around to see a middle-aged man standing by a winding metal staircase. He had pure white hair that was pulled into a ponytail, and a thick black military-style overcoat, the empty right sleeve pinned to his chest. In his left hand he held a torch, which he shone directly through Bits's translucent form.

'Elias,' said Joe. 'You bring me to the nicest places.'

Elias grinned, switching the torch off, content to let the scarab beetles light the conversation. 'Ruined seaside towns one month, abandoned Manchester nightclubs the next. The Lord moves in mysterious ways.'

'He does that,' said Joe. 'I'd shake your hand, but, well, you know.'

'I do,' said Elias. 'Only too well. I gather you solved the case I last met you on. Belated congratulations are in order.'

'Better never than late when it comes to that high-five,' said Joe.

'You find out who you really are in the way I did? Doesn't put you in much of a celebrating mood.'

'I hear of the great things you've done since then, though,' said Elias, 'and know of the great things you are yet to do. That's all that matters.'

Joe studied Elias in the bathe of blue provided by the beetles. He was even more gaunt than the last time they'd met. His face crawled with cheekbones, and blackened half-moon grooves were carved under his eyes.

Elias smiled at Joe's all too obvious once-over. 'I don't make for a pretty picture, it's true. I'm not dead yet, though, and while that's the case, there's still good I can do on this earth.'

Bits stared at him. 'If you're not dead, how come you can see us?'

'It's a long story,' said Joe.

'Not really,' said Elias. 'More of a short but interesting one. Allow me to feed these poor souls, and it will be one I'll gladly tell.'

Joe and Bits sat to one side, watching fascinated as the ragged collection of souls waited patiently in line. Elias stood ready to receive them, an oxygen tank at his feet. As each stranded soul stepped forward, he pressed a rubber mask over their face.

'Concentrated memory serum,' he said. 'It calms them.'

'You're running a soup kitchen,' said Bits.

'I run a *mission*,' said Elias, 'an extension of the Pen that cares for those who weren't able to cross over when they died. The small amount of comfort I can give them gives *me* a very great deal.'

'But how can you see them?' asked Bits. 'See us?'

Elias coughed, Joe wincing with every hack.

Finally he got himself under control, and continued. 'If

comedy is the art of timing, tragedy isn't very far behind. I'm dying, Bits.'

'Soz,' said the Mancunian.

'I'm not,' said Elias, smiling at him. 'It's a gift. It allows me to see souls like these. If I didn't have the cancer that I have – have it as aggressively as I do – then they'd have no one to help them. It's a privilege, and one I give thanks to God for every day.'

Bits shook his head. 'You're like an albino Gandhi, man. Me, I'd be raging against it, calling God every swear under the sun.'

Elias laughed. 'I have my raging days, believe me.' He got to his feet, wincing as he did so. 'Come. I want to show you something.'

Joe and Bits followed Elias up a winding flight of stairs, the scarab beetles lighting the way as they headed towards the tinny sound of music. Plastic sheeting acted as a doorway at the top of the stairs, the three men passing through it to find themselves in a smaller room than the one they'd come from.

An old-fashioned boom box rested on a DJ booth, the dusty disco ball hanging from the ceiling glittering in the scarab-beetle light. Four Dispossessed were dancing underneath it – although really it was more of a dad-dance shuffle – faraway smiles on their faces.

'This is perhaps the work I'm most proud of,' said Elias, nodding at the group. 'There's considerable evidence that music can help those suffering with dementia, which my own research bears out. These four used to be clubbers here – where they dance now is where they danced when they were alive – and playing electronic music stirs something in their memory. A couple of them have been able to recall their names, and even how they died.'

Joe shook his head. 'And that's without the oxygen tank or gum?'

'I find they work against it,' said Elias. 'When you've been on the soil for as long as these men and women have, the best you can hope for is that they give them some degree of solace. This type of therapy has longer-lasting benefits.'

'Clubbing ghosts. Fucking nuts, man,' said Bits.

Joe leaned into Elias. 'This is stellar work, Elias, but we're against the clock here. Where's our pickup? A young woman's life is at stake, and time's short.'

Elias sighed, his eyes searching the floor. 'There's something else I need to show you.'

If a late-night jogger (or early-night reveller) had decided to take the Ancoats canal that evening – in particular, the stretch between Tariff and Rodney Street – they would have been greeted by the sight of an emaciated, umbrella-wielding gentleman conducting a conversation with two blank slots of night air. As it was, the biblical downfall had cleared the canal of living souls, and so the unlikely trio were able to walk and talk in peace.

'Don't understand how you lose a ghost, man,' said Bits.

'They're considerably harder to find, believe me,' said Elias, 'and you lose them in the same way you lose the living.'

'Plus, the living can't walk through walls,' said Joe.

'Quite,' said Elias, raindrops pounding on his umbrella. 'And truthfully, they're not usually in the habit of wandering off. Stanley Veins was placid enough when I collected him, and as you well know, Joe, that's not often the case with pickups. Especially when they've been brutally murdered.'

'Did he remember anything?' said Joe. 'Anything about who kidnapped and killed him? Anything about his granddaughter?'

'Nothing,' said Elias. 'He was dazed, acted like it had

104

happened to someone else. It's a reaction I've seen many times before.'

'He didn't say whether it was this Generation Killer who had murdered him? Didn't give you a clue about his physical appearance, anything of that nature?'

Elias shook his head. 'Frustratingly, not. If I'd had more time with him – if I'd been able to use my music therapy on him, for instance – it might have been different.'

He stopped suddenly, peering at the rain-soaked canal floor. 'This is it.'

'This is what?' said Bits. 'Looks like concrete paving and rat's piss.'

'This is where I found Stanley's spirit body,' said Elias. 'Or rather, what was left of it.'

'Wait: you mean he's dead?' said Bits. 'Like, *dead* dead?'

'He does,' said Joe, nodding grimly. 'Which means our job just got a shitload harder.'

'Ever seen anything like this before?' said Bits.

Joe shook his head. 'Not on the soil, or in the Pen. It's like something's burned him away.'

They huddled around a dip in the canal paving, Joe giving thanks that this wasn't an earthly investigation; the incessant tropical rain would have swilled away any evidence that may have been left there. As it was, the Turin-shroud-like print of the spirit they'd come to claim lay there unaffected. It was as if his soul had been blowtorched into the brick.

'How the fuck do you kill a ghost when it's on the soil?' said Bits.

'There's plenty of ways,' said Joe, distracted, kneeling down next to the impression.

'Nothing earthly could do this,' said Elias. 'But unearthly? I'm sorry to say there are beings that could commit such a crime.'

'The Xylophone Man?' asked Joe.

Elias shook his head. 'He's contained by the ancient laws and attacks only those who break them. I'm thinking of something else.'

Joe and Bits looked at him expectantly.

'I'm thinking of wendigos,' said Elias.

Bits snorted. 'Thought this was Dying Squad, not Urban Myths Squad.'

'Why haven't I heard of wendigos?' asked Joe.

'Because they're Scooby-Doo bollocks,' said Bits.

'They're a little more real than that,' said Elias good-naturedly. 'I should know. I've seen one.'

'Bullshit,' said Bits.

'They prey on the type of souls I care for. I've seen the results of their feeding, if not their physical form.'

'Still waiting for a definition here,' said Joe.

'Wendigos, like the people back at the mission, are unable to cross over into the afterlife,' said Elias. 'Instead of slowly withering away, they mutate; they are able to survive on the soil, with their memories intact, by feeding off the dead.'

'So they're like ghost vampires?' said Joe.

'They're fucking fiction,' said Bits, 'so sure, why not?'

'They hunt in packs, feeding off the dead,' said Elias, looking grimly at Joe. 'They drain the soul out of them, leaving nothing but a smudge, like poor Stanley here. The physical mutation they have gone through is quite horrific. That doesn't mean they're brainless animals, though. That's what makes them so dangerous.'

'Absolute horseshit,' said Bits.

'Why are you so dismissive of them?' said Elias. 'You're dead and yet you walk in the living world. I'm alive and I can see and talk to you. Why are wendigos so difficult to believe in?'

'Nothing gets ruled out,' said Joe, foraging in his satchel, 'until the evidence demands it. One thing we can say for sure: whatever killed Stanley wasn't from the living world. *Ah.*' He pulled out a thin metal rod.

'That a glow stick?' said Bits, staring at it, fascinated. 'You kicking off a rave, Grandad?'

Joe waved the device and ultraviolet blue light flared from it, casting the canal in a ghostly pallor.

'Looks like the sort of light they use in train station bogs,' said Bits. 'So that junkies can't shoot up in 'em.'

You'd know, thought Joe.

'It's the same kind of kit a soil blood specialist would use,' he said. 'If something dead has left the merest trace at the crime scene, this thing'll pick it up.'

He waved the wand in front of Elias, and when it reached the living, breathing one-armed man, the blue light immediately disappeared.

'Clever, that,' said Bits.

'Very,' said Elias. 'What are you looking for?'

'Anything that shouldn't be here,' said Joe.

He took a step back and began methodically working the rod over the canal's brick surface. The raindrops hammered into the ground, the light in his hand giving them a flickering, strobe-like quality. Left to right he went with it, trying to unearth a hint of a clue.

Nothing.

Nothing.

Nothing.

'What's that orange shit?' said Bits.

Joe pushed the light closer to it, squinting.

'Fascinating,' said Elias. 'It looks like amber.'

Joe peered down, his nose inches from a small crystallised trail that led from what was left of Stanley Veins, along the canal path, to the steps leading up it.

'We're going on a bear hunt,' said Bits, his flattened Manc vowels lending the words insolence and aggression. 'We're going to catch a big one . . .'

The three men followed the trail up the steps. They led to a deserted side road, the only illumination a reluctant street light above them, the orange trail dribbling across the road like the vapid urine of a dying animal.

There, it ended.

'Whatever killed Stanley attacked him here,' said Joe, pointing at a spot a few feet from him. He turned on his heel, wand in hand, tracing back the trail. 'Stanley runs, or more likely crawls his way over the road and onto the canal path, then collapses at the point you showed us, Elias.'

'That makes sense,' said Elias. 'When a wendigo drains a soul of its remaining life force, it is said to be akin to trapping it in a sort of stasis. Much as a spider would when trapping a fly, it is then free to feed on it until there is nothing left to consume.'

'Say that's what we're dealing with,' said Joe. 'What's the best way of tackling it? What are its weaknesses?'

'They are so shrouded in myth, it's difficult to say,' said Elias. 'Crosses and garlic won't do much good, though.'

'Does it matter?'

They both turned to Bits.

'Harsh as fuck, but it's true. The missing woman's all that's important, right? Not what happened to a bloke that was dead anyway.'

'We're dead as well,' said Joe. 'It matters.'

'The way I see it, the dead have had their shot,' said Bits. 'Likes of me and you blew it. Megan Veins hasn't.'

Joe considered, then nodded. 'You're right. The problem is, our best chance of finding Megan – and the Generation Killer – died with her grandad.' He paced back and forth, an idea niggling at him. 'Or at least it died with his spirit.' He turned to Elias. 'I need to get to the morgue, see his soil body.'

'That may be something of a problem,' said Elias.

'Why?' said Bits.

'Because,' Elias replied, 'his body isn't being kept in a morgue.'

Chapter Seven

Tokyo, the Duchess believed, was just God showing off.

Twilight bathed the city in gold as she in turn bathed in the strangeness of the city. Even in the unhinged mania of the Pen, she'd never seen anything quite like Shibuya Crossing, an anthill with thousands of workers streaming over it, many wielding veiny, transparent umbrellas, rain or shine. At her unimaginable age, the place — the *newness* of that place — was a gift she felt she hadn't earned. She closed her eyes, allowing the warm swarm of humanity to pass through her. After the paralysing solitude of the Sea of Trees, she needed to feel something again, to reconnect with life, even if she herself was dead.

The traffic waited impatiently as thousands of people poured across the road, the whole operation a functioning, throbbing organism perfectly in harmony with the environment around it. It gave the Duchess peace, knowing that she couldn't be seen, that there was no one to order around, or be responsible for.

It won't last, screeched the voice of her long-dead grandmother, Oma Jankie, *and why should it? You've let that mad bitch of a sister break into the living world. Who knows what damage she's wreaking? You don't have space for any more blood on your hands. They're covered in it already.*

I'm working on it, the Duchess thought. The world's a big place, and Hanna's adept at making herself look small in it.

'It has been three days since the train crash outside Shibuya station,' boomed the voice of a newsreader above her, 'and the authorities are no closer to identifying the cause of the accident.'

The Duchess paused, looking up at the colossal video screen that loomed over the crossing, each one of its thousands of minuscule LEDs blinking with unease. 'Here at TCN, we have obtained a video recording from one of the carriages, taken moments before the fatal crash. The following clip contains footage that is difficult to explain, and that some viewers may find disturbing.'

Looking around her, the Duchess saw that the flow of people crossing had stopped. All were rooted to the spot, standing deathly still and staring up at the screen. The image of the newsreader cut out and was replaced by smeary video footage of a packed train carriage. The commuters wore their cattle-herd mentality well enough, with only a minimum of jostling as the train swayed slightly.

Then, at the bottom left of the screen, a window began to crack. It was just a spiderweb to begin with, but the fissure began to quickly spread to colonise the glass. Oxygen then sucked the pane from the carriage completely, the first time commuters were really aware of it.

A thick shard of glass hovered in mid-air.

'Do you see that?' a voice from behind the Duchess said.

'Hard not to,' said a man to the side of her. 'Don't know *what* I'm seeing, though.'

'It's like it's stuck,' said an old woman, a sense of wonder in her voice. 'Like it's got snared in the air.'

'It's not snared,' said the Duchess, knowing full well that no one would be able to hear her. 'Someone's holding it.'

Hanna.

A collective gasp went up as a male passenger on the screen was jerked backwards then yanked around towards the camera, his assailant invisible, the glass now inches from his throat.

She wants them to see, thought the Duchess. She knows where the cameras are, and she wants them to see. The living can't see her followers like I can – at least I assume they're her followers – but they can see the glass, and they can see that something is very, very wrong.

A soul-shredding scream went up from the crowd as the glass shard tore into the man's throat, the picture cutting out just before blood was shed, the crowd's imagination painting a far more horrific picture than the video ever could have.

A hungry silence stole over them.

Somehow, it was worse than the scream.

Gutsy electronica trickled in slyly from the west, but the Duchess barely heard it.

Her attention was consumed by the forensics team hunkering down amongst the ruins of the train wreck.

The passengers had long since been removed, their broken bodies taken to waiting morgues, and now only the forensic team remained. They worked methodically, sifting through the debris an inch at a time, trying to understand just why it was that a commuter train with a perfect safety record had careered off the tracks, killing every one of its passengers.

The CCTV footage would be pored over obsessively, the Duchess supposed. What conclusions could possibly be drawn, though? Were the authorities supposed to believe that spirits had caused the crash, as well as attacking the passengers on the train? It was a farcical idea. She could barely believe it herself, and she knew it to be true.

Had there ever been such a flagrant violation of the ancient laws? Hanna hadn't just interacted with the living; she'd incited murder against them. She would have known such an act was suicide, that it would draw the wrath of the Xylophone Man. Why commit such an act, then? What was her endgame? Because there *was* one, the Duchess was sure of that.

Moving forward, weaving in and out of the forensic workers, she continued her rootless search. She didn't know what she was looking for; she only knew that Hanna must have left some sort of clue behind her, a morsel that would reveal at least part of her plan.

Or she didn't, cackled Oma Jankie's voice. *She keeps making the impossible possible, so why would she let a silly old bitch like you pick up her scent? She learned from the best. She learned from me.*

So did I, thought the Duchess, and despite that, people still consider me competent.

So funny, said Oma Jankie. *You were always funny, Rachel; if only you were good, too. And think: if you hadn't thrown your title of Warden away like cheap confetti, you would have had the resources to track Hanna properly. Oh, what it would have meant to me, if you were capable of anything more than disappointment and failure.*

'Shut up, you old hag,' said the Duchess. 'It's because of your teachings that we're in this mess.'

Oma Jankie's voice fell silent at this, because the argument was so undeniably true, it didn't bear further discussion.

The Duchess stopped dead.

No. It couldn't be.

What she was looking at would have been missed by any forensics team, no matter how fastidious. Indeed, despite the shocking tableau in front of her, any living, breathing person would have been oblivious to it. The Duchess was neither, and so she saw, all too clearly, the fallen, broken body of a being considered unkillable. Someone had speared him, like a piece of meat, with a jagged metal stake. His back was arched, like his body had tried to expel it.

The Xylophone Man.

The Duchess let out a choked sob, but it wasn't for the fallen beast. Oliver Pipe had gloried in the pain and fear he'd created over the centuries, delighting in his role as afterlife judge, jury and executioner; he deserved as ignoble an end as possible. The sob was for the future, because when the old gods died – or in this case were murdered – where did that leave existence? Nature abhorred a vacuum, but the afterlife truly despised it; with the Xylophone Man gone, there was no one to stop the Hanna Jankies of this world from interfering with the affairs of the living.

Or cold-bloodedly murdering them.

The train was a trap, thought the Duchess. Hanna wanted to draw the Xylophone Man out so that she could kill him. I don't know how she did it, but I do know that one of the last lines of defence against her has gone.

There's only one left now.

Me.

She watched as a detective joined a huddle of forensic officers, engaging them in conversation.

It wasn't true to say that she was alone. There was another.

Whether he'd be willing to help was a different thing entirely.

Kisho Kurokawa's Nakagin Capsule Tower was a cultural rallying cry for the Japanese people, as well as an architectural application to rejoin the human race. Constructed in 1972 in just thirty days, the building embodied the country's growing confidence and post-war resurgence, and was based on the idea that the lives of humans in a post-modern megalopolis were similar to those of individual cells in the human body.

Those cells were close to ruin now. Only thirty capsules remained occupied, and those didn't enjoy the luxury of hot water. Not that Hanna Jankie minded; she'd never been big on luxury, and had little use for water, hot or otherwise. She'd chosen the building because it was the sort of place that looked like it was haunted by restless spirits.

Tonight, it was.

They'd filled the abandoned rooms, her new followers, because when everything was new (and death, truly, was as new as it got when you were dead), a person needed something familiar to moor themselves with. A roof over your head, even if that roof was low and the room small, was just the ticket, because the souls who had died in the train crash had a part to play. The performance would be far better if they weren't plagued by the madness of death.

They would do what she said, of course; the language of death she'd learned in the Pit ensured that. She liked to think that dead tongue was a component of their service to her, rather than the key motivating factor, though. It brought obedience, but it didn't bring true belief; it was Hanna's words and leadership that ensured that.

She sat in the room alone, a rare moment of solitude she would do her best to enjoy. Many of her Sea of Trees recruits were gone, necessary sacrifices to bring down the Xylophone Man. She was determined that those sacrifices wouldn't be in vain.

There was no one to stop her now. Or almost no one: the Duchess, foolish as she was, might try, but she was old, and she was no longer Warden of the Pen. It could be that she'd followed Hanna here to the soil – certainly Hanna had left booby-traps for her to discover if she had – but any power she still had would be dissolving by the moment on the soil.

That's where you are at a disadvantage, Rachel. When you know what I know, you have safeguards against your power diminishing. The soil can't stop you. In fact, all it does is make you stronger, because the undead you face won't have such knowledge.

It was knowledge that effectively made her a god, and although such titles didn't mean much to her, they meant enough to produce a small ripple of pleasure at the realisation. When you'd spend almost two centuries in the latrines of hell, godliness was a conceit you allowed yourself.

She sat on the floor, night neon filtering through the window, the rumble of the train overhead strangely comforting, despite the hell she'd unleashed days ago on a similar vehicle. She'd told the souls at the crash site that she'd freed them from their mortal coils, because coils was another word for manacles, another representation of servitude and slavery.

She breathed in, attempting to steady her thoughts as well as her undead breath, reciting the words in her mind.

Make thoughts words, and words actions. There is no such thing as amnesia because there is no such thing as the mind. There are only abstractions and consequences.

She took another breath, inhaling oxygen that should have been drip-feed poison to her.

My name is Hanna Jankie. I rose from the pits of hell to get here, and I will rise further before my work is done. The air here cannot touch me, because there are barriers in place that make that so. Everything else is a distraction. Everything else is noise.

They were like weights, these spoken-word enforcements, punishing, necessary workouts to reinforce her mind and keep it strong against the corrosive poison of the soil. Vital safeguards against losing her advantage over the Duchess, too, if she had indeed followed her here; her Warden power would mean she'd keep a firm hold on her memories, but she'd still be reliant on the gum. Hanna herself had no such need for a crutch.

It was in the Pit that she'd first learned the technique, sly mutterings from the Xylophone Man grooming her for his own nefarious, rabble-rousing means. Not that she hadn't been grateful; it had helped ease the greater horrors of hell, and meant she'd had the clarity of thought to plot the beast's downfall. He probably hadn't envisaged that downfall when his devil's tongue had whispered to her in the Pit, but then that was the problem with the Oliver Pipes of this world: they lacked vision. It wasn't a character flaw that could be levelled at her.

She exhaled, her reflection on the past at an end.

It was time to shape the future.

There was a thrill, Hanna had quickly discovered, that came from being invisible. It was unbecoming for a being of her stature to be so enraptured by such a childish thrill, but that thrill was there nonetheless.

Not that there was anything particularly thrilling about the man she was following. He wore his suit like it held a grudge against him, and his skin was pasty and stressed. He rolled his neck constantly, as if he was trying to knead out the kink, and looked like he'd stared mortality in the face and blinked. Knowing his profession, Hanna could believe that was the case.

It was that profession that had made her tail him to this bloated concrete high-rise in the Tokyo suburbs. She stood inches from him as the lift huffed and puffed its way upwards, her presence bothering the man in a way he couldn't quite understand. He drew his coat – a garment that was almost as ugly as the suit underneath it – closer, despite the clamminess of the day.

The lift pinged and Toki Sato sighed, stepping between the doors into a scrubland of a corridor, Hanna close behind him.

The area looked malnourished and ignored. Holes had grown in the faded red carpets, and only a smattering of the lights hanging from the ceiling were illuminated. A CCTV camera blinked at them, but Hanna thought it unlikely that it worked. Nothing else around here seemed to.

It was perfect. She'd chosen this man because the intel from her followers stated that he was of single status and minimal attachment. There was no family expecting him, no partner dutifully waiting with his evening meal. He was a humble man who lived in humbler surroundings, which made what she was planning a lot easier.

She waited as he fumbled for his keys, fatigue rolling off him in waves, fighting the instinct to simply walk through him and the front door.

Patience, she told herself. Patience.

Finally he found his keys, and then the lock with those keys. He swung the door open, revealing an apartment so modest it barely counted as inhabited.

A sofa sat at the back of the room, its plastic covering still in place. Three chairs were scattered randomly around – Hanna could have believed that they had been plucked from a skip, they were so ill-matching – and the only item that looked to be of any value was the floor-to-ceiling-sized television.

Perfect, she thought, smiling at the room. This is absolutely perfect.

Sato slumped onto the sofa, its plastic cover creaking in protest, and picked up a remote control, flicking it. The giant screen flared into life and he grunted contentedly, slumping deeper into the sofa's grooves.

Hanna knew she should wait till he fell asleep, that what she was about to attempt would be much easier if he was in a dream state, but she also knew she didn't have time. Someone would be on her tail, whether it was the Duchess or not. The slaying of the Xylophone Man guaranteed it.

Still, she paused as she looked upon the oblivious man. What she intended to do to him was yet another crossing of the line between the living and the dead, something spoken of in bad novels and worse horror films but rarely tried, let alone accomplished, by spirits such as herself. That wasn't just because of punishment from the recently slain Xylophone Man, either. It was because of the moral dimensions of the act, the aftermath of it. It would leave her scarred. There was no coming back from it, no forgetting it.

If he was lucky, this procedure would eventually kill the man on the sofa.

If he was unlucky, it wouldn't.

Possession is never really possession: that was what the Xylophone Man had said to her, shortly before releasing her from hell. *If done right, the invasion of a living soul is more an oppression of their free will. Possession is an act of rape. It is a brutal, despicable act that leaves the one you possess brain-damaged. Oppression, on the other hand, allows the victim to believe they have free will, that the decisions they are making are ones they have chosen to make, rather than ones you demand they make.*

Whether you intended to oppress a living soul or possess them, the initiation was the same: you clambered from your body into theirs. It was a procedure born out of violence, despite the differing levels of control, and was just as unpleasant for the spirit as it was for the living host. It was a trick employed by the most depraved, the most damaged spirits that haunted the soil, ones who had been driven mad by their exposure to the soil's air, or ones who had been mad to begin with. The act was beneath her.

It was also necessary, if her plan was to succeed.

Hanna crouched next to Sato as he stared obliviously through her. For this to work, there was no incantation to mutter, no spell to conjure; you slopped out your consciousness until it was a dribbling, crawling, biting monstrosity, and you let it do its work. It was the darkest of dark arts that only the satanic and the insane would even try to attempt.

Or the righteous, she thought. Those who were taught it in hell by a bored sadist called the Xylophone Man, never imagining it would be unleashed in the living world.

Muscle memory of vomiting hit her as something clambered up her throat. She gagged as it poked out of her mouth then dropped onto the floor and began crawling towards the unsuspecting Sato, leaving a trail of hissing, steaming fluid in its wake.

Slowly the twisted, mollusc-like creature began to crawl up his leg, the browned nails underneath it acting as millipede grappling hooks.

Sato noticed something without knowing what, and brushed his leg, his hand passing harmlessly through Hanna's crawling consciousness.

It's not harmless, though, she thought, watching with grim fascination as it crawled up Sato's chest. It's hideous. Is that because of the crimes I've committed? Would another spirit's look less demonic? I suppose it doesn't really matter, because when that thing embeds itself inside Sato, I'll know every bad thought he's ever had, along with the good ones. He'll do everything I ask of him, and serve the cause as faithfully as the most loyal foot soldier.

Sato blinked, confused, as the creature reached his mouth.

His jaw began to open against his will; a scream gurgled from the base of his spine.

Hanna closed her eyes as the monstrosity – her very essence – began to crawl down the man's throat.

Watch, said Oma Jankie. *Own what you're doing, and watch.*

For once, you're right, Hanna replied.

She opened her eyes.

She watched.

Chapter Eight

When it came to tracking down missing kids, you needed to find someone objective.

The Judge's domain was little more than a courthouse with a liquor licence. Daisy-May couldn't decide whether it was proof of the Dispossessed's burgeoning intelligence or a sign they'd reverted to subhuman levels of it.

The barn-like building was broken up into two parts: a de-militarised zone, branching off to the left of the open-plan main square, where the bedraggled Dispossessed drank, shouted, laughed and fought; and the main trunk, which operated as a courthouse, where order didn't so much reign as cling on with broken fingernails. At the centre of it all, presiding over the madness, was a man Daisy-May had to assume was the Judge.

His gown was white instead of the regulation black, giving him the look of an unhinged evangelical preacher. His lobster-red skin suggested he'd been hitting hell's tanning rooms, and he had an anorexic bolo tie slung around his neck, its thinness accentuated by the rippling layers of fat it had been strung around. His piggy green eyes shimmered with intelligence, taking in everything and nothing at the same time.

He looks mental, thought Daisy-May, but sharp-as-a-tack mental. No one's fool, even if he dresses like one.

The Judge slammed down his gavel (which Daisy-May saw was actually a hammer), demanding order, his Deep South drawl drawing the vowels out like they were prisoners on a torture rack. Two men stood in the dock in front of him, a ragged length of rope marking out the area, glaring at each other but keeping the peace, for now.

'I will sum up the facts of the case, then I will pass down my judgement,' declared the Judge, spittle flecks flying. 'My judgement is final. There is no appeal, and if you attempt to enter any, the punishment will be most severe.'

It's like he cheese-grates the ends of his words, thought Daisy-May. This bloke's every Christian evangelist I've ever seen on TV. Full of his own self-importance, twice as deluded, and triple-threat dangerous because of it.

'The allegation presented before me is the following,' continued the Judge. 'That Plaintiff A had a possession stolen from him – namely his dog, which I name as Item A – by Plaintiff B. Plaintiff B refutes that claim, stating that he couldn't have stolen the animal as the definition of *possession* cannot be applied in the afterlife.'

Plaintiff B stuck up a hand. 'If that means I couldn't have pinched his dog 'cos it weren't his in the first place, then you're bang on.'

'Silence,' screamed the Judge. 'There will be no interruptions to my summarisation.'

Summarisation-ah. This bloke hasn't met a word he doesn't want to make twice as long. It's like he's getting paid by the letter.

'The concept of possession in the afterlife is an interesting one,' said the Judge. 'For on the soil, the dead have few rights. They cannot marry, or divorce, or vote. The executor of an estate cannot sue for libel, or slander a deceased person. How, then, should a soul have rights in the afterlife if those same rights have expired on the soil?'

Daisy-May looked around at the seated members of the public, who were hanging on the Judge's every word. Even the revellers in the bar had quietened their ramblings to a dull roar.

'There is an argument to be broached, the court would argue, that legal rules concerning the dead are simply in place to control the actions of the living, and these soil breathers have no jurisdiction here. The court must concern itself with the rights of the dead, not the living.

'However, without law – without judges – there is only chaos . . .' the Judge paused here, to take a slug of neat whisky from a mucky glass decanter, 'and so this court rules that legal rights such as possession must survive something as trivial as death.'

'Possession's nine tenths of the law,' smirked the skinnier of the two men in the dock, 'so that dog's mostly mine now.'

The Judge hurled his hammer at the man, the sharp end connecting flush with his forehead. The man screamed and sank to his knees.

'There will be order in this court,' yelled the Judge. 'One more outburst and you will be held in contempt.'

Christ knows what contempt looks like, if disorder means a hammer being chucked at your head, thought Daisy-May.

'I rule that the dog must be returned to its rightful owner,' said the Judge. 'The whole dog. My judgement is final and immediate.'

The man got shakily to his feet, pulling the hammer from his forehead. 'Bit of a problem there, Judge. Dog's dead.'

'Course it's dead,' said the opposing plaintiff. 'It's in the fucking Pen. Don't mean it isn't mine.'

'Nah, *dead* dead. Ate some poison or something. Just a bunch of brown vines now.'

Plaintiff A didn't take this news well. He launched himself at the phantom dog stealer and the two men rolled around on the floor, searching for a punch to land.

The Judge, who had seemingly lost interest in proceedings, shuffled imaginary papers then beamed beatifically at the public gallery. 'Justice has been served. Court will break for recess.'

Fuck me, thought Daisy-May. The inmates aren't just running the asylum, they're writing its laws as well.

She stepped over the warring parties and headed for the Judge, who seemed to think the law was now best served from the bar.

'Minute of your time, Judge?'

He turned, jowls wobbling, gown rippling. 'On the soil, I once struck a legal councillor for calling me Judge. It's *Your Honour*, if it has to be anything at all.'

Daisy-May bit her tongue and the indignation resting on it. She needed this man, needed him to be onside even more. 'My apologies, *Your Honour.*'

The Judge sniffed. 'What may I do for a child such as yourself?'

'You can start by calling me ma'am,' said Daisy-May, motioning to the bartender, 'and letting me buy you a drink.'

The Judge retired to his private booth. Daisy-May sat opposite him, a bottle of half-drunk Scotch between them. The Judge swirled the contents of his glass.

Maybe he's trying to see into the future, thought Daisy-May. Can't be much worse than the present.

She took out another of Mabel's radiation tablets, popped it in her mouth and washed it down with a lick of Scotch.

The Judge rested his drink on the table, smacked his lips contentedly and considered the slip of a girl in front of him. 'And what do they call you, child?'

Ch-ild. Like he's a Southern preacher about to deliver me from the fires of hell.

'As of a few months ago, they call me Warden, but Daisy-May or ma'am fit just as well. Anything but *child*. Choose your weapon, mate.'

The Judge squinted at her. 'Someone so young should not hold a title that old. It is unjust, and no one knows injustice like I.'

'Won't get any disagreement from me,' said Daisy-May. 'The old girl that gave me the title would probably agree too. Just the way the cards fell.'

The Judge sucked in his cheeks. 'You should know, ma'am, that your power holds no sway here. We do not concern ourselves with the ruling class in the Downs. These are simple people, and I am their father, son and holy ghost.'

And there was me thinking you were just a slightly mental self-appointed judge. How quickly they grow up.

'Not interested in a power grab,' said Daisy-May. 'I'm fighting on enough fronts as it is. I'm here for something else.'

The Judge took the bottle of Scotch and liberated a third of the contents into his tumbler. 'Well then, tell me, ma'am, and I will help if I can, or at least help justice to be served. If you are on the right side of that, so much the better.'

Daisy-May leaned forward, her stomach settling slightly from the combination of medication and liquor. 'Got a Dispossessed female from the Downs in custody. She runs a gang that's been cutting up Dispossessed at the behest of a woman who doesn't glimmer. A woman who for some reason is ferrying Dispossessed through the Gloop to the soil. Kind of surprising that this woman just confesses and offers me the keys to the kingdom, she's that desperate for our help.'

'A move not prompted by a guilty conscience, I presume?'

'You presume right, Your Honour. This woman's son – lad

who goes by the name of Eric – is missing. Word is, lots of mothers' sons and daughters have gone missing, thirty, maybe more. All from here, all Dispossessed.' Daisy-May leaned forward. 'You know anything about these missing kids?'

The Judge considered. 'These rumours are not new to me. They do not ring *un*true. These people are too low to care about, there to be taken advantage of.'

'*You* care about them, though,' said Daisy-May, 'or you wouldn't be here in the first place, trying to keep order, trying to keep fair fair.'

'We all have a role,' said the Judge haughtily. 'I simply play mine.'

Don't lead the witness, that was one of the things Joe always said. Daisy-May wanted to ask the Judge about the woman who didn't glimmer, but she wanted him to offer up that information himself more. It would carry more weight, and independent witnesses were the gold standard in an investigation like this.

'You believe these rumours? About the kids, I mean?' she continued.

The Judge sighed, churning the contents of the glass around in a way that reminded Daisy-May of the Duchess. It was a tic she employed when she was playing for time.

'I believe it's easy to believe them. There is little evidence to contradict the plain fact that the children are gone.'

'Who could be doing it?' asked Daisy-May. 'You must hear every whisper in this place.'

The Judge took a drink and almost smiled. 'The inhabitants of the Downs are not ones to dabble in whispers, ma'am. Screams and shouts are more their vernacular.'

'What screams and shouts have you heard, then?'

He sat back, considering. 'Plenty, some of it believable, some of it not. The most common thing I hear is of a woman.

A kindly woman who offers jobs to the children of the Downs. If they accept this offer of employment, they are never seen again.'

'How do you know this, if they're never seen again?'

'You know how things work in the Downs,' the Judge replied. 'Rumours become facts in the shortest period of time.'

'Right,' said Daisy-May. 'Not many jobs in the afterlife, either. Kind of worth the risk.'

'What is a job but a means of giving yourself a better chance? These poor half-souls will grab for the grubbiest of baubles to alleviate the pain of everyday afterlife. You should know that better than anyone.'

He does know who I am, then, Daisy-May thought. No matter how naïve he plays it.

She looked away, trying not to think of a childhood that had involved teenage prostitution and drug addiction. 'I've heard the same thing about this woman. A few other things, too.'

The Judge looked around to make sure nobody was eavesdropping. The hum, chatter and chaos of the bar didn't pay them the slightest mind. 'That she doesn't glimmer, I suppose.'

Daisy-May nodded.

'That would, of course, be impossible, child, because you know what it would mean?'

'It'd mean she's come from the soil to the Pen,' said Daisy-May, 'so yeah, that shit hits *impossible* with a twelve-gauge shotgun. Strange how much impossible is about.'

The Judge laughed, seeing off the last of his whisky. 'A girl months dead convenes with a man years dead, and she talks of possibility and impossibility. That girl, if she thinks about it, will see the contradiction.'

'Nothing but contradictions, the afterlife. Fuck, is it wearying.' Daisy-May pushed her glass aside. 'You know where I can find her?'

'I don't know whether she even exists,' said the Judge.

'Well, *someone* exists. Someone's shunting the Dispossessed from the Pen to the soil, and that same someone's inciting them to butcher their own kin by kidnapping their kids. Whether that someone glimmers or not, they need bringing to justice.'

'On that, ma'am, we are in agreement,' said the Judge.

'So how do I find her?' said Daisy-May. 'Better yet – how do I have her find me?'

The Judge smacked his lips, like he was wrestling with his fidgeting conscience. 'I had a case on the soil, when I was simply a practising lawyer' – *loy-yah*, noted Daisy-May – 'rather than a court circuit judge. I was prosecuting a young man accused of murder, and if it's a crime to take pleasure in your work, child, then I was guilty. This man had killed children – young boys, to be specific. Poor ones of a skin tone that society simply didn't care for. Always strangled, always dumped on wasteland, and always with a calling card: a video camera, wiped clean of prints, set up on a tripod facing the victim, the tape inside containing the last moments of their life. The press christened him the Super-8 Killer.

'Do you know how they caught this alleged killer, child? Do you know the details of how they snared him, ones that were never released to the public?'

'I'm guessing they've got a relevance to our child abduction problems here,' said Daisy-May. 'Hoping they do, anyway.'

'They offered up bait. They took a poor black boy from a poorer orphanage in an even poorer part of town, and they put a tracker on him. They had him play outside, late at night, and waited. The first night drew no results. The second was equally barren. On the third, the police finally had success, if you can call it that. The officer who was supposed to be monitoring the child missed his abduction. When they realised he was gone, they followed the tracker and caught the man red-handed dumping the lifeless body.

'The Super-8 Killer was a high school janitor called Terrence Watkins. He proclaimed his innocence even when the judge sentenced him to death. I'm quite sure he proclaims it to this day, if he isn't already in the Pit.'

'Think it was worth it?' said Daisy-May. 'The life of that kid they tossed away, to catch him?'

'The question is, do you? It is a question only you can answer, Warden, but if you're serious about catching this woman, it is one you must carefully consider. When *I* considered the truth of it on the soil, I made a choice. If the public learned the police had used a poor black boy as bait, it would have derailed the case, and don't forget, we had our man. I made my choice. I chose to sweep the police's incompetence under the carpet, and that is why I was sent to the Pen, rather than the Next Place.'

The Judge looked down. 'I do not regret it. It was the wrong thing to do, for the right reasons. A foul criminal was kept off the street, saving dozens more lives. These are the decisions we must make. That you must make.'

Daisy-May nodded, sliding out of the booth and wondering whether coming here had become a good idea turned bad or a bad idea turned good. 'Thanks for the drink, Your Honour. And for the counsel, as much as it wasn't what I wanted to hear.'

The Judge nodded. 'If one were to employ similar tactics – and look for volunteers – one could do worse than journey to the docks. Many children of the Downs wait there for work, or the promise of it.'

'I might just do that,' said Daisy-May.

The Judge appraised her for the final time. 'Your predecessor would never have come to the Downs. You're a Warden of promise, and one that gives me hope in the way the Duchess never did. Know this, though: what is hope to me will be despair to many others, particularly those who do not embrace justice and change. You would be wise to remember that – and be wary of it.'

Chapter Nine

Megan had lost track of how long she'd been down here.

Hours?

Days?

Weeks?

Why had she followed George into the pipe? Everything about it had screamed danger, from the *DANGER, DO NOT ENTER* signs, to the flight-not-fight instinct in her gut. Her addiction had overridden them all, though, addiction to the perfect shot, the unique photo that no one else had captured before. She was paying for that addiction now. Kidnapped, tied to a chair, facing a wall, watching a film that made her eyeballs itch. Yeah, she was paying for it all right.

Closing her eyes made no difference, because she couldn't close her ears, and the images had become scorched onto her consciousness.

Her experience always followed the same pattern.

The film was on a loop, and started the same way each time: with the clip she'd seen on first entering the tunnel with George. The boy called Walter was given an injection, and then the balloon he'd been holding popped. The image would warp, and a title card would appear on screen, stating: *GIFT PROTOCOL: DAY 16.*

The same boy would be in the same seat. He would even be carrying the same red balloon. He looked different, though. More gaunt. Either his eyes had grown larger or his skull had shrunk back from them.

'How are you feeling today, Walter?' the same female voice as before asks off-screen.

Walter doesn't say anything. Instead, he just stares at the screen insolently, his hair sticking up in clumps.

'You're looking much better.'

Megan disagrees with this. He's looking far, far worse.

'Why are you here, Walter?' asks the voice. 'What is it we're doing here?'

Walter mumbles something unintelligible.

'I can't hear you,' the woman says.

'We're helping people,' he replies finally.

'That's right,' the woman says. 'We're helping people. Who do we help specifically, Walter?'

His vision is drawn to something off-screen. He closes his eyes. 'Those who need it.'

'That's not specific,' says the woman. 'Do you know what specific means, Walter?'

Walter looks at the camera defiantly. 'It means exactly.'

'Very good. Who do we help exactly, Walter?'

He doesn't answer. Instead, he squeezes his fist into the balloon, bursting it.

Megan always flinches at that. She's never quite got used to it.

Nor has she got used to the boy's screaming afterwards.

Although it's really more of a bark. Formless. Wordless. The noise a dog would make when it was taunted and tortured beyond all reason. A man in a surgical gown rushes in, and then the screen warps again.

GIFT PROTOCOL: DAY 30 appears on another title slate.

The boy again, although by this point he's more like a wispy ragdoll in a smock. His hair is patchy. His bones barely have the skin to cover them. The smock is like a tent on him. He doesn't have a balloon in this final shot. Megan assumes it's because he wouldn't have the strength to hold one.

'I have good news for you, Walter,' the woman off-screen says.

Walter makes no response. He's slumped in the chair, his head lolling forward.

'Today is your last day on the programme. You're free to go.'

He raises his head at this. It costs him a lot, but he manages it.

'I know what that means,' he croaks.

'It means you're free,' the woman off-screen says.

'Keep me,' Walter says. 'Keep me and let my brother go.'

Silence.

'Don't do this to my brother.'

Silence.

'Please.'

'This is what your parents wanted,' the voice off-screen says. 'To serve in the way that you are is a great honour. There is no greater thing one can do than to help others.'

'Please,' Walter says, for a final time. 'Not my brother.'

The image warps.

The film ends.

When it does, Megan always wonders how far away her own end is.

Manchester's best kept secret wasn't much of a secret.

Tucked away in Chinatown, amongst the chop shops pretending to be karaoke bars and the karaoke bars pretending to be restaurants, the building was unremarkable. True, the high walls and barbed wire hinted that something valuable had been hidden there once, but if anyone were to take a second glance, they'd assume it was just another relic of the city's past, on its knees and begging to be gentrified.

They'd have been wrong, because it wasn't what was inside the building that intrigued, but what was beneath it: a nuclear fallout bunker, constructed at the dawn of the Cold War and connected by four miles of tunnels, smack-bang under the city centre. Thankfully, there'd never been a need for the local movers and political shakers to use it.

'I have a contact on the police force who told me about this place,' said Elias, as Bits and Joe stood behind him, looking up at the soot-black building. 'When they found Stanley's body, it was pumped full of so much radiation they couldn't just keep it in the morgue. They had to isolate it until it could be disposed of properly, and what better place than a nuclear fallout shelter?'

'How do we find it once we're down there?' said Joe.

'As in all things, you simply follow the light,' said Elias. 'The tunnels are long, but they're straight, and they all meet in the middle. According to my contact in the police, that's where the body is being kept.'

He took a step back, rain splashing at his feet like it was applauding. 'This is where we part ways, gentlemen; only those with the highest security clearance can enter such a facility, and unlike you, I can't walk through walls.'

Joe nodded his thanks. 'One final favour to ask you.'

Elias smiled. 'Anything to help.'

'This contact on the force. Could he get us an address for the missing girl's flat?'

'You think you'll need it?' asked Elias. 'After you've examined Stanley's body?'

'Maybe not,' said Joe. 'Maybe so. The bad investigations are the ones where you only turn over half the stones.'

Elias nodded. 'I'll see what I can do.'

Joe wasn't alive, but that didn't stop him from being afraid.

He'd felt fear when he'd first encountered the Xylophone Man, he'd felt it when he'd first discovered the kind of man he'd been on the soil, and he felt it now, descending a ladder into a tomb of gloom, because a pitch-black nuclear bunker was still a pitch-black nuclear bunker, and that was true whether you were alive or whether you were dead.

He heard Bits breathing above him, grunting occasionally as his feet soundlessly found the ladder steps, the light getting a little less murky the lower they went.

He tried not to think of it as descending into hell.

'Where you taking us, man?'

'I'm not taking us anywhere,' said Joe, his hands firmly on the rungs. 'The case is. Sometimes that's not a place you want to go, but that's the job. A woman's life is at stake.'

'Agreed. So why are we here?'

'I need to see Stanley Veins' body.'

'Why?' said Bits. 'Not like you can question it.'

'You'd be surprised what you can – and can't – do in the Dying Squad,' said Joe. 'The Generation Killer murdered him. Touched his body, no matter how careful he was. It's the closest thing we have to a lead, so we follow it up.'

He hoped it would concentrate their minds, too. At the moment, Megan Veins was simply a missing woman neither of them had met, an image on a computer screen that had been kidnapped by a murderer with a pulp-fiction name. The body they were about to see was a cold, hard fact, a visual representation of what happened when bad people did worse things. It would do Bits good to see that.

It would do Joe good to see that too, because they couldn't let the same fate befall Megan.

If they did, it would show that Daisy-May had been wrong to rescue him from hell.

Elias had been right: there was really only one way to go, and that was forward.

The ladder had dumped them into a vast, horizon-less tunnel. The ceiling overhead was circular, with red globes peppering its length, their light bouncing off the miles of tiles ahead of them.

'This emergency lighting for something that's already happened?' asked Bits. 'Or for something that's about to?'

'Power you'd need to light an area this big must be terrific,' said Joe. 'This red stuff's the skeleton crew. It was built for an emergency that never took place.'

'Ideas above its station, Manchester,' said Bits. 'When the bombs fell, who'd have been important enough to bring down here? Man United's squad? The cast of Corrie?'

'They probably had elected officials in mind.'

He snorted. 'Last person I'd want in a crisis, them clowns.'

They'd been walking for ten minutes when they heard it. A mournful wail echoed around the tunnels, losing a little of its power each time it ricocheted off a concrete surface. Joe and Bits stopped, turning to each other, the red light giving their faces a distorted, nightmarish quality.

'Think that's a good scream or a bad scream?' said Bits.

'I don't think there are good screams,' said Joe.

He placed the satchel on the floor, released the clasps and ferreted around in it, finally bringing out a stubby object.

Bits squinted at it disapprovingly. 'That a water pistol?'

'It's a gun,' said Joe, handing it to him, 'that will make anything dead a fuckload deader.'

'Thought the Warden didn't allow guns.'

'She doesn't.' He brought out an identical weapon of his own. 'But the Warden doesn't find herself in underground bunkers these days. We do.'

Bits nodded, holding the gun with a side grip.

'You're not a gangster any more,' said Joe. 'Hold it like that and you'll miss a lot more than you hit.' He reached out, rotating the gun the right way. 'You aim, you shoot.'

The wail became louder.

The two men moved forward.

Another three hundred feet, and Joe realised they wouldn't need their guns.

A man was in the tunnel just ahead, slamming himself off the walls as if propelled by some unseen force. Joe was of the opinion that he wasn't, that it was the man's own will making him collide with the tiled tunnel surface.

It's like he's trying to get something off him, he thought, or trying to put something out. Either way, he doesn't look like much of a risk. Not to us, anyway, even if he is glimmering in a dead-as-doughnuts way.

'Put your gun down.'

Bits looked from the thrashing man to his outstretched pistol. 'Will I fuck.'

'This man needs help, not threats of violence.'

'He needs dealing with,' said Bits. 'Way I hear it, there was a fire in these tunnels back in the day. Couple of workers died in it. Think we're looking at one now.'

'I think you're right,' said Joe. 'With that in mind, I'd say he needs our compassion, wouldn't you?'

Bits shook his head, nevertheless tucking the weapon into the back of his jeans. 'Not kidding me with this saint act. Not sure you're even kidding yourself.'

Joe ignored him, pocketing his own gun and then walking towards the distressed man. His hair was long and unkempt, his jeans flared, his jacket brown corduroy.

'It's OK,' said Joe. 'I just want to help you.'

The man stopped thrashing, his wild, unfocused eyes switching between Joe and Bits. 'Did you see it?' he said. 'Is it here?'

'Is what here?' asked Joe, taking a step towards him.

'*I* saw it,' said the man conspiratorially. 'It only comes out at night, but it's always night down here, that's what me and my mates always used to say. Darker than the devil's shit, and stinks twice as bad.'

Bits circled his finger next to his head. 'Tapped this one, man.'

'How long have you been down here?' said Joe.

The man stared past him like he'd seen something in the tunnel.

Joe turned, despite himself.

There was nothing there.

'You can never sleep, 'cos that's when it'll come for you,' said the man. 'Orange eyes. Orange teeth.'

We're wasting time here, thought Joe. There's a woman who's alive and needs our help, and we're chatting with a soul who's been dead for decades.

That don't mean he's any less worthy of our help, mate, that was what Daisy-May would have said. *We don't pick and choose who we deal out care to. The person right in front of us is the one who needs it the most, and the soonest.*

He didn't agree with her, but that didn't mean she wasn't right.

He reached into his satchel, bringing out one of the syringes.

'This'll calm you down,' he said, smiling. 'It'll make you stop seeing things.'

The man looked at him suspiciously. 'It'll make the beast go away?'

'It will,' said Joe. 'My friend and I have to do something, but after that, we'll take you to safety. A man called Elias will be able to help you.'

The man nodded, sticking out an arm, his face twitching. 'I just want to be able to rest.'

'And you will,' said Joe, easing the needle in, then lowering the man to the ground.

They looked on as his eyes fluttered, then closed altogether. Joe noted the look on Bits's face. 'You disapprove.'

'Yep.'

'The serum helps those souls who have been here for a long time. Calms them when nothing else does.'

'That's not what I'm worried about.'

'What *are* you worried about, then?'

'That you assumed that just 'cos the bloke's a nutter, he wasn't speaking the truth.'

'You're talking in riddles.'

Bits looked behind them. 'The beast he described? Sounds like a wendigo to me, man. That shit you shot in his veins might make it go away for him; don't mean it'll make it go away for us.'

'He's disturbed, and he's soil addled,' said Joe. 'The only thing down here is us and the dead body we're going to see.'

Despite uttering those words, he still drew his gun.

The Silence of the Lambs, that was what the scene reminded Joe of. That, or some sort of high-level alien autopsy.

They'd eventually come to the main bunker, the huge floor-to-ceiling doors offering no resistance to their substance-less form, to be greeted by a warehouse-sized room with a translucent cube in its centre. Its surfaces were frosty, a body just about visible inside it, lying perfectly straight, a Lenin sleeping daintily in his tomb.

'Chilled, right? To keep the body from rotting?'

Joe nodded, transfixed by the incubator cube, feeling like a grave robber with nothing to steal. Although that wasn't quite true; he was looking for information, and with a girl's life at stake, he'd take that information any which way he could get it.

'You think he's still radioactive?'

'Come closer,' said Joe, 'and tell me what you think.'

Bits did, blinking as he arrived at the cube. 'Fucking hell.'

'Yeah. Radiation's as good for us as it's bad for the living.'

'I thought it was poison for us. Like the shit in the Gloop.'

'That's not radiation,' said Joe. 'That's soil air, weaponised exponentially. This here is the closest you can get to the Pen's air. Makes your memory pin-sharp. Your energy levels sharper than that. In short bursts, anyway.'

Bits inhaled greedily. 'Fucking around with those syringes when all the time you were keeping the good stuff for yourself.'

'This whole place is caked in radiation,' said Joe, surveying the room. 'God knows what they've done down here in the past, but it explains the soul we met in the tunnel. The amount of time he's been on the soil, he should have been a mass of vines, but he looked as fresh as me or you. For the dead, this much radiation is like a flower to a bee in springtime.'

'Good place to hunt, then,' said Bits. 'If you're a wendigo, like. Any spirit that wanders down here won't want to leave.'

'I thought wendigos were Scooby-Doo bollocks?'

'Even Scooby-Doo had real monsters to deal with now and again.'

Joe didn't reply. Instead, he peered into the plastic coffin, putting his head through its side until it was inches from the corpse of Stanley Veins.

It wasn't a pleasant sight.

The elderly man's body had been stripped naked. An autopsy had been either unnecessary, or, more likely, due to the amount of radiation he'd been forced to ingest, impossible. Ribcage fought with flesh, desperately trying to escape whatever damage had been done to Stanley's insides.

Joe walked around the cube, keeping his head inside it, looking carefully at the body for any distinguishing features.

Two knobbly blue knees.

Alabaster-white skin.

Tufts of grey straggling hair.

Gnarled hands.

And something else. A mark, on Stanley's left hand.

'Take a look at this.'

'It ain't right, man,' said Bits. 'Disturbing the dead like this.'

'We *are* the dead like this. Get up here.'

Bits did as he was told, shuffling next to Joe and leaning through the plastic.

'That a tattoo?'

'Looks more like a barcode,' said Joe, squinting at the collection of lines and the six digits underneath them.

'Reminds me of something,' said Bits. 'Need to think on what.'

Joe took a step back, reaching into his pocket and taking out a clear plastic box.

'More of those beetles?' said Bits.

'No,' said Joe. 'This is something else.'

He slid the plastic covering off to reveal two shiny silver coins. 'How's your Greek mythology, Bits?'

'Shoddy as fuck.'

'So was mine before the Dying Squad.' He eased out one of the coins, holding it up to the congealed-blood light. 'The Greeks believed that when a person died, their soul moved to

Hades. To get there, they had to cross a river known as the Styx. This river was guarded by an underworld spirit called Charon, although his stage name was the Boatman. As long as you had a single silver coin, the Boatman would ferry you over to Hades in his skiff.'

'What if you didn't?' said Bits.

'Then he'd leave your arse on the shore, and you'd haunt the living world.'

'That true?'

'I don't know,' said Joe, 'I wasn't alive in ancient Greek times.'

Bits nodded at the coins. 'So where do they come in?'

'The tradition remains in many cultures. You place two coins on the eyes of the dead for the ferryman.'

Joe moved forward, placing the coins on the irradiated eyelids of Stanley Veins. 'The Dying Squad being the Dying Squad, Mabel's souped up the process. This is new tech: let's see if she's delivered.'

I certainly hope she's delivered. Otherwise I'll just be a grown man with two coins on his peepers.

The coins sat there, gleaming in the Hades haze of red, and then began to glow. Faintly at first, then more aggressively, pulsing with a sort of heavenly white light.

'What are they supposed to be?' asked Bits. 'A mobile fucking disco?'

Joe leaned in a little closer. 'They're like afterlife CCTV tapes. They strip the last image imprinted onto the corpse's retinas; whatever Stanley saw at his moment of passing, that's what we'll see.'

'What if the last thing he saw was the floor? Or the ceiling?'

'Then we'll see the floor or the ceiling.'

The coins gave a final pulse, then returned to shiny silver normality.

'What do we do now?' said Bits.

'I lie on the floor and you place those coins on my eyes.' Joe lowered himself to the ground. 'Then I see what's what.'

Bits watched as Joe lay flat, crossing his arms over his chest. 'You done this before?'

'No.'

'So how do you know it's safe?'

'I don't,' said Joe, trying to sound calmer than he felt. 'That's why it's me lying here rather than you.'

'Touching, that,' said Bits, his fingers inches from the coins.

'They won't bite,' said Joe, sensing his hesitation.

''Bout the only thing in the afterlife that doesn't, then.'

Bits picked up both coins gingerly, as though he was afraid they'd be hot to the touch, and placed them on Joe's closed eyelids.

'What now?'

'Now,' Joe said, 'we wait.'

He didn't have to wait long.

The effect reminded him of a virtual reality headset he'd tried once; the way it suddenly immersed you in another time and place. This wasn't high definition, though, more a psychedelic simulator, the world around him blurred and smeared every time he moved his head – and his head moved constantly, hungry to take in every detail. Mabel had told him that the flashback wouldn't last for ever; like a Polaroid photograph in reverse, the effect would quickly fade. He had seconds to obtain the information he needed. That was, if there was any to obtain.

He was in a tunnel of some kind. It was different to the one he'd travelled along to get to Stanley's body – the ceiling was so high he couldn't see it – but the dim lighting and Victorian tiles definitely weren't of the above-ground variety. If he had to guess (and he did), he would have said it was a storm drain of some sort. He cursed the fact that the flashback didn't come with audio, or a three-hundred-and-sixty-degree view; he could only see what Stanley had seen, right at the end.

And Stanley had been looking at a drain, Joe was sure of it. A large figure hovered over him, so black and indistinct it could have been the Grim Reaper himself. There were no distinguishing features, nothing to feed into a computer, even if he'd had access to one.

There was something else, though, behind the black figure. Or someone.

A boy with a shock of bristle-top red hair stood in the corner of the image. He wore a green blazer over a woolly grey tank top, a grubby white shirt, grey shorts and thick, clumpy black shoes. There was a glimmering sheen to him, like he was a reflective sticker.

No kid alive would be seen in that get-up, thought Joe, which probably means he isn't. The glimmer he's got certainly suggests so.

There was something else about the boy, something that was familiar, a memory lodged deep.

The image began to fade and warp from the edges.

No, Joe thought. I need more time.

There was no sign of Stanley's granddaughter. Dead or alive, she hadn't been there when Stanley breathed his last. He took some comfort in that, because there was precious little else on offer.

But they were running out of time.

If the Generation Killer kept to form, Megan Veins had a matter of hours left before he injected her with a fatal dose of radiation. Being part of the Dying Squad wasn't about climbing up the greasy pole by massaging crime figures; it was about fighting for justice when there was no one else to fight. Or in

145

Joe's case, trying to wipe clean the stain of your previous life. Despite Daisy-May's death being on him, she had seen fit to give him this chance.

If he could save Megan, he'd at least justify his existence. As far as he was concerned, that was a job he had to keep applying for until someone told him he'd got it.

No one had told him that yet.

'So? What'd you see?'

Joe sat up, removing the coins and blinking furiously, trying to convince his eyes of their new reality. 'There was a boy there. Just before Stanley died.'

'What'd he look like?'

'He looked like a boy. Had a school uniform on, though. Old. Scruffy. Red hair. Familiar somehow.'

'You think he'd been kidnapped too?'

'That would make sense,' said Joe. 'But my gut tells me different.'

'Your gut?' said Bits.

'A hunch, then.'

'A hunch. Listen to Columbo.'

Joe got to his feet.

'So how'd we find this boy?' asked Bits.

'We hope Elias has got us the address of the missing woman. There has to be something there that the flesh-and-blood police missed.'

'Why?'

'Because if they'd done their job properly, there wouldn't be any need for us.'

As Daisy-May would say, that's Dying Squad 101, that is.

'You see Megan?' asked Bits. 'When you did your coin trick?'

Joe placed the coins back in their case. 'No.'

'Fuck.'

'It's not good news that I didn't and it's not bad news, it's *no news*,' said Joe. 'And with a missing person, that's often the best sort of news you can get.'

'Never knew you were so glass-half-full,' said Bits.

Neither did I, thought Joe. Though it's more glass-half-desperate.

The walk away from Stanley's makeshift morgue had been one of trudge and frustration, Joe leading, Bits slightly behind. If he hadn't known the tunnel would eventually come to an end, Joe would have feared they were back in purgatory.

'Shouldn't we have seen him by now?' said Bits.

'Seen who?' said Joe.

'Bloke you drugged up in the tunnel. One who was chatting about beasts coming for him.'

Fuck. That guy. Sometimes hard to think outside your self-centred box. Particularly if you're me.

'Maybe he went up to the surface,' said Joe.

'Amount of junk you shot him with? No chance. Something's wrong, man.'

Joe drew his gun. 'I'm sure he's just sleeping it off.'

'Shooter in your hand says otherwise,' said Bits, drawing his own gun.

'Better safe than dead.'

'Are there degrees of dead?'

'Shush now,' said Joe, as they neared a kink in the tunnel.

Bits obeyed, both men grateful for their soundless steps, the guns heavy and at the same time all too flimsy in their hands. They rounded the corner, undead hearts pumping, fingers flexing on triggers.

The distressed soul they'd seen earlier was right where they'd left him, slumped on the floor, his back against the curved tile of the tunnel. The angle of his head wasn't right, and Joe knew

Bits saw it too, because his partner had raised his gun a little.

There's something wrong with his body, Joe thought.

There's not enough of it.

As they drew closer, he saw that he was right. It was like the man's body was collapsing in on itself, his sunken pudding of a frame seeping into the tiles.

There was something else, too.

'You see the marks?' said Joe, pointing at two red pinpricks on the man's neck.

'Like something's bitten him,' said Bits.

'Maybe Elias wasn't so far off, with his talk of wendigos.'

'Knew this shit'd get supernatural, us being dead,' said Bits. 'But there's supernatural and then there's *supernatural*. Know what I mean?'

Joe scanned the barren tunnel, then crouched down next to the man's dissolving body. 'Yeah,' he said finally. 'I do.'

Chapter Ten

After the Duchess left the train crash site, she did something she should have done as soon as she'd passed through the Gloop.

She went to the police for help.

The Tokyo police department's headquarters were situated in the city's Chiyoda ward and stood indelicately on the street, almost as if it were afraid the thousands of people filing past it each day would tread on its toes.

The Duchess knew how it felt. The constant flow of people that passed through her meant she felt continually violated; she was used to the clinical quiet of the Pen's main compound, rarely venturing out into the frantic Dispossessed badlands.

And that's why you had to give up your title, cackled Oma Jankie. *You cut yourself off from life, and from the people you were supposed to lead, and that almost led to the end of everything. I hope you're not making the same mistake again, little Rachel.*

Me too, thought the Duchess.

She eased through the building's front doors, a low hum greeting her, so different to the New York police stations of her youth, which were more violent music halls than sober correctional facilities. Even the compound in the Pen was louder than this. It wasn't as if the police here could be short on work; Hanna's murderous rampage had seen to that.

The Duchess was beginning to see a pattern, though. The train massacre hadn't shown Hanna's hand, but it had allowed the Duchess to peek at the cards. What she'd seen meant she was about to do something that didn't come easily to her.

Ask for help.

There was a directory above the main reception desk that had been chiselled into the wall, its harsh symbols coalescing in front of her eyes. Those eyes wandered down the list, department by department, until she found the information she was after.

The basement. She should have guessed.

Walking past the lifts to the fire exit, she passed through the door and quickly descended the steps behind it. She'd never thought it would come to this, but then wasn't that true of life whether you breathed it in or not? It had a nasty habit of pulling your pants down, then inviting the world to look at your arse.

'The Pen extends from purgatorium to the living world,' Oma Jankie had told her, the best part of a hundred and sixty years ago. 'On the soil, our mission takes many forms. There are chapters that take care of souls who have been unable to pass over to the afterlife, living, breathing men and women who work in the service of the Pen. You will be responsible for these chapters, both here in the living world and then in what comes after.'

She had then beckoned for the Duchess to come closer.

'There is *another* arrangement between the living and the dead, one that has existed for as long as there has been law and order on both sides of the divide. It is neither spoken nor written of, yet it exists just the same, and those who do this work are born into it, in the same way you and I were born into our roles. You see, little Rachel, there are those in the soil police who know of the Pen, and of purgatory, and of the work that we do there. They are there to assist us when we need it. What do you think of that?'

The Duchess thought then as she did now: that it was a bad idea. The living and the dead weren't supposed to mix. The Eliases of this world, with their earthbound missionaries, had a certain merit, but the Dying Squad working with flesh-and-blood police was something else. No good could come of it.

No good *had* come of it.

The man she'd come here to see was proof of that.

The Gift Protocol had been implemented several decades before the Duchess was made Warden of the Pen: it took her until the one hundred and thirtieth year of her reign to end it.

It was its effectiveness that had given her pause. The ability for the living to see the dead – the ability for the dead to control who saw them, bringing the living into the all-encompassing embrace of the Pen – had proved invaluable, and difficult to discard.

Sometimes that ability to see the dead was used by men like Elias, ordained missionaries who were tasked with caring for those souls left behind on the soil. Sometimes it was for the Detective Hatoyamas of the world, men and woman placed into key soil law-enforcement roles, so an uneasy partnership between the two realms could take place.

Whatever position they took up, these men and women all had something in common: at birth, each of them had been given a genetically engineered death sentence.

Whether you considered it God's sick joke or the devil's healthy one, it had been discovered that living souls with fatal diseases could see the dead. The reason for this was uncertain, but it was speculated that the subject's crumbling mortality weakened the barrier between the living and the dead.

Whatever the reason, the Duchess's predecessors had deemed the ability too valuable not to use.

The Pen's reach was considerable in the living world. Physical churches were established that honoured its existence, its flock enacting the Warden's wishes on the soil. One of those edicts being the Gift Protocol.

To this end, the Pen's living emissaries on the soil set up laboratories, taking infant test subjects from the church's inner circle (of which the Jankie sisters were very much a part). The parents were recruited and given a small fortune – but more importantly, the knowledge that they were doing the Lord's work. That was their true gift.

To begin with, this 'gift' killed the test subjects before they reached their tenth year. The lab cancer was aggressive – it had to be, for the line of sight to the dead to be effective – and there was also the problem of logistics. If any of the children managed to contain the cancer ravaging their body, it was difficult for them to take up effective positions in the police or army. The best they could do was to become pilgrims, giving comfort to lost souls of the soil.

As the years went by, medical technology and the drugs that accompanied it became more sophisticated, and the life expectancy of the gifted grew longer. They began to take positions in various arms of the police and security services, and a working relationship took shape. The subjects were made aware of their condition from an early age (though not how that condition had been inflicted upon them in a lab – that little morsel was kept from them) and given the means of prolonging their health for as long as possible. Most welcomed it; it was a chance to serve. Their church needed them.

It wasn't his condition that potentially made Hatoyama a tricky customer to deal with, though; it was how his last case working with a Dying Squad member had gone. His partnership with Mabel had got results — they'd caught the most notorious serial killer in Japanese history — but the consequences and blowback had been so devastating that the Duchess had shut the Gift Protocol down a decade ago, ending the arrangement of the dead and the living working together.

She didn't know how Hatoyama had taken that news exactly, but if Mabel's description of him rang true, she didn't think it would be well.

The Duchess passed through the fire exit into a dimly lit basement. The clanking and grinding of machinery could be heard but not seen, giving off muscle-memory heat. It was impossible to believe that anyone could actually work down here.

She walked along the corridor, the noise of the machinery getting louder as she did so, following it around to the right. Other than the flickering tungsten bulbs above her, there was only one sign of life: a trail of light seeping out from a door on the left. She saw that a piece of A4 paper had been stuck to it, *Detective Hatoyama* scrawled on it in sprawling handwriting. Underneath was a crude drawing of a ghost. On closer inspection, she saw that it was attempting to swallow an engorged penis.

It was unclear whether the phallus was spectral.

She thought about knocking, then, realising the futility of such an act, simply walked through the door. A middle-aged man dressed apparently as some sort of Japanese cowboy lay slumped on the desk, his snores as unharmonious as they were loud. An ancient pale grey computer chuntered beside him and unfiled paperwork bled from every corner of the room. The Duchess was grateful that she could no longer smell, as she had no doubt the stale stench of body odour would have overwhelmed her.

It's fair to say Detective Hatoyama's career hasn't quite

worked out the way he would have wanted, she thought. Unless he wanted career oblivion and an office next to the boiler.

I hope that isn't down to me.

She coughed, eliciting nothing more than a broken snore from Hatoyama.

The slammed palm on the table had a little more impact.

No Xylophone Man. No consequences.

Which was exactly the problem.

Hatoyama lurched awake, looking wildly around then screaming when he saw the Duchess.

'Good morning, Detective,' she said calmly. 'It's nice to see you.'

'Get out,' he yelled, pointing a finger at her as if he were the witch-finder general himself.

The Duchess inspected a nail. 'Manners have clearly slipped on the soil in my absence. You could at least offer me a drink. Or failing that, a seat.'

Hatoyama frantically looked around, his eyes finally settling on his overflowing ashtray. He grabbed it and hurled it. It sailed clean through her, smashing into the opposite wall, butt ends and glass spilling onto the floor.

'Charming,' she said.

'I want nothing to do with you,' yelled Hatoyama, spittle flying. 'You've ruined my life.'

'There doesn't appear to be a great deal to ruin,' said the Duchess, looking disdainfully around her, 'and it's hard to see how I can take any credit for such ruination, seeing as we've only just met.'

'Don't be so modest,' said Hatoyama, a look of pure hatred on his face. 'You cancelled the arrangement between the living and the dead, didn't you? You deserve all the credit in the world.'

He marched towards the door, skirting around the Duchess as if she carried the plague, and swung the door open. 'Get out, and don't come back.'

'I can't do that, I'm afraid,' she said. 'Not until you've helped me.'

'I don't do that any more,' said Hatoyama, tugging at his stained tie. 'Thanks to you.'

The Duchess looked uncertainly at the chair opposite Hatoyama's desk, almost suspicious at its lack of paperwork and filth. '*Detective* is an extremely generous title, judging by the state of your office.'

Hatoyama stuck his head into the corridor, looking left and right, then swung the door shut, retreating back into the room. 'It's because of you people that I'm in this rabbit hutch.'

'You know, I was really expecting you to be a little more grateful,' said the Duchess. 'Us people – or rather, my sister Mabel – helped you catch the most notorious serial killer your country has ever seen.'

Hatoyama slammed his fist onto the desk, dislodging a Styrofoam cup and sending the acidic black coffee onto the floor. 'Helped? Is that some sort of joke?'

'Jokes and I have never been the comfiest of bedfellows,' said the Duchess, 'so it's probably safe to assume it's not.'

Hatoyama stared at her like she was the cause of every ill he'd ever experienced, and quite a few that were still to come. 'You have no idea, do you? What happened after your sister "helped" me?'

'Not really, no,' said the Duchess. 'Ruling a realm tends to consume one's attention.'

'That case finished me,' said Hatoyama. 'It should have been the making of my career, but it was the death of it. It's why I'm here, rotting in the fucking basement, without even enough self-respect to kill myself. That and you ending the

Gift Protocol.' He gestured to her. 'Shame that doesn't end me seeing the dead.'

It shouldn't have been that way. In truth, the Duchess was surprised that was the case. There'd been significant fallout from Mabel and Hatoyama's partnership, but her sister was the one who'd been drenched in the negative aspects of it; Hatoyama, she had assumed, would have launched his career from it.

She noticed the whiteness of Hatoyama's knuckles as he grasped the desk, and the look of fury in his eyes. It was fair to say her assumption was wide of the mark.

She nodded at the empty chair. 'May I?'

The fight seemed to leave him and he slumped down into his own chair. 'How could I stop you?'

'I'll take that as a yes,' said the Duchess, a conciliatory smile on her face because she needed this furious man, failed career and all.

'Take what you want,' said Hatoyama. 'Everyone else has.'

He dug out a packet of cigarettes from the jacket on the back of his chair. 'The famous Duchess. You know, there was a time when this would have been an honour. If only my mother and father could see me now. They had a picture of you on their mantelpiece, can you believe that? It was from when you were still alive. God only knows where they got it.'

'I heard nothing but good reports about your parents. The work they did – that you did too – was invaluable.'

Hatoyama snorted. 'So invaluable you shut the programme down. That you waited until I'd ruined my soil career was doubly delicious.'

'You're quite melodramatic,' said the Duchess. 'Why don't you tell me what happened after Mabel helped you catch the killer?'

Hatoyama dug under the mound of papers in front of him for a lighter, sparking the cigarette into light when he found it.

He inhaled hungrily, as if he were determined to eat the cancer stick whole. 'No, I don't think I'll do that.'

'You know those will kill you,' said the Duchess, nodding at the cigarette.

His laughter turned into an ugly cough.

He leaned forward, jabbing the cigarette at her. 'The dead have worked with the living for centuries, but suddenly that wasn't good enough for you. *I* wasn't good enough for you.'

The Duchess looked him dead in the eye. 'It was against the natural order, no matter what my predecessors thought, and as evidenced by Mabel's punishment, the consequences could be catastrophic.'

'I'm the one who's been punished,' said Hatoyama. 'I'm the one who resides in this store cupboard, shunned by my colleagues.'

The Duchess snorted. 'You're certainly punishing yourself with self-pity. Mabel, Detective, was sent to hell after she worked that case with you, and she displayed markedly less of it. You could do with a few days in the Pit. It might teach you a little perspective.'

Hatoyama tossed his spent cigarette into a glass of stale water, the bubbles in it breaking apart as the smouldering butt sank to the bottom.

He watched it, almost dazed. 'How is your sister?'

'You know Mabel,' said the Duchess, offering a small smile. 'She's never happy unless she's complaining. I see now why you got on so well.'

'Does she still work in the field?'

She shook her head. 'She lost her taste for it.'

'Does she miss it?'

'Do you?'

He swept the room with his arm. 'Why would I give up all this?'

'Perhaps you could put it aside for a little while. I need your help. Your colleagues may not put much store by your talents, but Mabel did. I need those talents. I need you.'

Hatoyama flinched slightly.

It's like a compliment is a slap in the face, it's so long since he's had one, thought the Duchess.

Then he sat a little straighter, his eyes flashing with something other than angry despair.

'It's been a while since anyone needed my help,' he said. 'I don't know whether the little I have to give is worth very much.'

'I'm willing to take that risk if you are,' said the Duchess.

Very few people went to the Hotel New Otani to stay; they came for the waterfall, and if not the waterfall, the gardens, because the location was a carved-out sea of green tranquillity in a Tokyo bustling with sound and fury. The Duchess gloried in it as she trotted next to Detective Hatoyama, the midday sun at their backs.

'This is a lot more agreeable than your office.'

'So's the abattoir.'

Time to rally the troops, she thought. With what I suppose you'd call small talk.

'Won't you be missed at work?'

Hatoyama laughed. 'Who would miss me? I catalogue cases that are as unsolved as they are unexplained.'

'It's unexplained cases I'm here to talk to you about.'

'The train crash,' he said.

Good. Back to business.

The Duchess nodded. 'You've seen the footage, I suppose?'

'Who hasn't? Caused quite the stink at the station, believe me. I'm out of the loop, but I don't need to be in it to know that.'

'What have they concluded?'

'Nothing they'd ever file in an official report,' said Hatoyama.

'What did *you* conclude?'

'I saw the spirits responsible for the attacks. What was I supposed to tell my bosses, though? They already think I'm a dime-store Fox Mulder. Hardly likely to firm up my case, saying I can see a spirit terrorist attack.'

'Yes, I appreciate your dilemma,' said the Duchess.

'Then I went to the crash site. Saw that dead monster. What did Mabel call him? The Xylophone Man. It was then that I knew. If something had managed to kill him, the law of consequences between the living and the dead was being rewritten.'

'A solid deduction for a detective with a basement for an office,' said the Duchess. 'It goes to show you can take the boy out of the Gift Protocol, but you can't take the Gift Protocol out of the boy.'

'I don't need to still be in the Protocol to know that's why you're here.'

They walked in silence for a moment, the birds in the trees taking up the slack.

The Duchess stopped. 'The train crash was my sister's doing.'

'Mabel?' said Hatoyama. 'Impossible.'

She shook her head. 'Hanna, the youngest of us and the one that was born to be Warden. She would have been if she hadn't killed herself and unwittingly passed the mantle to me. If I don't stop her soon, I fear the train will just be the start.'

'What's her plan?' said Hatoyama.

'My sister is wildly ambitious,' said the Duchess. 'Yesterday it was the train. Tomorrow? Put it this way, her actions are unlikely to become less aggressive.'

'How much chaos can one person really cause, though?'

'It's never just one person with Hanna,' she replied. 'My sister knows the language of the dead. Any spirit that hears her will do as she commands.'

'Including you?'

'Mercifully no. The Warden of the Pen – whether ex or current – is immune to such devilry. Or at least should be.'

Hatoyama blew out his cheeks. 'A small mercy, when we're looking for a big one. How do we find her before she next acts against the city? It's not like we can put out an all-points bulletin for her.'

'Quite,' said the Duchess.

'You think she'll know you're on her trail?' he asked. 'Will she be able to sense it somehow?'

'There's no supernatural reason that would be the case,' the Duchess replied, 'but she will be expecting *someone* to come after her.'

'Why?'

'Because I would, and she's ten times as cunning.'

'And you've come to me for help,' said Hatoyama. 'You must be desperate.'

'You're the last living contact I have here,' said the Duchess. 'So yes, I am.'

'I'm the punchline to a joke no one wants to hear. What can I possibly do?'

'Has there been anything in the last few days that's caught your attention? Any crime that's been out of the ordinary?'

Hatoyama stopped, a six-metre waterfall to the left of them, the sun plucking tiny rainbows from it. 'All crime is unusual in Tokyo in that it doesn't really exist. In the last twenty-four hours, though, there have been . . . incidents.'

'What sort of incidents?'

'Thefts. *Odd* thefts at that. A warehouse on the outskirts of the city had a generator stolen – a heavy-duty one – and the strange thing is, there was no sign of entry. The place was locked down. Still was the next morning, when the manager opened up. Normally I'd say it was an inside job.'

'This hasn't been a normal few days, though,' said the Duchess.

'No,' said Hatoyama,' side-eying the walking, talking ghost next to him. 'It hasn't.'

She looked away, chewing it over.

'There was something else,' said Hatoyama, 'though it was too small-time to fall on anyone's desk but mine. Too weird.'

'Weird's what we're after, Detective,' said the Duchess. 'The Dying Squad's in the business of weird.'

Akihabara was a technological riot of colour and sound that was as quintessentially Japanese as the most vivid cherry blossom, or the most ornate temple. Named after a former local shrine (because nothing said *shrine* like rabid technological commerce), the central Tokyo district housed row after row of electronic goods stores, each one offering up seductively cutting-edge tech.

The Duchess wasn't impressed.

'If I'm bound for the Pit, it will look an awful lot like this.'

'This is my country at its best,' said Hatoyama, smiling at the bustling Friday-night streets. 'Inventions your generation couldn't have begun to imagine fill these shops.'

'Perhaps they didn't imagine them because they weren't worth imagining,' said the Duchess, glaring at a pack of robotic dogs being shepherded by a man in a garish pirate costume. 'This place is evidence of the end times.'

'Appreciate it. It's one of the few places where a man talking to thin air won't elicit a second glance.'

She shook her head at a gaggle of girls in sailor costumes. 'Why have you brought me here?'

Hatoyama pointed at a squat store at the end of the street. It was far more modest than its extravagant, gaudy neighbours;

half the letters on its signage had failed to light, and there wasn't a sliver of glass in its resolute concrete front.

'Is that supposed to be a shop?' said the Duchess. 'It looks more like a bunker.'

'The man who owns it would take that as a compliment. He certainly thinks of it as one.'

'That wasn't the sort of unusual I had in mind,' she said.

'You haven't heard what he has to say yet,' said Hatoyama.

The shopfront, if it could be called that, paid no lip service to commerce, or even the outside world. Its concrete facade seemed to sweat in the clammy night air, and there was only the merest trace of a doorway within it. A digital keypad was carved next to that doorway, a faint red light flowing from it.

'I retract my earlier statement about this being a bunker,' said the Duchess. 'Clearly you've brought me to some sort of sex dungeon.'

'The man inside wishes it was.'

Hatoyama pushed the call button on the keypad, his podgy finger almost too large for the slender key. A shrill ringing sounded.

'I hope you're not wasting my time here, Hatoyama,' said the Duchess.

'It's a long time since you walked a beat, let alone ran a case.'

'By the sounds of it, it's a long time since *you* ran a case.'

'You follow the ends till they stop being dead,' said Hatoyama. 'The man who owns this shop can help us.'

An intercom flared into life.

'What?' barked a distorted voice.

'Charming customer service,' muttered the Duchess.

Hatoyama put a warning finger to his lips.

'He won't be able to hear me,' she said. 'It's one of the advantages of being dead.'

'Arata wouldn't let a little thing like death stop him being offended.'

'Is that you, Hatoyama?' the voice said. 'You finally decided to play at being a cop for once?'

'You call, I come,' said Hatoyama.

There was a non-committal grunt, and then a guttural buzz. The door swung open an inch.

'There's something you should know about Arata,' said Hatoyama. 'He's a little strange.'

'I'm sure I've met stranger.'

'Unlikely.'

'What does he have to do with my sister?' asked the Duchess.

'Maybe nothing, maybe something.'

'I don't have time for such wilful obtuseness.'

'You'll have time for this.'

'Why?'

'Because three days ago, the person you're about to meet was robbed by a ghost.'

The shop wasn't a shop in the sense that the Duchess understood it. There were no displays of goods, no counter hosting a friendly, attentive shopkeeper or signage explaining why failing to buy from their humble establishment would be the biggest mistake a customer would ever make.

Instead, there were racks.

Dozens of them, stretching from one end of the modestly sized room to the other. Bolted-together metal constructs holding hundreds upon hundreds of plastic boxes, those plastic boxes saturated with wires and circuitry and a variety of other hard-to-define electronic parts.

Music pumped beneath them, an industrial scream of instruments and pain that trembled the floor and made the thin red light stapled to the ceiling seem even more seedy.

'He's down here,' said Hatoyama, hugging the back wall and heading towards a barely visible set of stairs.

The Duchess wrinkled her nose as she followed. 'If it wasn't for the fact that I was dead, I'd feel rather nervous at the prospect of descending those stairs.'

'Like I said, Arata's a character. There's nothing he doesn't know about electronics, though, and nothing he can't invent using them. Whoever came here – whoever stole from here – must have been aware of that.'

Holding back on the dozen or so questions she wanted to ask, the Duchess trailed Hatoyama down the stairs, the wall of sound almost buffeting them back.

How can anyone work in that din? It's like he's trying to keep people out. What type of shop is this?

As they neared the bottom of the stairs, she was surprised to see that the room below was lit by candles. Hundreds of them, covering every surface, and those surfaces made an impression: it was as if someone had ripped the innards from a giant robot, then scattered them around the room.

Hunched over a table was a man so thin he could have qualified as a pencil. Twig arms held a soldering iron, a thimble of a head barely supporting a welding mask. Circuitry guts were splayed out in front of him, and he worried them, poking the glowing tip of the iron into their entrails. If he'd heard the arrival of his guests, he showed no sign of welcoming it.

Hatoyama walked over to him, tapping him on the shoulder. Arata shrugged him off, hunkering closer to the workbench.

I don't have time for this, thought the Duchess, scanning the room for the source of the musical apocalypse playing in the background. Three slender boxes sat on a stand at the back of the room, a speaker on either side. She walked towards them, leaning down and jabbing a finger at each device's off button. A perk Hanna has allowed me, she thought, by murdering the one creature that would have punished me for such a violation.

The music died and Arata swung round, soldering iron held out like a magician's wand. He raised the visor on his helmet, revealing alabaster skin and erratic clumps of greying beard.

'Who did that?' he asked, his eyes going from Hatoyama to the blank space next to the silenced stereo.

'You wouldn't believe me if I told you,' said Hatoyama.

Life flared in Arata's eyes, and he placed the soldering iron on the table. 'Do you have one of them with you?'

'Do I have one of what?'

'A ghost,' said Arata, the word dripping in awe.

'There's no such thing as ghosts,' said Hatoyama, looking nervously at the Duchess.

'Have you been speaking out of turn?' she said, a small smile on her lips.

'Is it over there?' asked Arata, squinting at the thin air next to the stereo. 'What does it look like?'

'Ask him about the break-in,' said the Duchess.

'I'm here about the break-in,' said Hatoyama.

'Is it a man or a woman?' asked Arata, taking a step towards the Duchess. 'Is she hot? I've always wanted to fuck a ghost.'

'Which village did you get this idiot from?' said the Duchess.

'The burglary,' said Hatoyama. 'I'm here about the burglary you reported, Arata.'

The shop owner gave the blank air a final stare, then turned his attention to the detective. 'I reported that three days ago. I tell you about my assistant who was killed on the train, how it's all connected, and you only come to me now?'

'I've had too many of your reports in the past,' said Hatoyama. 'I'm sorry for the loss of your assistant, though.'

'Benji was the best worker I ever had,' said Arata. 'Totally trustworthy. Brilliant in his way. It wasn't a coincidence he was on the train that day.'

'It was,' said Hatoyama. 'A tragic one.' He gestured towards the armada of candles that lit the room. 'Still eschewing electricity, I see.'

Arata belched. 'There's nothing wrong with electricity per se – the generator I built is proof of that. There's *everything* wrong with the government's electricity. Who's to say where it's been, what imperfections it's carrying? That's what this is about.'

He pointed to the workbench and the nest of components resting on it. 'A client of unusual vision – a man who truly appreciates what's important in life – tasked me with designing a power filter. He will attach it to the telegraph pole outside his house and so filter out the unclean current. He does this because, like me, he appreciates music. By cleaning the electricity he puts into his hi-fi system, that music will be reborn.'

'Hatoyama,' said the Duchess warningly.

The detective held up a placatory hand. 'We'll get there.'

Arata stared at him, fascinated. 'I always thought you were talking bullshit when you said you could converse with the dead. I mean, I believed such a thing was possible, but not by the likes of you.'

'The item you had stolen,' said Hatoyama, ignoring the bait. 'What was it?'

Anger clouded Arata's face. 'I call it the Dog Catcher. It's priceless. The next revolution in cybersecurity. Any network that employs it will be invulnerable to disruption, and completely impervious to foreign agencies attempting to hack into their operating system. Only a handful of people even knew of its existence.'

He struck the bench, a ripple of reverb sounding. 'Three nights ago, the prototype was stolen from under my nose. My alarm system is impenetrable, yet it didn't raise a peep. When I arrived the next morning, the device was gone. It was only a matter of time before spirits began to interfere in the dealings of the living. The question you should be asking yourself is this: why did they do it? Who's behind it? Because I guarantee you that somebody is.'

Hatoyama looked around, spotting the slick black CCTV camera attached to the ceiling. 'Did that record anything?'

Arata smiled grimly. 'That's where things get really weird.'

Arata's sleeping quarters were a sight to behold, and an even grimmer one to experience.

A bunk bed sat in the corner (it was difficult to believe that he ever tempted company down to share it, ghost or otherwise) and a bank of video screens colonised the back wall, each one depicting a different area of the city. The screen plum in the centre was the one to attract the Duchess's attention; every so often, a face appeared on one side of it, and a Rolodex of faces would spin opposite it, as if hunting for its twin.

Hatoyama and Arata's attention was concentrated on a more modest screen, planted on a large cast-iron desk. Arata's workshop could be seen on its LED panel. The time and date in the corner of the screen indicated that the colour footage was from three days before, and the workshop was shrouded in almost total darkness.

'If Hanna's on this, will we see it?' said Hatoyama out of the corner of his mouth.

'You don't have to hide your ghost from me,' said Arata. 'We're all friends here.' He frowned. 'Who's Hanna?'

'Tell him that doesn't matter,' said the Duchess.

'She says that doesn't matter,' said Hatoyama.

'Tell her that if some ghost called Hanna has been stealing my prototypes, it matters a great deal,' said Arata.

'Tell him that I can hear him perfectly fine, more's the pity,' said the Duchess. 'He just can't hear me.'

Hatoyama exhaled frustration. 'Why don't we all just watch the tape.'

'Here,' said Arata, excitedly jabbing a gnarled nail at the screen. 'This is where it happens.'

The group watched in silence as a plastic tray seemingly lifted itself off the rack it had been resting on, then drifted steadily away until it was set down on the floor next to a chair.

'Now watch the vent. It's like someone removes it, but there's no one on the screen.'

There was, though, because the Duchess could see them. There were two people.

The first was a teenage boy with a vivid green Mohawk, moving smoothly around the workshop carrying the plastic tray with Arata's Dog Catcher.

'You're seeing this too?' said the Duchess.

Hatoyama nodded.

'This assistant of Arata's, does he have green hair?'

Hatoyama asked the question and Arata nodded fervently.

Benji carried the tray to a woman secreted in the vent, who reached down and took it from him.

'That's her,' said the Duchess. 'That's Hanna.'

'Do you know what the funny thing is?' said Arata. 'The device they stole is useless.'

'How so?' said Hatoyama.

'I always remove the central microchip from the logic board a few days before a sale, reconnecting it when I've been paid.'

'Meaning what?'

'Meaning it doesn't have its brain,' said Arata.

'This microchip,' said Hatoyama, a small smile forming on his lips. 'Where is it?'

'In the safe custody of an unsafe man,' said Arata. 'This is a dirty business that I'm in, and it's necessary to play dirty. My partner keeps the location of the chip even from me; that way he bears all the risk. When it's time to do the exchange, he retrieves it.'

'How can you trust such a man?' said Hatoyama. 'What's to stop him from simply selling the chip himself?'

'Because he's a businessman,' said Arata, 'who knows I'm the very best at what I do. Why burn yourself after one deal when you can have a lifetime's worth of them?'

'What's this unsafe man's name?' said Hatoyama.

'Cujo,' said Arata. 'Just Cujo. Like Madonna.'

Hatoyama looked to the ceiling.

'What are you thinking, Detective?' said the Duchess.

'I'm thinking we find this Cujo and get him to tell us where the chip is,' said Hatoyama. 'Then we stake the place out and wait for Hanna to show up.'

'Police work,' said the Duchess.

'Police work,' agreed Hatoyama, smiling.

Genshiro Kawamoto was a favourite son who became an on-the-run outcast.

A billionaire real-estate warrior who didn't so much court controversy as French-kiss it, he had an empire of properties that stretched from Japan to the US. He was known for selling apartment blocks out from under his tenants and collecting mega-mansions like they were manga comics. Greed, ultimately, was to be his undoing; he received a prison sentence for tax evasion, meaning many of his residences went to rack and ruin.

Hanna felt there was a certain poetry in that. Where more symbolic to plot the next phase of her revolution than the crumbling jewel in a former tycoon's crown? Admittedly, there was an element of cliché to it all – she recognised that rotting mansions with room after room of beheaded marble statues were the last bastion of the lair-hungry super-villain – but she'd picked it for its location, not its originality. It was the perfect staging post for their final destination.

She walked from room to room, her followers looking up and smiling as she did so, all of them content in their tasks. The devil may have made work for idle hands, but there was nothing for him here; he could get his own lackeys. After all, it was one of his servants who had taught her the language of the dead; Hanna was grudgingly aware she wouldn't have been able to inspire such slavish devotion without it.

Taking the red-carpeted stairs two at a time, instinctively swerving the moss, leaves and dirt that had accumulated on them, she headed for the master bedroom. The floor-to-ceiling windows afforded panoramic views of the ocean, but she hadn't come for the views. She'd come to see one of her newest recruits.

The train crash had been a lottery in that respect – the commuters had included everyone from refuse collectors to record producers – but with Benji, she'd hit pay dirt. She smiled indulgently at him as the boy who was barely her senior (in soil years, anyway) hunkered over a gaudy ornate desk, the intestines of electronics spread out before him, his bright green Mohawk bobbing up and down.

It was luck she'd found him, not that she believed in such a concept. Benji was more a case of manifest destiny.

Manifest destiny turned and smiled nervously. 'We have a problem, ma'am.'

'There are no problems, Benji, merely solutions we haven't found yet.' She nodded at the device on the desk. 'Is it working?'

'Yes and no,' he said, smiling weakly. 'The chip has been removed.'

Hanna exhaled, digging her nails into the palms of her hands. 'What does that mean?'

'Arata? My old employer? He's *paranoid*. Thinks everyone's always trying to steal his prototypes.'

With good reason, thought Hanna, considering we just stole one of his prototypes.

'Just before he delivers them, he removes the chip,' Benji continued. 'The client only gets the chip – and so the working device – when they transfer the rest of the funds into his bank account.'

'And you didn't think to tell me this before?'

'Arata wasn't supposed to deliver this for another two weeks,' said Benji. 'The client must have moved the delivery date forward. Without that chip, this device is useless.'

Hanna tilted her head, considering him. It was tempting to simply tell him to eat his own eyeballs; the language of the dead was effective like that. She flattered herself her natural charisma would obtain the same result. Benji was a follower. A true believer.

Someone, in short, she still needed.

'Where does your former employer keep this chip?'

'I don't know where it's kept, but I know who *will* know. Arata and I squabbled about it. I didn't think he should deal with this person. He wasn't trustworthy. He *isn't* trustworthy.'

'Who isn't?'

Benji shivered. 'Cujo. A common gangster, who knows nothing of the purity of technology but plenty about abusing its commercial potential.'

'Where can I find this Cujo?' asked Hanna.

'There are rumours about him,' said Benji. 'Unnatural practices that he and his Yakuza brethren indulge in. He operates out of a disused cinema in Kabukichō. That's where I'd try.'

A Yakuza criminal who dabbles in the unnatural, thought Hanna. I like him already.

★

Kabukichō was a red-light district that had forgotten the red lights.

Disneyland for Yakuza gangsters and partygoers alike, Sleepless Town eschewed the hooker window-dressing of Amsterdam, but still found time to host over three thousand bars, nightclubs, love hotels, massage parlours and other dens of old-school iniquity. Hanna was looking for none of these things, though she held a bemused fascination for all of them.

The building she sought – and the people within that building – wasn't on the usual debauchery trail. To all intents and purposes, the Milano-Za movie theatre had been abandoned years ago, sold up to make way for a 225-metre skyscraper that stubbornly refused to be built. The doors were boarded up, as were the windows, the ghosts of letters hanging from the former cinema's front, the whole place looking like it craved the embrace of a wrecking ball.

If you knew the right people, though (and Hanna, with her ever-expanding network of converts, did), there was more to be discovered there, though it had little to do with wholesome celluloid entertainment.

She eased through the entrance, the baying of the crowd growing louder with each step, a sort of hysteria loaded within it. This was a mission she had decided to conduct alone, because her presence here would be noted if the wrong people saw her at the wrong time.

The cinema lobby was lit by a couple of construction floodlights, highlighting mouldy popcorn cartons and peeling film posters. Hanna moved quickly towards the sound of raised voices, surprised to find female ones meshed in with the men's. What happened here was unpalatable, savage. She failed to see the entertainment in it, but then there was much she failed to understand about this city and the world it festered in.

Quickly now she passed through the entrance of THEATRE I (its letters still hanging on for dear life) and was grateful to see that she'd come out onto the upper gallery. It would afford her some level of protection against the events unfurling below. As much as she wanted to act now, that wasn't the smart play. There was one of her, and a small company of Yakuza down below.

And unlike the people on the train, they'd actually be able to see her.

Hanna could just about cope with man's inhumanity to man (in fact she actively supported it), but man's inhumanity to the dead was something else entirely. That, she couldn't let stand.

She'd hoped what Benji had told her was a lie, but now, looking down into the belly of the movie theatre, she thought he'd undersold it. The Yakuza below – the tightly packed throng of businessmen and women, waving notes and cheering and screaming – were here for one thing and one thing only.

They were betting on a spiritual cock fight.

Two stranded souls stood on the stage below the abandoned, fractured cinema screen. A couple of stakes at opposite sides of the stage had long, thin steel cables running from them, each one lashed around the ankle of one of the warring parties. And these parties *were* at war; the larger, older man had been stripped to the waist and his younger, skinnier opponent was clothed, green vines wrapped around his fists like boxing gloves. Black-suited Yakuza foot soldiers hovered at either end of the stage, holding what appeared to be cattle prods. If the fighters began to retreat too much, they'd lash out with the weapons, a sulphurous crackle sounding when the prongs made contact with the spirits.

Animals, thought Hanna. Monsters.

Still, interesting that they have found a way to hurt us. Contain us. Such knowledge could be useful in time.

The younger fighter flung a left hook at his opponent, and it was immediately obvious that something had broken in the bigger man. He dropped to one knee, and no number of cattle-prod jabs would make him get up again. He keeled over, the crowd baying, money changing hands, fortunes won and lost.

It was the most exclusive of blood sports, those gifted with the ability to see the dead – those sick enough to enjoy it – paying top dollar to buy in and bet on ghost fights, spirits that had been stranded on the soil captured and broken by their Yakuza masters. It interested Hanna *how* these people were able to see the spirits – they couldn't all be on the verge of death – but what was undeniable was that there was a brisk trade in souls. She had learned from Benji that they were bought and traded like cattle between the different gangster houses. When they became too broken-down to fight, they fetched top dollar as dogsbody slaves for those with the sight.

Not for much longer, though, if she had anything to do with it.

She hunted for the man she'd come here for, her eyes passing over the Yakuza royalty until she found him.

Cujo.

Short as he was round, a lolloping dollop of flesh with a shimmering purple suit and pale, sweating skin, Cujo was every inch the conquering Japanese warlord, content in his fiefdom, fanning himself with a sheaf of banknotes.

Enjoy it while you can, thought Hanna. There's no place for the likes of you in the future I'm going to build.

Someone else caught her eye, too. A blonde woman. Almost regal-looking, very much at odds with the sweaty Yakuza gangsters. She wasn't watching the fight (indeed, her body language suggested she was faintly appalled by it); instead, her attention was drawn to the heavens. Drawn, in fact, straight to Hanna.

She can see me. Perhaps she can explain why the rest of them can see me too.

The blonde woman held Hanna's gaze, then nodded imperceptibly to her left.

The target was Cujo. Hanna could afford herself a little detour, though. You never knew what good places those detours would lead you to.

As Hanna made her way down the upper atrium's sagging stairs, she caught sight of the blonde woman again. Or rather, the back of her. She upped her pace as she followed her down the corridor, her curiosity growing by the minute. The barbarism on display in the main auditorium would need to be punished, and the woman she was now following into some dank, crumbling toilets had played a part in that barbarism simply by being there, but she'd hear her out first. Professional curiosity demanded it.

The woman stood waiting for her, arms crossed, leaning against a grimy set of sinks, a small smile on her lips.

'Hello, Hanna.'

Hanna wasn't used to being taken aback. She was the one who set the pace, kept those around her off balance by always planning ten steps ahead.

She wasn't sure she cared for it.

'How do you know who I am?'

'The famous Hanna Jankie, the force of nature that almost toppled the Pen itself? I would have thought it stranger if I *didn't* know who you were.'

'But you're one of the living,' said Hanna.

'Unfortunately,' said the woman. 'I keep my hand in with the dead too, though. Think of myself as an equal-opportunities employer.'

'I'm not looking for a job,' said Hanna.

175

'And I'm not looking to give you one. I'm looking for a partner.'

Hanna shifted on her feet. 'What's your name?'

'I'm not big on names.'

'I'm not big on trusting people who don't tell me them,' said Hanna.

The woman considered for a moment. 'Lucia.'

Hanna took a step towards her. 'What's a woman called Lucia doing at a Yakuza ghost cock fight?'

Lucia stood her ground. 'Providing the cocks, darling.'

'You're responsible for this outrage?' Hanna said quietly, her fists clenched.

'You think me barbaric,' said Lucia, and Hanna couldn't fail to be impressed by the way she didn't flinch under her glare. 'The men in there *are* barbarians. I hate this as much as you do, I assure you.'

'Yet you enable it, by bringing these poor souls to this god-forsaken place.'

'Oh, I'm not sure God has forsaken it,' said Lucia. 'It's more like he's ignoring it.'

Hanna took another step forward. 'Give me a reason why I shouldn't rip your throat out.'

Lucia smiled. 'Because I can not only return you to the Pen, I can also install you as Warden.'

Hanna unclenched her fists. 'Impossible.'

Besides, I have my own plans, and they don't involve traipsing back to the Pen.

Lucia inspected a nail. 'I've heard that word so many times over my lifetime. I've never paid it much mind.'

'The Gloop's poisoned,' said Hanna.

'The Gloop's for third-class tourists and cattle-class heathens,' said Lucia. 'I have something much better. You see, Hanna, I don't bring the spirits you see fighting here out of cruelty; I bring them here for research.'

Hanna laughed. 'You're a scientist.'

'I'm an entrepreneur. One who's been gifted with the ability to see the dead. I'm intent on not wasting that ability.'

'You're a pimp for the poor souls out there, selling them to the highest bidder.'

'The Yakuza pay me well for the spirits I smuggle through the Gloop,' said Lucia. 'I won't deny that, even if I apologise for it. It's the journey that's important, though. Their money funds my research into the dead – allows me to study the impact the living world has on them. In time, I believe I can eradicate the memory loss the dead suffer on the soil. Think what that could mean.'

Hanna did.

'The dead could return home,' she said.

'Precisely,' said Lucia. 'For good. And now that you've removed the means of punishing them for interacting with the real world, think how wonderful that could be.'

Hanna tilted her head. 'How exactly does that philanthropy extend to me? Why have me installed as Warden?'

Lucia folded her arms. 'Because the current one is making a pig's ear of it. She'll be removed shortly, meaning there'll be a vacancy.'

'Making it even easier for you to conduct your little experiments. *How* are you smuggling these spirits from the Pen to the living world?' said Hanna. 'You've been remarkably light on detail.'

Lucia smiled. 'That's the sort of information partners share.'

Hanna considered. It was an attractive offer, there was no doubt about that, and this Lucia was intriguing.

She was also a living soul, though, and so not to be trusted.

'The technology binding the spirits in place while they fight: that's yours?'

Lucia nodded. 'That's old tech. The new wonders I could show you. The men and women in the auditorium; they see the dead because of me. Because of a drug I've developed. That's just the start of what I can do.'

It was tempting to throw her lot in with this Lucia. She clearly had potential.

No, she'd come too far. She needed to stick to her own plan. Lucia was a rogue agent, not to be trusted. A last resort, at best.

One that was worth keeping onside, though.

'I need something from you,' said Hanna. 'An item that shows me you're worthy of my trust.'

'Name it,' said Lucia.

'Your friend Cujo has information I need. I can't get it from him here, he's too heavily guarded. When's the best time to hit him?'

Lucia told her, along with a way she could be contacted in future.

Hanna walked to the toilet door, then turned back.

'If I were you, I'd get on the next plane out of Tokyo.'

'Why?' asked Lucia.

'Because in twenty-four hours' time, I'm going to raze it to the ground.'

The Gion district was perhaps Japan's most famous deliberate time warp, traditional bars and restaurants peppering the streets along with the tea houses, cherry blossom tumbling down, buffeted this way and that by the wind, a five-pronged temple on the horizon, its spires stretching up to the afternoon sky.

The living don't deserve this world, thought Hanna. Which is why it's so important I take it from them.

On Lucia's advice, she'd trailed Cujo here from the abandoned

178

cinema. She had been surprised to learn that the Yakuza didn't enjoy second sight himself, instead relying on his four slabs of bodyguard meat for the task. An aversion to getting high on his own supply, perhaps. Hardly the best advertisement for Lucia's drug if so.

The bodyguards had stuck to him closely after they'd left the cinema, four bristle-topped, fat-necked heavies who eyed the tourists swarming the area suspiciously, as if each and every one of them was a trained killer desperate to display those skills. Such was Cujo's infamy, Hanna could have believed that they were.

The Yakuza chief stopped abruptly, causing his escort to lurch to a halt. He gestured to them impatiently and they followed him into a low-roofed, wood-drenched tea shop.

Hanna whistled, and several of her followers eased through the crowd and joined her. It was time.

Hanna was relieved to see the diners being quickly shepherded out of the front door by the apologetic geishas, Cujo waiting impatiently by the kitchen hatch, daring anyone to cross his line of sight. When the last person had exited and the party had taken their seats on the floor, Cujo grabbing the backside of the nearest geisha and slapping it firmly, Hanna nodded to her followers and gave a simple one-word command.

'Now.'

Her team sounded a war cry, rushing towards the seated bodyguards, who felt something before they saw it.

Tables flipped over, seemingly of their own accord, chairs scattering like mice.

The bodyguards spotted the onrushing swarm and formed a defensive shield around Cujo.

'Spirits,' said the bodyguard closest to him, his gun held out in front of him, his finger caressing the trigger. 'Demons.'

'You're here because you can see them,' spat Cujo, his jowls frantic, his neck hairs standing to attention. 'So shoot them.'

The bodyguard who'd correctly identified them was the first to go.

He grunted as his gun hand was bent backwards, his face showing surprise his mouth couldn't catch up with. As his trigger finger was yanked back, he had just enough time to yelp before he blew his own face off.

His three colleagues took one look at each other – and one look at Hanna and her team – and threw their guns to the floor.

'Cowards,' screamed Cujo as they rushed towards the exit. 'I've paid for *cowards*.'

Hanna grabbed him by the shirt, pulling him forward, her unseen face inches from his. What she was about to attempt was the barely possible side of impossible, a feat talked about in legends and fairy tales, not in modern-day Japan, with its technology and wonders. It was precisely that technology she was planning to use, and not a little wonder.

Concentrate, she told herself. This is no harder than making a long-distance phone call.

The television behind the tea room's counter began to flicker, warring with its karaoke offerings. Cujo continued to struggle, pinned by Hanna's invisible arms.

The picture on the television became ragged, a snowy trickle of static across it. Hanna, projecting pure will, yanked Cujo round by his collar. Her face appeared on the screen, ghostly to begin with, but then growing in power and clarity.

I'm doing it, she thought. I'm actually doing it.

She readjusted her grip on Cujo, grabbing a clump of his hair and marching him towards the television so that he was mere inches from it. He stood slack-jawed, drool sliding down his chin as he took in the pixels and the girl they represented.

'Can you hear me?' she said, her words echoey and tinny,

filtered as they were through the television's speakers. 'Can you see me?'

He whimpered, nodding.

'I need information from you,' said the grainy, pixelated image on the screen. 'The location of a microchip you're keeping for an inventor, Arata. If you tell me you don't know who this Arata is, or where you're keeping the chip, I will kill you. Do you understand?'

Hanna looked down as the front of Cujo's trousers darkened.

'Do you understand?'

'Yes,' he whimpered.

'Good.'

She asked her question.

Cujo answered it.

Hanna Jankie smiled.

She was still smiling as she pile-drove Cujo's head into the TV screen.

Chapter Eleven

A woman who didn't glimmer. A woman who wasn't dead. Was such a thing possible? How could someone from the soil travel here and interfere with the affairs of the dead? Daisy-May felt a pang of longing for the Duchess. She may have been harsh and officious, but her knowledge and experience would have been invaluable now. And didn't her pilgrimage to the soil prove such a thing was possible? If the dead could journey to the land of the living, why couldn't the living journey to the land of the dead?

Facts, Daisy-May, that was what Joe would have said if he was here. *All there is is the facts. Keep to them and the truth will come, cowed and willing.*

One irrefutable fact was that, just like the case that had taken Joe to the soil, children had gone missing.

Another irrefutable fact was that it was her duty to find them, including the son of the woman in custody. Find the person responsible for abducting them, too. Could she do it? Could she use children as bait to draw out this woman who didn't glimmer?

I'll do it differently, she thought. The Judge may have told me it as a cautionary tale, but it's only a cautionary tale if you don't employ caution. The copper on the soil lost the boy because he didn't value his life enough. I value any kid's life here more than my own.

The docks.

Daisy-May wasn't sure whether they'd always existed and she hadn't been aware of them, or whether they were a recent Dispossessed construction. What she did know was that instead of boats, commerce and industry, the docks represented little more than a stubby outcrop in a desert: a half-collapsed pier, a flotilla of sunken oil tankers, and the almost overpowering stench of chlorine. The bleach-like smell was always present in the Pen, but never was it more noticeable than here.

What is this place? she wondered, as she peered down at the scant traces of water pooled under the hole-ridden boats. Another thing I should have found out from the Duchess before she left. It wasn't much of a handover. She didn't even give me the Wi-Fi code.

She turned away from the parched land and trained her attention on the dock itself. Dispossessed bustled to and fro, oblivious to her or pretending that they were, the whirl and click of their language softer than she remembered it, another thing that had changed in the last few months.

Around a hundred yards away were a group of children, a ragtag mix of teens and those not yet troubling double digits, all of them talking, teasing and bullshitting while music played, piped in from somewhere unseen.

Music, in the Pen, thought Daisy-May. World's changing, and it hasn't even asked my permission.

She strolled toward the group, trying to remember what it was like to be that age, with that amount of loose-shouldered insolence. She couldn't, because she'd never had it. It had been beaten out of her before it had a chance to take.

183

The children quietened down as she drew close, eyeing her warily.

One of them in particular was familiar.

'Chestnut?'

The girl looked up. Daisy-May knew her.

It was the girl she'd saved from the Gloop, months ago that felt like years. The one who had been half poisoned and she'd dragged back to the Pen. Mabel had given her some sort of antidote, and Chestnut in turn had saved all of them, because she was a visual representation of what the new regime would be like under Daisy-May, how the Dispossessed would be cared for and considered equals.

They had a bond, Chestnut and her. They always had.

'What the fuck are *you* doing here?'

Well, they used to.

'What kind of welcome's that?' said Daisy-May, digging her hands deep into her pockets, hunching her shoulders against a wind she couldn't feel.

'Only one you'll get round here,' said Chestnut, looking at her coldly. 'And Chestnut's a kid's name. Go by Francesca now.'

'You'll always be Chestnut to me,' said Daisy-May, smiling.

'I said it's Francesca.'

'You remember who I am, right?' said Daisy-May, confused.

'Fucking difficult to forget,' said Chestnut, hair matted with dirt, eyes burning with vulnerability and front. 'What do you want?'

She was different, and not just in the way she spoke, or her desire to go by a different name. She *looked* different. Older. If she didn't know that such a thing was impossible, Daisy-May would have sworn she'd aged. You didn't age in the Pen, though, at least not physically. That was a given. That was a fact.

Except facts seemed to have pissed off recently. Someone like me isn't supposed to be the Warden of purgatory, yet here we fucking are.

'What's with the attitude?'

'What attitude?' Chestnut bit back.

'We used to be tight, you and me.'

She scowled at that. 'What do you want?'

It's like she's aged three years in three months. Proper teenage stroppy.

'Your help. Got a job for one of you. Easy money.'

Chestnut snorted. 'No harder job than one that offers easy money.'

'Who told you that?' said Daisy-May.

'You,' said Chestnut.

'You with the woman that don't glimmer?' said a tall girl lurking behind Chestnut.

Here we go.

'Who's the woman that don't glimmer?' said Daisy-May.

'She's like an angel,' said the girl. 'Comes to the Downs and gives jobs out.'

'What sort of jobs?'

'Dying Squad jobs,' interrupted Chestnut. 'Figured I'd be in line for one of those from you. Apparently not.'

Daisy-May flinched. There was a lot of truth to the girl's words. She hadn't thought much about Chestnut. She'd be lying if she said she had.

She'd thought plenty about the woman who didn't glimmer, though: like how she was snatching kids to induct their parents into her murder squad. Now she knew she wasn't having to snatch them at all; she was bribing them.

Come into my parlour, said the spider to the fly.

Still, least that means Chestnut will be safe. No one to leverage if she's taken, considering her folks aren't here. Which gives me an opportunity.

'Have you seen this woman who doesn't glimmer?'

'Nah, but that's why we hang out here,' said Chestnut.

'Reckon the longer we do, the better the chance we have.'

'Reckon that sounds right,' said Daisy-May. 'Not sure how good an idea it is, though. She's bad news, mate.'

'Who isn't, in the Pen?' Chestnut replied.

'Bit young for the Dying Squad, though, aren't you?' said Daisy-May.

'Wasn't too young to be poisoned in the Gloop, was I?' said Chestnut, lifting her chin. 'And help you save everything.'

'Fair point,' said Daisy-May, smiling. 'All right, Francesca, I've got a deal for you. If you're in the game for one, that is.'

Good policing's having the patience to hang back and let the villains catch themselves, that was what Joe said. This usually happened through stupidity, or greed, or desperation. Sometimes it was a heady mix of all three. The point was, all you needed to do was to get out of their way and let them fuck up.

Using Chestnut as bait, then, was the smart play, no matter how much waiting was making her brain curdle. Whoever this non-glimmering woman was, she wouldn't be able to resist such juicy temptation. It wasn't like she was risking the girl's life, because Chestnut was never going to be out of her sight.

The woman who didn't glimmer. The fact that she was using the Dying Squad as a lure was interesting, a sign that the opportunities Daisy-May had created were making an impact – like partnering Joe with Bits. It had been her first act as Warden, a means of trying to bridge the gap of inequality and give the Dispossessed some hope. She hadn't imagined it would be used to snatch their young.

What had been Chestnut's problem? She'd reeked of attitude. Seemed angry at the world, and in particular Daisy-May and what she represented. Maybe she'd expected that they'd stay in touch. Maybe Daisy-May should have made more effort to ensure that they did. She had a fucking realm to run, though, and no frame of reference for doing that. She didn't have time to roam the Pen looking for play dates and chatting about old times.

Which was exactly what the Duchess would have said. Which was exactly why Daisy-May had been lumped with the job of Warden in the first place.

She slouched down against the wall, pulling her cap lower. The docks had quietened somewhat, what passed for night in the Pen casting everything in a red-tinged gloom. The crumbling tops of the oil tankers could be seen in the distance, and beyond that, the indistinct circular smudge of the Pen wall itself.

I command all of this, she thought. Every time I see somewhere new here, that becomes clearer. What am I supposed to do with it? How do I know what I'm doing is right?

She felt a surge of anger at the thought of the Duchess. The Pen's matriarch had spent a lifetime preparing for the role. Daisy-May had enjoyed a few days, and was now dependent on the Remuses of this world.

I should be back at the compound, she thought. Mabel was right: there are teams here to do this for me. This isn't me taking my eye off the ball; this is me acting like the ball doesn't fucking exist.

Still, it bothered her that so little concern had been shown for the missing children. Their parents had been terrified into silence, there was little doubt about that, but the disappearances had still been noted: the Judge and Mabel were both aware of them, even if nothing had been done. It was that sort of neglect that had meant Joe Lazarus and his ilk could run county line drug gangs on the soil, hoovering up vulnerable teens like herself. She wouldn't let the same thing happen here.

The group of children fifty feet away were now kicking a

football around, Chestnut at the centre, trying to retrieve it. No woman who didn't glimmer.

Not yet, anyway.

Time, then, for a little more telekinesis practice, this time on something heavier than a pink teddy bear. Chestnut wasn't far away; she'd be able to hear and see her if any mysterious non-glimmering women appeared.

And now that she was out here on her own, doubts had begun to creep into Daisy-May's mind. She was gallivanting around the place like she was the bad-ass bitch of an afterlife realm rather than a newbie intern who couldn't so much as push a doorstop around with her mind. She had no idea what awaited her when she caught up with this mystery woman. She was going to a gunfight with a water pistol; the least she could do was learn how to aim.

There was a clump of stones several feet away from her. She glared at them, holding out a furtive hand.

Move, she thought. Move.

The rocks stayed where they were.

She closed her eyes, keeping her arm outstretched.

I'm the Warden of the fucking Pen, she thought, and I command you to move.

She opened her eyes.

They hadn't.

She felt the anger begin to rise in her again, a hot, liquid gloop of rage that surged through her veins and frothed in her stomach.

Anger at the Duchess, for inflicting such a burden on her.

Anger at being so unprepared for it.

Anger at being kept from the Next Place, where she would finally have experienced some peace.

Anger at being left to fend for herself, a child in a realm full of adults where she was expected to be an uncrowned god.

Anger at never having control of her own destiny.

Anger at being abused by the destiny she'd been handed.

A high-pitched whine filled her head, and it was as if she'd paused the world somehow, knocked it down to half-speed. She saw the rocks slowly begin to rise from the ground, sand falling off them as they did so.

Then, as quickly as it had begun, the whine died and the rocks tumbled back to the ground.

It's a start, though, Daisy-May thought. It's not breaking the Xylophone Man's neck, but it's a fucking start.

She shuddered, noticing for the first time that she was bathed in ice-cold sweat.

Then she realised something else.

Chestnut was gone.

Fuck, thought Daisy-May. Fuck, fuck, fuck, fuck.

'Where'd she go?'

The children looked up as she strode towards them. Fear sweat slid down her back, panic smeared in with it too.

'Where'd who go?' said the tall boy at the back, football cradled under his arm.

'Chestnut,' said Daisy-May.

'Went with the woman, didn't she?' said a girl of around ten, jamming a grimy finger up her nose.

'Which woman?'

'The one that don't glimmer.'

Daisy-May's stomach slalomed.

This didn't make any sense.

Chestnut didn't have anyone to bribe into butchery. There wasn't a reason in the world why she should have been taken.

Unless . . . the woman was taking the children for a purpose *other* than blackmail. Or she knew Daisy-May was on her tail and had kidnapped Chestnut as leverage.

Whatever the reason, it's my fault she's been snatched.

'Where'd they go?'

The girl withdrew her finger from her nose and pointed past the pier into the wasteland of dissolving oil tankers and parched land.

Stupid, thought Daisy-May. Stupid, stupid, stupid, stupid.

She'd told herself she wouldn't get distracted, that she'd watch the children at all times, and she'd failed within hours. Attempting to conjure up the power that was hers by right may have been done with the best of intentions – it would have allowed her to actually take the woman down when she'd shown up – but it had made her (literally) take her eye off the ball. When it came down to it, she was no better than the cop in the Judge's story.

I won't let this end in the same way, she swore to herself. Besides, he probably just fucked off on a doughnut break. I was moving fucking rocks with my fucking mind.

She reached the end of the pier, the dusty wood creaking ominously under her feet, the sky blood-red above her.

It was going to be all right. She'd only taken her eyes off the kids for a couple of minutes, and the landscape in front of her was featureless and pancake flat. They couldn't have got far, and the far they had got, she should be able to track.

That's if it was *only a couple of minutes*, a voice barbed with judgement said to her. *You lost all sense of the outside world when you were messing around with those rocks. It was like a trance, so how do you know how long you were out of it for? Could have been minutes. Could have been an hour.*

Could have, should have, would have, thought Daisy-May. My past's been built on that shit. Sort of hoped the future would be different.

She squinted at a flicker of colour on the landscape,

accompanied by a faint tumble of dust. It could be some sort of vehicle, she thought. It could be a germ of nothing conjured up by guilt and desperation. Either way, I need to find out.

'You all right up there, girl?'

'I'm not big on titles,' said Daisy-May as she looked down to see a man at the bottom of the pier, 'but would it kill any of you bastards to call me ma'am now and again?'

The man offered nothing but a toothless grin. He was slouched in the hull of a rowing boat, his feet resting on one of the seats, a cigarette dangling from his lips like it was getting up the courage to jump. A fading tattoo of a skull covered his face, piercings jutting haphazardly from his inked flesh.

Daisy-May put her hands on her hips. 'You seen a woman and a young girl go past here?'

'Done more than seen 'em,' said the man. 'Talked to them. Sold to them.'

'Sold them what?'

'My last boat,' he said.

Daisy-May looked from the man to the cracked, parched desert behind him. 'You taking the piss, mate?'

'Don't sound like something I'd want to take,' said the man, 'so I'll say no.'

'Not sure which bit to disbelieve first, but I'll probably start with the boat bit. Not much water out there, unless you're counting dry-fuck earth.'

'Why'd you need water to sail a boat?' said the man, half a smile on his face.

''Cos that's the way it usually works,' said Daisy-May.

'Find much use for "usual" in the Pen?' he asked, tossing his cigarette away. 'I never did.'

She bit down on her lip, looking out at the horizon. 'How long ago did you sell them this boat?'

"Bout thirty minutes ago,' said the man, his rolling West Country accent lurching this way and that.

So I did lose track of time, thought Daisy-May. A hair on that girl's head gets mangled, it's on me.

'Can I buy a boat from you?' she said.

'Already said, they took the last one.'

She dug her nails into the palm of her hand. 'What about the one you're sitting in?'

'That's *my* boat,' said the man, patting the seat next to him affectionately. 'No one uses my boat but me.'

'Hate to use the *do you know who I am* line, mate, but do you?'

He took another cigarette from underneath his cap. 'You're the new Warden. Still not letting you use my boat, though.'

'How about I hire you and the boat, then?' said Daisy-May, her teeth gritty.

'Sounds *more* like it,' said the man, sitting up straight. 'Not much use for money in the Pen, though. More into favours.'

'So, what favour do you want?'

'Hop into my boat, let us get on our way, and I'll tell you.'

Daisy-May frowned, looking at the distance from the pier to the boat.

'You can jump from a hot air balloon, you can drop into a boat,' said the man.

'You saw that?' asked Daisy-May, remembering her plunge into the mass of Dispossessed that had helped her save the Pen.

'Everyone saw that. Least, that's what they say. Like the Sex Pistols in Manchester, your little swan-dive.'

'Don't know what that means,' said Daisy-May, jumping off the side of the pier.

She landed on the boat and the man reached forward, catching her before she could tip over the side. She took a seat opposite him, then looked at him expectantly. 'So, what do they call you?'

'Toll man seems to fit well enough.'

'All right, toll man,' said Daisy-May. 'Toll me.'

He grinned, the tattoo skull mouth smiling with him, the piercings slathered over his face jingling. He reached out, taking the wooden oars that jutted from the sides of the boat, then shifted in his seat. 'Might want to hold on, Warden. Gets choppy out there.'

Daisy-May looked doubtfully at the cracked land facing them. 'Hope you're not wasting my time here.'

The toll man began to rotate the oars, and as a dull whine began to sound, Daisy-May noticed he was careful that they didn't touch the ground. Around and around they went till they were a whirl of bone-dry wood and blurred vision. After thirty seconds or so, he took his hands away, but the oars paid him no mind, continuing to whirl and thrash.

It's like he's starting an aeroplane, she thought, one of those old-school twizzle-your-own-propeller jobs.

'You ready?' he yelled over the noise of the rapidly rotating oars.

'Ready for what?' Daisy-May shouted back.

He smiled again, reaching past her and pulling out a thick oak lever.

'Best duck.'

She did, just in time, as a flimsy-looking sail swung out over her head and popped into position.

'You've got to be fucking kidding,' she said.

'Never joke when it comes to sailing.'

Daisy-May cried out in surprise as the boat lurched forward, tipping her out of her seat. The oars smashed into the ground, pitching them forward again and again, each time the boat jerking a little further, the tips of the oars getting a little higher.

Like a dog on a fucking leash, she thought. One that's just seen a chaseable-as-fuck cat.

The toll man reached backwards and placed a hand on the rope that attached the boat to the pier.

'Here we go,' he said, smirking.

As he yanked it from its mooring, the effect was instantaneous. The boat lurched once more and Daisy-May was tossed backwards, the toll man grabbing her leg and preventing her from toppling over the side. Her stomach lurched with the boat as the tips of the oars scraped against the cracked ground, a cloud of dust billowing up around them.

Wind ripping at her, the world a blur of speed, she hauled herself up once again, looking in wonder as the docks rapidly became a speck on the horizon. 'Shit, this thing can motor,' she shouted.

'Fastest boat in the Pen,' the toll man shouted back, his left hand holding the rudder and easing it left, then right. 'Where we going?'

'Wherever the woman and the girl are going,' said Daisy-May, shifting in her seat and looking out into the distance, the boat chugging and whining underneath her, her purple hair yanked that way and this by the wind.

'Don't know where that is,' said the man. 'But know how to follow 'em.'

'What do you want for this ride?' she asked. 'Anything sleazy, and I'll sling your arse in prison.'

'Want you to get a message to someone.'

'Who?'

'Mabel,' said the man, winking.

'How do you know Mabel?'

'Reckon that's no one's business but mine and Mabel's.'

Daisy-May nodded. 'Reckon you're right. OK.'

She looked away and took in the landscape. The ground was like dried skin, parched and lumpy, stretching endlessly in every direction. She could just about glimpse the Pen wall in the distance, so indistinct as to be little more than a half-finished pencil sketch. The only thing truly definable was the smell, the almost overpowering stench of chlorine violating her nostrils.

'Still getting my head around the fact I've never heard of this place before, let alone seen it.'

'Know about everywhere on the soil, do you?' said the toll man, that same knowing half-smile playing on his lips. 'Why'd the Pen be any different?'

'I *am* the fucking Warden,' said Daisy-May.

'Pen's endless. Endless ways to surprise you, for good and bad. Woman you're chasing, she surprises.'

She leaned forward, struggling to hear over the grinding revolutions of the boat's oars. 'Surprises how?'

'Heard the rumours, I'm guessing, on how she doesn't glimmer?'

Daisy-May nodded.

'Ain't quite right when you see her in person. She don't glimmer, that's true enough, not like you or I would anyway, but she ain't totally solid neither. Like you're watching a TV show of her, but one where the picture's not too clever.'

'Like a hologram, you mean?'

'Nah, she's real enough,' said the man. 'Took my arm when I helped her into the boat. Hard to say exactly, but it's like she ain't been coloured in right. You'll see when we catch up to them.'

'What'd she look like?'

'Blonde. Stank of privilege. Looked like you could grate cheese on her cheekbones.'

Daisy-May considered this. 'She give you a name?'

'She didn't,' said the man.

'You helped her before, shifting these kids?'

The man bristled, the metalwork on his face jingling.

'Weren't me. Used to be others with boats here. They're gone now. I'm all that's left.'

'You think that's down to the woman who doesn't glimmer?' said Daisy-May. 'These others being gone?'

'What I thinks and what I know, they're two different things.'

She pointed to the infinite horizon. 'What's out there? Where could they be going?'

The toll man stared past her. 'Nowhere good.'

Chapter Twelve

Megan had never been one for company.

It wasn't that she disliked people; it was that she distrusted them. There was a difference. She liked them on her periphery, liked the noise and the smell and the energy of them. It was when interaction was necessary that she recoiled. All the people in her life had let her down, and there came a time when that shit was on you. If you knew they'd let you down, yet you let them do it anyway, whose fault was that?

That was why she liked the dead so much. They were usually so grateful that someone could hear and see them; they fell over themselves to be kind. Growing up shorn as she had been of friends of her own, they'd been a lifeline, and rarely something to be scared of. They were all she knew, and there was nothing scary about the known.

Usually nothing scary, anyway. Sometimes a terrified and terrifying soul would cross her path, one doused in rage and confusion and looking to infect those around them with that bile. Never, though, had she met a spirit who had fooled her like the boy had.

When she'd first seen him loitering in the train station, George had seemed like a stray dog looking for its owner. It had almost seemed to scare him when he realised she could see him.

He'd followed her for several hours before finally plucking up the courage to talk to her.

When he did, it had seemed like he'd being waiting decades for the chance. Her unfamiliarity with the city – she was only weeks into her photography and digital media masters – gave him free rein to show her that city and all of its nooks and long-forgotten crannies. She'd felt a degree of guilt at this. She knew she was using him and his loneliness, but she was producing the best work she'd ever done. The Ghosts Never Die series, in particular, showed a side of the city that only a select few people would see. Only people like her, with their ability to see the dead, would be able to glimpse the image of the spirits she'd captured in the photographs. It was like a secret society, with an even more secretive membership.

She looked at the three lines tattooed onto the back of her hand.

The longer she sat here in this dank toilet of a cell, its walls dripping, water roaring in the distance, the more Megan realised something. She hadn't been taking advantage of George. He'd been taking advantage of her. Or, more accurately, grooming her. Earning her trust to the point of leading her here.

Why, though? What did he hope to gain?

Why had she been tied to this chair? Why was she being shown this film, again and again? What relevance did it hold for her? The off-screen scientist claimed the boy on-screen had the same ability Megan herself had: he could see the dead too.

A test facility where you were made to see the dead?

It didn't seem credible.

'I'm sorry, Megs.'

Megan looked to her left – the bindings at least allowed her to do that – and saw a chunky steel door with a slit cut across the top of it. She could just about glimpse George's eyes peeking through it.

'Why did you do this?' she said. 'Why did you lure me down here?'

'I had no choice. Mind if I come in?'

'How could I stop you?'

'Don't want to be rude.'

Megan laughed. There was a smattering of hysteria to it, but could she be blamed for that? She was arguing courtesy do's and don'ts with a ghost. A child ghost that had lured her into the arms of a kidnapper.

'It's a free country,' she said. 'At least I thought it was.'

George passed straight through the door and walked in front of her, blocking the images projected onto the wall.

'Why did you trick me down here, George?'

'Can't tell you.'

'I'm in danger, aren't I?'

He didn't reply, but she didn't need him to. Getting kidnapped and locked in a storm drain was its own answer.

'You can make this right,' she said, 'if you can get me out.'

'There's no way out,' said George. 'I can't open doors. Can't move soil things, not the way some spirits can. You know that.'

'I thought we were friends,' said Megan. 'So I don't know really know anything, do I?'

'You look like him, you know.'

'I look like who?'

'Your grandad.'

Goosebumps erupted on Megan's back. 'I don't have a grandad.'

'Yeah, you do,' said George. 'He sat right where you're sitting now.'

She swallowed. 'Why would you say that?'

''Cos it's true. It's why he takes them.'

'It's why who takes them? Who's keeping me here, George?'

'Can't say,' George replied.

'Can't, or won't?'

'Both.'

'Why has he taken me, then?' said Megan. 'At least tell me that.'

'The youngest and the oldest,' said George. 'Always that way.'

'The youngest and the oldest what? What makes me so special?'

'I'm not supposed to say. I'm sorry,' said George, walking backwards towards the wall. 'For everything.'

The shelter.

Bits and Joe's arrival barely warranted a nod from the dozing homeless souls, stupefied as they were on purgatory gas and air. Elias stood at the back of the room, one of his lost souls sitting in front of him, looking to all intents and purposes like a customer at a dive-bar barber's. Elias held what looked like a small blowtorch in his hand, and was patiently cutting away the tangle of vines on the stranded spirit's face.

'That shit's beyond the call of duty,' said Bits.

Elias smiled as a clump of vines fell to the floor. 'It's a small kindness that gives fellows like this some of their dignity back.' He held out the mini solder. 'I can show you how, if you like.'

Bits held his hands up. 'Made my peace with the fact that I'm a selfish fucker. God knows my limits and loves me for them.'

'Maybe you'll surprise yourself one of these days,' said Elias, returning to the task at hand.

Joe noted the modest camp bed in the corner of the room, and the rows of pill bottles on the shelf above it, carefully sorted by order and colour. *He even sleeps here. Amount of pills he's on, I question how many more times he'll wake up from that sleep.*

'Wondered if you'd managed to get us an address for the girl,' he said.

'Stanley's soil body didn't help in the way you hoped?' said Elias.

'It helped,' said Joe, 'but you can never have too *much* help in an investigation like this.'

'I'm sure.' Elias put down the blow torch and patted the newly shorn spirit on the shoulder. 'The missing woman's flat is in Moss Side. You gentleman should feel right at home; that place is *awash* with ghosts.'

Manchester City Football Club's spiritual home – and literal one until 2003 – was a ramshackle cowshed slapped down in one of Manchester's toughest neighbourhoods. Maine Road's stands creaked with the cigarette smoke and sweat of decades of Mancunian passion, most of it dashed on the rocks of hope and despair. If you were a neutral (and you weren't from the red half of the city), you loved City and their ability to fuck things up.

Then their grubby old shrine to football just wouldn't do any more, so they decamped to Eastlands, a wasteland that needed a shiny new state-of-the-art football stadium but didn't know it yet. As petro-billions fluttered their eyelashes at everyone's second favourite team, the old Maine Road stadium was bull-dozed, replaced by flats, another relic from Manchester's past desecrated and destroyed.

'This is the final straw, man,' said Bits, looking at the ship-shaped block of flats built on the stadium's corpse. 'Feels like someone's shat on my grave.'

Joe stood next to his partner, head tilted slightly to one side. He'd never seen City's old ground before, but if he hadn't known of its existence, he would have been able to sense it. It was like the air around the new flats was wounded. Scarred.

There didn't have to be a hole in the sky for there to be a hole in the sky. You looked at the space, and it was like it was framed wrong.

'Never go back.'

He turned to Bits. 'What?'

'That's what my grandad always used to say. Never go back, whether that's football managers scuttling back to a former club or wives taking back a cheating bloke. There's always a reason you left in the first place, and it's usually a good one. He was right. Shouldn't have come back here, man. It's fucked up. It's wrong. Not my Manchester any more.'

'I get it,' said Joe. 'We still have a job to do, though.'

'Then let's get on and do it,' said Bits. 'Place gives me the creeps.'

The plod on the door made Joe grateful to be dead.

It was sometimes difficult to remember the advantages that state of being brought, because the disadvantages were all too stark: a lack of being able to touch anything, the paucity of resources to call upon, the feeling that truth and justice were always three steps ahead of you. On this occasion, though, being dead was something to celebrate, because the policeman on the door didn't need to be shown a badge, or cajoled into letting them in. Bits and Joe could simply walk through him.

The copper shivered, despite the balminess of the evening and the boredom etched on his face.

'Be glad you were never police on the soil,' said Joe. 'Half the job is standing outside empty homes waiting for a body to turn up, dead or alive.'

'Not sure I'd have passed the entrance exam, me,' said Bits. 'Been more likely to nick the pen. Or snort it.'

'Elias said 503, the girl's flat number,' said Joe. 'Which means the fifth floor.'

'Sharp as a tack, you,' said Bits.

They made their way through the fire exit door, taking the steps two at a time, the case in Joe's nostrils now.

'What you hoping to find in here?' said Bits. 'That the flesh-and-blooders will have missed, like?'

'Until I see it, I won't know,' said Joe, his feet hitting the steps with a soundless sigh. 'Though I'm willing to bet anything that it has to do with the boy.'

'One you saw when you used the coins?'

Joe nodded. 'Only reason there'd have been a boy present when Stanley died is if he was a prisoner, or in on it somehow. Maybe he's the killer's son. Maybe he's some poor lost soul who's in too deep. He glimmered, which probably means he's dead. Either way, there's a connection. We just have to find it.'

They huffed and puffed their way to the fifth-floor landing. There was neither sight nor sound of another soul, living or dead. It was like the place knew a wrong had happened and was hiding from the consequences.

Bits pointed to a door with two slashes of police tape strung across it. 'Almost like the soil bizzies knew we'd be coming. Wanted to gift-wrap the place for us.'

Joe said nothing.

'How'd you want to do this?'

'Professionally,' said Joe.

With that, he walked through the door.

The two partners stood next to each other, letting the room take a good look at them. It fascinated Joe how their presence had made the air shift. There was no earthly reason for this to have occurred, yet it had.

That's what people mean when they say they can feel a presence, he thought. And it works both ways, because the girl might not be here any more, but it's like some of her still is. Some impression. An idea of her.

It felt like buzzing, a tingle under his skin.

A collage of old gig tickets sat proudly on one of the walls. A café's loyalty card had been discarded on an ancient-looking coffee table, just one stamp short of a free drink.

Megan would get the chance to earn that free coffee. Joe was going to make sure of it.

There was something else here, too. Something they couldn't see.

'You smell that?' said Joe.

Bits nodded. 'Rank. Smelled it before.'

'When?'

Bits considered. 'When I went to see the Roses play. Spike Island. Gig was on an old toxic waste dump. Band came on, and everyone lost their shit. Rushed to the front and kicked up a proper cloud of fuck knows what.'

'Chemicals, then,' said Joe.

Bits nodded. 'Shouldn't be able to smell them, though, should we?'

'We can smell a feeling sometimes,' said Joe. 'Get a sense of something. But this isn't that. This place is caked in the dead.'

'What could have caused that?' said Bits.

'Nothing good,' said Joe. 'Tread carefully.'

The walls nodded to Manchester's industrial past with their exposed brickwork and pipes. The furniture was sparse and cobbled together. Half of it looked like it had come from a skip.

It was the stuff hanging on the walls that caught their attention, though.

'Our girl's a photographer,' said Bits. 'Fuckin' shonky one.'

Joe felt he had a point.

Manchester was laid out before them, framed and spaced a few inches apart. Photo after photo of the city. Crumbling

Salford side streets and shining new glass buildings tattooed onto the skyline. Market stalls in the Arndale. Canals on Deansgate. All of them devoid of a single human soul.

'What's she got against people?' said Bits.

'Same thing she's got against framing a shot, apparently,' said Joe. 'It's like she's missed half the background out on each photo.'

'Not supposed to be understood by the likes of me and you,' said Bits. 'For arty cunts, isn't it?'

Joe frowned. It was more than that. Something bothered him about the photos more than simply the artistic choices the kidnapped girl had made, or their composition.

Or rather, it *was* their composition. It was wrong, but deliberately wrong. It hovered in front of him, the truth he was seeking, then sprinted away when he reached for it.

It'll come, he thought. It'll come, if I let it.

'Let's check the rest of the place out.'

The bathroom was just a bathroom, the kitchen barely that.

The bedroom, on the other hand, was a gallery in all but name, and a gallery dedicated to a very specific subject.

'The Lads Club,' said Bits. 'In Salford.'

Joe leaned in to a picture of the red-brick facade. 'Everyone's heard of the Lads Club.'

'Went there for a bit, me,' said Bits. 'Part of the city. It'll outlast us all.'

Joe made his way along the display of photographs, noticing that the chemical stench was even worse here than in the living room. The framing of the photographs was worse too, if that was possible. A wall cut out here. A door frame butchered there.

It's like she was hammered when she took these, thought Joe. Hammered, or blind.

Bits was studying a bit of paper stuck to the wall. '*The ghosts that haunt us*, it says. What the fuck does that mean?'

Something clicked.

She's not blind, thought Joe. I am.

He hauled his satchel off, then dug deeply inside it.

'You brought sandwiches?'

'I thought you did,' said Joe, gifting his partner a rare smile.

He withdrew a small plastic bottle. Blue liquid swilled around inside it, and a nozzle sat at its top. It looked like the sort of sprayer you'd use on the windows.

'Bag of tricks you've got,' said Bits. 'Fucked if I know what that's for, though.'

'It's a different flavour of UV, like the wand I used earlier,' said Joe. 'Watch.'

He squeezed the bottle's trigger, and blue liquid hit the surface of the picture closest to him.

'Fuck me,' said Bits.

'Yep,' said Joe.

The photograph showed an ancient sports hall with even more ancient green paint. It was lit moodily by a single dangling bulb. Standing beneath it was a boy in a battered school uniform, a nervous expression on his face.

One who'd been invisible before Joe had doused the photo in UV spray.

'That's him. The boy I saw when I used the coins.'

He moved from picture to picture, soaking them all in the UV spray.

The boy outside the Lads Club.

The boy next to a mosaic homage to the Smiths.

The boy on a flight of dimly lit stairs.

The boy on a raised gantry in the club, musty punchbags circling him.

'She's not a shit photographer,' said Bits. 'She knew exactly what she was shooting. She was snapping the boy. We just couldn't see him before.'

Joe nodded. 'Which means the boy's dead. Which means the girl who's been kidnapped can *see* the dead. Feels significant, that, doesn't it?'

He marched through to the living room and squirted the pictures in there too. The previously empty photographs now hosted a roll-call of spirit waifs and strays.

An old woman in a Salford street. A young man staring nervously at the camera.

The boy again, outside the neo-Gothic grandeur of the Rylands library.

'This is mental, man,' said Bits. 'A photo exhibition of ghosts. What's the point if no one can see them?'

'Maybe some people can see them,' said Joe. 'Maybe that's what got Megan kidnapped and her grandad murdered.'

Bits sniffed the air. 'You smell that?'

Joe frowned. 'Burning. From the bedroom.'

As if waiting for such acknowledgement, the picture next to him burst into flames. Joe sprang backwards as blue fire licked and tickled the image. It spread quickly and hungrily.

'They're not normal flames,' said Bits, backing away. 'Not giving off a lick of heat.'

'You're right,' said Joe, moving towards the window, not taking his eyes from the blue fire.

'Think they could hurt us?' said Bits.

'Think I'm not willing to find out,' said Joe. 'That's what the chemical smell we noticed was, though. Pretty sure we've just tumbled into a fire trap.'

Bits took a further step backwards. 'Fucking hell.'

'What?' replied Joe.

'This is hellfire,' said Bits. 'Seen it before in the Pen. Eats through anything dead in seconds.'

'We're dead,' said Joe.

The flames had colonised the room, backing the partners into the corner.

'Thanks, Sherlock,' said Bits, 'and it's scheming to eat through us. Time to skedaddle.'

He reached for the window, crying out in surprise when his hand struck it.

Frowning, Joe copied the action. He got the same result. His solid fist hit solid glass when it should have passed clean through it.

'That should be impossible,' he said.

'Tell the window,' said Bits.

They both took a final step backwards as the flames surged several feet forwards.

'Trapped like rats in a chute,' said Bits. 'You got any suggestions?'

Joe coughed. Whatever the fire was, its smoke was capable of choking him. And if it was capable of that, the flames were capable of burning him too.

'Drop.'

Both men fell to their bellies, smoke gathering over their heads.

'Now what?' said Bits. 'This is how I went out the first time. Not going to be killed again by a bunch of fucking flames.'

Joe stared at the chunky wooden coffee table in front of them. Its legs were woodlouse-nibbled but looked sturdy enough. He reached out a hand and closed it around one of the legs, shuddering when he got the same result as the window. It was like he was still alive.

'Something's been triggered in this room,' he said. 'Something that makes us solid. Something that's torched the place. It was when I used the UV spray. It's like it knew we were undead.'

'So?' said Bits, coughing up a lungful of hellfire smoke.

'So if someone's made us solid, it means we can interact with things on the soil.'

Joe rose to his knees and dipped his fingers under the lip of the coffee table. 'Give me a hand with this.'

'Won't that break the rules?' said Bits, getting reluctantly to his feet. 'Call the Xylophone Man?'

'Way those rules have been bent already, I don't think so,' said Joe. He risked a look at the room. The flames were inches from them. 'Besides, what choice do we have?'

Bits nodded, reluctantly helping Joe to heave the table up. 'Where'd you want it?'

'Through the window,' said Joe.

They were lucky, in that the window gave them plenty to aim at. It stretched from the floor to the ceiling, letting in acres of artificial street light.

'On three,' said Joe.

He counted and they rammed, the flames reaching for them, the end of the table juddering the glass but not breaking it.

'Fuck,' said Bits. 'Didn't even dent it.'

'Again,' said Joe.

This time they had more luck. Spidery cracks spread from the impact point, but the window didn't cave in.

Smoke filled the room, clawing at their lungs.

'One last time,' said Joe.

One last time didn't get it done. The window was a mass of cracks but still intact.

'We're going to have to go through.'

'You're mental,' said Bits.

'Better than dead,' said Joe.

He felt the fire snag the back of his coat. It was more effective than any starter pistol.

He slammed his shoulder into the glass, the force knocking

the undead air out of him but also smashing the window. The road below rushed up to meet him, and he prepared himself for the bone-splintering impact of tarmac.

It didn't come. He hit the road as weightless as he'd ever been, and immediately rolled, trying to put out the heatless flames that were spreading over his back.

When they were out – and when he'd confirmed that they hadn't caused any permanent damage – he looked for Bits. His partner was sitting several feet away, coughing but seemingly unharmed.

'Fun, that,' he said. 'Fancy another go?'

Joe looked at the policeman who'd been left to guard the front door. He was staring up at the broken window and reaching for his radio. 'Disturbance at the missing woman's address. Possible break-in. Proceeding to investigate on foot.'

'He doesn't see the flames,' said Bits. 'Just sees a busted-open window.'

'What did you expect?' said Joe.

'Didn't expect to have to break through a glass window,' said Bits, 'or be able to.'

He got to his feet, dusting himself down. 'Something dead set that trap for us. Still think it's not wendigos?'

'I was doubtful before,' said Joe, 'and I'm a cast-iron cynic now. This is way beyond some supposedly vampiric undead creature. This was a trap set by someone who doesn't want us getting closer than we've already got. This was the Generation Killer. And the more I see, the more I think he's as alive as we are dead.'

He rose wearily, cursing his creaking undead bones. 'We know more than we did thirty minutes ago at least. We know the kidnapped woman can see the dead, and we know she knows the boy. The boy's the key. We find him, I'm convinced he can lead us to Megan.'

'How do we find him then?' said Bits.

'Almost every photo of him was at the Lads Club in Salford,' said Joe. 'I suggest we start there.'

Bits turned his nose up. 'Sick twist, this. Firebomb assassinations I can just about handle. Salford, though? It's the devil's playground, man.'

Chapter Thirteen

'My God.'

'You're welcome to him,' said Hatoyama, 'if this is the handiwork of his children.'

The Duchess and the detective lurked on the edge of the tea-house crime scene, taking in the death and destruction Hanna had left in her wake. A skeleton crew of pathologists were at work, the scene consisting of a dead man with no face, and a shorter, deader man with a television for one. Cracks in the screen spidered away from the hole Cujo's head had made, a flickering imprint of a girl's face framing him like a halo. The whole thing could have passed for a modern art exhibition if there hadn't been a pool of blood around Cujo's expensive loafers.

'That's her all right,' said the Duchess, glaring at the image of Hanna on the TV screen. '*How* it's her, I can't begin to imagine.'

The pathologists were beginning to pack up, one of them taking final snaps of the television screen, ignoring altogether the strange sweaty detective who lurked at the crime scene's edge.

They can see her on the screen, thought the Duchess, in the same way I can. How can that be? How can she make the impossible possible?

'So much for our link to Hanna. We're back to square one.'

'Hardly,' said Hatoyama. 'We're closer than we've ever been.'

'How so?'

'Because now we know for sure that she's after that chip.'

'Yes,' said the Duchess, 'but the man who knows where the chip is being kept is currently modelling a television set. And we have to assume he told her where it's being stored, or his usefulness wouldn't have come to such an end.'

'Agreed,' said Hatoyama.

He took out his phone and pointed it at the fractured TV panel with its flickering image of Hanna.

'It's hardly the time for a selfie, Detective.'

Hatoyama ignored her, tapping a button on the phone. The device responded with a click.

'What are you doing?' asked the Duchess.

'I'm thinking that if Hanna can be seen on this television by pathology cops like these,' he replied, 'then she can be seen by facial profiling systems too.'

'Only the dead can see the dead,' said the Duchess, 'and even then it's not a given. It's not an exact science.'

'What if she's made it an exact science? What if she changed something when she imprinted herself on that TV?'

'That seems something of a stretch, Detective.'

'This is *all* a stretch,' said Hatoyama. 'Fact is, the other police at that crime scene, they could see her image on the TV. Who's to say Arata can't see her now too? Or more importantly, his facial profiling system?'

77 Bank, in Tokyo's Chuo City, was notable for how little currency it actually carried. Like most banks in the modern age, the money that filtered through its system was electronic, paper notes rarely touching a teller's hands. To those in the know – which now included Hanna Jankie – the real value

was to be found a hundred feet below the bank floor, in a room surrounded by several feet of reinforced steel. That is, if Cujo had been telling the truth.

Hanna started walking towards the bank's front entrance, knowing the trio of followers behind her were untroubled by doubts, that after hearing her language-of-the-dead sweet nothings, all they wanted to do was follow her to the ends of the earth. If things went to plan, they wouldn't need to: the ends of the earth would come to them.

She passed through the entrance, noting the security guards on the other side of it, as well as the two at the entrance to the vault. There would be no bloodbath this time, no showy use of force and steel.

Her eyes scanned the room for danger.

Twenty or so people stood patiently in line, waiting to be served by the bank tellers.

Six windows, a teller behind each one.

Five security cameras overlooking it all.

She eyeballed each and every one of them, a small smile on her lips.

If they could somehow see her, what of it? Though in truth, the way she'd managed to infect the TV screen troubled her slightly, made her question whether she'd changed something by committing such a sacrilegious, scorch-the-earth act. When it came to the dead, seeing wasn't believing; it was convincing yourself you hadn't seen anything at all. It was less scary for the living that way.

No, it was the dead that troubled her.

She'd lost contact with her follower in the Sea of Trees. That could only mean one thing: someone had tracked her there. Fingers crossed, the suicide bomber she'd left behind there would have killed that someone, but she couldn't rely on it. She had to assume that someone was hunting her down.

You know who that someone is, Oma Jankie's voice said. *It's Rachel, the sainted Duchess. She's a dog, and you're her bone.*

If that's true, Hanna thought, then it's time that dog was put down.

The rush-hour traffic pushed and pulled at Hatoyama's Honda, oblivious to his screaming siren, the Duchess's foot tapping in frustration.

'Can't this thing go any faster?'

'It could,' said Hatoyama, 'if there weren't a thousand cars in front of us.'

'This might be our last chance to catch her,' said the Duchess.

'I know that,' he said, drawing deeply on his cigarette.

Arata's facial profiling system had come up trumps, sighting Hanna entering one of the city's largest banks. Fortune had favoured them in its location – it was close – but had then evaded them by clogging the roads with traffic, slowing their progress.

The Duchess frowned as she saw Hatoyama grind his cigarette into the smouldering mini mountain of butts, then chain-light a new cigarette from it. 'You flesh-and-blooders. The damage you willingly do to yourselves.'

He laughed. 'When you've got what I've got, you don't worry about cigarettes. Quitting would be like trying to put out a forest fire with a glass of water.'

The Duchess looked out of the window, taking solace in the teeming life outside. 'What *have* you got?'

'Cancer,' said Hatoyama. 'The type that doesn't care for remission.'

'I'm sorry.'

He barked out a laugh. 'You sound it.'

'You still haven't told me what happened with you and Mabel,' she said, the knowledge that it was the Gift Protocol that had given Hatoyama his death sentence – knowledge he was ignorant of – guiltily yapping at her.

'Deliberately,' he replied. 'Pouring over injustices I've received isn't one of my favourite hobbies.'

'Injustices?'

'Ask me again when we're not on the trail of a psychotic spirit.'

'I'll hold you to that. So: what are we going to find at this bank?'

Hatoyama drew deeply on his latest cigarette, then blew smoke towards her. 'I haven't the first clue. There are rumours, though, about Yakuza vaults. Old gangster wives' tales that tell of defences designed to keep out the dead as well as the living.'

The Duchess looked out of the window, formations of traffic either side of them. 'It's not an impossibility. The Yakuza are an ancient institution.'

Hatoyama cursed as an elderly man stumbled out into the road, squealing the car's brakes.

'Agents like yourself received a field kit,' said the Duchess. 'Do you still have it?'

'I should have thrown it away when I learned you were closing down the initiative,' said Hatoyama.

'But you didn't.'

He nodded towards the glove box.

No penalties for interacting with the living world, thought the Duchess.

She still flinched a little when she pressed down on the glove box. It popped open, revealing a yellow plastic case. She reached forward, taking it out and placing it on her lap, a tingle going through her as she handled something she had no earthly (or unearthly, come to that) right to.

On first inspection, the weapon in the case looked like a crude toy for a cruder child. It was shaped like a gun and made of moulded grey plastic, with a vivid yellow trigger and a similarly coloured muzzle. It was only when you lifted it that you realised it wasn't a plaything; the weapon had heft, and a sense of barely constrained power. She held it to her ear, smiling at the almost subliminal hum it gave off. 'Have you ever fired it?'

Hatoyama shook his head. 'That thing's an abomination. It should never have been built.'

The Duchess held the weapon up, allowing the sunlight to bounce off its plastic casing. 'You should meet my successor in the Pen. You'd find plenty of common ground.'

She returned it to its case, then placed it on the dashboard. 'We should go over the plan again.'

'There's a plan?' said Hatoyama, finally able to push the Honda forward.

'If you have a better idea, then by all means let's hear it.'

'A better idea than a ghost waltzing into a bank trying to stop another ghost from stealing a microchip? Impossible.'

'All I need you to do is wait in the car. It's a feat even a burnout like you should be capable of.'

'So I'm the chauffeur now,' said Hatoyama.

The car chugged up a steep incline, its engine coughing and spluttering. A towering building revealed itself on the horizon, its arrival so sudden it was as if it had jumped out from behind a curtain.

'That's it?' said the Duchess.

Hatoyama nodded.

'Stop here,' she said, shifting in her seat. 'I'd like the element of surprise.'

He slowed the car, then brought it to a stop, yanking up the handbrake. 'You're a ghost; how much surprise do you need?'

'None when it comes to the living. As much as you when it comes to the dead.'

Hatoyama nodded at the case on the dashboard. 'You're not going to take the bolt-cutter with you?'

'If I need it, it will already be too late.' The Duchess rose from her seat, her head passing straight through the roof of the car. 'That shouldn't stop *you* bringing it if I'm not back in twenty minutes.'

Hanna walked towards one of the tellers, passing through the booth and the woman sitting behind it. On first glance, the room looked like a typical bank strongroom; safety deposit boxes lined the walls, but they weren't the sort of riches she was after. If Cujo had been accurate in his description, those were behind the wall in front of her.

Beckoning her followers, she strode to the floor-to-ceiling door at the back of the room. A vast metal circle was pressed into the door's centre, a smaller steel wheel taking pride of place in its middle. It would have taken a tank to batter through it, or at the very least a master safe-breaker.

Or someone who could pass through solid objects. Whoever designed this safe hadn't figured on the dead.

Didn't they? said a voice in her head.

I stopped listening to you centuries ago, Oma Jankie, thought Hanna.

And see where that's got you, said Oma Jankie. *Flouncing around on this ridiculous campaign of yours. You make me so ashamed. You were never worthy of the title of Warden.*

I bet you said the exact same thing to Rachel, thought Hanna. Mabel too. You never had my vision. You never had my nerve.

Nerve has always been a jumped-up word for stupid, cackled her grandmother. *And that's what you'll be if you waltz straight into that safe. The Yakuza are an institution almost as old as our own — do you really think they'll trust their riches to computer alarms and soil-breathing guards?*

Hanna paused at this, because although the old crone's words were like dragging nails down a blackboard, there was a kernel of common sense to them. If anyone knew how to capitalise on the dead, it was the Yakuza; the fighting gangs she'd witnessed at the cinema were testament to that.

'Ma'am.'

She turned to see one of her followers jogging towards her. Annoyance crackled; she'd specifically ordered this one to stay as lookout on the bank's main entrance.

She'd be even more annoyed if she actually had something to report.

'An old woman spirit has entered,' said the lookout. 'She glimmers in a way I didn't believe possible.'

Hanna squeezed her fists together. 'Does she have grey hair, this woman? Scraped back from her face?'

The lookout nodded.

The Duchess. Hanna had to admit she was impressed. She'd feared it would be her sister who would follow her to the soil – Rachel would view her as a mess she needed to personally clean up – but that didn't mean she had hoped it would happen.

She had to be quick.

Quick, yet careful.

She turned to the group waiting patiently behind her, commanding them to move through the steel door, the language of the dead sweetly seductive in their ears. They nodded gratefully, then walked forward, the mighty metal door swallowing them whole.

Seconds became a minute.

A minute doubled.

The Duchess had to be close.

Something's wrong, thought Hanna.

A hand appeared through the door's metal hide, the skin on it rabid and bubbling. An arm and a body quickly followed, the

219

woman they belonged to soundlessly screaming, her body dissolving before Hanna's eyes. She dropped to all fours, chunks of her skin clinging to the floor with each desperate drag forward.

Barbarians, thought Hanna, smiling. Which means I'm in the right place.

Anything with that amount of protection has to be worth stealing.

Detective Hatoyama hated feeling useless. Which was unfortunate, as feeling useless was pretty much his default setting.

He fiddled with the radio, chopping and changing stations, unable to settle on one, then picked up and discarded the three-week-old newspaper rotting in the back seat.

Twenty minutes, that was what the Duchess had said. If she wasn't back in twenty minutes he was to ride in like the cavalry and save her. From what, he didn't have the first clue, but she had seemed similarly uninformed.

He smiled, despite himself. It had been a long time since he'd been in a situation like this, his right knee jiggling with nervous tension, his eyes wandering everywhere and nowhere, his mind racing with thoughts and deeds not yet done. Something was at stake, and that felt good. He reached over to the yellow case on the dashboard, placing it on his jiggling knee. He probably wouldn't need it, but for once he was glad he had it.

In ten minutes, he'd find out whether he'd need to use it.

The Duchess had passed through the front of the bank and through the teller's windows with the minimum of fuss, the line of customers patiently waiting for their turn oblivious to her. The room behind that had contained rows of safety deposit boxes and two bodies; they lay in front of a mighty steel door, glimmering, smouldering and steaming.

She kneeled down, looking at but not touching their bubbled, sheared skin. *It's like they've bathed in acid, a dip I doubt they took willingly. Although Hanna's always had a knack for convincing people they should flout common sense and follow her into battle.*

She took a step towards the steel door in front of her, thinking of Hatoyama's warning of Yakuza defences designed to keep out both the living and the dead. There was every chance the room was booby-trapped. The corpses behind her were brutal proof of that.

She flexed a hand and pointed it at the body nearest to her. It shifted slightly then clumsily sprang to its feet, a puppet for her to control. She shuffled it over to the door, then dipped its right hand through the solid metal structure. As she mind-twitched it back out again, she heard it hiss and sizzle.

I still have some power then, she thought as she peered down at the corpse's freshly smoking hand. I only hope it's enough to get me through whatever hell is behind that steel door.

When you'd journeyed through the fires of hell and swum through the poisoned Gloop, an acid bath in a bank vault was child's play, or at the very least, a young adult's.

That didn't mean it hadn't hurt.

Still, she was through it now, and the squat samurai on the other side almost looked pleased to see her.

The warrior facing Hanna wore a suit of vivid red armour, gold engravings bobbling out of his chest plate and shoulder pads. A quiver of arrows hung from the back of his war suit, and his left hand held a curved sword loosely, as if the power in it was a curse as well as a burden. His ankle was what interested Hanna the most: attached to it was a thin metal wire that stretched all the way to the far left-hand wall, where it was wrapped around a pole jutting out from the floor.

He's trapped here, she thought. Just like the cock-fighting

souls at the cinema. I wonder if that's Lucia's doing. Perhaps she's more than just words and promised wonder.

The samurai lifted his head, a horned helmeted thing of fierce, horrific beauty. A pair of deep brown eyes peered out from a gold faceplate, its nose hooked, its mouth stretched into a rictus snarl.

'Are you alive?' he croaked. 'Or are you dead?'

'That depends on how you view those two states of being,' said Hanna.

He laughed, the sound bone dry. 'A philosopher. Most who come here are thieves.'

'I'm more interested in what I can give to people,' said Hanna, 'rather than what I can take.' She nodded at the wire tied around the samurai's ankle. 'You are a prisoner here.'

'I am a servant to my master.'

'A servant who's kept in chains.'

'It is not for me to question the will of those I serve,' said the samurai. 'It is for me to defend their honour, and to uphold my own. It is to show loyalty.'

'And what of your master's loyalty to you?' said Hanna. 'He keeps you bound here. Does he trust you so little?'

'You are just a girl. What do you know of trust?'

'More than you could imagine.'

The samurai placed one foot back, then leaned forward with the other, raising his sword above his head, his body vibrating, ready to attack.

I could make this warrior parade around on all fours if I wanted to, thought Hanna. The language of the dead would certainly allow it. Better to use it to curry favour than cause humiliation, though.

Particularly with a duchess in the building.

'How long have you served your master?' she asked.

'Masters,' said the samurai. 'The Yakuza have endured for thousands of years. When they wither and die, so will I.'

'That's the only way you'll be released?' said Hanna. 'If the Yakuza are no more?'

'It is an honour gifted to very few, to serve in such a way.'

'There's a whole world out there,' she said, 'and you could be anyone in it, yet you choose to rot here, defending some grubby soil breather's gold. What honour is there in that?'

'You would not understand.'

'I understand perfectly. I was bound like you once; not physically, but shackled mentally, by my family, by duty. Then something wonderful happened. I realised I didn't need to be, that the only person keeping me in bondage was myself. We are the same, you and I.'

'There would be no honour in betraying my master,' said the samurai, 'and no amount of words could persuade me otherwise.'

Hanna smiled.

We'll see about that.

Clunk.

Clunk.

Clunk.

Hatoyama opened and closed the soot-grey Honda's door, all the while looking at the clock on the centre dashboard. Ten minutes ago, he'd been willing time away, but now, with just sixty seconds of the allotted period left, he wished he could dial it back. What was he supposed to do, waltz into the bank and ask for his ghost back?

Still, he *was* a detective, or at least that was what the badge in his back pocket said. There'd been a time when he'd even been considered a good one. Good detectives didn't make excuses and shirk danger. When innocent lives were at stake – and if this Hanna was as dangerous as the Duchess said, they absolutely were – you walked towards it.

Time's up, he thought, picking up the chunky yellow case. One way or another.

There had been a few seconds when the Duchess thought she might be all right.

Three pain-free steps had taken her into the safe, and she dared to dream that the bodies she'd seen outside would have soaked up most of the room's supply of poison. It made it worse, somehow, when that turned out not to be the case: it was like bathing in a shower of fire, unseen liquid blistering her soul and skin. It must be some sort of gas – though she dreaded to think who could have created something so deadly to the dead, and why. It almost felt like a novelty, so long was it since she'd felt pain. There was a chance that this was for nothing, that Hanna could have gone a different way, but her instincts and eyes told her it was the only way her sister could have come. Anything with this level of defence *had* to be worth stealing.

I'm too old for this, she thought, as the room dropped her to one knee. Too old to be alive. Too old to be traipsing around with soil in the treads of my boots. Too old to be chasing a younger sister who's frozen in time while I'm embalmed as the old crone I really am. I've done my duty. I've earned my retirement.

You've earned nothing while your mad sister gallivants around the place, Oma Jankie's voice said. *She's your responsibility. If you fail to stop her, who knows what damage she'll wreak? Or how many innocent people will die?*

'I'm here, aren't I?' the Duchess replied.

Then get on with it, little Rachel, said Oma Jankie. *Get on with it, and get up.*

The Duchess struggled to her feet, gritted her teeth, and cursed the truth of her long-dead grandmother's words.

Hatoyama tugged at a tie he wished were cleaner and strolled through the bank's main entrance, swinging the yellow gun case like it held his lunch.

He stopped, taking in the surroundings, grimacing at what they portrayed. Queues ten people deep trailed back from the various teller windows, and there was a bustle and buzz he could have done without.

Get a grip, he told himself. You're a detective with every right in the world to be here. You just need to tell your face that.

He glanced around for someone in authority, picking out a bored-looking security guard loitering by a long wooden bench. Removing his badge from his back pocket, Hatoyama marched towards him.

As she staggered through the wall, leaving the room of poison gas behind her, her skin steaming and smoking, the Duchess was grateful for the pain. Without it heightening her senses, she might not have heard the air being sliced in two.

She did, though, jerking away just as a sword blade flashed past her skull, tungsten light tickling its razor edge. She dropped to the floor, the sword missing her by inches, the poison from the previous room obliviously eating through her clothes and flaying her skin. Blinking out the pain, she focused on her attacker.

A stubby, laced-with-power samurai stood there, sword raised now above his head, his brown eyes burning in the slits of his mask. The room she was in was if anything even sparser than the one she'd just left; a metal spike stood isolated, a tether hanging from it limply.

A single safe sat in the room's dimly lit centre.

The samurai swung his blade at her once again, but this time the Duchess was ready, rolling to the right, the blade spitting sparks onto the cold floor.

'She said you'd come,' said the samurai, crouching in an attack position.

'*She*, I'm guessing, is a young woman called Hanna.'

'The girl's name matters little,' he said. 'All that matters is her mission.'

'It *was* Hanna, then. She has a way of getting others to fight her battles for her.'

The samurai swung again, the Duchess rolling, the blade singing the air where she'd just been.

They crouched, both of them ready, a few feet away from each other, the samurai looking for an opening, the Duchess looking to close it down.

'It is an honour to serve,' said the samurai.

'Except you don't have to serve at all,' said the Duchess. 'She's tricked you. It's a devil's trick, one she learned from a monster. She's left behind a legion of bodies that testify to that.'

'She said *you'd* try to trick me,' said the samurai. 'She said not to listen to you.'

He lunged forward, eschewing grace for brute force. The bluntness of the attack took the Duchess by surprise; she stumbled backwards, slamming against the vault's steel wall.

He's got me.

'I'm not trying to trick you,' she said. 'I have no quarrel with you. All I want is my sister.'

The samurai tensed.

The Duchess sighed.

I may have some power left. This may not be over yet.

'Fine then,' she said, raising her hand. 'We'll do this the hard way.'

'This is most irregular.'

'Yes,' said Hatoyama. 'Crime tends to be.'

'You want to see inside the vault,' said the portly bank manager, the security guard looking from Hatoyama to his employer like he was watching a tennis match, 'because you've had reports of a crime you can't disclose the details of.'

'That's about the size of it,' said Hatoyama, aware of the sweat clustering at the top of his brow. 'Do you want me to show you my badge again?'

'That won't be necessary,' said the bank manager. 'I've seen it three times already.'

'Strange that we're talking and not walking, then,' said Hatoyama, trying to dredge up authority he didn't feel. 'Time is of the essence in these sorts of cases.'

'What sorts of cases exactly?' said the bank manager, fiddling with his monogrammed cufflinks. 'I hardly think my clients would be pleased if I exposed their riches to every badly dressed detective who wandered in off the street.'

Hatoyama looked down at his watch, saw that it was thirty minutes since the Duchess had left him, and tried to remember what courage was. 'Funny you should mention your clients. They've long been of interest to my department.'

The bank manager flinched. It was only for a second, but that was all flinches ever were. 'My clients—' he began.

'Your clients have links to some of the biggest crime families in the country,' interrupted Hatoyama.

Or so the rumours go.

'Outrageous,' said the bank manager, confirming them. 'A slur.'

'I don't want to tell you how to do your job,' Hatoyama continued, 'but I can't imagine such men would be happy if they learned their money had been stolen.'

The bank manager swallowed. 'The vault is impenetrable. There's not a man or woman alive who could get into it without us knowing. Without *me* knowing.'

'Crime isn't what it was,' said Hatoyama, 'and you don't need to be flesh and blood to commit it any more.'

'A cyber attack?' asked the security guard, remembering that he was alive, and that that state of being meant he was supposed to be earning a wage too.

'Worse,' said Hatoyama, as if the gravity of the situation was almost too much to mention. 'At least, worse for you, because you'll have lost your clients' money.'

The bank manager shifted on his feet, then nodded to the security guard.

'Open it.'

Something was wrong, the Duchess knew, and it wasn't just the crazed samurai who was charging towards her.

She'd lost her power.

She had her hand outstretched and her mind stretched further than that, visualising plucking the warrior from the ground then crashing him into the walls of the vault. It would have been the simplest thing in the world to do if she were still Warden of the Pen.

You're not, though, are you, little Rachel? cawed Oma Jankie. *You gave your title away, then you thought you'd do some sightseeing on the soil. You've been running on the fumes of your former power for a very long time, and that little acid shower took the last dregs. What can a broken-down old woman do against an ancient warrior trained to kill?*

It's over.

When the first vault door swung open, the relief the bank manager felt at the seemingly untouched room contrasted sharply with the panic felt by Hatoyama. His second sight showed a very different scene: whereas the bank's employees saw rows of safety deposit boxes safely locked up tight, the detective saw the smoking corpses of Hanna's followers, and heard the Duchess's screams coming from a room he hadn't yet entered.

He pointed at the steel door at the back of the room. 'Open that, please.'

The bank manager frowned. 'That's really more of a storage area. The real wealth's in here, and as you can see, it's quite safe.'

The Duchess screamed again, unheard by the bank manager and his faithful security guard, but all too heard by Hatoyama.

'Please don't take me for a fool,' he said, swallowing hard. 'There has to be three feet of reinforced steel standing between us and that storage area. I need it open now, or by God, your Yakuza benefactors will be the least of your concerns.'

On the third sword swing, logic took over. It dictated that the Duchess was a centuries-old woman shorn of power, rather than an all-powerful demi-deity. The samurai's blade sliced through her left shoulder, ripping an anguished scream from her and dropping her to one knee.

He loomed over her, pushing the blade in deeper.

She screamed anew.

'The blade is treated with soil nitrate,' he said, his voice muffled by his faceplate. 'I believe you use something similar in your own weapons.'

The Duchess gasped. 'I believe . . . we do.'

She raised her head, trying to control the pain, remembering that real pain couldn't be controlled or cajoled. 'You don't have to do this. This is what Hanna wants.'

'It is what *I* want,' said the samurai, withdrawing the blade with one swift movement and allowing her to topple over onto the floor. 'It is my mission to protect the riches of this place.'

'Did you protect them from the girl?' she asked. 'From Hanna?'

'I need not protect them from Mistress Hanna. She knows all. She sees all. When I have struck you down, I will finally be free. It is her command.'

'You're already free,' said the Duchess. 'My sister has convinced you otherwise, through the language of the dead, but there's nothing in this world or the next to stop you walking out right now. And there's no one better placed than me to show you where to go.'

The samurai raised the sword above his head, light glinting off its serrated blade. 'Quiet now,' he said. 'Quiet, and I'll make it quick.'

Hatoyama was grateful, when he thought about it later, that he'd already begun loosening the clasps on the bright yellow gun case. If he hadn't, he would never got the gun out in time.

When the steel door had swung wide to reveal a sword-wielding samurai and the felled form of the Duchess, training he didn't remember submitting to kicked in. He flipped the case open, tugged out the grey slub of plastic shaped like a gun and pointed it at the samurai.

The security guard and the bank manager, who saw nothing but an empty room, looked on nonplussed as the strange man who claimed to be a detective aimed what appeared to be a toy gun at thin air.

The Duchess had thought it unlikely that she'd ever look upon Hatoyama with anything but withering scorn, but she was delighted to be proved wrong. He'd got there with seconds to spare and had even had the presence of mind to bring the bolt-cutter with him. It was almost enough to take her mind off the searing pain in her shoulder.

The samurai whirled around, glaring at the unwanted interruption. 'Are you alive,' he asked Hatoyama, 'or dead?'

'That's a question I've asked myself many times over the years,' said the detective. 'Today, I believe I feel alive.'

He fired.

The Duchess heard – and smelled – the blast before she saw it or the samurai felt it.

There was a shift in the atmosphere, a crackle and a fizz and a thrum she recalled when she'd been alive on the soil, one that signified the imminent arrival of a storm. The weapon in Hatoyama's hand had begun to vibrate, the two gawking bank employees feeling something without realising they were feeling something, the smell of molten sulphur pungent in the air.

Then there was a crack, like lightning wielding a bullwhip, and the samurai spasmed violently, landing heavily, his sword tumbling to the floor. The shot, the Duchess saw, had passed through his right shoulder, and this wasn't a wound of green vines and crumbling essence like you'd find in the Pen; this was as if God himself had plunged a hand in there.

Hatoyama fired again, but the shot was wild, clearing the samurai's head by a good foot.

The detective cursed, steadying himself and bringing the gun level with the warrior's face.

He pulled the trigger.

The gun coughed apologetically.

He frowned at it as the samurai hauled himself to his feet.

Hatoyama fired again.

The gun whined, then juddered slightly, like a misfiring stolen car.

Hatoyama struck it, cursing, trying to beat it back into life.

The Duchess raised a useless, feeble hand in the direction of the samurai. The warrior gave her – and the spike in the ground – a final look, then passed through the back wall.

Hatoyama went to follow.

'Leave him,' said the Duchess, shaking her head wearily. 'It's Hanna we want, not her followers.'

Hatoyama turned to the bank manager and his security guard. Both of them were staring at him open-mouthed. He couldn't really blame them.

'What's that?' he said, nodding at the wallet-sized Peli case in the bank manager's hand. Noting too the open safe.

'This is the only thing that's been touched,' said the bank manager. 'It was removed from the safe.'

He undid the clasp, then opened up the case.

It was empty.

'She got the chip,' said Hatoyama. 'What does that mean?'

The bank manager looked at him, bemused.

'It means we have a big problem,' said the Duchess.

Chapter Fourteen

Daisy-May had never been on a boat before. If the last half-hour was anything to go by, she didn't feel like she'd missed out.

Her stomach churned as the vessel hovered inches above the famished desert floor, powering forward at a rate she found difficult to judge, feeling as it did both fast and slow. She leaned over the side, dry-heaving up what felt like her stomach lining.

The toll man chuckled. 'Proper landlubber, you.'

Daisy-May wiped her mouth with the back of her hand. 'I grew up on a Nottingham council estate, mate. We didn't have running water Monday to Wednesday, let alone a boating lake.'

She reached into her pocket, withdrawing the medication Mabel had given her, then tossed it over the side when she saw that it was empty.

'Don't like your colour, girl,' said the toll man.

'Don't like it much myself,' said Daisy-May. 'Like the chundering even less.'

'Not the boat causing it, then?'

She shook her head. 'Not the boat.'

The stomach cramps had started twenty minutes ago, far worse than before she'd started taking Mabel's remedy. It felt like each one of her cells had been buffed with poison, her vision doubling, then tripling at random moments. She squeezed her fists together, trying to flex some circulation into them. She didn't have time to be ill. There was too much at stake.

She turned to the toll man, who was frowning fiercely at the landscape. 'How much longer till we catch up to Chestnut and the woman she was with?'

'They ain't my worry,' said the toll man.

'What is?'

'Them.'

Daisy-May followed his finger and saw a small dust cloud on the horizon, similar to the one she'd seen from the pier.

'Under your seat's a harpoon gun,' said the toll man. 'Get it.'

She squinted at the dust cloud. It was getting larger by the second.

'Today, girl.'

She bit her lip and did as she was told, her hand finding the weapon's smooth wooden skin. She brought it into the light. 'You expecting whales?'

'Whales are gentlemen,' said the toll man. 'What's tracking us ain't.'

Daisy-May lifted the harpoon gun, staring down the sights at the incoming dust cloud. 'What *is* tracking us?'

'Something hungry,' said the toll man. 'Something fast. Something you can't sweet-talk. Something that doesn't care about wardens or toll men or heaven and hell.'

'Hate a straight answer, people in the Pen,' muttered Daisy-May.

'I judge six, maybe seven,' said the toll man, standing now, his hand still on the tiller.

'Six or seven *what*?'

'Maxillas. Can't give a better description than your eyes, and they'll be talking to you soon enough. Pack creatures, vicious, desperate ones at that. They'll be on us in minutes.'

'So what do we do?' said Daisy-May. 'Shoot 'em?'

'Never get all of them,' said the toll man. 'Need to take out the pack leader. You'll know him, 'cos he'll be bigger than the others. You hook the alpha, tie the harpoon off on the boat, drag the corpse along with you, it'll discourage the rest.'

Her finger found the trigger. 'Doesn't sound so hard.'

The toll man laughed, a sound starved of mirth. 'You find it easy, means you've done it wrong and we're both dead.'

'Thought we were already.'

'No you didn't.'

Daisy-May took a breath. The dust cloud blotted out the horizon now, the odd furry limb just about visible.

'Any tips on how to fire this thing?' she said.

'Aim it at the biggest monster and pull the trigger,' said the toll man, his West Country vowels singing, his face painted with gallows humour.

'You remind me of Mabel,' said Daisy-May.

He smiled. 'Tell her I'm sorry. That's the favour I want from you. Tell her I'm sorry.'

Just as Daisy-May went to reply, a parched scream filled the air and the creatures responsible for it finally became visible.

The maxillas were a surrealist homage to a bad dream. Their bodies were like that of a wolf, four powerful legs propelling them towards the boat, but their heads looked like someone had stripped the skin from a dolphin then bathed it in acid. Their jaws were elongated, shaped almost like a beak, with dozens of razor-sharp teeth laced down both sides, snapping at thin air. They didn't appear to have eyes; instead, a crown of bone sat there, gleaming and compact.

'Fucking hell,' said Daisy-May.

''Bout sums them up,' said the toll man.

'Why they called maxillas?'

'Why you called Daisy-May?'

The pack was just a few short feet away from the boat now, snapping and worrying at the whirling oars whenever it started to pitch towards them. Daisy-May raised the harpoon gun, trying to pick out the largest of the creatures.

The toll man growled, stretching out an arm and pushing the weapon down. 'Normally be trying to swarm the boat by now. Something's wrong.'

'This hardly feels right, to be fair,' she said, daring to look away from the pack for a moment, to the opposite side of the horizon. 'Bloody hell.'

The toll man followed her gaze. A pack of fifteen maxillas, at least double the number of the first group, was surging towards them.

'Wily bitches,' he said. 'It's a bloody ambush.'

'Going to need more than harpoons, mate. I count twenty, and that's with my dodgy maths.'

'There.' The toll man pointed towards the new pack, and the mighty snapping beast at its centre. 'That's the alpha.'

Daisy-May lifted the harpoon gun again, trying to get the creature's torso in her sights. 'Difficult shot. Have to try and go through three others to get it.'

She heard that same parched scream again, along with the sound of grinding teeth.

'Best get shooting then,' said the toll man. 'I'll hold them off as long as I can.'

'I hate guns,' said Daisy-May, her finger nevertheless on the trigger, flexing over it.

'You'll hate those teeth on your spine more.'

She didn't disagree. The alpha loomed large in her sights. She pulled the trigger, the gun kicking against the crook of her shoulder. A bright orange rope tore from the barrel, a silver tip gleaming from it. One of the maxillas roared in pain as it punctured its skin, unspooling under its thick fur, digging itself in.

'Jam the gun into the side,' yelled the toll man, who was attempting to steer the boat with one hand and lash out at the baying pack with a sharpened cleaver in the other.

Daisy-May was dragged forward, almost dropping the harpoon gun due to the dead weight it was now attached to. Like catching fish, she thought as she spied a solid silver hoop in front of her. Except the fish are all wolves with the heads of sharks, and they want to eat me.

She wrestled the gun down towards the hoop, shooting a look at the pack. One of the creatures was dead and being dragged along by the boat, the gun it was attached to fighting Daisy-May every step of the way.

'Did I get it?'

The toll man grimaced. 'Hard to say,' he replied as he slid the hoop open.

She jammed the gun into it and the toll man flicked it closed, a reassuring clunk sounding in response. The boat listed to the right slightly as the slain creature was dragged alongside it.

The pack on either side didn't pay it the slightest heed.

'Bollocks,' said the toll man. 'That weren't him.'

'What do we do now?' said Daisy-May. 'What other weapons do you have?'

The toll man never got the chance to reply.

He screamed as teeth gripped his flesh, one set, two sets, a sea of biting and rending and ripping jaws. He was pulled backwards off the boat, Daisy-May looking on in horror as he disappeared under a hairy mountain of monsters.

The tiller was unmanned.

She lurched towards it at the precise moment that the boat rolled to the left, slamming into the maxillas that hadn't stopped to pick the toll man's bones clean. It turned over, and all Daisy-May could hear was the sound of broken bones and primal screams. Her trapped leg saved her, pinning her to the boat as it flipped endlessly, rampaging through the monsters and finally coming to a stop, right side up, roughly two hundred feet from where it had first capsized.

She allowed herself several seconds of staring up at the sky, then got shakily to her feet. She'd been lucky, no question about that, not only to emerge virtually unscathed, but also because the boat seemed to have taken out all the pursuing monsters; a dozen or so maxillas lay twitching on the floor. One of the oars had speared two of the creatures, pinning them to the cracked ground as if they were a ceremonial offering.

Luck's changing, she thought, as she blinked out dust.

A gurgling growl came from behind her.

Maybe not.

She turned slowly to see one of the maxillas watching her, or at least she assumed it was, shorn as it was of eyeballs. Its body was tensed, its skeletal jaw open, an ominous snarl coming from whatever passed for its soul.

The alpha. Of course, that would *be the one that survives.*

Her eyes flicked away from it for just a second, hunting for a weapon. Her backpack had been thrown free in the crash. It lay thirty feet away.

I'll never make it, she thought, and there's nothing in there that could pass for a weapon even if I could.

The creature growled again, then took a step forward.

Actually, that's not right, she realised. There's the flare gun Mabel gave me. If I get close enough, that thing should do plenty of damage, and plenty might just be enough.

It was still thirty feet away, though. The alpha would only need ten to be at her throat.

Except she was supposed to be able to move things with her mind. She should be able to ping that bag into her hand just by visualising it.

'How about we call it quits, little doggie?' she said. 'I killed your mates and you killed my toll man. Sounds about even.'

The alpha growled again.

'All right then. We'll agree to disagree.'

The creature started to bound towards her, and Daisy-May continued to stand her ground as she thrust her hand at the dropped backpack.

Come on, she thought. Come on.

The creature kept coming, gobbling up the distance.

Don't have time to get angry to make this thing work, she thought. Wonder if shit-scared will do?

Dust kicked up from the alpha maxilla's paws as it surged forward, and although every last instinct in her dead body told her to run, Daisy-May held her nerve as well as her ground.

'Come on, you fucker,' she said, her sickness forgotten in the face of her surging adrenaline, a statement to herself as much as the creature and the makeshift weapon she was trying to spirit into her hand. '*Come on.*'

The maxilla leapt at precisely the same second as the bag, the backpack dragging itself out of the dirt and snagging itself on her hand. As the creature's teeth gnashed and tore, she used the canvas bag as a shield, the only thing separating her from the maxilla's judgement.

Got some judgement of my own to give it, she thought grimly.

As the maxilla continued to chomp and bite at the bag, Daisy-May freed a clasp on it, and the top fell open.

Going to get one shot at this, she thought. Let's hope it's a lucky one.

There was a pause when she could have believed the eyeless creature looked right at her, then she plunged her hand into the bag, finding the stocky handle of the flare gun just as she felt the creature's jaws clamp round the canvas. She squeezed down on the trigger as the maxilla began to tighten its grip.

There was a fraction of a second of a whine, and then the creature was propelled high into the air, its legs pawing at nothing. At two hundred feet, the bottle rocket the maxilla's jaws were clamped around exploded, ripping the beast in two. Daisy-May looked up in wonder as hundreds of scarab beetles poured from the rocket's casing, their wings beating out a bright red hue as chunks of the maxilla fell to the ground below.

There's something you don't see every day, she thought. Trouble is, that little light show told Mabel where I am, but there's a good chance the woman who snatched Chestnut saw it too. Better than good.

Plus, I'm down a boat and haven't got the first idea where I'm going.

Although that wasn't true, because the toll man had simply been following the tracks left by the woman in her boat; there was nothing to stop her doing the same on foot.

An inspection of what was left of the boat showed that there wasn't much to be salvaged, except a splintered oar. It would do as a makeshift weapon, she supposed, if she ran into any more maxillas. Though if she ran into any more maxillas, she knew it wouldn't really do at all.

Two hours into her trek, the tracks getting fainter by the footstep, Daisy-May saw it.

It began as a black smudge on the horizon, but one large enough to be visible in the flat, barren landscape. The Pen wall could be seen behind it, and two thin trickles of smoke rose from the squat monolith, the whole thing looking like a discarded Lowry sketch.

Shouldn't be any type of civilisation this far out, thought Daisy-May. The Dispossessed, maybe? She hadn't seen any Dispossessed for hours, though – since leaving the docks, in fact – and it seemed unlikely that they'd build anything this far out from the Dispossessed settlements and the Dying Squad compound.

Only reason anyone would, she thought, is because they'd want to keep it a secret from people like me. And judging by the tracks of the boat that had come before her, whoever had been sailing it had headed straight towards that secret.

A wave of nausea crashed over her, the force of it buckling her to her knees, which hit the cracked desert floor. The attacks were getting more pronounced. More regular, too.

She took a breath, then looked at the black building on the horizon. It was a two-hour walk at least. There was no shame in waiting here for Mabel. She'd be in some crazy mash-up vehicle, no doubt, and backup was never a bad thing to have when approaching a bad-vibe building that had no right to be there.

Except Eric doesn't have any backup. Chestnut neither. I was her backup, though I was more of her fuck-up, because I let her get snatched. And if I wallow here kicking my heels, I won't even be that. I don't know why that woman's taken her, but that building doesn't celebrate her good intentions.

The stomach spasm passed and Daisy-May levered herself up with her oar spear.

There was nothing else for it.

She started walking.

Chapter Fifteen

'Salford, man. I don't care how much glass and steel they throw up. Place is still full of cunts.'

'You should work for the tourist board,' said Joe. 'Not one for change, are you?'

'Not when it involves this dump.' Bits shook his head as they made their way along the Quays, Media City's twinkling edifice behind them, the Lowry squatting on the dock opposite. 'Think we're wasting our time here?'

'You tell me,' said Joe. 'It's your city.'

'Salford's never been my city, pal. I'm from *Manchester*.'

'What's the difference?'

'Geography.'

Bits gestured at the glut of new buildings around them. 'All of this is new. In my day, only reason you'd come to Salford would be to watch United, score pills or go to my grandad's.'

'How's the Lads Club fit into this brave new world?' said Joe.

'Badly, I reckon,' said Bits. 'If it's how I left it, though, it's an oasis of decency in a town fuckin' parched of it.'

Even in a city peppered with musically iconic locales, the Salford Lads Club took some beating.

Situated in the Ordsall area of the city, the club had been

keeping boys – and later girls – on the straight and narrow since 1903. The Hollies had practised there, and the Smiths famously posed outside its hallowed entrance, forever immortalising the club and ensuring it remained a permanent fixture on the city's heritage music crawls. It was easy to believe that when new Salford eventually crumbled into dust, the Lads Club would stand firm and resolute amongst its rubble.

'Place hasn't changed a bit, man,' said Bits, eyes shining as he took in the red-brick building, its mighty green doors locked tight for the night. 'Probably got the same people running it an' all. Priceless, these places, for keeping kids on the straight and narrow.'

'Didn't seem to do much good in your case,' said Joe, deliberately not noticing Bits wipe at his eyes.

'They're decent people, not miracle workers,' his partner replied. 'Your childhood could have used a bit of the old straight and narrow, by the sounds of it.'

'I'm not judging,' said Joe. 'My dad was a vicar, and I still came off on the first bend.'

'Probably time we had another hit of the bad stuff,' said Bits, nodding at Joe's bag. 'That type of memory won't hang around for long if you don't.'

Joe nodded. 'Shows how great this shit is. Before, with the gum? You'd be able to get maybe thirty minutes before your memory started fading. This keeps you frosty for hours.'

He rooted around in the bag, handing Bits a syringe. 'Three left. Six hours' worth, if we're lucky.'

'Let's hope we don't have to use them all,' said Bits. ''Cos that missing girl's fucked if we do.'

As they passed through the green iron doors, it felt like the room held its breath.

Joe couldn't blame it.

It was as if the city's whole history — its hopes, schemes and broken dreams — was captured in the club's four walls. Visually, with the photo-tapestry celebrating the music pilgrims who'd visited the club, but also in the bricks and mortar, the sweat and tears that had been expelled over the years then soaked into its foundations.

Bits crouched down, breathing deeply.

'You OK?' said Joe.

'There's nostalgia, then there's this,' said Bits. 'It's a head-fuck, pal. Haven't thought of this place for thirty years, yet here I am back here. Need a minute.'

Joe patted him on the back. 'Take five. Know what it was like from when I did my own trip down memory lane. It's brutal but necessary.'

'Necessary things always seem to be brutal,' said Bits. 'Why aren't they ever just nice?'

'Because that's not the way it works,' said Joe. 'If it did, we'd be kicking it in heaven rather than trying our level best to stay out of hell.'

Leaving his partner to his panic attack, he walked into the club's main sports hall. It was cloaked in darkness, the fire exit signs giving off just enough light to show the balcony encircling the space. Pale green paint clung to the walls, two black basketball hoops facing each other.

Joe stood in the centre of the room, waiting and listening for he didn't know what, because sometimes — a lot of times — that was what police work entailed. You watched, and you waited, and you listened, because if you did, people spilled secrets they couldn't keep, and clues dusted themselves down and put on a show for you. Clues, in his experience, always wanted to be discovered; the question was how much you wanted to discover *them*.

As his eyes adjusted to the dark, he looked up to the balcony.

He could just make out the outline of a figure hidden in the gloom.

'Hello?' he said. 'Is there anyone there?'

'Question for the ages, that,' said a voice from above, its letters buffed softly with Mancunian shammy. 'Feels like there isn't sometimes.'

Joe took a step back. He hadn't actually expected an answer to his question.

He held his hands up in the universal language of surrender. 'If you can hear me, I'm guessing you're not of this world any more.'

'Been stuck in this place for forty years,' said the man, staying in the shadows. 'Sounds pretty *of this world* to me.' His words were soft, like they were scared of each other.

Something's wrong here, thought Joe. If he's been here for forty years, he should be riddled with amnesia, a walking, squawking zombie.

'I'm looking for a boy,' he said.

The man chuckled, the sound a thing of nicotine and cancer. 'Aren't we all.'

Joe took a step forward, trying to hook a better look.

'Stay where you are,' said the man. 'I like you right there.'

I don't want to like anything this bloke likes, thought Joe. I don't know him, I don't know anything about him, but I do know that.

'I'm with the Dying Squad. I'd hold up a badge if I had one.'

'Heard of them,' said the man. 'Do-gooders. Couple have come across my path. Don't last long.'

The tip of a cigarette flared into life. Joe squinted to try and see the man behind it.

'That down to you?'

The man laughed again. 'I never take credit that isn't due. Think they breathed something that didn't agree with them.'

There was something about the words that made Joe's dead skin crawl. It was like he'd dipped each vowel in sour milk.

'Come up if you like,' said the man. 'Probably best you know, though, that I never give anything away for free.'

Joe looked for Bits, but his partner was nowhere to be seen.

'Alone,' said the man. 'Crowds make me jumpy.'

Joe walked towards the doorway, the man's words sticking to him. He knew he shouldn't do this – knew there was nothing right about the man upstairs – but he also knew his partner had street smarts and was in the next room. If things went wrong, he had to believe Bits would have his back.

As he walked up the darkened steps, he slipped the gun from his belt, then lowered his sleeve over it. If this man had truly been here for forty years, he was something Joe hadn't encountered before, or hadn't been told about. Either possibility made him nervous.

He reached the top of the stairs and found himself in a boxing gym, lit only by a single exit sign. Punchbags hung from the ceiling, each one creaking with an almost apologetic whisper. Hundreds of photographs decorated the walls, boys and girls down the decades embalmed onto the plaster.

'Over here,' said the man's voice.

Joe turned and flinched. The man was still shrouded in shadows, but his form was more easily recognisable. Up here, he seemed to be twice the size, with a linebacker's frame and an air of barely suppressed menace. Green cigarette smoke trailed from his silhouetted shape. It was like his lungs had poisoned the smoke that passed through them.

Joe took a step towards him.

'That's far enough,' said the man. 'Words walk by themselves. No need for you to carry them.'

'All right,' said Joe. 'I'm looking for a boy. He was here

246

before, with a woman. A flesh-and-blooder. She was taking photographs of him.'

'I remember,' said the man. 'Don't get to see many new things at my age, but that was new to me. Living soul able to see the likes of us. Had mediums here that couldn't see as much as a hair on my head. That lass could see it all.'

'You talked to her?'

'Wasn't much of a conversation. Never is when people get to know me. Remember the boy, though. Pretty little thing.' He chuckled and it sounded like rotting meat. 'I know all the pretty dead boys around here.'

Something tightened in Joe's gut. 'Is that right?'

'It is, for my sins. Red crew cut. Green blazer. Grey tank top and shorts. Old school uniform. That the lad?'

'It is,' said Joe.

The man's shape nodded. 'He's been in. Scared. Jumpy, like he'd seen something he shouldn't. Something with the fangs to bite him and the will to do it.'

'What did he tell you?'

'Only where he was hiding out. Me telling you where that is? That's where the favour comes in.'

The shadow man threw his cigarette to the floor. Joe heard a crunch, then saw the outline of the man putting something in his mouth.

He began to chew. 'I help you, you help me. Fair barter.'

'I'm not really in the bartering game,' said Joe.

'Everyone's in the bartering game when they want something badly enough.'

Joe half sighed, grinding his teeth with frustration. 'All right then. What do you want?'

The man stepped out of the shadows, and as Joe took in the sight, his hand instinctively tightened around his concealed gun.

He'd been wrong when he thought he'd been talking to a man. He'd actually been talking to a monster.

Green vines covered every square inch of the man's skin, binding and turning back on themselves. It was the worst case of soil infection Joe had ever seen; a consequence of the dead being exposed to the living world's air.

He really has been here for decades.

The man monster laughed. 'Oh, I know I'm pretty. You take it all in.' He snapped off one of the vines protruding from his arm and threw it into his mouth.

Joe's stomach lurched.

'Bad habit, I know,' said the man. 'One of many.'

'I bet.'

'Want to know what turned me like this? Other than the soil air?'

'Not really,' said Joe. 'Doubt it's a PG friendly tale.'

'You've got that right,' said the man, smiling through his pinched lips, 'though it does involve kids.'

Joe felt a presence behind him.

'Jesus,' said Bits, as he took in the blizzard of vines and dead flesh.

'I'm a long way from that, son,' said the man. 'You a Manc like me?'

Bits nodded. 'Wythenshawe, when I was breathing.'

'I was Burnage.'

'Must have stood out there with looks like yours,' said Bits. 'Extreme even for that shithole.'

'This gentleman can help us find the boy,' said Joe, interrupting, 'but he wants something in return.'

'Course he does.'

'It's nothing fancy,' said the man of vines, absent-mindedly knocking off some of the branches on his hand. 'Not for men of your calibre.'

'What does *nothing fancy* look like, then?' said Joe.

'It looks like you taking out that gun, pointing it at me and shooting,' said the man. 'It looks like you killing me.'

During his time on the soil, Joe had played a greatest hits set of criminal acts. When reflecting on this, he always felt grateful he'd never got his deadly sins number one; murder was the big league, and the fact that he'd never committed it was the main reason he'd been dumped in the Pen rather than the Pit.

Murder was what was being asked of him now, though, and the fact that the man who'd done the asking wasn't actually alive wouldn't make that murder any less cold-blooded or calculated.

'Why do you want us to kill you?' he said.

'Take a good look and answer your own question,' said the man, breaking off another clump of vines from his arm and tossing them into his mouth. 'Think this is a life?'

'How come you've got your wits?' said Bits. 'Forty years here, you should be tapped in the head.'

'Because hell isn't a pit carved into the earth's bowels,' said the man, 'not for people like me. It's places like this, where I can't forget.'

'Why did you end up here?' said Joe. 'What were you being punished for?'

'What's it matter?' said the man. 'I tell you where the boy is, then you end my existence. Everything else is noise.'

'It matters because I'm not in the habit of carrying out executions,' said Joe. 'It's a quick trip back to the Pit if I start now.'

The man smiled, revealing, just, the traces of a mouth. 'Then I'll tell you why I'm here, and when I do, you'll be begging to fucking shoot me.'

'I doubt that.'

'Doubt it all you like. You haven't heard it yet.'

It's like he wraps his words in velvet, thought Joe. Then crushes them under his boot.

'When I was breathing, I worked here, in the Lads Club,' said the man. 'Jobs never stuck to me, but this one did. I gave boxing lessons. Always loved boxing, me, always wanted to be around it, but blokes never took me serious. Had a lot to give the sport, but the sport weren't interested. Something about me just seemed to put people off.'

'Can't think what,' mumbled Bits.

'Then I came here,' the man of vines continued. 'Told a couple of white lies about my experience, and there weren't no CRB checks in those days. Truthfully, they were short-staffed, and I said I'd work for pennies. How could they say no?'

I know where this is going, thought Joe, and it's nowhere I want to go.

'I told myself I was going to be good, to give the boys no bother. Got in trouble a couple of times before for that sort of thing, but I thought it'd be different, 'cos I liked the boxing a lot more than I liked the boys. I was sure it'd go OK.

'I was wrong. First couple of boys it happened with, there was no drama. They were poor as fuck and came from bro-ken-back homes.'

Joe felt his hand tightening around the handle of his pistol.

'But that Bobby with the pretty eyes, he was the ruin of me. He told his grandad what I'd done. Like it was something I had a say in, like it was something I wanted to do, like the voice in my head gave me any sort of choice. Tried to make the grandad understand, but he wouldn't. Said he was going to the police. Didn't leave me much choice. Had to top myself. That fucking Bobby left me no choice, did he?'

'Are you honestly asking me that question?' said Joe.

Bits squinted at the man, trying to see the human face be-hind the tangle of vines. 'I know you. I *know* you, man.'

'You don't know me.'

'Yeah,' said Bits, 'yeah, I do. Heard of you, at least, 'cos of my mate Jamie. He came to the club. Said there was a nonce there that topped himself. You never touched Jamie – least that's what he said – but he knew the boy you *did* touch, the one with the grandad. Malkey. Your name's Paedo Malkey.'

'Not much of Malkey left,' said the man. 'Rest's true enough. You'll see why I don't deserve to live. Be doing the universe a favour killing me.'

Be doing you a favour too, thought Joe, and I can't help thinking that's a bad thing for us. No one comes out clean in a deal with a scumbag like you.

'So why arc you here?' he asked. 'Crimes like yours should have been a free pass to hell, yet you're here, compos mentis, wandering around unpunished.'

The thing that used to be called Malkey laughed. 'Think I look unharmed? Think I wouldn't give anything to forget the things I did, the things I'd still do, given the chance? Think this isn't hell, being trapped in a place teeming with fucking kids, ones I can't touch, a place I'm never allowed to leave?'

'It sounds like you're being punished for your crimes, and we can't interfere with that,' said Joe. 'It's not for me to release you from your sentence.'

'I could do it,' Bits interjected. 'One quick shot to the nonce's head, it'll all be over.'

'No doubting you could.' Joe didn't like the look in his partner's eyes. 'I'm just saying that you shouldn't.'

'Only way you're going to find out where that lad is,' said the man.

'Was it the Xylophone Man that put you here?' Joe replied.

'If that's the bloke with the elephant skull for a head, then yeah. You know him?'

'We go way back,' said Joe. 'Got no love for him.'

He looked away, his body language suggesting he was weighing up the dilemma.

Having apparently solved it, he raised his gun, pointing it directly at the man's head. 'If shooting you's going to fuck him off, then that's an idea that appeals. Tell me where the boy is, and I'll do it.'

'You swear it?' said the man. 'You give me your word?'

'I do,' said Joe. 'In our line of work, our word's all we've got.'

From the corner of his eye, he noticed Bits take a step forward, all the better to see the execution.

The man nodded, the vines encircling his neck sighing sickeningly. 'He's at the John Rylands library. Lots of kids go there. Something to do with its vibe. You know it?'

Bits nodded. 'Can't say I visited it much when I was breathing, mind.'

Joe's finger tensed on the trigger.

The man closed his eyes.

Bits kept his open.

Finally Joe lowered his gun, holstered it.

'What are you doing?' said the man.

'Following up your lead.'

He took a step forward. 'You gave me your word.'

'Yeah,' said Joe. 'I lied. Lot of that in the afterlife.'

'You're supposed to be Dying Squad,' said the man. 'Supposed to stand for truth and justice.'

'Truth is, I'd be doing the world an injustice by taking your life,' said Joe. 'You've been given your punishment: who am I to let you out on early release?'

'You gave me you word,' repeated the man softly.

'I'm a recovering bent copper who used kids to sell drugs,' said Joe. 'My word doesn't mean a fucking thing.'

'You piece of—'

Joe never got to find out what he was a piece of, because at that precise second, the man's head exploded. The top of it was blown clean off in a mush of vines and ghostly tissue, causing him to sink to his knees, then fall flat on what was left of his face.

Joe turned to see Bits with his arm outstretched, stubby gun enclosed in his right hand, smoke leaking from the barrel.

'What the fuck was that?' asked Joe.

'Justice,' said Bits.

When you were on the soil trying to crack a case that was the definition of time-sensitive, day and night lost some of their meaning. That didn't mean Joe didn't enjoy the precious snatches of daylight when he could get them; after months of the cauldron-and-soot Pen sky, a Manchester dawn suddenly became the most precious thing in the world. Rain, tropical or otherwise, was swerving the city again, the temperature swelling already.

The two Dying Squad members walked down Deansgate, Beetham Tower looming over them, a glass giant overseeing a street full of concrete midgets, fierce red sky bouncing off its windowed coat.

'Don't know what your problem is, man.'

'That's the problem.'

'That bloke was straight-up scum,' said Bits. 'Filthy paedo deserved putting down.'

'Wasn't your call to make,' said Joe.

'And it was yours?'

'On cases like this, with you green and untested? Yeah. We're not a hit squad, and that man had already received his punishment. Not for the likes of us to release him from it.'

'Fucker messed with my mates,' said Bits. 'Couldn't let that stand.'

'He was being punished,' said Joe, 'and in a more brutal way than the one you just handed out. It's not the way Daisy-May wants things run.'

'Think she'd give a shit? Probably stick a medal on me chest.'

'*Through* your chest maybe. She was made Warden because she's got a moral core you can only dream of.'

'I'm a fucking angel.'

'You're a fuck-up, Bits, just like me. We do this job to try and change that, to redeem ourselves, but beating up prisoners and shooting suspects isn't going to get you there.'

'Fucking pious, you.'

'If not wanting to shoot people in cold blood makes me pious, then yeah, I suppose I am,' said Joe. 'You have to be better. Daisy-May took a risk making you part of the squad. Plenty were against it.'

'And I'm supposed to be grateful for that?' said Bits, stopping dead, the sleepy commuters who traipsed the pavements alongside them oblivious. 'Making me a charity case is supposed to make me feel part of the team, is it?'

'I'm just saying you've been given an opportunity to better yourself, and you're not taking advantage of it.'

'How much of an advantage do you think this is?' said Bits. 'I was happy before, me. Didn't think there was much need to better myself. You whole-souls, you think everyone else wants your life. Then your Warden comes along like a fucking missionary, changing us, the way we think, the way we live.'

Joe looked down at his wrist. 'We're wasting time we don't have.'

'*Fuck* your time. You know the main reason I took this job? I thought if I understood whole-souls like you better, maybe that'd be a good thing, maybe it'd be better for everyone. I understand you now all right. Problem is, now that I do, I want nothing more to do with you.'

'We don't have time for this,' said Joe. 'We've got a job to do.'

'Get your mouth to tell your brain that,' said Bits, "cos you've done everything to stop me doing it.'

'I've been holding your hand from day one,' Joe spat back. 'The only time I didn't, you used it to beat a witness.'

'You're the past, man. Pretending to be something you're not, but I see you. You're just like me. A fucked-up soul faking that he's not.'

'I'm nothing like you,' said Joe. 'Thank Christ.'

Bits went to answer, then turned on his heel and stormed away.

The John Rylands library had been a gift Manchester hadn't asked for or expected, but one it appreciated nonetheless.

Founded by Enriqueta Rylands in 1900 as a neo-Gothic memorial to her late husband, even in modern-day Manchester there was an air of reverence about the place. Its pew-like seats and stained-glass windows reminded Joe of church and worship. As he passed through the gift shop's glass entrance, he offered up a prayer of his own. Time was running out, along with the kidnapped girl's chances of survival.

Megan, that's her name. Megan Veins. She needs a name – needs me to use it – otherwise she's nothing but a problem to solve. That's not good policing. You need to let that shit get under your fingernails so that it's not just another job. Problem is, that was never how I did it when I was breathing. I didn't care about catching the bad guy because I was the bad guy.

A murkily lit stone corridor faced him, its walls curving inwards and meeting in a thatch of stone at the top. From habit, Joe looked for Bits, then remembered. *I'm fucking this up. Daisy-May makes it look easy. She always knows what to say, or at least what I need to hear. Can't seem to find the words for Bits, and when I do, they're the wrong ones.*

If Daisy-May had been there – and he was grateful that she wasn't, so she could be spared witnessing his incompetence – she'd have told him to focus, to drown out the noise and the things he couldn't control and instead focus on what he could.

That began with finding the boy, because Joe was convinced the boy would lead to Megan.

Joe came out into what he assumed was the main trunk of the library. A huge stained-glass window shepherded in light so dim it identified as dark, and the ceiling looked like a ruptured wooden ribcage. Two marble statues of the Rylands sat at opposite ends of the room, judging what Manchester had become.

This place is like a church that's been built for anyone but God, thought Joe. Why can't these investigations ever take me to the Maldives? Why do they always involve eerie-as-fuck crypts, or abandoned farmhouses?

He removed the UV wand from his backpack and activated it with a flick of the wrist. It spilled blue light onto the stone floor, but little else; no footmarks, or signs of ghost children fleeing supernatural coppers.

Place this old has to be festooned with spirits. Crawling with them, yet I'm not picking up a single fingerprint.

He moved away from the main hall towards a flight of cold-looking stone steps, unholstering his gun because something had changed in the air, a ripple of unease that the UV wand wouldn't pick up. It was one that came from being a copper – sometimes a vaguely competent one – a gut instinct that whispered danger was close.

And that's fine, because on a case like this, the truth is often hiding behind danger. All you need to do is show it that you're not afraid, and it'll peek its head out.

256

As he made his way up the stairs, gun in hand and a chill down his back, he felt a sense of excitement that moments like this were still possible, a little reminder of what it was like to be alive, with something at stake.

Light dribbled from the room at the top of the stairs, the lanterns blinking in wind he couldn't feel. He heard a scraping noise, like a knife digging the last remnants of a meal from the floor, and swallowed as he inched closer towards the room. A faint whimpering was now audible. He stopped when he got to the door, looking around to see if there was another way in.

There wasn't.

Something's wrong here, he thought. Something that feels like death.

He hovered at the door. Going through it screamed *ambush then kill me*, but the only person who knew he was coming was a dead paedo who looked like a tree. There was a chance that he was actually ahead of the game here.

Taking a deep breath, he entered the room.

There was someone here, but Joe couldn't immediately see who. It was more a sensory skin prickle.

The room he'd walked into was vast, and more crypt-like than the one he'd just left. Tungsten tulips flowered from its stone walls, dappling the dozens of glass displays in harsh, jaundiced light. The atmosphere was different, too. It felt like it had spikes. He moved forward, imagining an unseen crosshair on his back, feeling like the room was watching him.

The whimpering got louder.

Rounding a particularly large bookcase, he saw what was making it.

A boy lay on the floor, his face drained of colour, like science and God had forgotten to ink him in. His right leg twitched, his mouth gasping for air, his hands against his stomach, like he was trying to stop his guts from spilling out. There were marks on his neck, just like the man in the tunnel.

Joe scanned the room, looking for the boy's attacker. If he was still here, he was hiding amongst the shadows.

Jamming his gun out in front of him, he moved forward. He crouched down next to the boy, his eyes doing laps of the room, almost pleading with it to strike.

Red hair. Green blazer. Grey tank top and shorts. It was the boy from Stanley's retina flashback all right, and the one who featured in the missing woman's photos. That nagging sense of familiarity was back too, needling and taunting him.

I know you, he thought. How?

Whoever he was, he was the only witness they had.

Which was the reason, Joe supposed, that he'd been attacked. The timing was significant, wasn't it? Their sole witness, eliminated just as the net was beginning to tighten. He'd half wondered whether the lad had set the booby-trap at Megan's flat himself. Maybe he had, but Joe was willing to bet it was on someone else's orders. And now that someone had taken care of the boy, removing him from the equation altogether.

It had to be the Generation Killer.

If nothing else, it meant they were getting closer to him.

Or her. Women are just as likely to kill you where you stand, Daisy-May's voice said in his head. *Just look at your wife.*

The victims the Generation Killer was choosing were puzzling too. The pattern of taking the youngest and the oldest would be easy to dismiss as mere madness. But if he could figure out the motivation behind it, he'd be closer to finding the killer.

He took the boy's hand with his left while his right pointed the gun out into the room, ready to fire. 'Who did this to you?'

The boy croaked an unintelligible reply.

Joe leaned in closer. 'A young woman called Megan Veins

was kidnapped,' he said. 'An old man too. I know you were there. Where's she being kept?'

'I'm sorry,' the boy croaked.

'That's OK,' said Joe. 'I need an address, lad.'

'The . . .'

'Yes?' said Joe, panic in his voice.

There was a final glimmer in the boy's eyes, then it was gone. He began to crumble and collapse into the stone floor, his frame no more solid than sand, his words no louder than gasps.

Within seconds, apart from the stain he left behind, it was like he'd never been there at all.

Part Two

When you embark on a journey of revenge,
dig two graves.

Confucius

I'd rather be dead than cool.

Kurt Cobain

Chapter Sixteen

We don't get the case files for this sort of shit. That was what Daisy-May had told Joe when she'd briefed him back in the Pen. *Going to be up to you and Bits to piece how it all fits together.*

Easy for her to say, a lot harder for him to actually do. Especially now that he was down not only a partner, but also a witness. Bits was stropping around the city, and the boy, who was his only lead, had been killed by persons (or wendigos) unknown. Joe had reached a dead end, but there was no time for him to retrace his steps. He needed to plough through, because dead ends weren't always dead ends. Sometimes they were sneaky bastards hiding where you needed to go.

It was that sense of hope (or punch-drunk desperation) that brought him to the city's largest police station. He stood considering it, dawn mewling all around him, Manchester unable to decide whether it was too late to go to bed or too early to get up.

He'd been to this station when he'd been a living, breathing copper. A drugs network that had spanned Nottingham, Manchester, Liverpool and London had been subject to a multi-jurisdictional investigation, and he had made sure that he ended up on that task force, which had meant effectively investigating himself.

Needless to say, he didn't get his man.

That was the past, though, when he'd been good at being bad. Now he was trying to do the right thing. Good was hard. Good made you work for it. Bad made it easy for you. Catching villains was a lot trickier than helping them. Or being them.

He walked towards the building's entrance. The city had several police stations, but the Greater Manchester Police Headquarters would be the nerve centre for a kidnap investigation of this importance. Particularly, as with the other cases, because that kidnap had the potential to escalate into murder.

If the detectives on Megan's case were any good – and only the best would have landed a case so media friendly – they should have substantial case files on the other murder victims. There had to be something in those files that would offer up some sort of clue, something that would lead him to Megan. A lead only the dead could see, then act on. That was why he was here, wasn't it? To go where the flesh-and-blood police couldn't. It was time to prove it hadn't been a wasted journey.

Passing easily through the front door, he saw that the station's reception area slumbered. A duty sergeant sat behind a murky glass screen, a book in his hand, its spine cracked and bent. A woman, emaciated and spindle thin, slouched on a bench directly opposite the window, a nodding dog whose head slouched, then snapped back upwards.

Joe passed through the sergeant's window, then through the sergeant himself, causing the man to frown and tremble slightly. Ignoring him, he walked to the back of the room and the whiteboard attached to the wall. If this was like every other large station he'd ever been in, there should be a list of teams and the respective cases they were working on. It wouldn't be named the Generation Killer – that was the press's gaudy title for the case – but it would contain the victims' names.

There.

Stanley Veins. And below, *Megan Veins*. They'd rolled the kidnapping and murder together.

Because they know the same person's responsible for both, thought Joe.

That is, if it even is a person.

It was a long time since Joe had been in an incident room. From the look of this one, they hadn't changed much.

He didn't need to physically smell the mushy aroma of coffee, sweat and nicotine to actually smell it, because the place twanged a muscle memory in his mind. He'd been in rooms like this on nights like this, minds huddling together in the pursuit of justice and truth. Or in his case, obfuscation and skulduggery.

Still, there was no one here now. The room was deserted, early-morning sunlight elbowing through blinds that covered the modesty of the floor-to-ceiling windows. Rows of empty desks sat untouched, their computer monitors winking and blinking cheekily. Either everyone was out looking for the missing girl, or they'd given up any chance of finding her.

Have to believe it's the former, he thought. And if it's the latter, that's OK, because she's still got me.

The room may have been empty, reeking of an operation in its death throes, but the three noticeboards that had been shunted together at the back were full, engorged with photographs, newspaper cuttings and printouts.

That's what I'm talking about. A pick-and-mix of clues and leads, just for me. Don't even have to crack open a file.

He jogged over to the display, instantly recognising many of the images; he'd seen them back in the Pen, when Daisy-May had first presented him with the case. Victims of the Generation Killer, old and young, lay in a variety of locations, their names pinned underneath their photographs. His eyes darted between them. *Deceased* was written next to each.

Deceased.

Deceased.

Deceased.

Deceased.

I can't let Megan join this list.

Deceased.

Deceased.

Deceased.

He stopped. There was a boy on the board who didn't have that dreadful word next to his photograph. Tony Fisher. Twelve years old, according to the text under the photo. His grandfather, Greg Fisher, had been found in a church five weeks ago, Tony several days later.

Joe's eyes hungrily scanned down the text. There had to be something here he could use.

Tony Fisher discovered outside the National Football Museum, Todd Street, at 3.03 a.m., 08/06/22. Biohazard team attended due to Fisher's potential exposure to toxic and hazardous materials. Team later confirmed the child had been subjected to radiation. Fisher was unable to recall the details of his kidnapping. Unable to confirm where he was taken. Unable to confirm the identity of his kidnapper.

Currently receiving palliative end-of-life care at the Royal Manchester Children's Hospital.

He blew undead air from his lungs. The child was still alive. He couldn't remember anything, but he was still alive.

And if he's still alive but on the brink of death, he might be able to see me. Talk to me. Might remember something when he couldn't before. I have to believe that. I have to try.

God does love 'em, that's what Daisy-May would say.

Time to put that to the test.

Moorgate Towers was a gazelle flung uncaringly amongst the Salford lions.

A forty-floored slab of brutalist architecture, it had been built in the seventies, when the seventies didn't know any better, dragging the city's inhabitants out of their crumbling terrace slums and into the modern age. Unfortunately for its residents, the 'modern age' had been just as neglectful as the post-war one. The Towers had been allowed to fall into rack and ruin, its ageing inhabitants increasingly isolated by the erratic lifts and the swarms of low-level criminals waiting to take their pound of dole-cheque flesh.

For Bits, though, there was nowhere more special.

On the many occasions he'd been unceremoniously tossed out of home for stealing (or for not stealing the right thing), the Towers had been his sanctuary. His grandfather, a Salford veteran of piss, vinegar and fierce protective love for his oldest grandson, called the place home. Bits would stay there for days at a time, doing the old man's shopping, watching TV with him on the good days and hearing his war stories on the bad. What would have been dreary to many was utter heaven to Bits, a shelter from the day-to-day horror of his life. It was one he'd maintained right until the end of that life; he could roll in at midday from an all-nighter at the Hacienda, and there was always a place for him at his grandad's.

It had been difficult to believe the old place could look any shabbier, but it had somehow managed the feat. Paint had long since peeled from the wooden reception area, and many of the windows on the lower floors had been boarded up, graffiti tags splayed across the wood.

More desperate than the fucking Pen, thought Bits. More lost souls. Less hope.

He didn't know what had brought him here after the argument with Joe, other than his own two feet and a sense of nostalgia. Now that he was here, though, he felt glad. It seemed to him that Moorgate Towers was one of the last beacons of old Salford – and by extension, Manchester – a line in the sand against the area's gentrified sell-out. But then he didn't have to live in the building; chances were any one of the remaining inhabitants would give their right eye (their left one too) to sell out into one of the city's gleaming glass apartment blocks.

The surrounding area was deserted, the malnourished children's playground outside the entrance broken down and neglected, a nest of broken bottles and fast-food wrappers. It would never have happened in his grandad's day; the old man had waged war against neglect in the building and its grounds, spending hour upon hour collecting rubbish the council didn't care to.

Walking towards the entrance without really knowing why, Bits knew on one level that he couldn't afford this diversion. It had been a good sixty minutes since his last hit of the amnesia drug, and when it wore off, the crash would be brutal, and it would be final.

On another level, he couldn't give a donkey's fuck.

Joe's like every boss I ever had, he thought. Thinks he's always right. Thinks people like me are always wrong. That paedo had it coming, and if Joey boy wasn't man enough to step up and do what needed to be done, it was lucky for him he had me there. Not that he'd ever thank me. He'd never have the wit to.

He passed through the door. The lights in the foyer had been smashed, shards of glass lying on the floor like they'd given up, along with everything else in the building. Vomit-yellow walls added to the sense of a structure gone to seed, the *Out of Order* slashed violently on a sheet of A4 paper and sellotaped to the closed lift door completing it.

What was he doing here? he asked himself as he began to take the stairs two at a time. His grandad would be long dead, and even if he wasn't, he wasn't going to be able to see him. At best, the flat would have new tenants; at worst, it would be boarded up and left to die. It was an exercise in self-torture.

Torture, but also a chance he knew most souls didn't get.

The chance to go home.

When he reached the fortieth floor, he wondered whether it was the muscle memory of exhaustion he was feeling or the real thing. Certainly he didn't believe he was imagining the burning in his calves or the shortness of breath.

Nostalgia rippled down his spine as he walked through the fire exit and into the corridor. Everything was the same, from the stained, cigarette-scarred carpet to the dim lights smeared on the walls. It was like the place had been embalmed since his last visit.

His grandad had lived at number 23, and as Bits arrived at the door, he hesitated, listening for sounds of life, or even death. Nothing, except the faintest crackle of static.

So what if someone's there? Not like they're going to shop me to the pigs for breaking and entering. Most they'll get is a chill.

Still, he felt a strange sense of nervousness as he walked through the door, a sense that he'd been waiting outside the headmaster's office and had now received the call to enter.

Inside, the hallway was totally still, like it had been some time since anyone had stepped into it. The small mound of letters by the front door reminded Bits of a dog patiently waiting for its daily walk.

He began to move down the hallway. It was just as he re-membered; even the pictures on the wall were the same. He allowed himself a smile at the framed photograph of himself, aged five, with the world at his feet rather than at his throat.

Wish I could talk to that lad, he thought, placing a finger on the glass. Tell him what's right and what's wrong. To turn left when he went right.

He moved down the row of pictures, soaking up the mem-ories. His mother as a young girl (tellingly, none of her as the woman she'd gone on to be), his grandma gurning for the camera, his grandad giving her a long-suffering, long-loving smile. The old man on his final day at the factory, the sort of place that would now house young professionals and the professionally young, arrested-development trust-funders who knew nothing of the real world or the people that lived in it.

The final picture in the row gave him pause.

It was him as a boy – ten, possibly eleven years old. He was in a boxing ring, gloves too big, vest bigger than that, helmet covering most of his face, which carried no trace of his big shit-eating grin. An older man stood behind him, arm placed proudly around his shoulders.

He felt panic surging, closing up his airway in the same way it had in the boxing club.

He dropped to his knees, his vision blurring, memories charging at him, unprompted.

Long-term memories repressed by pain and death battered their way up.

There was no friend called Jamie who'd told Bits about the paedophile boxing coach at the Lads Club.

He was the one who'd gone to the club.

He was the one who'd been abused.

The late-night training sessions with Malkey.

The things that came with those late-night sessions.

The way he could never get clean afterwards.

The first spliff he'd smoked, and the way it took the edge off his shame.

The ecstasy that sanded those edges completely away.

The smack that cured him until it didn't.

Seeing Malkey again at the Lads Club – even in his horrifically altered undead state – had triggered the shame and anger once more. It had always been there, waiting to be reignited. Death hadn't been able to cure that.

Nothing would be able to cure it. Killing Malkey certainly hadn't.

Joe was right. Malkey being cursed to walk the Lads Club's halls was a fate worse than the one Bits had handed out. By killing him he'd released him for ever, and where was Bits's own release? He'd still carry the damage around with him, and no amount of Dying Squad do-gooding would change that fact.

Maybe it could take the edge off, though, in the same way as drugs used to.

Maybe it could do that.

Bits surveyed the hallway again, with its unchanged trinkets and its old-man dressing. Perhaps the council never sold the place after his grandad died. Maybe they couldn't rehouse anyone here. Maybe no one *wanted* to be rehoused here. You'd have to be desperate to want to live in this shithole.

His grandad hadn't been desperate, though. He'd loved his flat, modest as it was, and that love had been infectious: Bits had caught a dose too.

As he walked into the living room, Bits saw that it too was much the same; shrouded in gloom and dust, imperfectly preserved. The same furniture stood in the same places. The same TV sat in the corner, a hulking wooden monstrosity whose screen danced with waving lines of static.

Weird, that, he thought. This whole fucking deal's weird. Why's all my grandad's stuff still here? He'd be a hundred and five years old if he were still alive. Bang strange that whoever's living here now would keep his things. Weren't great to begin with, let alone end with.

He approached the back of his grandad's special chair. It was right where it belonged, opposite the television. He frowned as he got closer; there were white wisps jutting over the top of the chair, dancing slightly in a wind he couldn't feel.

As he reached the chair, he let out a cry of anguish. A mummified corpse, shrunk by age, time and malice, sat there, its skeletal hands on the armrests, its skull staring straight ahead, traces of warped skin clinging to its fragile-looking bone. He allowed himself a few seconds of believing it wasn't his grandad, and then he saw the old man's cardigan. Burgundy, moth-eaten in all the right ways, with his war medals attached to the front. He had always been utterly unabashed at wearing them.

'People say I'm showing off,' he used to tell Bits, 'and they're bloody well right. I wear them for those that were lost, and I wear them for me. Anyone that's got a problem with that can go off and fight their own bloody war.'

Bits had felt burning pride at those medals when he'd been a young lad, and his wasn't a life that had been full of pride. He looked forward to Saturday afternoons round at his grandad's, the gas fire burning, raindrops rattling the windows, the old man doing the football pools while Bits polished his medals.

'Get 'em good and shiny, lad,' his grandad would say. 'Want to be able to see my face in 'em. Yours too, 'cos you're going to do great things, I know it.'

I didn't, though, did I, Grandad? Every year that went by was one where I fucked up more than the year before. You pretended not to know what a fuck-up I was, but you were shit at pretending. You were too good for it. Your soul was too good.

Bits crouched in front of what was left of his grandad. How hadn't he been missed? Why had no one checked on him? Bits's mother was flaky, but not abandon-her-own-father flaky. Or maybe she was. How many parents' evenings did she ever go to? How many school nativities? She'd treated Bits like the dog-isn't-just-for-Christmas accessory you weren't allowed to toss in the canal. Was it so impossible to believe she simply wouldn't have visited?

Sorry, Grandad. Sorry you had to die like this. Hope it was quick, in your sleep. Hope you didn't suffer.

The bang from the kitchen – out of sight, just around the corner from the living room – made Bits cry out in swearing surprise. There was no way anyone could have come in after him, and no way anyone would have come in before; the place had all the buzz of a seance. It was unlikely people cared to share their downtime with a mummified corpse either.

'Cept that's messy bullshit, thought Bits, 'cos I've seen people squat in worse. After a mad one, plenty just want to get their head down and couldn't give a fuck how mucky the pillow is. That don't even count junkies. They'd kip down with the rats and think it was a treat.

The bang came again.

Feeling for his gun, knowing just how useless such a weapon was in the living world, he stepped out of the living room and into the hallway.

The kitchen was one door down, and still had the same curtain of wooden beads fastened to the doorway. Bits flinched as he walked through them, then instantly saw what had made the noise.

His grandad's flat was unique in that it allowed access to the roof. It wasn't access that had been granted willingly by the council, but it was access Bits had gladly taken anyway; it was possible to see across all of Salford from there, and if you squinted hard enough, you could just about make out United's ground, as well as the sprawling Manchester skyline. It had been the perfect place to smoke and see what was what.

Wind must have shaken open the door, he thought. Probably been banging to and fro for months. Years, even.

He walked over to it and saw that the ladder was still in place. *I'll take a quick look for old times' sake. Maybe I'll even spot Joe being pious as fuck.*

Jumping up, he caught the fourth rung, hauling himself out to be greeted by a blanket of sky. The promise of the red sunrise had given way to a sea of mottled grey and a film of fine drizzle. As his head popped out, he saw him. An old man with his back to him, standing at the lip of the roof.

'Grandad?' he said, instantly recognising the old man's grey cardigan and stooped posture.

The man turned, and Bits realised he'd been right but also utterly wrong. Because the creature in front of him was barely his grandfather any more. He was barely even human; his hair was a tangle of vines, his face a beard of them. They erupted from his withered fingers and shrivelled hands, worse even than the abuser Bits had shot at the Lads Club. He'd at least tried to keep the vegetation under control; his grandad clearly hadn't.

The old man's eyes were free of clarity, devoid of comprehension. 'Who are you?'

'It's me, Grandad. It's Bobby.'

'Don't know a Bobby,' said his grandad, his words muffled by the moustache of vines around his mouth.

'Bits,' he replied. 'You used to call me Bits.'

A light cleared in his grandad's eyes, a flash of recognition, and then horror to go with it.

'It won't end, lad,' he said, suddenly aware of how he looked. 'No matter what I do, it won't end.'

274

Then, without a second's hesitation, he stepped off the edge of the roof.

'You're a daft old sod.'

'Plenty'd say I was a daft young one.'

'How many times have you done that?' asked Bits, helping his grandad to a chair pointed away from the one containing his mummified corpse.

'Can't remember my name,' said his grandad, sighing and closing his eyes. 'Hardly likely to remember how many times I've tried to top myself.'

When he'd seen his grandad throw himself from the top of the building, the fact that he was already dead hadn't stopped terror surging through Bits. There were some things your brain couldn't adapt to, no matter how much common sense and logic you fed it, and that included your nearest and dearest jumping off buildings.

The old man looked at him suspiciously. 'Who'd you say you were again?'

'Bits,' he said patiently. 'I'm your grandson.'

His grandad laughed. 'He's been dead years. Got himself blown up, didn't he, the silly twat.'

'Yeah, that was me, Grandad. I'm dead, just like you.'

The old man snorted. 'Dead, is it? You sound alive to me, lad. That blather's coming from somewhere.'

He turned to Bits, his face a tangle of vines. 'Won't complain about the company, mind, as long as you don't mither me too much. Gets lonely up here.'

'Bet it does,' said Bits, looking around at the crypt of a flat.

'Knock the wireless on, would you? Might take the edge off my bloody thoughts and your bloody prattle.'

The radio was right where he remembered, underneath the grimy window that looked out onto the rain-lashed city skyline.

It was an ancient beast of wood and dials, covered liberally with a layer of dust. A row of numbers was etched on the top, suggesting, Bits supposed, the radio stations it could be tuned into. He wondered if any of them were still in service.

As he reached towards the on switch, he heard Joe's warning about not interacting with the living world. His hand hovered over the dial.

'You sorting that radio or not?' barked his grandad. 'You look slow-witted, but you should still be able to turn a bleeding wireless on.'

Wondering why exactly he'd bothered coming, Bits decided to risk it and turned the dial. A haze of static greeted him, ghostly voices scratching their way to the surface. He continued to rotate the dial, chancing upon a local news station.

'The search continues tonight for Manchester student Megan Veins,' announced the newsreader. 'Megan and her grandfather, Stanley Veins, went missing several days ago. Mr Veins' body was discovered in the Moss Side area of the city, and police say they're following several lines of enquiry. They have refused to either confirm or deny that the individual dubbed the Generation Killer is their prime suspect.'

'Don't want that rubbish on,' called his grandad. 'If I want bad news, all I need to do is look out of the bloody window. Or find a mirror.'

Hiding a curse under his breath, Bits carried on turning. He needed to get out of here, needed to find Joe and put the pettiness behind him. A girl's life was at stake.

'That'll do,' said his grandad as Bits tuned into a mournful concerto. 'Music to kill myself to.'

Bits nodded, then took a seat across from the old man. Despite himself, he smiled at a painting on the opposite wall. It depicted the face of a pinched, parched man who gazed out with a look of scorn or mournfulness, depending on how you caught the angle, or your mood.

'That painting scared the shit out of me as a lad. Always used to think it were looking at me when I kipped on the sofa.'

His grandad leaned forward. 'Who are you again?'

'Bits,' he said, weariness sneaking into his tone. 'Your grandson.'

'Pah.' His grandad rubbed at his face, his hands getting caught in the mass of vines. 'You're too big. Never called him grandson anyway. We're not royalty here.'

'That's right,' said Bits, nodding. 'You always used to call me your grand*boy*.'

A flicker of recognition appeared in his grandad's eyes, then faded almost immediately. He put his hand to his face, tugging at the vines. 'Need a bloody shave, me. Got to keep my standards up. See so many blokes my age that don't, that just let themselves go.'

Bits smiled sadly. 'Why don't you let me help you with that?'

Bits had largely ignored the field kit he'd been provided with (the gun he'd been very unofficially provided with had been the main item he'd used), but now he was grateful for it, containing as it did just the item for his grandad's shave. The small metallic object looked like a pen torch, but when you pushed down on the button at its centre, a thin lick of flame came out rather than a puny beam of light.

'You're not putting that thing anywhere near my face,' barked his grandad. 'Looks bloody lethal.'

'It'll be fine, Grandad. Trust me.'

'I never trust anyone till they give me a reason to, and I'm not your grandad, no matter how many times you claim it.'

'Fine,' said Bits. 'Just think of me as help the fucking aged, then.'

'Got a lip on you,' said the old man, half a smile visible. 'Never hated anyone for having spirit to go with it, though.' He closed his eyes and tilted his head towards the ceiling. 'Go on then. Do your bloody shaving.'

Maybe you'll surprise yourself one of these days: that was what Elias had said in the shelter when he'd been performing a familiar service for the souls under his care. Well, maybe he just would.

His face was fixed with concentration as he began to burn the thick sprouting vines from his grandad's face. The vegetation browned and curled as if it were trying to wriggle free from the fire's tickle.

'I called him Bits because of the food.'

Bits didn't reply, hiding behind silence as he went about his task. He was afraid anything else would throw off his grandad's recollection.

'Later on, he'd tell his mates he got the name because of all those bloody drugs he took, but that weren't true, not to begin with, anyway. It were me that gave him the name.'

Rain fell gently against the window, and with the radio playing scratchily, Bits could almost believe he was eight years old again.

'It was because of the way he ate food,' said his grandad, a sense of wonder in his voice at the fact that he was able to recall these facts. 'I'd give him a chocolate bar every week – although let's have it right, it was a Caramac, one of those funny thin light brown ones – and instead of wolfing it down in one go, he'd break it into dozens of little bits. Kept them in the fridge. Saved it, like. Made it last. Always fascinated me, that. My little Bits.'

Tears prickled at Bits's eyes. He killed the flame and looked at a face that was discernibly his grandad's again. He gently brushed away a scattering of vines still clinging to the old man's face. 'That was me, Grandad.'

His grandad stared ahead, his own tears sparkling. 'My grandboy's dead.'

He's too far gone, thought Bits. Been breathing this soil air poison for too long. There's no coming back from it.

He thought about the suicide pill that was included in every field pack. It was in case you got stranded on the soil and didn't want to end your days like his grandad here, confused and amnesia-riddled. It would be a kindness, in a way, to give it to him. A few seconds of pain and then he would be at peace for ever.

He walked to the window, placing his head against the glass as he'd done so many times on the soil as man and boy.

He couldn't do it, no matter how much of a mercy it might be. His grandad wasn't the paedo he shot at the boys' club, nor the suspect he'd beaten back on the soil. He was a simple, kind man who'd never harmed a living soul. A dying one, come to that.

Which left only one other option.

Chapter Seventeen

Bōsōzoku was the Japanese term given to delinquents who aspired to be outlaws.

The closest Japan had to Hells Angels, Bōsōzoku gangs made it their life's work to create havoc in the city's intricate traffic ecosystem. In homage to the biker gangs of America, packs of young men on motorbikes and scooters set out to cause the maximum disruption to civilians, racing through red lights, speeding, and generally making a nuisance of themselves.

Hatoyama, unlike many of his colleagues, considered them Hells Angels with stabilisers; he'd seen enough real crime to recognise kids being kids. Certainly they were harmless compared to crazed ancient samurai.

As they entered Bōsōzoku ground zero, he looked over to the passenger's side. The Duchess sat there, hand on her shoulder, eyes in the twilight between open and closed.

'You don't look so good.'

'You try being hundreds of years old,' she replied. 'It takes the edge off your lustre somewhat.'

'That why you didn't go after the samurai?' said Hatoyama. 'Not enough juice in the tank?'

'I didn't go after the samurai because the samurai is irrelevant,' said the Duchess. 'It's Hanna we seek, not her followers.'

She looked out of the window as the uniformity of the high-rise suburbs blurred by. 'She'll be long gone, you know.'

'I do know,' said Hatoyama, 'but that doesn't mean it isn't worth checking the place out. You chase down the leads. You turn over every stone till you catch a break.'

The Duchess closed her eyes. 'Careful, Hatoyama. You're beginning to sound like a detective again.'

He tried to hide his smile.

When they'd left the bank – the Duchess battered and bruised, Hatoyama engaged and enthused – a message had been waiting for them. Arata had managed to pull up another sighting of Hanna, this time retrospectively; she'd been recorded a day ago at a nondescript block of flats in Bōsōzoku-ville. Hatoyama was of the opinion that an old lead was better than no lead at all, and this was a lead with teeth, because the footage had captured her entering a specific flat.

'It's unfortunate that your friend couldn't find intel on who owned the flat,' said the Duchess.

'Unfortunate but telling,' said Hatoyama. 'Someone's gone to great lengths to get off the grid.'

'Meaning what?' said the Duchess.

'In my experience, anyone with a non-existent digital footprint is usually Yakuza, or government. Top-secret, national security government at that.'

She pursed thin, cracked lips. 'Neither possibility sets my mind at ease.'

'It shouldn't,' said Hatoyama.

The car sat idling, the high rise looming over them.

'How do you want to play this?' said Hatoyama.

'You have no reason at all to enter that apartment,' said the Duchess, 'and I don't need one. Warrants aren't required when you can walk through doors.'

'Doesn't sit well with me, just being a taxi service for you.'

'But you do it so well,' said the Duchess, a touch of playfulness in her voice.

Hatoyama crossed his arms, pouting.

'We're always trailing in Hanna's wake. Reacting rather than being proactive. With your friend Arata on the case, we know we can get a location on her now. When we do, we need to move quickly.'

'Told you he was useful,' said Hatoyama. 'He has access to systems the police can only dream of.'

'That *you* can only dream of.'

He nodded towards the towering building ahead of them. 'You still here? Because that apartment isn't going to search itself.'

The Duchess eased out of her seat. 'You suspect something about whoever owns this apartment. Something you're not telling me.'

'It's because I haven't told myself yet,' said Hatoyama. 'Do your snooping, and let's see if we reach the same conclusion.'

The stench hit her as soon as she stepped out of the lift.

Acrid, as if vomit had been heated up in a microwave then liberally smeared around the hallway. And if she could smell it, it meant nothing living had caused it. This wasn't muscle memory of the living world; this was something of hers.

When she reached the door, she stopped, listening for signs of life, human or otherwise. Silence greeted her. Her eyes watering, her fists balled in readiness for anything, she walked through the door.

The Duchess hadn't quite known what to expect, but it hadn't been banality. The flat was so sparse, it was difficult to believe anyone could live here.

A sofa covered in plastic.

Three forlorn chairs.

A television that dwarfed the room, playing contentedly in the background.

She felt her stomach lurch and shimmy. Whatever had caused the smell had happened here in this room.

Holding her sleeve against her nose, she walked towards the sofa. Sweat was mixed with blood, filtered through something sharp and tangy. *This room reeks of violence.* It wasn't just the smell, either; it was like an imprint had been left, a purple bruise discolouring the air.

She kneeled down next to the sofa. There was an impression on the right-hand side, two hollow grooves that could have been left by a man's backside. They looked recent, like the plastic hadn't had a chance to pop back into place. Or they could just as easily be heritage. Grooves carved over months. Years.

The area beneath the sofa caught her eye. There were two dust-free circles, like it had been pushed back from a spot it had rested on for months.

Maybe it has, she thought. So what? This is circumstantial evidence when I'm looking for a smoking gun. Although when it comes to Hanna, a smoking gun's the last thing I actually want to find.

A picture frame rested on the windowsill nearby. It showed a middle-aged man and a woman so ancient she made the Duchess feel young.

Is that him? she wondered. Is that the man Hanna came here for yesterday? He looks so nondescript, he'd struggle to remember his own name. If it is, where is he now? If she came here with murder in mind, where's the body? Arata couldn't find any CCTV footage of him leaving. Did Hanna know to avoid the cameras?

She climbed to her feet, the stench of decay and anger still there, her system steadfastly refusing to get used to it.

There was one other room she hadn't been in, separated off by a thin shoji partition wall; thin enough to punch a hole through if she'd been so minded. She wasn't – the threat of the Xylophone Man's reach hadn't quite left her, despite his murder – so instead she slipped quietly through it and into the bedroom on the other side.

This room was as trim and sparse as the one she'd just come from. A single bed sat underneath a slim window cut into the wall. A wardrobe, similar in design and style to the partition wall, stood opposite, its doors closed. A small desk was the only other furniture. It stood bare and neglected, save for a row of black folders underneath it.

The Duchess kneeled down, plucking one out from the end, her guilt and fear spasming at this interaction with the living world. Just because she could get away with it didn't mean she wanted to. Fetching Hatoyama would waste time they didn't have, though.

She placed the folder on the desk and peeled back the cover to reveal what looked like a sheaf of payslips. The name *Toki Sato* was printed at the top left of the uppermost document, the address of the apartment she was currently standing in beneath that. Her eyes scanned down, stopping when she saw who the payslip had been sent by.

The Daiki Gin Power Plant. That has to be what Hannah was here for, because this Toki Sato doesn't have a single memorable thing about him. Only his job.

The question is, why?

On 11 March 2011, nature had decided enough was enough and had taken revenge on man for his nuclear folly. Specifically, she'd directed her ire towards the Daiki Gin Power Plant.

One of the most powerful earthquakes in Japanese history (or any other country's history, come to that) had struck the facility, a hit the plant's reactor took squarely on the chin. The authorities didn't know the quake was a sucker punch: nature's killer blow came from the fifteen-metre tsunami the quake generated. It killed over 19,000 people, decimated coastal ports and towns, and destroyed over a million buildings. It also hit the Gin nuclear plant, disabling the three active reactors and causing a nuclear meltdown the consequences of which would still be felt in a hundred years' time.

Hanna Jankie felt a hundred years wasn't quite good enough; she was in the legacy business.

She stood in the ruined Reactor 3 building. It was the reactor that had received the least damage when the tsunami hit, the one that could have limped on if necessary. A team of three young men sat at the control desk, ghost fingers slashing at man-made keyboards, spools of electronics feeding into the back of the desktop computers.

Her possessed puppet Toki Sato faced them, a thin film of drool hanging from his bottom lip. It already seemed a lifetime ago since she'd snatched the plant's lead clean-up technician from his non-descript apartment.

She hadn't yet got used to the sensation of watching herself through another's eyes. It was disconcerting, possession, like flicking between two television channels, the blur of the last channel still present when the new one popped up. Sato's memories clashed with hers, oil mixing with water, making her brain prickle. It took considerable discipline to keep control of him, a defiant horse bucking against her reins.

She noticed that one of his eyes had slid down lazily in its socket. But then was that so surprising? There were two consciousnesses existing in one body, and Hanna knew that a little of her went a long way. The effort of living with her was stretching Sato out of shape from the inside.

It was an effort worth making. He was vital, this man, to what came next. Then his usefulness would be at an end. She had to admit she was looking forward to that moment; the jarring, disorientating flashes of his consciousness that assailed her were troubling.

'Tell me again,' she said, because having Sato talk to her was easier and less painful than accessing the memories from his subconscious, 'how this is going to work.'

He looked at her with clouded eyes. 'We black-start the plant.'

'In plain Japanese.'

'The nuclear plant was taken offline remotely when the tsunami hit,' he said, his voice monotone, scraped free of emotion and life. 'To bring it back online, we need to jump-start it. We connect the battery and generator you stole several days ago. The battery fires up the generator. The generator will be sufficient to bring the reactor back online.'

'What about the authorities?' said Hanna. 'When they see the reactor is back online, what's to stop them shutting it down again?'

'The security disruptor module you and Benji stole,' said Sato. 'Now that you have the primary microchip for the Dog Catcher, the device will block any outside signal hitting the system. It's like a catcher's mitt with a baseball.'

Hanna smiled, though in truth she didn't like it, because it seemed to suggest Sato could read her mind, just as she could read his. It was a mild inconvenience. As soon as her plan had come to fruition, she would kill him, and then he'd be useful in a different way. 'What is the projected damage Tokyo will suffer?'

286

'The temperature failsafe on the reactor is irreparably damaged,' said Sato. 'The reactor will explode hours after it's brought back online. Hundreds of thousands will die.'

'Many more will be given the opportunity to truly live,' said Hanna.

She turned to the men at the control desk. 'Are you ready?'

They smiled, grateful for the attention and the chance to be of service. 'Say the word, ma'am.'

Ma'am, thought Hanna. How the dear Duchess would get a kick out of me being called that.

She turned to Sato, who stood patiently waiting, a tablet in his hand.

'Do it,' she said.

The neon of downtown Tokyo waved in the rear-view mirror. The Duchess was almost tempted to wave back. She had no idea whether she'd see it again.

Hatoyama looked from his ghostly passenger to the road ahead, unable to decide which required the greater attention. 'I just think I should call someone.'

The Duchess sighed, placing her hands on her lap while looking out at the crimson sunset, the city behind them, ridges of terraced rice fields to the side, the red sun glinting off their pools of standing water. 'Who would you call?'

'Someone at the nuclear plant. The police. The army.'

'And tell them what? A homicidal ghost is planning a terrorist attack?'

'No,' said Hatoyama, a certain prissiness creeping into his voice. 'I could tell them I'd received an intelligence report of an imminent attack, a potential hack of their systems.'

'Be my guest,' said the Duchess. 'The words of a detective who shares his office with the building's boiler carries gravity, I'm sure.'

'You're even snarkier when you're in pain,' said Hatoyama, nodding at her ravaged shoulder.

'I merely want to emphasise the reality of our situation. There is no one to turn to, amongst the living or the dead. We're the only thing standing between Hanna, and whatever's she's planning.'

A sign whizzed past them on the right, announcing that the Daiki Gin Power Plant was a mere thirty kilometres away.

'My God,' said Hatoyama.

'On this occasion,' said the Duchess, 'he's unlikely to help us, I'm afraid.'

'The Daiki Gin nuclear power plant has been decommissioned,' he said. 'It's a graveyard. According to Arata, Sato will be on the skeleton crew, closing down the last few sections.'

'That's what worries me,' said the Duchess. 'What better place for a ghost? Decommissioned or not, the government were paying Sato to do something important. If Hanna's taken him – and we have to assume she has – she has access to his knowledge. That terrifies me. It should terrify you too. What's her plan?'

'Do you want my hunch?' said Hatoyama? 'Or the facts?'

'The facts I know,' said the Duchess. 'Your hunch I don't.'

'I think she's going to reactivate the plant.'

'To what end?'

'Other than the murder of hundreds of thousands of people? It received fatal structural damage during the tsunami; reactivating it will be like throwing petrol on a bonfire. Your sister is a terrorist – everything she's done screams it. What bigger terrorist act is there than creating a nuclear winter in Tokyo?'

The Duchess shook her head. 'It would be extreme even for Hanna.'

'I think she passed extreme when she murdered a trainful of people, don't you?'

'Yes,' the Duchess said eventually. 'I suppose so.'

Hatoyama's hands gripped the steering wheel as another five-kilometre marker went past. Above it was a sign that declared aggressively: *EXCLUSION ZONE: 20 KM. NO UNAUTHORISED PERSONNEL BEYOND THIS POINT.*

'I'm the definition of unauthorised personnel,' said Hatoyama. 'There are armed guards at the barrier. No way am I getting past those.'

'You'll get through,' said the Duchess.

'How do you know?'

'Because you have me with you. And I have the password.'

Hatoyama snorted. 'Are you serious?'

'In our short time together, have you known me to joke?'

'Fair point.'

'The arrangement between the living and the dead that you and I enjoy —' Hatoyama wrinkled his nose theatrically at this — 'is not a unique one. There are many tendrils connecting the world of the living and that of the dead. National security is one such tendril.'

Hatoyama bark-laughed. 'I'm supposed to believe high-ranking generals seek counsel with ghosts?'

'You're not supposed to do anything but drive.'

He shook his head, the nuclear power plant on the horizon swelling to a malignant size.

'Think about it,' said the Duchess. 'What assassin, what thief is more effective or deadly than one who cannot be seen, touched or hurt? There has to be communication and cooperation between the two worlds, or the defensive barriers will fall. It's why beings like the Xylophone Man are so important; without them, you have soldiers with machine guns trying to shoot something they can't see or hurt.'

'And you think Hanna knew of this arrangement?'

'I know she did,' said the Duchess, 'because I was there

when she was told about it. She was supposed to be Warden, remember.'

'We have a more pressing concern,' said Hatoyama, pointing ahead.

The guard with the outstretched arm and the machine gun started as a dot, then quickly became a life-sized smear. Whatever his size, his you-shall-not-pass attitude was unmistakable.

'This chump doesn't look like he'll settle for your password,' said Hatoyama, easing his decrepit Honda to a stop. 'Unless it's *I will shoot you.*' He turned to the Duchess. 'So? What's the password?'

'*Oppenheimer.*'

'Seriously?'

'*I'm here to see Oppenheimer.* The guard will ask who sent you. You reply, *The Duchess.*'

'This feels like the sort of practical joke where a camera crew will jump out.'

'I wish it was.'

Hatoyama sighed and pulled up on the handbrake. The guard's eyes were trained on him as fiercely as his gun was. He eased his way out of the driver's side, making sure to keep his hands – and badge – in view.

'Do you know what this place is?' said the guard, whose gun, Hatoyama couldn't help notice, was pointing directly at his head.

'I do,' said Hatoyama. 'I'm here to see Oppenheimer.'

Don't wink, thought the Duchess.

Hatoyama winked.

The guard frowned. 'Are you trying to be funny?'

Hatoyama swallowed. 'I was told to ask for Oppenheimer.'

'There's no Oppenheimer here. No anyone except for a few robots and a wall of radiation. I need you to get back in your car, turn around and drive away.'

'But the Duchess sent me,' said Hatoyama, only the merest trace of desperation in his voice.

'I don't care if the emperor himself sent you,' said the guard, 'you need to—'

His mouth formed an *o* of surprise, and he slumped to the ground. Standing behind him was the Duchess, bolt-cutter in her hand, held like a club.

'What happened to the password?' said Hatoyama.

'You didn't believe that nonsense, did you?' she said with a slight smile.

Hatoyama glanced from the crumpled body of the guard to the frail-looking Duchess.

'What about the arrangement between the living and the dead?'

'Oh, it exists,' she said, 'but it's hardly likely to include low-level guards for radiation graveyards.'

'You played a prank on me,' said Hatoyama wonderingly.

'I believe it's my first,' said the Duchess, trying not to smile too widely. 'In this life or the previous one.' A cloud passed across her face. 'The Xylophone Man's death carries some benefits.'

'A little gallows humour never hurt anyone, I suppose,' said Hatoyama.

'It usually stings for the person standing at the gallows,' said the Duchess, stepping over the unconscious guard.

Sweat prickled across Hatoyama's back as he raised the barrier next to the guards' hut, the warped power plant watching him judgementally as he did so.

With a final grunt, he fixed it into position, then stood, hands on hips, looking at the cracked, desolated road stretching out in front of them. 'Can you feel it?'

'Unusually for a soil-based phenomenon, yes,' said the Duchess. 'A great tragedy happened here, and I don't need to see bodies to appreciate that.'

Something else, too. She could feel some of her strength returning: whether that was because of the radiation she couldn't be sure, but what she could be sure of was her burgeoning sense of power.

She'd need it.

'There are no birds,' said Hatoyama.

'I would wager there's no living thing within twenty kilometres of here,' said the Duchess.

'Who we're after isn't living, though.'

'No.'

'I, however, am.'

The Duchess looked at him with something like sympathy in her eyes. 'Yes,' she said. 'You are.'

Hatoyama folded his arms, looking at the power plant in the distance. 'This is why you still need me. What better driver than someone with my condition?'

The Duchess lowered her head.

'You didn't just need my ability to see the dead, or my police database. You needed someone with nothing to lose.'

'I did need all those things, Detective. They have proved to be invaluable, as have you yourself.'

'Not as invaluable as my disease, though.'

'No,' said the Duchess. 'Not as invaluable as that.'

She took a moment, then continued.

'I didn't know what Hanna's plan was, but I knew it had to be something big; she'd come too far and committed too many atrocities to rein in her ambition. You, of course, are free to leave. To return to your life.'

Hatoyama scowled, went to reply, then instead wiped the sweat from his brow.

The reactor loomed large. 'At least this way it's on my own terms.'

'Thank you, Detective,' said the Duchess, the slightest tremor in her voice. 'I wish I'd had a hundred of you on the Dying Squad.'

'No you don't,' said Hatoyama, smiling.

'No, I don't,' said the Duchess, smiling back.

Chapter Eighteen

The building at the end of the world didn't have any doors. That was the first thing Daisy-May noticed. It was like God had hurled down a black rectangle, one without windows, entrances or exits, a building block for the offspring of deities to play with. The engineering was way beyond any of the Dispossessed, way beyond the living souls on the soil even. It was also enormous, comfortably the size of three football pitches, and the height of the stadiums housing them.

It hadn't taken her the two hours she'd feared it would to reach the monolith, but the sickness she now felt on a minute-by-minute basis gave her no chance to appreciate it. She didn't know how much longer she could continue for, only that she had to, until she'd found Chestnut. The gang leader's son, Eric, too, along with all the other missing kids. Once she'd sprung them – and taken down the cow who had kidnapped them in the first place – the Pen would be safe again.

First of all, though, she had to find a front door.

Leaning on the broken oar she'd taken from the ship, she considered the building, as well as her options. She could wait till someone left: the woman who'd taken Chestnut had to have got in somehow. The trouble was, there was no telling how long that wait would be, and also no telling how much danger Chestnut was in while she waited.

Never had the patience of a saint, me, she thought. Barely got the patience of a sinner.

Which meant she was going to have to break in, if she could work out where *in* was.

Moving quickly, trying to keep her feet light, she approached the building. She checked for cameras but saw none; if she was being monitored, it was covertly. Which didn't mean it wasn't happening.

Having reached the building safely, she put a hand against its cold black structure, and found instead warmth tickling her hand. Where she'd expected to touch concrete, instead she found a supple, almost fleshy texture.

What the fuck is this place? she wondered. Wall feels like it's made of human skin. Or the devil's.

No one asked for my permission for it to be built. Whatever unholy shit's going on inside, I'm going to pull this place down brick by brick.

She tried to drag her hand back, then frowned when she realised the building had other ideas. Setting herself, she tried again. Dust kicked up from her heels as she pulled as hard as she could, *as hard as she could* apparently woefully insufficient.

This isn't good.

It got worse.

She cried out in surprise as something dragged her forward, the wall swallowing half of her arm. She didn't feel pain, but she'd have been hard pressed to describe the sensation as pleasure; the pressure was firm, with the same moist feeling she'd experienced when touching the wall for the first time.

She was tugged forward again, her whole arm now consumed. She tried to yank it back, resulting in nothing more than dirt on her Converse trainers and the feeling that her shoulder was about to pop out of its socket.

I'm fighting this when I should just go with it. After all, it's not like I don't want to get in there. Getting in there's the whole fucking point.

She took a step forward, her shoulder going through the wall, the feeling like she was walking with the current, rather than fighting against it. Another step and her head was half in, half out. Another, and she was all the way through.

Daisy-May stumbled as she passed through to the other side, feeling like she'd been gobbled up then spat out by some great unseen monster. She blinked, smoothing out her clothes, trying to get the feeling of wall spit off her.

She was in a huge courtyard. At the far side of it was a boat, much like the one she'd travelled in. It sat empty, listing to the right without water or oars to keep it afloat. The wall behind it was translucent, showing the barren desert that she'd come from, a trick that was replicated on all four of the structure's walls.

This is way beyond anything we've got in the compound, she thought. *It's like someone's taken that tech and shoved a genius pill up its arse. Has to be this woman who doesn't glimmer: that mad cow gets everywhere. Can't be a coincidence that all this weird shit started happening as soon as she came on the scene. Something this massive, though, she had to have help. Lots of it.*

Can't wait *to meet them.*

The courtyard was mostly empty of buildings, save for what appeared to be an enormous concrete barn on its far-right hand side. A thick wooden door had been carved into its centre, the height sufficient for a giant to walk through, if it was so minded.

What is it with doors in the Pen? Never seen one that couldn't be twenty foot lower.

Jogging over, grateful that her stomach had settled – at least for now – she pushed against the barn door. Where she'd expected resistance, she found none. That was where the good news ended.

The stench – death filtrated with decay – hit her immediately.

A scar of a window allowed watery light to illuminate dozens of beds. All were empty, all neatly made, all unused. She walked uncertainly to the centre of the room, her footsteps landmines of noise, listening for anything that wasn't a hollow echo. This room could hold two hundred people: where had they gone? There was something in the air that still spoke of occupation, even if she couldn't see what that something was.

A draught ruffled her hair, picking up strength before dying away completely.

Daisy-May walked over to the apology of a window, holding her hand over it. Not so much as a whisper of a breeze; indeed, it was as if it had been vacuum-sealed shut. Dust drifted across the thin shaft of light, the room's ghosts keeping their counsel.

As it tugged at her again, Daisy-May followed the breeze towards the opposite side of the room. One of the beds failed to comply with the regimented lines of the others, jutting out at an angle. A quick inspection showed why it had been dragged out of position: underneath was an open hatch, the lip of a ladder sticking out.

Where's Mabel? Daisy-May wondered. Emergency backup ain't what it should be.

The smart play, she knew, was to wait for help rather than tramp down a ladder leading to who knew where.

She'd never been a fan of the smart play.

She began her long descent.

She heard the humming before she saw the light.

A subconscious drone shivered in fillings she never knew she had, loosening her grip on the seemingly never-ending ladder. Grasping the cold metal tighter, she continued downwards into the light, its warm glow bathing the bleached-white floor tiles that drew ever closer in its heavenly hue. When she ran out of ladder, she hopped off, her feet hitting the ground with a muffled thud, the flickering tungsten lamps overhead illuminating a room so sterilised it was almost virginal. She clicked her fingers, the echo that responded shorn of its strength.

Soundproofed.

At the end of the corridor was a white door, with a thin metal grille for a window.

She approached it cautiously, trying the handle, knowing it would be locked but still feeling disappointment when she confirmed it was. I miss the soil, she thought. I'd be able to just walk straight through the fucking thing.

This wasn't the soil, though, and even if she'd had a key for the door, it hadn't demeaned itself with a visible lock. A peek through the grille revealed nothing but a tumble of steel with a blackened slab of glass behind it. If she squinted and looked down, she could just about see a bolt on the other side of the door, but that was it.

Anything *that* hidden is something I need to find, she thought, wincing at the ever-present hum. Whether it turns out to be something I want to find's another matter.

She glared at the locked door, breathing in, then out.

Never tried to move anything that big before. It'd be tough if it was already open, but locked and that chunky? Gonna take some serious willpower. Or brainpower. Or whatever-the-fuck power it is that lets me move things with my tiny dead mind.

She closed her eyes, then stretched out a hand. Anger had

been her defining emotion when she'd moved the rocks, fear when willing the bag and flare gun into her hand. What was she supposed to call on now, in this strange place that hadn't asked her permission to exist, with its smell of death and sterility? Desperation? Hope?

She visualised the door ripped from its hinges, metal buckling in on itself then casually tossed aside. Sweat erupted on her brow and a whine sang in her ears as she replayed the door doing what she needed it to do again, and again and again.

It was too big. One day she might wield such power, but not today.

She had to think smaller. Smarter. Sometimes you needed a fist, and sometimes you needed to slip that fist into a velvet glove. There was no way she could yank the door off its hinges, but she didn't need to; she just needed to pick its lock, and there had to be one, despite there being no visible sign of it.

She looked again at the sheet of glass, testing it with a jabbed elbow. Thick. Certainly too thick to break with her weak mind and even weaker elbow.

She peered through it again, looking down, the bolt on the other side of the door just visible.

A smile broke out on her face.

Growing up, Daisy-May had a lot of uncles.

These men came in many shapes and sizes. Her mother didn't seem to have a type, unless you counted rancid louses who treated women like shit.

There was one of her mother's beaus she did like, though. Ted was a wrong'un, but a wrong'un with his heart in the right place. He was a petty thief, but one good enough not to get caught, and he treated the women in his life with respect. For this reason, Daisy-May knew it wouldn't last.

It didn't, but before her mother's lack of self-respect spoiled things, Ted taught Daisy-May a few tricks. Like how to pick a lock.

'Way they do it in films, with a hairpin? That'll not work more than it will,' he told her once. 'All you need's a shoelace, love.' He bent down to her, slipping the lace from her supermarket no-brand trainer. 'See, it's simple.'

Daisy-May watched, fascinated, as he created a slip-knot bow at the top of the lace, then wiggled it through the minuscule gap between the car's window and its frame. Once it was in, he lowered it towards the lock button.

'Not as difficult as threading a needle, this.' His tongue stuck out, one eye closed in concentration as he looped the knot around the jutting lock button. 'But it ain't far off. Need a steady eye and a calm heart. You got a calm heart?'

Daisy-May – still a few years short of ten – would nod fiercely, hand on said heart.

Once he'd lassoed the lock, he carefully tightened the knot.

'Moment of truth,' he said, smiling at her. 'You imagine it unlocking with your mind, and it will.'

He pulled slowly on the shoelace, and the tightened slip knot dragged the lock button upwards. She'd cried out in triumph when the lock had given a resounding unlocked *click*.

Hacking a Ford Cosworth was one thing. Jimmying the lock of a mysterious afterlife compound was quite another, though.

Is it fuck, Ted would have said. *A lock's a lock's a lock.*

As she guided the slip knot of her grimy Converse shoelace over the steel bolt on the other side of the door, Daisy-May hoped he was right.

She could feel the sweat gathering on her forehead as she began to tighten the knot. The bolt was a lot weightier than a car lock, and instead of dragging it upwards, she was attempting to tug it to the left.

Same principle, though, she thought, as the bolt grudgingly

began to move. Bet the Duchess never had to do this shit.

She smiled at the thought of her trying.

At last there was a faint grinding noise, like the bolt was desperately trying to escape its metal prison, and then the telltale glorious click.

She pushed against the door.

It opened.

Cheers, Ted, she thought. You always were my favourite.

Daisy-May hadn't frequented many laboratories in the afterlife – even fewer in her soil days – but she was certain the one she'd just walked into wasn't typical.

Nine metal gurneys rested in perfect symmetry, trolleys containing surgical tools standing beside them and large, slightly curved needles angled down from the ceiling above. A thick strap had been fastened around each table, the clasps closed. The tables were, mercifully, empty.

They hadn't always been. You didn't need to be Sherlock Holmes to work that out. Who had built this place? And why?

She moved away from the tables to the wall behind them. Dozens of clipboards adorned it, all full of charts with numbers and terminology that meant nothing to her.

The Duchess had to have known about this place, whatever *this place* was, thought Daisy-May. No way had it just sprung up in the last few months.

A few feet away from the unintelligible charts was a door, and she winced at the thought of having to pick another lock. She reached out to the handle, braced for the worst.

The door opened.

Thanks, God. Trying my best here, but I appreciate the assist.

This is going to be OK. Whoever this woman is, there's no benefit in killing kids: she just needs them to use as leverage with their parents.

Yeah. Leverage to kill.

The statement popped into her head unprompted and unwanted. The woman had taken the kids to motivate their parents to murder; she was unlikely to be too concerned with their welfare.

She needed to be quick.

As Daisy-May stepped through the doorway, she was instantly reminded of her last case with Joe. Their investigation had taken them to a secondary school science lab, and the room she'd just entered shared the same sense of formaldehyde and sterility. Something told her that it wasn't locusts or frozen mice that were stored here, though. It was something much, much worse.

Lights flared on, alerted by her presence, and she let out a cry.

It was like someone had painted a roomful of children's corpses. Boys and girls, all with their arms outstretched as if they were reaching for something unseen. They filled the space, their colours those of an exploding rainbow. Daisy-May reached out to a shimmering impression of a boy in front of her. Like someone had made a jelly mould of them, she thought, some instinct making her snatch her hand away at the last moment. Were these real kids? Was she too late?

They can't be.

I can't be.

She made her way past the children, telling herself it was just her imagination that their eyes followed her as she moved.

How did I get here? she thought. Warden of fucking purgatory, with jelly-mould ghosts and Frankenstein laboratories. Least when I was a junkie back on the soil, the world made sense. A horrible, brutal, fucked-up sort of sense, but sense all the same. I have no frame of reference for this. I don't want one.

Still, there was no point in crying about it. She was here now, and she was going to do something about this bitch who didn't glimmer.

When Daisy-May had finished with her, she'd glimmer just fine.

At the back of the room was a tunnel, bathed in red light.

Wondering what fresh hell it would lead to, she began to walk down it.

At the end of the tunnel was a room the size of a warehouse.

The ceiling, hundreds of feet up, slumped in on itself, its brutal lighting reminding Daisy-May of a chicken battery farm she'd worked on one summer. That wasn't where the inhumanity or the analogy ended.

Throughout the room, spaced three feet apart, were transparent plastic boxes, though only the briefest of glances revealed them to be cages.

Within those cages were children.

Boys and girls alike strapped to steel chairs; needles – Daisy-May counted eight in total – inserted into their arms; wires stretching from the cages to the ceiling.

All were unmoving.

Fucking monsters, thought Daisy-May. If I close my eyes then open them again, that's all they'll be, monsters in a nightmare that'll fade. These children can't have suffered on my watch. I'll open my eyes, and none of this will have been real.

She did.

It still was.

The kids were here, at least. They weren't like the jellymould monstrosities in the previous room. She was in time. She could still save them.

The boy in the cage nearest to her stirred. His eyes met Daisy-May's and he began to silently scream, in fear, in anger, in joy – it was impossible to tell which. The cry was taken up by the other children, their bound bodies shaking from their exertion, all of them making not a whisper, soundproofed ghosts in waiting, a fact only their physical form was unaware of yet.

There's no glimmer to them, thought Daisy-May. No shine. How can that be?

She walked towards the nearest cage. It had a small door carved into the front, a rash of tiny air holes above it. A handle sat at the bottom of the cage.

Dampening her feeling of nausea, Daisy-May reached for it. She pulled and it opened easily, almost as if were keen to please her.

She swallowed, ignoring the smell that wafted through, and stepped into the cage. The boy's body screamed surrender. His skin was bleached white, all trace of glimmer drained from him. He sat hunched over in the seat, muttering something she couldn't catch.

'I didn't hear you,' she said gently, leaning in.

The boy lifted his head up.

'Kill me,' he said. 'Please.'

'I'm not in the business of murder, mate,' she said. 'Got my mind set on liberation instead.' She looked over her shoulder at the other cages. 'Who took you?'

'A woman,' said the boy weakly, his skin clammy. 'She was strange. Didn't glimmer.'

Of course she didn't, thought Daisy-May. 'This woman nearby?'

He shook his head. 'Never seen her after she brought me here.'

'Have you seen a girl here? Goes by the name of Francesca.'

'Lots of girls here,' the boy croaked.

He was right.

'What else can you tell me about this woman?'

'She said my mum worked for her. That if I tried to escape, she'd hurt my mum.'

Daisy-May crouched down. 'What job did your mum do for this woman?'

The boy closed his eyes. 'She made her hurt other Dispossessed.'

She gripped the bars. 'And what's your name?'

His reply was barely a whisper. 'Eric.'

It's him. He's still alive, if you can call this living.

'Hello, Eric, I've met your mum,' she said. 'She sent me to find you. Really glad I have, mate.' She took the boy's hand and his eyes flickered with life. 'Now, I'm going to get you out of here. Where are the people in charge?'

With great effort, Eric raised his head and nodded towards a booth on the far wall. It sat roughly a hundred feet in the air, sticking out like a defiant tongue. 'Never see faces, just shadows,' he said. 'New kids that are brought in, that's where they go first, before they're put in here.'

Daisy-May smiled gratefully at him.

'I'm going to take care of them, then I'm coming back for you.'

Eric let his head drop. 'Don't leave me. Please.'

'I'll be back, I promise. I'm going to make the people who did this to you pay, then I'm going to free every last one of you.'

It was tall-as-fuck talk, Daisy-May knew, because just how she was going to make them pay was up for debate. As she walked past the last row of cages, energy seeping from her like oil from a ruptured engine, she was aware of every inch of her emaciated sixteen-year-old body. She had no idea what she was walking into, and no weapons to walk in there with.

She should go back to the compound for reinforcements, get Remus to round up the troops and come back to hit the place hard. She should wait for Mabel, at least.

Except those kids were in the cages now.

They needed help now.

Chestnut needed help now.

And I'm the bloody Warden of a realm. If the bloody Warden can't kick arse from time to time, who the hell can?

As she marched towards the door at the back of the room, she felt like a character in a fairy story, a Grimm soul whose ending would be as horribly imaginative as it would be deserved. She'd let these kids down. This had happened on her watch, but she'd make sure it ended on her watch too. Those responsible would be made to face justice.

Old Testament, wrath of God justice.

She reached the door and peered through the crack. There was a winding, dimly lit staircase and not much besides. She eased through the door, unsure whether the churn of her stomach was due to nerves, her ongoing sickness, or what she'd witnessed in the main room.

Slowly, carefully, she began to make her way up the stairs.

Daisy-May came upon another room.

There was a girl in the corner, uncaged but strapped to a chair. Her head was as slumped as her shoulders, and an IV drip ran from her arm to a piano-sized metallic object at the back of the room. The dials on the machine whirled frantically, like they were picking up a signal.

The girl jerked awake and turned her head, looking straight at Daisy-May.

Chestnut.

She was all right, or as all right as someone in those circumstances could be. She had a different complexion to the children in the cages; there was still life and glimmer to her, contrasting sharply with the dull-skinned kids downstairs.

I'm in time. She's OK. Because all that's important is my fucking conscience, obviously.

Daisy-May raised a finger to her mouth, indicating that Chestnut should be silent; then, as quietly as she could, she eased the door all the way open.

'I'm going to get you out of here,' she whispered as she crept into the room, the machine squatting behind Chestnut chugging. 'Are you hurt?'

Chestnut pointed at the IV jutting from her arm. 'Nah, since they hooked me up to this it's all been shits and giggles.'

'She's a sarky cow, this new Chestnut,' said Daisy-May, lifting the girl's arm up, and examining the IV. 'I remember the old Chestnut, who used to put flowers in my hair.'

'It's Francesca.'

She was about to reply when footsteps sounded outside, a muffled voice with them.

Terror erupted across Chestnut's face. 'She's coming back.'

Daisy-May looked desperately around the room. If there was a time for a throw-down confrontation with an unknown number of attackers, this wasn't it.

On the left-hand side of the room was a steel cabinet that ran the length of the wall. Giving thanks, on this occasion, for her spindly frame of bag and bones, Daisy-May slid open one of the doors (all the time being reminded of the sort of industrial cabinet you'd find in a hospital kitchen), then contorted herself inside it, sliding the door shut, leaving the tiniest spy crack. She noted that Chestnut had slumped down, feigning sleep or unconsciousness.

Footsteps stalked into the room, light, the steps of a ballerina. Daisy-May caught sight of a leg, but little else.

'I appreciate you trying to manage my expectations,' said a woman's voice. 'I just wish you didn't have to.'

German accent. The vowels rough, the tone laced with authority. The voice reminded Daisy-May of the Duchess, without even a hint of the warmth the former Warden of the Pen occasionally employed. The woman stood with her back to the cabinet, a smudge of a person.

A smudge that didn't glimmer.

A man's voice replied, tinny and indistinct.

'That sounds very much like an excuse,' said the woman.

The man laughed, the mucky sound of curdled milk, his reply too quiet to hear.

'You didn't create it, though, did you?' said the woman. 'My scientists on the soil did.'

A scratchy response.

'You were supposed to have secured the Pen by now. The ability to journey between it and the living world is useless until you do.'

That can't be true, thought Daisy-May. It's impossible.

A change in tone from the man. Anger now, amongst the unintelligibility.

'She's sixteen years old,' retorted the woman. 'How hard can it be?'

Daisy-May's dead blood ran ice cold.

Don't think it's too narcissistic to think she's talking about me.

A muffled reply.

'I'm not underestimating her,' said the woman, 'and I'm aware the Duchess made her the ruler of the realm for a reason. That doesn't mean she should have bested you so comfortably.'

Guess that settles it, thought Daisy-May. Only one of me.

The woman snorted, turning and finally coming into focus.

Joe was right. I didn't listen, and he was right. She doesn't glimmer. She's like the kids in the cages below. Although that's not quite right

308

either: her colour's wrong. Kind of like she's been photocopied. It's a good photocopy — photo-realistic good — but a photocopy, none the fucking less. She's just flat-out not supposed to be here.

The woman's startlingly clear blue eyes flicked to the left, and Daisy-May's heart raced as she felt them take her in.

It's just my imagination, she thought. I'm in a fucking cup-board, in the dark. No way can she see me.

The woman's eyes passed over her. 'Then get rid of her, and let's make this happen.'

As the man replied, Daisy-May noted the copper wire curled over the woman's ear. It looked almost like the spout of a miniature gramophone player.

'My work here is almost at an end,' said the woman. 'My research is complete. There are only so many children I can take before my woman-who-doesn't-glimmer legend cripples me.'

The man replied. Daisy-May cursed the fact she couldn't hear his words.

'No more excuses,' said the woman, beginning to move towards the door. 'This needs to happen tonight.'

That's my freaky, scary ice queen, thought Daisy-May as the woman walked out of the room. Clear out so we can get this rescue mission going.

She levered herself out of the cabinet as quietly as she could, cursing her trailing foot as it caught on the lip.

'One last thing,' said the woman, her silhouette lingering in the doorway. 'I've found your missing Warden.'

No, thought Daisy-May.

She launched herself forward as a gate slid down over the doorway, shutters slamming down behind her over the room's windows.

The woman smiled through the slats covering the door. 'Daisy-May, I believe.'

Daisy-May flexed her fists, anger surging through her. 'And who the fuck might you be?'

'Such language. Hardly becoming of the Warden of the Pen.'

'I say what's becoming or not,' said Daisy-May, 'and you talk mighty tall considering you've got a room full of tortured kids down below.'

'Those children are already dead,' said the woman. 'How could I possibly torture them?'

'They're souls who can feel pain as well as joy. But you know that already.'

'I know a great many things,' said the woman. 'I just don't care about most of them.'

'When I get out of here, I'm going to make you care.'

'You have spirit,' she said, nodding approvingly. 'If only that was all it took.' She turned to go.

'What are you planning?' said Daisy-May. 'What is this place? What's the purpose of these experiments you've been carrying out?'

'So many questions and so little motivation to answer them,' said the woman.

'If you've got designs on taking my job, you can fucking whistle,' said Daisy-May. 'I'd never abdicate to someone like you.'

The woman smiled like indulgence was a gift to give out. 'Oh, you will. When the time comes, you'll beg me to take the title from you. If you don't, every child in this facility will be killed. And what's more, you'll be the one to kill them.'

'This rescue fucking sucks.'

Daisy-May looked up at Chestnut, who was still bound tightly to the chair. 'Thanks for the notes, they're appreciated.'

'So how are we going to get out of here?' said Chestnut.

'Figure you've got some sort of Plan B, being the Warden and all.'

'Yeah, you would think that, wouldn't you,' said Daisy-May, wandering over to the window. She peered through the gaps in the steel shutter, looking down at the rows of cages below. There was no sign of the woman who'd imprisoned her.

She turned back to Chestnut. 'You've been a ball of attitude since I met you at the docks. What's your problem? Anyone'd think I'd left you in the Gloop rather than pulling you out of it.'

'Most of the time, I wish you had,' said Chestnut.

'Don't say that.'

'It's true. Know what it's been like for me since that day? People treat me like some sort of freak. They follow me around. Touch me, like I'm a god they could catch intelligence from. Half the crazy bastards think I can get them to fucking heaven. Not sure how, exactly, but that's what they think.'

'What was I supposed to do?' said Daisy-May. 'Just leave you in there to die?'

'You were supposed to not abandon me,' said Chestnut, vulnerability infecting her anger. 'I used to see you every day, then the Gloop happened and I didn't see you at all. Got no mum and dad here. All these Dispossessed want a piece of me, and there's no one to turn to. That's why I went to the Downs. The docks. Figured if this woman who didn't glimmer was Dying Squad, she could get me back to you.'

'You acted like you didn't give a shit when I saw you at the docks,' said Daisy-May.

'Pissed off at you, wasn't I?' said Chestnut. 'What was I supposed to be like? Happy 'cos you finally showed up? I liked what she had to say. She actually listened to me. Respected me.'

Daisy-May looked down. 'I'm sorry. This job I've been given's massive, and I'm small as fuck.'

'Bigger than me, though.'

'Keep growing like that, and I won't be for long,' said Daisy-May with a smile. 'You *are* growing, right? You seem older, but you look it, too.'

Chestnut shrugged her shoulders. 'I'm just me.'

You're more than that, thought Daisy-May. Just like I am. Wonder what that means.

'So?' said Chestnut. 'What's the plan?'

Right. Because as fascinating as Chestnut's backstory is, we're still trapped here.

Could what the woman who didn't glimmer said be true? Could the living now travel to the Pen? The repercussions were staggering if so. Why, if the information became public knowledge, if the afterlife became a documented fact rather than a place of belief and faith, that knowledge would make the Dispossessed's revolt look like a playground scrap. Daisy-May had had plenty of those fights in her soil days, but they'd rarely ended with the collapse of the Judaeo-Christian belief system.

She rested her forehead against the wire mesh, flicking the surface with her finger.

'You all right, Warden?' said Chestnut. 'You look fucking peaky.'

Nope, I'm not, Daisy-May thought. Something in me broke when I came through the Gloop, and it hasn't come close to being fixed. Not even sure it *can* be fixed. Mabel's drugs helped for a bit, but I think what I've got goes beyond cough medicine. I think what I've got only ends one way.

That blonde cow should have cooled her jets. In a few weeks, she would have become Warden without having to lift a finger.

That's a few weeks, and this is now: what exactly are you going to do about now?

That was what the Duchess would have said, and Daisy-May wouldn't have had an answer for her, just as she didn't have an answer for Chestnut, or the gang leader's missing son in the cage below.

I don't know, she thought, *because I'm young, and I'm stupid, and I'm sick, and I have no idea what I'm going to do next.*

She'd played her hand.

She'd lost.

'You hear that?' said Chestnut.

Daisy-May frowned, her ears pricking up. She *did* hear something, an almost subliminal buzz in the distance. They both turned to the door, their ears straining along with their curiosity.

The buzzing got louder.

'You think this is a good thing or a bad thing?' said Chestnut.

'Things can't get any worse,' said Daisy-May. 'Which usually means they will.'

They waited impatiently.

Then, finally, they saw it.

A swarm of insects were gliding down the corridor, perfectly in formation and heading straight for them.

'Fucking hate wasps,' said Chestnut.

'They're not wasps,' said Daisy-May, a dare-to-hope smile on her face.

The buzzing became louder and a mass of scarab beetles slipped between the bars and into the room. They hovered in the centre, almost as if they were weighing up their next option, then headed en masse for the back wall, coalescing together on it.

'That a face?' said Chestnut, wonder in her voice.

'Yep,' said Daisy-May. 'One I've never been happier to see.'

The scarab beetles settled, and the impression of Mabel could be clearly seen within them.

'That's the old woman from the hot air balloon,' said Chestnut. 'The one who saved me.'

313

Daisy-May nodded.

The insects began moving again, crawling and chivvying for space on the wall. As they did so, letters began to form along with the smile on Daisy-May's face.

'*Be ready*,' Chestnut read out. 'What's that mean?'

'It means that help's on its way,' said Daisy-May, grinning. 'And woe-be-fucking-tide anything that gets in its way.'

Chapter Nineteen

Joe weaved unseen between Oxford Road's early-morning stragglers. There was still a pleasant buzz at the city's student ground zero as the sun peeked out from behind its nightly veil. No fights, or the rumblings of them, no cross words or angry fists. A reminder that the living world and those within it were capable of peace, and that peace was worth fighting for.

Megan Veins was worth fighting for.

Joe passed through the children's hospital's closed front doors. This wasn't a take-all-comers infirmary; it was a place where sick children would be transferred after their condition had been assessed elsewhere. There was no one around, save for a couple of nurses on the front desk, and a bored security guard. Their lack of urgency annoyed Joe; didn't they know there was a missing girl out there? Why didn't that fact plague them, make their skin crawl with panic? How could they look so unaffected?

He checked himself. *Because they don't know her. Because it didn't happen to them. Because if you lost your shit at every bad news story, the only position you'd ever be in is the foetal one.*

Because it's not their job to be affected by it. It's mine.

Joe found the Generation Killer's only living survivor on the building's top floor.

The other wards had contained little more than fitfully sleeping children and a few anxiety-ridden parents, but when he reached the building's peak, and saw how it had been cleared of beds and human beings, he understood why the boy had been isolated from the general hospital population.

Tony Fisher, Megan Veins' last, best hope, was in a radiation tent.

It wasn't quite as dramatic as Stanley Veins in his underground fallout bunker, but it still made an impression. Tony was propped up in bed, his face bathed in light from the TV suspended above him. He stared up at it, occasionally looking down at the table that jutted across his bed, where he appeared to be sketching something. Dozens of sheets of paper were stuck to the wall behind him, shrouded in darkness, their pencil lines vaguely visible.

Technology sprouted from the boy's arms and chest, a slow, patient *beep* shattering the silence. A woman slept on a small metallic cot several feet away. His mother, Joe presumed.

Has to kill her, not being able to touch her son because of the radiation. Hold him. Comfort him. It's another form of torture. Hasn't she had enough? Hasn't Tony?

Joe crept in, not wanting to draw attention to himself yet. There was a good chance Tony wouldn't be able to see him at all, but if he could, he didn't want to spook him. As he walked forward, he seemed to grow stronger the closer he got to the radiation. It had been one thing when the source of that radiation had been the already dead Stanley Veins, but it made Joe feel guilty here: it felt like he was stealing life force from the boy.

There was a seat next to the radiation tent, and Joe sank into it. How many hours had Tony's mother sat here? Cursing the Generation Killer? Mourning the loss of her inexplicably murdered father while being drip-fed the slow-motion death of her son? By the look of Tony, it was a death that now hunted for him thirstily; the boy was a bundle of grey skin and jutting bones, his brittle chest rising and falling, the pencil in his hand a blur, despite his fluttering eyelids.

Is he close enough to death to see me? Because if he isn't — or he simply can't — this lead is dead, and Megan Veins with it. This boy was taken by the Generation Killer. He remembers something. I know it in my gut.

'Tony?'

The boy's eyelids fluttered, but there was no sign that he'd heard.

'Tony.'

Louder. More authoritative. Same lack of response.

Then Joe noticed the headphones. Two small black buds wedged deep inside the boy's ears. Maybe he just hadn't heard him. Maybe there was still a chance.

He leaned forward, his arm poised at the edge of the tent's plastic shell. *Don't want to scare him. Better he thinks I'm a real-life, flesh-and-blood bloke rather than a supernatural copper, and real-life blokes can't stick their hands through isolation tents.*

He got to his feet and walked round to the front of the tent. He waved at the boy.

This time, there was a reaction.

Tony blinked, almost as if he'd imagined the man in front of him, then yelped in surprise, although it was really more of a startled croak.

The woman on the cot stirred.

'It's OK,' whispered Joe, raising his hands to quieten the boy. 'Let's not wake your mum.'

'Who are you?' croaked Tony.

'I'm a policeman,' said Joe. 'One of the nice ones.'

Tony said nothing, closing his eyes. 'I'm sick of policemen.'

'I don't blame you,' said Joe. 'I get sick of them too.'

He returned to the seat beside the bed. He needed information quickly, but this boy screamed slow and steady. He needed to be handled with finesse, and with patience.

Joe had never been blessed with either.

He looked up at the TV screen. The movie playing on it made him smile; there was nothing like irony, especially when it was this delicious. 'Have you seen *The Sixth Sense* before?'

Tony nodded. 'A hundred and fifty-six times.'

Joe laughed. 'That's impressive. I think.'

'It was my grandad's favourite. We always watched it together when I stayed over.'

Tony carried on watching the film, the pencil in his hand moving over the paper, almost as if he were sketching from instinct.

'Loved ghosts, my grandad. Always made up stories about them, even when I was young. Although they never really felt like stories. Always felt real.'

Joe shifted in his seat, leaning forward a little. 'How do you mean?'

'He said that in real life, there were people like the boy in this film. Ones who could see dead people.'

Joe watched the screen. A man hung from the ceiling, a small boy wincing in horror at the sight.

'Grandad said the film got some things wrong, though. In the film, ghosts don't know they're dead, and they can't see other ghosts. But in real life, that's different. They can see each other. Talk to each other. Then one day I began to see dead people. They'd talk to me. I'd talk to them. And I realised my grandad was, like, preparing me for it.'

'Huh.' Joe looked down at the boy's right hand, which continued to score the piece of paper. Three bars were etched into the skin.

Like Stanley Veins. Like all the other kids and adults in the photos.

'He sounds like a cool bloke, your grandad.'

'He's dead.'

'I'm sorry to hear that.'

'I'll be dead soon as well.'

'I'm sorry to hear that too.'

'You're here about me being kidnapped.'

Not a question, thought Joe. More a statement of fact. 'I know you find it hard to remember what happened.'

'Still can't remember, not really. I have dreams, though. 'Cept they're more like nightmares.'

'What do you see in these nightmares?' Joe asked, his voice level.

Tony closed his eyes. He stopped sketching, letting the pencil drop. 'I see the monster that took me.'

The space Bits had described as a soup kitchen looked different in the daylight.

Bits supposed that this was for the better, though the light that slashed its way through the room's solitary nod to a window highlighted unflatteringly the paucity of the facilities. The row of camp beds looked even more grimy and unloved than under the light of the scarab beetles, and a family of rats patrolled the space, seemingly without fear. His grandad didn't seem to mind the humble surroundings, though: he was deep in conversation with a couple of elderly women, a smile on his face and a twinkle in his eye.

'How's your investigation going?' asked Elias.

'You'd have to ask my cunt of a partner.'

'You gentleman have had a disagreement?'

'Polite word for it.'

'What would an impolite word for it be?' said Elias, smiling.

'That we had a fucking barney 'cos he didn't think we should execute a child-abusing piece of filth and I did. *I did* won.'

Elias looked at Bits curiously. 'You're talking about the man of vines. At the Lads Club in Salford.'

'Flowery name for a paedo monster, but yeah, I am.'

'My job – my purpose – is to care for people,' said Elias. 'Give them comfort where I can. The man you killed should have been a soul under my care, but he was perhaps the most truly lost man I've ever met. For what it's worth, I think you did the right thing.'

Bits smiled as his grandad looked over and gave him a thumbs-up.

'I'll take good care of him,' said Elias. 'Visit whenever you like.'

Bits looked at the watch on his wrist that spun ever forwards. 'Time's running out to solve this thing. If we don't do that soon, you'll be spoon-feeding me gum along with my grandad.'

'Do you know where your partner will be?' asked Elias.

'Knee-fucking-deep in worthiness,' said Bits. 'I'll probably check out that Rylands library first, though.'

Elias looked at him, concerned. 'Your eyes seem a little unclear.'

Bits blinked. 'Memory's going. Almost two hours since I had a hit.'

Elias nodded gravely. 'I have something to help you with that. Follow me.'

Joe leaned forward in his seat. 'This monster,' he said. 'The one you see in your nightmares. The one that took you. What does it look like?'

The boy didn't reply. His eyelids remained closed, his face sporadically twitching in pain.

'Tony,' said Joe, louder than he wanted. 'Wake up.'

The boy's eyelids opened.

Joe hated waking him up, hated the pain on his face even more. Tony's life had been taken already, though, stolen by the Generation Killer weeks ago. Megan Veins' life was still her own.

At least he hoped it was.

'I need to know about the monster, Tony. The one in your dreams. What does it look like?'

'Not it . . .' said Tony. 'He.'

His eyes closed.

The heart monitor began to scream.

No, thought Joe. No, not yet.

Elias led Bits to the bar area. Behind it was a metal oxygen canister with a rubber mask hanging off it.

'This is an invention of my own,' he said proudly. 'A purer concentration than the substance you've been putting into your veins. More organic.'

'All about healthy living, me,' said Bits, taking the face mask from him. 'Hit me.'

Elias turned a dial on the canister, and Bits heard the sound of gas escaping. It was as if some unseen figure had flicked his brain; thoughts and memories pinged into crystal-clear clarity, energising and renewing him.

What have we been messing around with needles for? he asked himself. This is the real shit.

The woman on the metal cot screamed.

Nurses ran in.

Tony lay deathly still.

Joe yelled his name again and again, but he knew it was no good.

The boy was gone. And there was no spirit left behind. He'd already passed on.

To the Next Place, if there's any justice. Longer I do this job, the more it feels like there isn't, though.

There'd been a man in his nightmares, Tony had said. Not a monster, but a man.

The boy's mother sobbed as a nurse tried to console her. The second nurse checked the heart monitor, but its insistent screech suggested there wasn't much to check.

Not a monster, but a man.

Joe frowned, seeing properly for the first time the piece of paper the boy had been drawing on. He had dismissed it as mindless scribbling – Tony hadn't even looked at the page most of the time – but the closer he got, the more he saw it had been anything but.

It was an intricately sketched drawing of a man.

No, thought Joe.

It isn't possible.

Bits was having a bad trip.

The gas Elias had given him had brought clarity to begin with, but now it brought only confusion and nausea. The room had become muddy, Elias little more than a smudgy one-armed puppet.

Bits yanked the mask away.

His knees buckled.

The ground gave way beneath him.

He lay on his back, his throat constricting, his body useless.

'Help,' he croaked. 'Help.'

Joe stared at the picture next to Tony's lifeless body.

It showed a man with a long mane of hair and a thick military-style coat. The boy had coloured the coat in black, the pencil strokes so thick they'd almost scored through the paper.

The man's right arm reached out, an effect so lifelike it looked like he was reaching off the page.

His left arm didn't exist. The sleeve was empty, pinned to his coat.

Joe rose from the chair, walking to the back wall and its tapestry of sketches. He'd dismissed those at first glance too, blanketed as they were in darkness. The closer he got, though, the better he could see them. A few were of superheroes, others of robots and footballers.

Most – at least half – were of a man with long hair.

Long hair and one arm.

Elias.

He sank against the wall.

The drawings are of Elias.

He closed his eyes, unable to accept it.

The man from Tony's nightmare, the one who kidnapped him, is Elias.

Bit's vision began swimming in and out.

Elias crouched down next to him, a strange smile on his lips.

'You shouldn't have come back,' he said.

It was the last thing Bits heard.

Chapter Twenty

'You must have seen some sights in the Pen.'

'Like you wouldn't believe.'

'Anything like this, though?'

'No,' the Duchess admitted. 'Nothing like this.'

Hatoyama had driven them through the power plant's exclusion zone without interference or, indeed, the sight of a single living soul. Animal carcasses were another matter; their skeletal remains formed a macabre guard of honour as the car had slowly rolled towards the punch-drunk facility.

It was the vehicles and scatter-fire debris that made the real impression, though. The Duchess saw the twisted shell of a school bus, as well as a collection of objects so random it was like a bomb had detonated in a film's prop department. Bikes, pushchairs and garden furniture were all strewn before them, a sailing boat the cherry on the displaced cake. It sat smack in the middle of the road, as if patiently waiting for a surge of water to ferry it away to safety.

'Heard rumours of this,' said Hatoyama. 'When the tsunami hit, cows ended up in trees, trees ended up on roofs, roofs ended up in—'

'I get the idea,' said the Duchess.

Hatoyama killed the car's engine.

They sat in silence, the only noise the odd creak of metal in the poisoned wind.

'Nature's a savage beast when riled.'

'It takes a lot to rile her,' said Hatoyama. 'Although I'm the first to admit that the human race is a lot.'

'I didn't think I'd miss the Pen when I left it,' said the Duchess. 'This place, here and now, has made a liar of me. It's as if the air itself is damaged. Unable to heal.'

Which was in stark contrast to her physical condition. She couldn't deny it: the closer she got to the reactor, the more energised she felt. The poison in the air was repairing her somehow. Long-term, that couldn't be a good thing. Until she'd stopped Hanna, she'd settle for its short-term benefits.

Hatoyama looked down at the bolt-cutter resting on his lap. 'It's a pity we don't have two of these.'

'That's all right,' said the Duchess. 'Guns aren't really my style.'

'You think Hanna will have help here?'

'Yes.' She turned to him. 'Before we walk into certain death, I have a last request. I want you to tell me what happened between you and Mabel. What was so bad that it ruined your career? She's been unwilling – or unable – to talk about it. I only saw the fallout, not what caused it.'

Hatoyama began playing with his bolo tie, wrapping the weathered leather around his finger, wrestling with the question, determining whether he should submit to it.

Finally he spoke.

'Osaka was under siege when I first met Mabel. Over thirty women murdered, their corpses covered head to toe in paint. The post-mortems showed it was paint that had killed them too. They'd been forced to drink it.'

'Unimaginable,' said the Duchess.

'There seemed to be no pattern to the killings,' continued

Hatoyama, his voice distant. 'The women were from every walk of life, some young, some old, some poor, some rich. In the deaths we linked to the Painter – the press's name for him, not mine – we never discovered a single shred of physical evidence. It was when the thirtieth body turned up that Mabel got involved.'

The Duchess nodded. 'I was most reluctant to approve the transfer, but the edict came down from on high. We all have superintendents to answer to, Detective.'

'Thing is, I *wasn't* reluctant,' said Hatoyama. 'I saw the benefits. She could go to places I couldn't. She didn't need warrants, and she didn't need to play politics. And she had a nose for it. She's smart, Mabel.'

'Her mouth certainly is.'

'We walk the old crime scenes, because I'm hoping she'll find something us flesh-and-blooders missed, and that's when we get our break. A girl gets snatched from a nearby park and bundled into a car by a man in his early twenties. She somehow manages to escape, raises the alarm. This is it. I can feel it.'

He picked at a stray stitch on the steering wheel.

'The suspect's vehicle is parked in Southern Higashiyama. We pile in, arresting the remarkably calm gentleman sitting in his car. He's listening to a baseball game, looking like he's ditched every care he ever had. On the way to the station, we discover his name is Tuko Yakomoto. Means nothing to Mabel, but plenty to me; his father's a millionaire who controls every branch of Kyoto's media, as well as having influence in our department.

'Within an hour of reaching the station – and without us having asked a single question – Yakomoto's lawyer swoops in and swoops his client out. Threats of wrongful arrest are bandied about and Yakomoto, despite matching the description the girl gave to a T, is free to go. Know what my biggest problem with this is?'

The Duchess didn't.

'He confessed to us in the car. He gave us details about the murders only the killer could have known, times, places and facets of the deaths that hadn't been released to the public. The superintendent didn't want to know. It was above his pay grade to go against the financial might of the Yakomoto clan, no matter what confession had been made in the back of a police car. Me and Mabel, well, we couldn't let that stand. I knew we'd never get a search warrant for Yakomoto's house, but who needs one when you've got a ghost as a partner? Mabel would go in, thoroughly case the joint, and report back.'

He turned to look at the Duchess. 'The rest, I can only go by what Mabel told me later, before she ran. She searches the place. Finds nothing but trust-fund knick-knacks. She's about to leave when she hears a scream. Parched, raw, and undeniably coming from a woman.

'There's a cast-iron door at the back of the house, and as Mabel passes through it, the screams get louder, but no easier to hear. She walks down two dozen steps in darkness so total, she tells me it's like descending to the Pit. When she reaches the bottom, it takes her eyes several moments to adjust to the darkness. Her ears don't need that long; the woman keeps up a steady stream of *help me* pleas. Then, just as her eyes hunt out an outline of a human being in the darkness, the room is scorched in light.

'Yakomoto's standing at the top of the stairs, but it's the woman tied to a metal bench in the centre of the room who gets Mabel's attention. She's naked except for the paint that's been daubed on her hands and feet, like she's been marked for death.

'Mabel's torn. If she rushes to fetch me, she leaves the girl de-fenceless. What can she do if she stays, though? You physically interfere with the living world, you end up in the Pit. Then she realises Yakomoto means to kill the girl, and although hell will be waiting for her if she interferes, watching him kill her then living with the consequences would be its own type of hell.

'So she knocks him out. She tells me where I can find the woman, and she runs. I storm the premises and find the kidnapped girl just where Mabel said she'd be. She's terrified out of her mind and has borderline malnutrition, but she's physically unscathed. I call it in. My colleagues arrive. Yakomoto is arrested.'

'The hero cop saves the day,' said the Duchess.

'Hardly,' said Hatoyama bitterly, blowing a cloud of smoke out of the window. 'You don't understand how powerful Yakomoto's father is. Ultimately, he couldn't fight the charges – the kid had literal red hands from the paint he'd applied to the woman's body – but he could make sure he ruined my life. I faced disciplinary charges for unauthorised entry to the property, and much of the evidence was inadmissible because I didn't have a warrant. There was also the small matter of how I knew the woman was down there. *A ghost told me* was a surprisingly flimsy explanation.'

'You must have had your defenders,' said the Duchess. 'You caught a serial killer, for goodness' sake.'

Hatoyama nodded, digging out another cigarette from its pack like he held it responsible. 'That was what saved me. When it leaked that I faced expulsion from the force, even Yakomoto's father couldn't spin the narrative aggressively enough against me. I survived, if you can call this surviving. I think of it as his drip-feed revenge.'

'What happened to Yakomoto?' the Duchess asked. 'I assume he was executed.'

'Do you?' said Hatoyama. 'Well you'd be wrong. I had no search warrant. We had no reason in the world to be there. He received a conviction for kidnapping, for which he served two whole years in a cushy hospital, on the grounds of diminished responsibility. The last I heard he was living in a penthouse apartment in Tokyo. You should see where I live. Even the rats shun it.'

He considered lighting the cigarette, instead returning it to the pack.

They sat in silence, which Hatoyama eventually broke. 'Mabel went to hell for helping me?'

The Duchess nodded. 'I was able to free her eventually, but she suffered a great deal before I could. Not all of her came back from the Pit.'

Finally having the missing piece of Mabel's story couldn't change what had happened, but the Duchess felt it bridge something between her and her sister.

Lay the foundations to bridge it, at least.

'I never got to say thank you,' said Hatoyama.

'Say it now,' said the Duchess, 'by helping me take Hanna down. I may not know what her intentions are yet, but if it involves this reactor, it's bad news for everyone in this city.'

'How bad can they be?' said Hatoyama. 'It's been shut down.'

'I think your hunch is right. I believe Hanna intends to re-activate it,' the Duchess replied. 'Think about it: she's got the former lead technician of the plant, along with Arata's micro-chip and this Dog Catcher blocking device. I don't pretend to know how she's going to fire the reactor back up, but I wager that's her intention.'

'We have to stop her then,' said Hatoyama.

'Yes,' said the Duchess. 'We do.'

The crushing silence reminded the Duchess of the Sea of Trees. Like there, she had the feeling of being watched, unseen eyes inspecting them as they walked towards the reactor. Its smelted steel splayed outwards, reaching for the sky as if seeking refuge in it.

'How many souls were lost when the tsunami hit?' she asked.

'Thousands,' said Hatoyama.

'And when the reactor fell to it?'

'That's not something that was made public.'

'Why not?'

'Because the government doesn't know. They're unlikely to ever know. How do you quantify how many people drank irradiated water? Breathed radiation-stained air? It may be many years before the first cancerous symptoms begin to show. A disaster like the one that happened here isn't showy. It's slow-burn.'

'My sister doesn't have the patience for slow-burn,' said the Duchess.

Two white pylons stretched out above their heads, relatively unscarred and highlighting two gashes in the structure that faced them. One branched left, one right.

'You're going to say something stupid like *let's split up*, aren't you?' said Hatoyama.

'Time is of the essence; we'll cover twice the distance that way,' said the Duchess. 'It's the obvious course of action.'

'It's the suicidal course of action, but that seems to be about par for the course when it comes to you.'

She offered a small smile.

'They don't call it the Living Squad, Detective.'

'They're here.'

Hanna looked up, away from the wall-sized control room with its newly blinking lights and freshly whirling dials.

'Who's here?'

'Your sister,' said the lookout, 'and the soil detective.'

She did survive, then, thought Hanna. Good old Rachel. 'There's only two of them? I'm almost insulted.'

'The detective has a weapon.'

'And my sister has her Warden power, at least what's left of it. It won't be enough. The reactor's cooking nicely. There's just my state of the union address to make, and then we're done here.'

'Will you deal with your sister first?' said the underling.

'No,' said Hanna, smiling. 'I think I'll leave that to our new friend.'

Hatoyama couldn't decide whether he liked the silence or feared it. He liked that no one was trying to slit his throat or shoot at him, but he trusted his gut when it told him that neither of those things was far away. In a way, he'd welcome them. The anticipation was almost worse than the reality.

Still, he had a gun in his hand and a Western shoot-out gait to his walk, and he was making a difference. Better to die quickly here from radiation poisoning and a heroically stupid last stand than rot like a coward in his basement office, a figure of ridicule and not much else.

The wind whispered.

He turned quickly, finger on trigger, to nothing.

An afterburn trail of a giggle, perhaps. A cough from an irradiated rat. Nothing more.

He inched forward, the path he was walking down narrowing with each step. Parts of it looked almost man-made, as if human hands had taken the radiation-blistered metal and bent it into a walkway.

Or a slaughterhouse chute. Cattle never know they're being led to their death until they see the knife. Is that what Hanna's doing? Corralling us into the abattoir?

A sound came from ahead.

Hatoyama looked up.

Three men and one woman, their hair unkempt, their

robes flowing, strange hooded caps adorning their heads. Each wielded a large rip-taut bow, a chiselled arrow resting snugly against it.

There's something of the forest about them, he thought. Something ancient and wild. Not wild enough to be untameable, though, if they're here in the service of Hanna.

'Turn back, soil breather,' said the man at the front, his Japanese decipherable even if his accent was so heavy it almost consumed the words within it. 'Turn back, or it will end badly for you.'

Hatoyama reached out with his left hand, steadying his bolt-cutter-wielding right.

'Stand down. I have Dying Squad dispensation.'

The man at the front turned to the others and nodded. They shifted slightly to the left, lowering their bow and arrows, allowing a sliver of space in the narrow walkway.

Maybe I'm going to get away with this, thought Hatoyama, his grip on his gun loosening a little. Maybe they respect the rule of law. Or respect getting blasted out of existence at least.

Then he saw why they'd stepped aside.

Crouched at the back was a teenage boy holding a long cylindrical object. If it hadn't been for its wooden exterior, Hatoyama could have believed it was a rocket launcher.

I may have underestimated their respect for the rule of law, he thought, as the end of the device exploded.

The Duchess didn't know why she was feeling stronger, only that she was. Every step she took further into the reactor seemed to breathe life into her undead cells. Perhaps it was the adrenaline. Perhaps it was being in the field rather than just barking orders from behind a desk, but she felt empowered. Certainly she felt ready to take on Hanna's followers.

What about Hanna herself, though? said Oma Jankie. *Do you feel up to facing her?*

'Let's hope I have the chance to find out,' said the Duchess, striding towards the reactor's ruptured entrance.

The advantage of not existing in a physical sense was that mountains of smelted debris were really just life-sized balloons, waiting to be walked through. It wasn't as if the experience was pleasant, but it wasn't as if it was new either. The Duchess had been dead far longer than she'd been alive, and so was well used to the disconcerting prickle that came from walking through walls. Or in this case, radiation-soaked slag heaps.

She gave an inward shudder as she passed quickly through them, the dark total except for the odd shaft of daylight elbowing its way through, revealing skeletal remains untouched since the original reactor meltdown.

What was Hanna's play here?

When she returned to the Pen, it had been her younger sister's intention to take over the realm, and the revolution she'd inspired amongst the Dispossessed had meant she'd almost succeeded. Mass murder – which was what, essentially, reactivating the reactor would be if Hatoyama's theory was correct – didn't seem to fit her win-hearts-and-minds MO.

Maybe she doesn't want to win hearts and minds, said Oma Jankie. *Maybe she's seen enough of heaven, and of hell, and of the soil to believe that they should be razed to the ground. She has a point, no?*

That's not her decision to make, thought the Duchess. No one made her judge, jury and executioner of the human race.

It's not a job you apply for, said Oma Jankie, *it's one you reach out and take. Hanna is ambitious, and she's clever. There are worse traits to have when reaching for immortality.*

You'd certainly know, thought the Duchess, as she finally passed through the last of the debris and dropped into the guts of the power plant.

The room was enormous, a cathedral-sized shrine to the folly of man, the devastation it displayed suggesting nature had punished it for that folly. Steel girders were splattered over the structure's curved roof, and a steady stream of water sloshed its way around the floor far below it, reaching the Duchess's knees. At the back of the room was a large cylindrical tube that stretched halfway towards the ceiling. Yellow ladders covered each side, all of them ending their journey before they reached the top, because there wasn't a top, at least not any more; it had been ripped clean off, a few steel splinters left and not very much besides.

This must be one of the damaged reactors, thought the Duchess. One the government shut down as soon as they realised the extent of the damage.

Do you think? cackled Oma Jankie. *With a steel trap of a mind like that, it's a miracle you haven't caught Hanna already.*

The Duchess ignored her, despite the truth of her words.

Hanna wasn't here.

In his thirty-five years of service in the job, it was the first time Hatoyama had been fired upon. He'd always assumed the day would never come – certainly he'd never craved it – but the fact that it came from an ancient gunpowder-fuelled *bohiya* rather than a conventional handgun or semi-automatic gave him a strange sense of pride.

Admittedly, that pride ended when his suit jacket caught fire.

The teenage boy had aimed the weapon at him like it was a bow and arrow, but it was old-fashioned flame and gunpowder that propelled the petrol rocket. It landed just a few inches away from him, immediately exploding into hungry, grasping flame.

Hatoyama fell to the floor, instinct rolling him over onto the blaze that was threatening to devour his arm. Seeing a small canopy of steel behind him, he scrabbled backwards, throwing himself under it just as another rocket landed above his head, raining fire. Sheltering under the metal lip, he inspected his arm. His leather sleeve was blackened, but he'd managed to put the flames out before they'd done too much damage. That was the good news.

The bad was that he'd dropped the bolt-cutter. The weapon lay several feet away, exposed in the middle of the path.

He cursed himself. Better to have singed skin and a gun than all his arm hair and nothing to fight back with.

This is the consequence of the Xylophone Man's death then, he thought. The dead taking pot shots at the living.

He stared at the dropped bolt-cutter, willing it closer.

It was a mistake splitting up. All I'm doing is providing these devils with target practice. That might be enough, because if they're firing at me, they're not firing at the Duchess. Maybe this will help clear a path for her.

Maybe that was her plan all along.

He glared again at his fallen weapon. To clear that path, he needed to do more than be a human pincushion.

You can make it, he told himself. Dive, roll, fire, just like they taught you at the academy. The academy may have been thirty years ago, and nowadays your paunch has a paunch, but fuck it: you're a Japanese cowboy who has truth and justice on his side. What could go wrong?

On five.

Four.

Three.

Two.

One.

Hatoyama dived rather than rolled, lurching for the stricken bolt-cutter, his hand closing round it just in time for him to scream out in pain as an arrow pierced his wrist, skewering it to the irradiated ground. One of the archers stood there, already reaching for another arrow, his colleague training one at Hatoyama's midriff, another reloading his ancient rocket launcher.

White-hot pain gave Hatoyama focus. He grabbed the bolt-cutter with his uninjured left hand, raising it up and firing, the kick almost jerking the weapon from his hand. He got as lucky as a terminally ill man with an arrow sticking out of his hand could get: the blast hit the archer who was preparing to fire, the air sizzling as it wrenched him from existence. His forged-on-the soil arrow dropped to the floor, almost as if it had never been held at all.

Hatoyama ripped the arrow from his hand, yowling with pain, another whizzing by his shoulder, just missing. Blood he couldn't feel flowed as he lurched for the gun, a fire rocket exploding over his head, showering him in gasoline and embers.

Tightening his grip on the gun, he tried to size up a target through the haze of pain and smoke, and fired once more, not caring which of his attackers he hit, as long as he hit *something*. Someone gargled pain, then disappeared.

Hatoyama rolled back to the metal lip as another arrow thudded into his knee.

He took it as bad news that he barely felt it.

Chapter Twenty-One

Death didn't give a fuck. This was the universal truth Daisy-May had discovered. It was the last truly democratic thing. It didn't matter how much money you had, how thick a wall you built against it, or how bloody-minded you were when it came to the concept of mortality. When it was your time, it was your time, and that was as true if you were a duchess or a member of the Dispossessed.

Was it her time? As she festered in her cell, was her female jailer planning on scrubbing her clean from existence? What about the children in the cages in the laboratory below? If the boy she'd spoken to was typical, they craved death, because death meant they were freed from pain. Maybe they were onto something. Maybe all this struggle wasn't worth the effort. Struggle was all her soil life had been, and all this one had been too.

But then there was Chestnut, a girl who reminded Daisy-May of herself before the responsibility and the burden. She had fire in her eyes and rebellion in her soul. Chestnut wasn't ready for death. Would spit in its face if it came for her, then shoe it in the nuts for good measure.

There was the caged boy downstairs too. Eric. She'd promised his mum that she'd bring him back. She intended to honour that promise.

And there was Mabel. *Be ready*, that was what the scarab beetles had said. *Be ready*.

'When's this rescue coming then?'

'Always thought I was anorexic when it came to patience,' said Daisy-May, turning to Chestnut. 'You're fucking bulimic.'

'Lovely comment, that,' said Chestnut. 'Very statesmanlike.'

Daisy-May gave her the finger.

'Knew I shouldn't trust you Dying Squadders,' said Chestnut. 'Great talkers, but nowhere to be seen when the chips are in the shit.'

'That's not the expression.'

'It's *my* expression.'

'Look, it's going to be all right,' said Daisy-May. 'Mabel's got *mad* gadgets. Our worrying days are over.'

Chestnut snorted. 'She's anything like you, maybe she can talk 'em to death.'

Daisy-May bit back her reply. It wasn't so long ago that she'd been this girl, hiding behind quips and insults when all she really felt was fear and awe.

Then again, it could just be that Chestnut had turned into an arsehole.

'What I don't get is how you couldn't see this coming,' said Chestnut. 'That blonde cow looks like a Nazi nurse.'

'That *I* couldn't see it coming? You went with her after I warned you she was dangerous. You were supposed to come get me.'

'You were supposed to have my back,' said Chestnut.

'I'm not saying I haven't fucked up,' said Daisy-May. 'I'm just trying to do my best. All of this is new to me.'

'Brilliant. I get the deity with training wheels.'

Daisy-May closed her eyes, trying to tune out Chestnut's barbs, and visualised the gate in front of her. By rights, all she should need to do was raise a hand and rip it from its frame. She'd made the rocks move. She could do this.

'Warden.'

She looked up to see the blonde woman at the mesh gate, a playful smile on her face.

'Not sure whether I should be honoured you're still calling me that, or insulted.'

'I'll refer to you by your official title for as long as you hold it,' said the woman. She grinned, revealing bleached white teeth. 'Admittedly that won't be for very long.'

If you try anything, the girl dies.

That was what the blonde cow (called, of all things, Lucia – Daisy-May had had her down as a Helga) had said shortly before releasing her, and Daisy-May had no reason to disbelieve her; the laboratory with the caged children was proof enough of that. So although it was tempting to slam the woman into the nearest wall, it would also have been foolish. She needed to bide her time and wait for Mabel.

Once they'd left her temporary prison, she'd been led down a seemingly endless concrete corridor lit only by dumb slabs of lights on the walls. It reminded Daisy-May of an underground dungeon, the sort a government might use when they were under attack.

'You'll be happier, you know, when you renounce your title,' said Lucia. 'The Duchess did you a great injustice when she foisted it upon you.'

'Yeah, but the point is it was her injustice to foist,' said Daisy-May. 'It ain't yours to foist back.'

'You're a child. You wouldn't understand.'

'Body might be young, but my soul's old as fuck. I'd understand things you wouldn't have the first clue about. It was the point of picking me. New blood, that's what the Duchess said.'

'It's your blood that's the problem.'

A wave of tiredness and nausea hit Daisy-May. She stopped, leaning against the door, catching her breath. 'Nothing wrong with my blood. Pure Nottingham lionheart, me.'

'I don't refer to the unworthiness of your lineage,' said Lucia, 'as utterly unworthy as that is. No, I refer to your condition.'

Daisy-May stood a little taller, squashing down the pain. 'What are you chatting about? I'm fit as a fucking fiddle.'

'You're dying.'

She winced. 'I'm already dead, love.'

'Your soil body is, and your soul will soon follow. You have your precious Duchess to thank for that.'

'Don't know what you're talking about.'

'The Dispossessed I smuggled through the Gloop needed deep-sea diving suits; you did it without an oxygen tank. I'd give you another week, if that.'

'Thanks for your concern,' said Daisy-May, 'but I'll see you into your grave before hopping into my own.'

'Defiant to the last,' said Lucia. 'I respect that.'

Daisy-May considered her coolly. 'How about translating that respect into some answers? Figure I'm owed some.'

Lucia shrugged. 'Why not? They won't do you a lot of good now.'

'I know you're behind smuggling Dispossessed through to the soil. Know you've been inciting them to cut each other to bits, and know you've been experimenting on these kids, too. What I don't get is *why* you're doing any of it.'

'You don't want to ask me that,' said Lucia.

'Don't I?' said Daisy-May.

Lucia shook her head. 'Because I could give you a dozen different answers. I'm doing it for research. For financial gain. To understand the Dispossessed's increased intelligence and the potential for that intelligence to grow further. For the greater good of scientific exploration – I could cite the moon landing, and the other technologies that came out of it, such as water purification and polymer fabric. Goodness, I could say it was to simply see what would happen. All are true; none help you. No, *you* want to ask me about the Generation Killer.'

Daisy-May's polluted blood ran cold. 'How do you know about the Generation Killer?'

'Oh darling,' Lucia said, smiling warmly. 'I made him.'

The film had changed.

Megan almost didn't notice at first, because the framing was identical, as was the room the film had been shot in. It didn't help that she had lost all sense of time. There had been no more visits from George, the boy who had lured her down into this underground hell in the first place. No sign of who had kidnapped her, either. All there was was the chair she was tied to, the roar of water in the distance, and the ever-growing thirst and hunger. She'd kept her fear in check, but now it was fighting for a hearing, because whoever had taken her wanted her to die either slowly from starvation or quickly from the fear of what was yet to come.

That was why she felt almost grateful when the film changed. For a while, it gave her something else to focus on. Think about.

GIFT PROTOCOL. TEST
SUBJECT 2.
DAY 1 flashed up on a black slate.

A boy was projected onto the wall in front of her. Similar in age to the boy in the first film. A little younger, perhaps. No more than two years. He sat in the same chair, facing the camera directly. His left hand held a red balloon. He was healthy. Smiling. His skin shone and he radiated goodness. It was like he was grateful for the opportunity to be there.

Megan had a feeling he wouldn't be grateful for very long.

'How are you today?' asked the woman's voice off-screen.

'Fine, thank you.'

English accent.

'Such excellent manners. Tell me, what is it that we're doing here?'

'Helping people, ma'am.'

'Exactly right. And who are we trying to help?'

'The dead, ma'am. Those who were unable to pass over, who were stranded here on earth.'

'Again, very good, although we call it the soil, rather than earth.'

'Why?' the boy asked politely.

'We just do. How, then, do we do that? How do we help those poor souls?'

'You empower us,' said the boy. 'You give us special medicine that means we can see the dead. Help them. Make them more comfortable. It's what our church does. What the Pen does.'

'That's a perfect answer,' said the woman off-screen. 'Tell me, why is it important to help stranded souls in this way?'

'Because no one else can,' said the boy. He leaned forward. 'We're the only people these poor souls have. It's an honour to serve them. A privilege.'

'Yes,' said the woman. 'It is. Do you know what, Elias? I have a feeling you're going to be our best pilgrim ever.'

The film ended.

The picture warped.

'What do you think of my little film?'

Megan whipped around, trying to locate the man who had just spoken. The voice had come from behind the door to her left. She couldn't see anyone. Couldn't see much of anything, apart from a dull red glow.

'Felt like I'd seen it before,' she said, fighting to keep her

342

voice steady. 'It was just a shot-for-shot remake of the original.'

The unseen man laughed. 'Of all the old and young I've had stay with me here, none has been quite like you.'

'I'll take that as a compliment,' said Megan, craning still to see who he was.

'You should.'

'*Stay with me* is stretching it, though, don't you think? You make this sound like a bed and breakfast.'

'It gives me no pleasure to imprison you in this way.'

'Yet you do it anyway,' said Megan.

'I do. It's necessary. Tell me: do these tapes mean anything to you? Do they make you remember events in your past, perhaps?'

'You're joking, right? Why would they?'

The unseen man said nothing.

'George, the boy you used to lure me down here,' Megan continued, 'said you had an old man in this cell before.'

'Not an old man. *Your* old man.'

'I don't have an old man,' she said. 'I don't have any family.'

'You did, you just didn't know them. It's why it took so long to find you.'

Megan's throat went dry. 'Why were you even looking?'

'Because of the mark on your hand.'

She looked down at the barcode smudge on the back of her hand. It was dotted with scabs, but still clearly visible.

'He hid you well, your grandfather. He must have loved you very much.'

Tears prickled against Megan's eyes, brought about by a description of a man she'd never met. 'You're going to kill me, aren't you?'

'*I'm* not going to kill you. The radiation will, eventually.'

'Why?' said Megan. 'What did I do to you?'

'It's not what you did,' said the man. 'It's what your

grandfather did. Him and all the other grandfathers like him.'

'This isn't the first time you've kidnapped someone.'

'No, but it's the last.'

He walked into view, and Megan swallowed.

The man had a mane of hair pulled back into a ponytail. His face was porcelain white, stretched tight against his skull.

He only had one arm.

'What do you mean, you made him?' Daisy-May said.

'Precisely that,' said Lucia. 'I took a damaged man called Elias – damaged, I should say, by your sainted Duchess – and remade him into something better.'

'Better? He's murdered innocent people.'

Lucia nodded. 'He's certainly developed a taste for it. My little Oswald has exceeded my wildest expectations, bless him.'

'Oswald?'

Lucia wagged her finger. 'Not a girl who's up on her history, clearly. Lee Harvey Oswald, darling: if you wish to remain in the shadows, send a patsy to do an assassin's job. The results are the same, but the madness of the patsy camouflages your true intentions.

'*Why* do it, though? Because you could?'

'Oh no, there was method in my genius,' said Lucia. 'A certain group of people needed disposing of. People like Megan Veins' grandfather, monsters who experimented on children.' Her eyes flashed with something only a few decades of therapy could unpick.

There was something to this woman that Daisy-May couldn't understand. Something more than the bogeyman child-snatcher she seemed to be.

Did that matter? She wasn't sure.

There was something she *was* sure of, though.

'*You* experimented on children,' she said.

'I experimented on *dead* children,' Lucia replied. 'Find me an ethics statute that violates, and I'll gladly repent. A hundred different discoveries will come from that research, discoveries that will allow us to treat the living who are sick and ease the pain of those who are dying.'

Daisy-May snorted. 'Bending over backwards to justify yourself, love. Don't care how fake-noble your intentions are; you've brought pain to those who didn't deserve it.'

'I hope you're not referring to the Generation Killer's victims,' said Lucia. 'The men and women I had Elias kill were worse than Nazis. Half of them *were* Nazis. They infected Elias and countless others like him with inoperable cancers that would allow them to see the dead. They deserved everything they got.'

'What about the kids he's murdered? What did *they* do to deserve it?'

Lucia's smile frosted over. 'That, I didn't foresee. Regrettably something appears to have fractured in the poor man's mind.' She looked Daisy-May dead in the eye. 'Still, it's proved to be something of a happy accident. Eventually the authorities might have made a connection between the people Elias murdered. The children muddy the water nicely; nothing distracts from the truth quite like a Halloween ghoul, and the Generation Killer is surely that.'

'Muddy the water?' said Daisy-May incredulously. 'They were innocent kids, you bitch.'

'Now, now,' said Lucia. 'Some of them were grown adults. Megan Veins, for instance, who your man Lazarus is trying to save. A pity he's going to fail. A pity too that he'll pay for that failure with his afterlife.'

'You don't know Joey.' Daisy-May scowled defiantly. 'Chances are he's already found her. Then he'll be coming for your psycho Elias.'

Lucia smiled. 'I'm absolutely counting on it.'

It was roughly a twenty-five-minute walk from the hospital to Elias's sanctuary. Joe did it in an eight-minute sprint.

As he reached Ancoats' deserted streets, he slowed. This was partly to allow his burning lungs some respite, but mainly because he had no idea what he was about to walk into.

It had been Elias in the dying boy's pictures. There was no doubting it, because the pool of one-armed men with shoulder-length hair and military-style coats wasn't a deep one, particularly in Manchester. That didn't mean it made sense. The Elias he knew was selfless, concerned only with helping others. How did you reconcile that man with the serial killer Joe now suspected him to be?

How could Elias be the Generation Killer?

He wiped the sweat from his brow and looked up at the remains of Sankey's nightclub.

It was time to ask him.

As soon as Joe passed through the club's scaffold-clad wall, he knew something was wrong.

It was the air. It was malignant. Poisoned.

He made himself stop and listen. Deathly silence answered back.

He'd come out into what he assumed used to be the coat-check area. The booth was dark, despite the daylight outside. Naked coat hangers clung to a rail behind him. Dust floated in the air.

He drew a gun he knew to be useless, because sometimes objects were reassuring, especially ones you held in your hand and fired. If Elias was here and things turned nasty, it would be useless against his flesh-and-blood form. If he wasn't and things turned nasty anyway, then who knew? Something was wrong here, and sometimes the solution to that wrong was a gun.

He passed through the booth into a corridor untroubled by light, natural or otherwise. Reaching into his satchel, he pulled out the box containing the scarab beetles. They pounded against their plastic prison, but he didn't release them. He wanted their light, but not too much of it, because he didn't know what he was going to find when he walked through the door at the end of the corridor. He only knew he didn't want it to find him before he knew what it was.

Slow step by slow step, he walked towards the door.

A smell hit his nostrils.

Bleach.

No, chlorine.

Like in the Pen.

Nothing of the Pen should be on the soil, thought Joe. Which makes me a hypocrite, because I'm here.

He reached the door.

He pressed his ear to it.

He heard a whimper from the other side.

He swallowed, tightening his grip on the gun.

He walked through the door.

Joe had thought there wasn't much that could shock him any more. He'd been wrong.

He slid through the door into the main room of the club. Weak sunlight punched through a skylight in the roof, illuminating the dozens of cots that had been set up for the homeless souls Elias had taken in. Those same souls were still in those beds. Or at least what was left of them.

The amber husks of thirteen men and women lay on the cots. It was like they'd been stitched into the fabric of the mattresses. Their faces were just visible. Some of them still had some sort of physical form – a lump here, a scoop of flesh there – but most had dissolved completely into the surface.

Like when we found Stanley Veins, a million years ago, on the canal. Elias professed ignorance as to what had happened to him. Fed us that bullshit about wendigos. Played us for chumps.

Played me for a chump.

And now he's cleaning house. Wiping out the witnesses. Massacring those he's supposed to protect. Like the boy at the Rylands library. These poor bastards have all died in the same way.

And I don't have the first idea where to find him, let alone stop him or rescue the girl.

'Help.'

He started, whirling round to his right. A voice so small it barely counted as one.

An old man. Not on a cot, but lying against the stage. Fully formed, almost. Raising an arm and his head at the same time.

Joe rushed over. The man's ancient eyes were infused with orange, and no small amount of terror. His skin bubbled. It looked like hell was trying to force its way through his body.

Joe crouched down next to him.

'Who did this to you?'

'Bastard with one arm. My grandboy said he'd help me.'

'Elias?' said Joe.

The old man nodded. 'He took my grandboy.'

'Took him?'

'Dragged him out of here. My poor Bits.'

Joe frowned. He must be due a hit of the memory drug.

The man had said something about . . . Bits.

Bits was Joe's partner.

'You know Bits?'

The old man coughed, then continued. 'Course I bleeding do.'

'Where did this one-armed man take him?'

With an effort that looked like it cost him a great deal, Bits's grandfather raised himself up on his elbow, and pointed towards the DJ booth. 'There.'

He sank back down, cursing. 'Know what the funny thing is? Didn't know who he was, Bits. He came to my flat, brought me here, and I didn't have the first clue. Only remember him now, at the end. Ironic, right? That's the word for it. Ironic.'

Joe looked towards the DJ booth.

'You're not going to leave me like this.'

He turned back. The old man was pointing at the gun in Joe's hand.

'In more pain than I know what to do with. *You* can do something about that.'

Joe looked at the man's blistered skin, and saw how he was slowly dissolving into the club's stage. This wouldn't be murder. It would be mercy. It would be gifting him a quick, painless death, rather than inflicting a longer, more painful one.

'I'm sorry about what's been done to you,' he said. 'Bits has done you proud. I'm going to make sure I tell him that when I find him.'

'You do that,' said the old man.

He closed his eyes.

Joe pulled the trigger.

Chapter Twenty-Two

The voices were indistinct to begin with, whispered words on an irradiated breeze that had no right to be there. The Duchess followed them, because who she was looking for had no right to be there either.

The nuclear facilities corridor was painted in various shades of bleak. A sliver of water ran through her feet, and the ceiling tiles were fractured and intermittent. The whole place reeked of the end of days, and those were days the Duchess knew only too well. Took comfort in, in a way. The living hadn't signed up for them, though, and although it might not have been her duty to protect the living, no one else would.

Think you're up to it, do you? said Oma Jankie. *A broken-down old bitch like you?*

I think I'm what the world gets for the next thirty minutes, the Duchess replied, because that's how much longer I can keep going for.

Was that true, though? She felt powerful, like God was giving her the kiss of life. Why was that? Something about the reactor, perhaps?

The voices got louder, and when they did, the Duchess realised it was actually only one voice.

Hanna.

Creeping now, going slowly when her fizzing bloodstream demanded she speed up, she came to what looked like a classroom. A ragtag collection of chairs had been piled in front of the door, while every one of its windows had been punched in and shattered.

She kneeled down, peering over the window frame's edge.

Hanna stood at the centre of the room, addressing a camera that had been placed a couple of feet away from her. A teenager with a purple Mohawk sat in the corner of the room, a laptop on his knee, a wire snaking back to the camera.

'Old woman.'

The Duchess closed her eyes.

It was never easy, was it?

She stood, then turned towards the voice.

Standing there was the samurai from the bank vault.

'You shouldn't have come here,' he said, the eyes behind the mask slits burning bright. 'Because now I have to cut you from existence.'

She allowed herself a weary smile. 'You can try.'

This is the end, thought Hatoyama.

He had his back to the metal platform, shielding himself from further attack, blood flowing from his hand, an arrow planted into his left leg, staunching, he assumed, gore that would flow as soon as it was removed. There was no pain in his body, which told him that he had gone into shock, and he'd been gulping radiation for the last half-hour. And there was at least one archer left.

Still, at least he was out of the office.

He laughed, because he had an arrow in his leg, and if that didn't give you a pass for the odd unhinged giggle, he didn't know what did. He also had the bolt-cutter, which he'd take over a primitive bow and arrow any day. The archer may have been a better marksman, but the blast radius of the device meant that Hatoyama had to be anything but deadeye with it. Point. Aim. Shoot.

Or he could just sit here. Sitting here meant no one shooting at him, which was an infinitely better state of affairs than when they were. He could just close his eyes, get a few seconds' rest, and go again.

His eyelids drooped, already on board.

Except the Duchess is counting on me.

A lot more people besides her, if Hanna is as dangerous as she said.

And the cowboy doesn't die in the dirt. He dies in a hail of bullets, if he has to die at all.

He thought he might have to – that the injuries he'd already sustained would make that decision for him – but there was still good to be done before the final curtain. Firstly, though, he needed to see what he was shooting at. Brave didn't have to mean stupid.

At his feet was a shard of glass. He lunged for it and raised it, hoping to catch sight of his attacker in the reflection. He angled it slightly, revealing nothing.

He heard a crunch above his head and looked up.

A pair of ancient eyes looked down.

The face they belonged to held a knife in its teeth.

The archer dived down towards Hatoyama, the detective raising his gun in greeting.

He fired.

Nothing happened.

The archer, his face contorted in triumph, plunged the knife towards him.

In all the Duchess's hundreds of years of existence, the one truth she knew was this: the bigger they were, the harder they fell. Many would have been intimidated by the samurai's fearsome garb, his blade flashing this way and that, each step he took towards her bringing that blade closer.

Many didn't have her newly restored power.

Many didn't have her will.

Many were afraid to die.

The Duchess raised her hand, and the samurai's blade's stopped dead.

He grunted, trying to free a sword that appeared to be stuck in thin-air quicksand.

'You're a witch,' he said, wrestling with the blade.

'No,' said the Duchess. 'More a deity with a death wish.'

One whose power seems to be growing by the second.

She flicked her hand to the left, wrenching the sword from the samurai and slamming it into the opposite wall. The blade trembled up and down, as if it were a toy moulded from plastic.

'That was your sword,' said the Duchess with half a smile. 'Imagine what I could do to your neck.'

The samurai tensed, adopting a crouching stance. 'I don't need a sword to beat you.'

'No, you need a great deal more, and you don't have it. Stand down.'

'There's no honour in surrender,' said the samurai.

'There's no honour in suicide either.'

A throwing star arced through the air towards her, so fast that a lesser god wouldn't have seen it. The Duchess did, though, a blink of her eye halting the weapon's flight. She reached out, plucking it from mid-air treacle. 'Are you convinced yet?' she asked, examining the ninja wheel. 'Or would you like a further demonstration?'

'I would like you to fall at my knee, slain,' said the samurai.

The Duchess sighed, tossing the star aside. 'Yes, most people seem to want that.'

She flicked her hand, slamming the samurai into the wall

and making him cry out in pain and surprise. Suspending him three feet above the floor, a butterfly pinned to a board, she then flicked her hand from left to right, ragdolling him from one wall to the other, chunks of masonry tumbling off with each throw.

Finally she raised her arm, levitating the dazed warrior to the ceiling then dropping him head-first into the floor.

'I'll be slain soon enough,' she said, walking over the samurai's unmoving body, 'but it won't be by your hand.'

The bolt-cutter was heavier – and stronger – than it looked. Hatoyama was as grateful for this as he was ungrateful that it hadn't fired when he wanted it to.

As the archer swung the sickle towards his head, the gun acted as an unlikely, if effective, shield. Steel clashed with whatever the weapon was made of, the *clang* echoing through Hatoyama's teeth. The archer grunted, trying to prise the sickle's point from the gun's barrel.

I'm doing this all wrong, thought Hatoyama. Trying to fight a ghost on its terms rather than my own. It can pick up physical objects, but that doesn't mean it's a physical object itself.

He reached through the archer's formless hand, grasping the sickle's handle and freeing it from his gun barrel.

The archer blinked in surprise.

Hatoyama pulled the trigger.

The bolt-cutter whined, coughed, then blasted the archer in the face.

A smell of sulphur, a scream on delay, and he was gone.

Hatoyama stood bleeding, his gun arm trembling, his eyes hunting for other attackers. When he didn't find them, he pulled himself up, then emptied the contents of his stomach.

Could be because my body's in shock, he thought, or it could be because of the radiation I've inhaled.

His body decided it didn't very much care what the reason was, and Hatoyama decided he didn't care either. He stood up straight, wiped his mouth, and then began limping towards the only doorway he could see.

The reactor control room.

Hanna stood at the back, huddled with three of her followers over a console of flickering lights and digital endeavour. A glass partition wall loomed above them, all the better to see the reactor core behind it. In contrast to the one the Duchess had seen earlier, its unsullied appearance suggested to her that it was working, or at least had been before the authorities had taken the decision to shut it down.

She stood watching for a moment, gathering herself. The battle with the samurai had been mercifully short, but she had no way of telling how much it had taken out of her, or of knowing how much longer her power would last. Though truthfully, she hadn't felt this good in years. It was like the place was invigorating her somehow.

Which was just as well, because she couldn't rely on Hatoyama. She had to assume she was on her own.

Perhaps that's for the best, she thought. On my own is all I've ever really been.

'How is the reactor functioning?' said Hanna.

'All systems online,' replied one of her followers. 'For now.'

'Has a remote shutdown been attempted?'

'If it has, the Dog Catcher we stole countered it successfully.'

'Of course it did,' said Hanna. 'We have right on our side, and when you have right on your side, it's impossible to fail.'

Enough, thought the Duchess. Enough.

She rose from her hiding place, power humming inside her. 'Hanna.'

Her baby sister turned, as did the followers alongside her.

355

'You can't stop me,' said Hanna, smiling. 'You're too late.'

'Too late for what?'

'To prevent the inevitable.'

'I'm beginning to understand my former colleague's loathing of riddles.'

'When you see what I've done, you'll thank me,' said Hanna.

'I find that difficult to believe.'

'The reactor's back online,' she continued, 'and thanks to the prototype we took, a remote shutdown is impossible.' She smiled, taking a step towards the Duchess. 'The reactor is under my complete control, and there's nothing you can do about it.'

'And what exactly do you intend to do with that control? Why have I been chasing you all over Japan, stepping over the trail of dead bodies you left for me to find?'

'Don't tell me you have sympathy for these soil breathers?'

'I have sympathy for any innocent you've killed.'

'*Innocent.* What a creative use of that word.'

'How would you describe them?'

'No one on the soil is innocent,' said Hanna. 'They don't deserve this world. That's why I intend to take it from them.'

'Take it how?" said the Duchess.

'You'll see,' said Hanna. 'You're already feeling the benefits, I wouldn't wonder. I bet that frail old body is positively singing with power.' She smiled at the Duchess. 'I'm right, aren't I? If you got past the samurai, I must be.'

'You haven't been right about anything for a long time.'

'The old era is over, and the new one is about to begin,' she said. 'Embrace it. Join me.'

'You're good at that,' said the Duchess. 'Getting others to fight your deranged battles for you.'

'Deranged?' said Hanna. 'The Dispossessed were mistreated slaves under your rule. I showed them another way.'

'Your "other way" almost toppled existence. The end never justifies that kind of means.'

'It's that sort of thinking that's held the Pen back.'

'It's that sort of thinking that's ensured there's a Pen *to* hold back,' said the Duchess. 'You won't be happy until the world of the living and the dead are both razed to the ground.'

'I won't be happy,' said Hanna, 'until the world of the living and the dead are the same thing.'

Chapter Twenty-Three

Some fuckers just wanted to show you how clever they were.

As Lucia led her down a seemingly endless white corridor, Daisy-May concluded that that could be the only reason for the information she'd just been gifted. There was nothing she could do from here to help Joe, no way of getting word to him that Elias was the Generation Killer. He was on his own.

Just like me, then. Let's hope he's not equally as fucked.

Lucia reached the door and placed a hand on it. 'You probably think I've launched this coup against you.'

'Well, yeah,' said Daisy-May. 'You seem the type, to be honest.'

Lucia smiled. 'I am. This isn't my doing, though.'

She pushed against the door.

It swung open, and Daisy-May cursed her escaping gasp.

They were back in the main laboratory, the children just where she'd left them, caged and docile. Standing at the centre was a man. Or at least the approximation of one.

At first glance, he had the face and skin of a man. It was like that face and skin had been stretched, though, wrestled clumsily onto something much larger underneath. His eyes were wider than they should have been (longer, too, Daisy-May realised; it was as if the pupils didn't fit properly in his eye sockets) and his skin was paper-thin and translucent. The whole look reminded Daisy-May of a grown man trying to jam on a toddler's jumper.

Then there was his height.

He had to be almost seven feet tall, and that size seemed to bow his back, making him look like a pensioner leaning in for a closer look at a priceless antique. His torso bulged, not with muscles but with something that seemed shapeless and formless, almost like it was desperately searching for solidity.

'Greetings, Warden,' the thing pretending to be a man said, its voice squelchy and wet. 'I am Uriel.'

'That might be *who* you are. *What* are you?'

The thing began walking towards her, its footsteps heavy, like there were rocks in them. 'A friend. One who's here to help.'

'I've got plenty of friends,' said Daisy-May. 'Don't need any more.'

'None are like me,' said the man thing.

'You're fucking right there, mate, 'cos we're standing in a room full of caged children, with the woman that put them there, and you claim you're here to help. Tough sell, that one.'

Uriel opened his arms and smiled. The facial contortion made it seem like black sweat was streaming down his forehead. 'I come merely to offer service.'

'I've got no need of your service.'

'Oh, but you do.'

A man's voice.

One she knew.

One that had no right to be here.

Daisy-May turned.

Remus was standing there.

Her faithful number two, counsel for countless Wardens over the centuries.

'What's going on, Remus?' she asked. 'This your idea of a rescue mission?'

'It's a rescue mission all right,' said the old man, a grave expression on his face. 'I'm trying to save the whole of purgatory.'

'From who?' said Daisy-May.

'From you, you stupid girl,' he said, a snarl on his lips. 'Do you know how much damage you've done to my realm?'

'*Your* realm?'

'Yes,' said Remus, taking a step towards her. '*My* realm. Wardens come and go every century and a half, but I am the constant that remains. I have guided the Pen's leaders for a millennium. Would have guided you too, if you'd let me. You always thought you knew better, though. *You*, a gutter rat from a council estate.'

Daisy-May looked from Remus to Lucia. 'Wait: *you're* who I'm supposed to abdicate to?'

Remus looked away, tugging at his tunic. 'I am ready to serve. It has never been more necessary.'

Daisy-May shook her head. 'Why'd you want my job, mate?'

'I don't. It's a responsibility I will reluctantly accept, though, for the sake of the Pen.'

'It was me the Duchess wanted,' said Daisy-May defiantly. 'You were supposed to help me, not stab me in the back.'

'I tried to help you,' said Remus, 'as I tried to help your predecessors over the centuries. They knew my advice would help protect the balance of things, of existence itself. I warned you against this ridiculous obsession with the Dispossessed, how bringing them into the fold was a huge mistake. After what happened with Hanna, how could you even countenance such madness? A race of half-souls that almost destroyed existence as we know it, and you rewarded them for such an insurrection with employment. They should have been wiped, or at least culled. That would have kept them in line for another millennium.'

Cogs whirred in Daisy-May's brain.

She thought back to the conversation she'd had with Remus just before leaving the compound. 'This is what you were talking about. The Gabriel Initiative.'

'I wanted to give you one last chance,' he said. 'If you had accepted the need for the Initiative, I would have been happy to work alongside you, to guide you away from the mistakes you've made.'

'Those mistakes were mine to make, not yours to correct.'

'On the contrary, I'm the only one who can correct them. Which is why I've been forced to enact the Gabriel Initiative. It is to be activated in times of crisis. A dying Warden, an agency on its knees: what bigger crisis is there than that?'

'I'm not dying,' said Daisy-May. She looked up at the hulking Uriel. 'You some sort of soldier, then?'

'From a simplistic perspective, my colleagues and I could be viewed as soldiers, yes.'

'You look like a rotting sock puppet,' Daisy-May replied. 'We don't need your sort of help in the Pen.'

She turned back to Remus. 'Hide this in as much fancy wrapping as you like, mate. You're staging a coup.'

'I'm staging an intervention,' Remus replied, 'and Uriel and his friends are going to make sure that intervention sticks.'

'I'll never abdicate to you. I'll die first.'

'That, I believe,' said Remus. 'What about the children here? Will you let them die as well?'

Daisy-May looked out on the row of cages. 'Wondering when we'd get to them.'

She fixed her gaze on Remus, letting the anger rise within her. 'I can just about buy the whole saving-the-Pen bollocks. It *is* bollocks – I'm not the right flavour of ice cream for you – but you're not the first bloke to have his head turned by power, and you won't be the last. What did these kids do, though? They're innocent.'

'They're not kids,' said Remus, 'and they don't have the wits to be guilty, let alone innocent. They're animals.'

He smiled at Lucia. 'Lucia and I share certain goals and world views. I don't like the existence of this place, but I accept the need for it. With that in mind . . . Lucia?'

She nodded, and walked over to the nearest cage, its translucent plastic shell twinkling under the fluorescent lights. The boy inside it, like all the children in the cages, was slumped unconscious in his seat. The non-shimmering woman placed her hand against the cage, and it began to glow softly.

The glow became a red pulse that began to beat faster.

Now the boy was awake, groggily raising his head and looking around in fear. He began to scream, and even though Daisy-May couldn't hear it through the soundproofed cage, she could feel it: his fear, his pain, his hopelessness.

'All the cages have this feature built in,' said Remus, hovering next to her. 'Useful if the test subject proves to be less so.'

The boy continued screaming, desperately thrashing against his restraints.

Uriel, it seemed to Daisy-May, was getting off on the child's pain. His eye sockets were even more stretched than before. The black sweat dripped down his face.

Remus leaned closer. 'I'll kill each one of these children, right in front of you, if you don't abdicate. Then I'll kill the girl upstairs. Then your friend Lazarus. Save their pain. Save your own. All you need to do is renounce the title. Help me to help you.'

Daisy-May's hand went absent-mindedly to the pin on her black Ramones T-shirt. A thin sliver of red and gold, it was the closest she'd got to adopting an official uniform. The Duchess had gifted it to her when things were at their darkest in the Pen; could she have possibly known then that they would become darker still? Perhaps she had. Perhaps that was why she herself had abdicated. Close to two centuries of crushing responsibility had to have been exhausting.

Daisy-May had been doing it for all of two minutes, and she felt fucked.

The cage was shrieking red now, if colours could shriek. Daisy-May was of the opinion that they could. Certainly the child inside was.

'I'll do it,' she said, closing her eyes. 'Stop hurting the boy, and I'll do it.'

Remus nodded at Lucia, and she raised her hand to the cage once more. The thrashing red became a more sombre yellow, then died away altogether.

The boy slumped back down, his body spasming and twitching.

Daisy-May stood up straight, opening her eyes.

That's the last child you'll ever hurt, she thought, glaring at Remus.

'The ceremony is a simple one,' said Uriel, his words pregnant with ooze. 'You will repeat the words Remus says to you, and the title of Warden will pass to him.'

Daisy-May nodded, trying to keep the look of hope off her face.

She'd seen something on the far wall.

A small rash of scarab beetles had formed on it, more of their friends joining them by the second. You pick your moments, Mabel, she thought. You might act like you've got no airs and graces, but you're a right drama queen. This is going to be quite the entrance. Least I hope it will be.

She had to play for time.

363

'Not one for pomp and fucking circumstance, is he, the Almighty?' she said. 'Always thought he'd be a choir-of-angels fella when it comes to this sort of thing.'

She risked a look over Remus's shoulder. The scarab beetles had formed a huge *B* on the wall, and their colleagues were well on the way to shaping an *O* next to it.

Whatever you're going to do, Mabel, now's the time. This ceremony's mighty fucking quick, and there's only so slow I can play my part.

'Raise your hand,' commanded Uriel.

Daisy-May did as she was told.

'Repeat after me,' said Remus. 'I, Daisy-May Braithwaite . . .'

'Feels like I'm at some sort of fucked-up wedding,' said Daisy-May, smirking at him. 'You're the vicar, and Quasimodo over there's my blushing groom.'

'I have little patience left,' said Remus, 'and the children in those cages will be the one to suffer for that.'

'All right, rim-job, all right.'

Her eyes flicked to the wall, noting that a third letter had been formed.

B . . . O . . . O . . . Hope that's going to spell what I think it's going to spell. Hope that word comes to pass even more.

'I, Daisy-May Braithwaite,' she repeated.

'Anointed Warden of the Pen,' continued Remus.

'Anointed Warden of the Pen.'

Remus licked his lips. 'Hereby renounce that title.'

'Hereby renounce that title,' said Daisy-May, risking an eye flick at the wall.

BOOM had been spelt out. Lucia had noticed it too.

'Remus,' she said.

'Not now,' Remus barked, keeping his eyes firmly locked on Daisy-May. 'And bestow it upon Remus Hans Killion.'

'Killion?' said Daisy-May. 'Fucking hell, if I'd have known

that was your surname, I'd have been able to guess you were a wrong'un. It's right out of evil genius central casting.'

'Say the words,' screamed Remus.

'Remus,' said Lucia, more urgently this time.

'One more word from you, and you'll go in the cage,' said Remus, not looking at Lucia but pointing a gnarled finger in her direction. 'Say the words, girl.'

Daisy-May looked at the wall. Saw too how Lucia was inching away from it.

'I hereby renounce that title,' said Daisy-May, 'and bestow it upon Remus Hans Killion.'

That wasn't quite it, though, she knew. Until she pinned the badge on Remus, the ceremony, modest as it was, wouldn't be complete. Whatever you're going to do, Mabel, you better do it now, she thought, reaching for the red and gold pin.

Before her fingers could close over it, she extended her arm, and her middle finger along with it. 'You're a child-torturing cunt, and I'll never renounce my title to the likes of you.'

Remus snarled in rage, just as a gut-punching roar tore through the world, the wall behind them ripped apart in an explosion of masonry and light, its shock wave snatching gravity from everyone in the room, knocking them clean off their feet and onto their backsides, the cages full of children left mercifully untouched.

Daisy May heard a guttural rumble cutting through the afterbirth of the explosion. She coughed and spluttered and squinted, trying to see through the billowing cloud of dust.

A human form appeared – or rather, an almost human form. It was larger than any human, larger even than the monstrous Uriel, who had been thrown thirty feet away and lay motionless amongst the rubble.

Is that a robot? thought Daisy-May as the dust began to clear and the whirl of machinery sounded loudly.

She got to her feet, her eyes stinging, coughing madly, and saw that it wasn't a robot, because robots didn't exist here. It was Mabel, in one of the diving suits Joe had used to get through the Gloop.

The suit had been modified, though; where there should have been a lumpy gloved right hand sat instead a machine gun.

No guns, thought Daisy-May. I specifically said no fucking guns.

The helmet on the suit was different too, in that there wasn't one; instead, Mabel's reassuringly thick head poked out from the suit's rusted metal hide. 'On your feet, girl,' she called out, surveying the damage she'd left in her wake. 'That won't keep 'em down for long.'

Daisy-May did as she was told, fighting off the fatigue and nausea that galloped inside her. 'Took your sweet time.'

'Didn't know I'd have to traipse all the way to the end of the bloody world to come and save you,' said Mabel. 'Might have left you to stew if I had.'

She looked around at the row of cages. 'Wouldn't believe this place existed until I saw it with my own eyes. Now that I have, I wish I hadn't.'

'You knew about it?'

'Knew the rumours.' She squinted at Daisy-May. 'You look bad, girl.'

'Thanks.'

'You been taking that stuff I gave you?'

'Till it ran out.'

Mabel shook her concerned-looking head. 'Come on. We're getting out of here.'

'Not without the kids in these cages,' said Daisy-May. 'Not without the girl upstairs neither.'

'Don't have time for that,' said Mabel, her eyes hunting the

366

wreckage, seeing a clump of rocks stirring by the now collapsed wall.

'Lucky that time has no meaning here then,' said Daisy-May,
winking at her would-be saviour then looking up at the caged
observation window. 'That gun on your arm as mean as it looks?'

'Meaner,' said Mabel.

Masonry swirled as Daisy-May lurched into the room that held
Chestnut, the far wall punched out by Mabel's firepower.

'Could have been killed,' coughed Chestnut, covered as she
was in head-to-toe wall.

'*Could have* never counts,' said Daisy-May, taking the girl's
weight as she stumbled from her chair. 'Now come on, you
lump, we're leaving.'

'Who you calling a lump?'

They staggered towards the doorway, Daisy-May supporting
Chestnut's jelly legs.

'How we getting out of here?' asked Chestnut.

'On Mabel's ship.'

'Who's Mabel?'

'The old bird with a ship.'

'Do I know her?'

'Yeah,' said Daisy-May. 'She saved your life once. It's sort of
her thing.'

As they returned to the main laboratory, Daisy-May saw that
Mabel had done as she'd asked: the children had been freed
from their cages and were shivering in the corner.

'They don't glimmer,' she said. 'Notice that?'

'Hard not to,' said Mabel, her suit clunking and crunching as
she headed towards the blown-apart wall. 'Whys and hows of
that I'm happy to discuss when we're out of this concentration
camp.'

'I can walk fine,' said Chestnut, as Daisy-May reached to stop her falling.

'Can you fuck.'

'Getting carried like a baby's embarrassing.'

'So's getting killed 'cos you're acting like one.'

Daisy-May looked behind her as they stumbled towards the open entrance.

A pile of bricks had begun to move.

'Let's pick up the pace,' she said.

'Walk faster then,' said Chestnut.

The girl cried out as they reached the entrance and looked up. 'The fuck's that?'

Daisy-May knew, although she understood Chestnut's reaction.

It was an airship.

Metal girders were cut into its black balloon skin, and four ropes dangled from its belly, supporting a sturdy-looking command module. The rust on the Zeppelin reminded her of the Gloop-diving suit Mabel was wearing, past its best and cannibalised for another purpose.

Nothing's new here, she thought. We get the shit that nobody else wants, and have to make do. Big shock. That's how we all ended up here in the first place.

'How'd we get up there?' said Chestnut. 'Don't see a step-ladder.'

'Going to take a wild guess and say in that,' said Daisy-May, pointing at a large skiff-like boat a few feet away. A sail billowed from the front of it, with a dozen or so propellers recessed into its left and right sides. It would hold them all – the kids too – but she doubted it would be able to take off. The weight, surely, would be too great.

'It'll get you up,' said Mabel, as if she'd been listening to Daisy-May's thoughts. 'Stronger than it looks, old *Myrtle*.'

'You named a ship *Myrtle*?' said Chestnut.

'Gotta name it something,' said Mabel.

'Woman.'

All three women turned back towards the laboratory.

Uriel was standing in the blown-apart entrance. His skin, it seemed to Daisy-May, was even harder to look at than before, like it had shrunk in the wash. There was barely enough of it to cover the tissue and bones beneath.

'Bloody hell,' said Mabel. 'Uriel. Who died and let you in?'

'It's been a long time, woman,' said Uriel, each word dripping in poison. 'I knew I'd see you again one day.'

'More's the pity.'

Daisy-May looked at Mabel. 'You know this freak?'

Mabel nodded. 'They go by a few names, but fallen angel is as good as any. God chucked them out of heaven for being shithouses. Some went straight to the Pit, some of them got lucky and ended up in the Pen. Wasn't good enough for them, though, was it? The Duchess ended up booting them out. Looks like Remus needed their muscle and found a technicality to bring them back.'

Right, thought Daisy-May. One I vetoed him on. I got that right at least, even if he did it anyway.

Mabel looked at her. 'Get those kids on the boat and get up to the ship. You want no part in this.'

'I'm the Warden,' said Daisy-May. 'It's my job to have a part in this.'

'Your job's running the realm,' said Mabel. 'Not fighting devils.'

Chestnut tugged on Daisy-May's sleeve. 'Those kids need you.'

Daisy-May nodded.

'Amusing that any of you think you have a chance to escape,' said Uriel. He began pulling at his skin. 'Once I'm done with this old bitch, you'll find it amusing too.'

Chestnut began herding the children into the boat, but Daisy-May couldn't resist watching Uriel. He was tearing off his skin like a too-tight-to-breathe suit, and when she saw what it concealed, she realised why it had been necessary.

Two pink eyes, far bigger than a human's.

A jagged mouth that appeared to have been scored on with a blunt knife.

A torso that looked hot to the touch, oozing tar.

Five talons jutting out from shovel-sized hands.

She could believe that this creature, whatever it was, had been born in the fires of hell itself.

Mabel waved a hand at her, and she reluctantly turned away, heading for the ship.

'You ain't got much prettier since the last time I saw you,' Mabel said behind her. 'Rachel was right to throw you and your mates out.'

Uriel smiled, bits of him dripping and sizzling onto the ground below. 'Our presence has never been more necessary. The Pen is in ruins. The Dispossessed run amok as if they are your equals.'

'They *are* equals,' said Mabel. 'The new Warden taught us that. It's why Rachel gave her the job.'

'They are cattle,' said Uriel. 'After I kill you – and the Warden renounces her title – measures will be put in place to remind them of that.'

'Come on then, handsome,' said Mabel. 'Let's be having you.'

The children were weak, and they were beaten, and that made it easy for Daisy-May and Chestnut to corral them into the boat. What was more difficult was getting the boat to start.

It looked simple enough. It actually had a motor, but no

matter how hard they pulled at the rope hanging from it, it refused to offer up the slightest cough.

'What are we doing wrong?' asked Daisy-May.

'A fucking oil demon's fighting an old woman in a metal suit, and she asks what we're doing wrong.'

'We're in a solutions place, not a snarky place,' said Daisy-May.

'My solution's to be snarky.'

Mabel's scream put all ideas of snarkiness aside.

Mabel stared down at the pitch-black monster with the talon round her throat.

Uriel had been too quick and her suit too heavy and her body too old and her bones older than that. She hadn't been able to so much as raise the suit's gun arm before he'd mangled it in one of his fists.

Quicker than I remember, she thought, or maybe I'm just older. He's just as strong, though. That's the thing about fallen angels: just because they've fallen doesn't mean they don't retain the power of the righteous. It's why Rachel banished them in the first place. Anyone with such a disdain for power, and a healthy supply of their own, is bad news.

Still, she had a couple of tricks left up what remained of her sleeve.

Well, one.

Her flesh-and-blood finger found a button in her metallic gloved fist.

'You should have worked with us,' said Uriel. 'It's the last mistake you'll ever make.'

'Bollocks,' choked Mabel. 'Got plenty more fuck-ups to make before I go to the Next Place.'

A sharp blast of green gas enveloped Uriel, causing him to release her. She managed to land on her feet, the heavy boots compressing the ground beneath them. Quickly now, as Uriel coughed and searched for her blindly, she flicked another button and a faint whine began to sound.

The suit gave a piston-pump sigh and the back of it swung open, allowing her to hop out just as Uriel's grasping hands found it.

Lean in close, she thought. Give it a kiss.

The suit whimpered and then exploded, throwing Mabel away with a flick of its aftershock. She landed fifteen feet away from the boat, singed but alive. There was a tower of flames where the suit had been, dancing green and black waves reaching for the charcoal sky.

Mabel dusted herself down, then turned to Daisy-May and the others. 'You blithering idiots still here?'

Daisy-May looked down at the flames as the boat rose steadily into the air. She told herself that the shivering would stop soon, and that the feeling of every last one of her cells bleeding would soon be staunched. The children to her left, all silent and dead-eyed, had endured far worse. If they could stand it, then so could she.

'What was that thing?' asked Chestnut.

'An angel,' said Mabel. 'Or to have it right, an ex-angel. Don't think Uriel's done much of God's work lately.'

She frowned. Something was emerging from the lingering flames.

Something enormous and tar-covered and angry.

'Thought you'd killed it,' said Daisy-May.

'You never kill something like that,' said Mabel. 'Not really.'

Uriel appeared to be as untouched as he was angry.

Daisy-May put a hand to her mouth as two enormous wings unfurled from his back. Black liquid dripped from them, eating into the floor beneath him.

'You've got to be fucking joking,' said Chestnut.

He beat his wings and took off, the smudges of his pink eyes just visible on his tar face. Each downward motion of the wings powered him closer to them.

Daisy-May looked up. They were almost at the slab of metal that was dangling from the main body of the Zeppelin. Mabel picked up a length of thick rope that lay on the ship's floor. 'Moor us up. I'll hold it off.'

'With what?' said Chestnut. 'Bad language and prayer?'

Mabel reached down and brought up a long metallic pipe. 'A lot more than that, girl.'

The sound of cracked leather. That was the noise Uriel made as his wings bore him closer to the boat.

Mooring to the Zeppelin had been easy enough for Daisy-May, getting the children to move similarly easy, considering the black demon that was heading straight for them.

Chestnut reached down a hand for her. 'Why doesn't she shoot?'

Daisy-May hauled herself into the Zeppelin's cockpit, looking down at Mabel, who stood with one foot on the edge of the boat, the long metallic pipe resting on her shoulder. 'Because she's afraid of what's going to happen if she misses. So am I.'

At the exact moment Mabel fired – Uriel mere feet from them – a gust of wind tugged at the Zeppelin. It wasn't a big tug, but it didn't need to be: the smallest of breaths was sufficient to nudge her aim off-kilter, the gas-fired rocket soaring past Uriel's veiny left wing.

The fallen agent of God hovered where he was, smiling as Mabel huffed and swore, desperately trying to reload.

Fallen angels are probably worse than old demons, thought Daisy-May, 'cos there's no going back for those fuckers. They've made their evil bed and they've got to lie in it.

Uriel landed on the boat, tipping Mabel towards him. He grabbed the rocket launcher from her grasp and pitched it over the side.

'Stand back,' Mabel called, taking a knife from her belt. 'Don't want you having no part of this beast.'

Got to know I won't do that, thought Daisy-May.

Mabel slashed out with the knife, a movement that was easily blocked by Uriel, an oozing black hand wrapping around the old woman's wrist. She smiled through the pain, and Daisy-May saw why: she wanted the opening such a move would create. Her left arm swung forward, smashing a glass jar into the angel's cheek. A blizzard of beetles flew from it, latching themselves onto Uriel's face.

As he screamed, his hands trying to claw the swarm away, Mabel saw her next opening. She swung the knife at him, stabbing him again and again in the chest, like she was decimating a whack-a-mole.

Uriel dropped to one knee.

On the ropes, thought Daisy-May. Don't fuck with my Mabel.

Mabel kneeled down, bringing the knife to Uriel's neck.

Finish him, thought Daisy-May. Finish the fucker.

But Mabel wasn't the only one capable of bait and switch: Uriel wasn't reeling to the extent that he'd sold. He shot out a hand, wrapping it around Mabel's throat, grunting with exertion because he was injured, but not fatally so. He got to his feet, Mabel dangling from his clawed hand as if she were the lightest of ragdolls.

Can't beat this fucker with weapons, thought Daisy-May. He's too powerful. There's only one thing that *can* beat him.

Me.

★

Daisy-May had been four years old when she'd discovered the concept of power, and the fragility of life when faced with it. This wasn't the type of power that came with the title of demigod of a realm. She couldn't move things with her mind, much less hurt them. That didn't mean her chubby four-year-old fingers couldn't dispense their own brand of wanton destruction, though.

Her mother's house backed onto a tiny concreted yard of cracked slabs and determined weeds, an unlikely sanctuary from Mum's four-day benders. It was in the guts of one of these sessions that one of their 'guests' took pity on Daisy-May.

'A beautiful girl deserves a beautiful garden,' the reveller said, cigarette in hand, her sobriety trailing far behind. 'Next time I come, I'm going to bring you a window box. Do you know what a window box is?' Daisy-May didn't, but she took an educated guess, and for one with such a startling lack of education, she guessed close, her reward being said window box the next time the reveller darkened their doors.

'You've got to water them, all right?' the woman said. 'You water them, and just you see the insects you'll get coming to them. Nature, love. It's important.' She looked around her, gazing at the debauchery amongst the ruins, almost as if waking from a dream. 'It's important.'

Daisy-May *had* watered them, dragging a stool up to the sink and fastidiously filling empty beer cans with water, her own makeshift watering cans. And as promised, the insects had come, drawn to the petunias, geraniums and begonias. She liked the ladybirds best, with their handsome red wings and the pretty black dots that adorned them.

One day, after a particularly violent party, she was sheltering outside even though there was a tropical deluge of Nottingham's finest rain. She crouched in front of her window box, allowing a ladybird to crawl onto her finger, its wings extended for flight.

I want those wings, she thought. I don't want to just look at them from time to time. I want to be able to look at them whenever I feel like it.

She had no toys worthy of the name, so was it so wrong to want her own insect to play with, and its beautiful wings? She was of the opinion that it wasn't. So she took those wings between her fingers and she tore them off.

What was left of the ladybird fell to the floor, and the wings dissolved in her fingers. There was nothing left to keep. Daisy-May was sad about this, but she also found she was something else. Excited. Because for a second, she'd held life and death in her hands, and for that second, she had also held power. There was no sense of control in her life; she was buffeted between strangers in a way she didn't understand. For that moment, though, things had been different.

She'd enjoyed it. She'd wanted it again.

That was what she thought of now, with a hand extended and a demon-angel frozen in mid-air at her behest.

She'd been getting it wrong all this time. Begging desperately for the power when it was hers all along. She couldn't even hear the dog-whistle whine that usually accompanied her efforts. A feeling of peace and serenity coursed through her, verging on bliss.

He's just an insect, she thought as she looked wonderingly at Uriel. He's nothing to me and what I can become.

Flesh and bone and tissue tore, and Uriel screamed, a sound of pain and shock and indignation. Daisy-May smiled as she visualised the angel's wings being plucked from his back, just as she'd done to the ladybird all those years ago. He tried to reach back, to somehow keep them attached, but to no avail. Finally they were ripped clean off, a steaming black substance spraying from his back in slow motion.

Mabel blinked, gathering herself, then plunged the knife into his chest.

He staggered backwards and pitched over the side of the boat, plunging hundreds of feet down, the ground waiting patiently for him below.

Daisy-May laughed. 'That felt good,' she said. 'That felt really fucking good.'

She blinked rapidly, let out the smallest giggle, then collapsed.

Chapter Twenty-Four

There was a hole underneath the DJ booth.

That hole had dropped Joe into a tunnel that ran underneath the belly of the club. He and Bits had been just a few feet from it and they'd never known.

How could they have?

How could they have suspected Elias? It still made no sense.

Neither did taking Bits. It made sense, he supposed, that his partner would have returned to the club; it was a place he knew could care for his grandfather. But why would Elias subdue him then take him away? Why not kill him, as he'd done with the other poor souls?

Joe worked his way down the endlessly dank corridor, its clammy brick ceiling only a few feet from his head. There was no sign of Elias, no trace of the missing girl. No sign of anything except small pepperpot lights that spilled tungsten onto the tiles underneath his feet. Water rushed in the distance. Moisture passed through him from the tiles above. The tunnel started to curve to the right, light seeping out from a source he couldn't see.

There was something else, too. As he got closer to the light, he felt the subliminal hum get stronger. It was like it was on his skin. In his teeth. Poking at his eyelids.

He'd felt it once before. At the missing girl's flat, shortly before it had turned into a fireball. It had made him solid then. Had it done so again?

He clenched his fist, then struck it against the tiled ceiling above him. He winced when the ceiling struck back.

Solid as rock. What technology could cause that?

The unholy kind. The sort that shouldn't be in the hands of the good, let alone the bad.

The light was coming from a door. The room behind it reminded him of an abandoned war bunker.

Another door – closed – was embedded within the tiles of the back wall. A mighty chunk of machinery sat to Joe's left, water pooling around it, rust sleeping on its chrome surfaces. It looked like some sort of control desk. A tumble of dials were carved into it, with a battalion of fat steel buttons sitting beneath them. An insignia was embedded in it, too, smeared with dust and grime.

The insignia depicted an eagle. Its talons were wrapped around a wreath, which had in its centre the crooked cross of the swastika.

Looks old enough to be Second World War issue, thought Joe. What's a Nazi control console doing down a Manchester storm drain? The thing's ancient – how did it get here? And how did Elias find out about it?

There had to be someone else behind it all. Nothing else made sense.

The woman who didn't glimmer, perhaps?

Now you're out-and-out guessing, mate was what Daisy-May would have said.

That didn't mean he was wrong. Though this machine was clearly ancient, and the woman he'd seen back in the Pen had looked barely older than Joe himself, that didn't mean they weren't connected somehow. The wriggling in his gut spoke to that.

One of the dials on the console was larger than the others, and set a few inches away from them. Before he had time to think about what he was doing, Joe reached over and turned it.

The hum that had tap-danced on his teeth died away completely.

He reached up, slapping his hand against the brick ceiling, watching as it passed clean through it.

This is the machine he does it with. This is how he makes us solid. Makes us real.

This was too big. This machine. This room. Whatever was happening down here was above his unpaid pay grade, and maybe even above Daisy-May's. He needed to find Megan Veins and get her out. Nothing in this room would help him achieve that.

He reached out, turning the dial back. He could believe that the constant humming would drive him insane in time, but that time wasn't now, and it might not be a bad thing to retain his solidity. If Elias had somehow subdued Bits, he had the ability to hurt him in his spectral form.

Maybe he'd find it harder to do that with a solid size ten shoe at his throat.

A small wooden desk stood at the back of the room, an LCD lamp perched on it, giving off a soft, heavenly glow.

False advertising, thought Joe. There's fuck all of heaven in this place.

He winced. His brain tingled, a foggy whine sounding in his head. His thoughts became clammy, like someone had smeared them in vagueness.

Serum's wearing off. Running out of supplies as well as clarity of thought.

He took the satchel off his shoulder and searched through it for one of the memory syringes. Rolling up his sleeve, he grimaced at the tracks that had guiltily gathered on his arm. Maybe Bits was right. Maybe the stuff did turn you into an addict. He eased the needle in nonetheless, because if he was going to get Megan out, he had to remember that was his endgame.

As his focus sharpened, he turned his attention to the desk. It was a mess of files and photographs, and he had too much cop in his veins to not want to review them. He slid onto the seat, spreading the photos out in front of him.

Old man, young girl.

Teenage boy, old woman.

Old man, infant boy.

Pictures of the subjects taken at long range, the photographer presumably unseen, then pictures of the subjects taken together from a variety of angles, scared faces and terrified eyes.

These are the Generation Killer's victims, thought Joe. Elias's victims. That's still hard to believe, but the evidence is overwhelming.

And there was something else.

They all had three-line tattoos on their hands. The same one the old man in the morgue had had. What did that mean?

One final photo hid at the bottom of the pile. It was smaller than the others, a Polaroid. The colours were washed out and impermanent. A woman smiled coyly at the camera. She was blonde, with cut-glass bone structure and a sense of authority in her eyes.

That's her, thought Joe. The woman who didn't glimmer, the woman I saw back in the Pen. Daisy-May said it was impossible, yet here I am looking at her photograph, and there's no way it wasn't taken on the soil. Feels like I've bought a jigsaw with half the pieces missing.

Megan Veins didn't care about jigsaws, though. Neither did Bits. All they cared about was freedom, so that was all he should care about. Daisy-May could take care of the rest. This was his case, and it was high time he solved it.

The top drawer of the desk was open. Why wouldn't it be? Elias would hardly have been expecting company.

There was a set of keys in the drawer. Long, slender lengths of metal held together by a spindle of wire. And they weren't alone; a collection of plastic bottles had been tucked away at the back. Joe had seen them before, at the abandoned nightclub.

At Elias's so-called sanctuary.

The doorway at the back of the room might have been small, but the room it led to was considerably bigger.

It had the same moist brickwork as the room he'd just come from, but this was very much the go-large version: the ceiling stretched out far above Joe's head, the walls keeping a respectable distance from each other, the floor angular. He realised he was on a stubby tiled mezzanine. An eight-foot drop to the floor, if that.

Another machine, identical to the one in the room he'd just come from. Better preserved, the Nazi insignia gleaming on it.

A metal table sat in the middle of the room below, the oversized syringe hovering above it seeping in menace. A young woman was perched on its edge, looking at something Joe couldn't see.

And she wasn't alone. Bits was a few feet away, unconscious and unmoving.

I'm not too late, thought Joe. I can still salvage this.

Elias walked into view.

No denying it now.

He was unarmed, and paler than the last time Joe had seen him.

Because he's dying. That part wasn't a lie. I've been around death long enough to be able to smell it.

Elias had his back to Joe. Fifty feet away, give or take. If Joe was quick – and as quiet as his newly solid form would allow – he could drop down from the mezzanine and sneak up behind him, overpower him. It was the one advantage of not being formless any more.

It gave him a chance to fight back.

With the barrel of a gun resting in the small of her back, Megan Veins had walked.

It had been a silent walk, every step feeling like a march towards the gallows. After a few moments of clammy low-ceilinged corridors dripping with moss and mulch, they had arrived at the cavernous room she'd first seen with George. The metal gurney – and the large needle that hung above it – sat below them.

It hadn't got any less intimidating.

There was a new addition to the room: an unconscious man, lying a few feet away from the table.

He glimmers, thought Megan. *Which means he's dead. Which means he's going to be fuck-all use to me.*

The gun jabbed into her back again, aiming her towards a flight of stone steps.

She swallowed as she began to descend them, each step taking her closer to the table and needle.

'There's no reason to be afraid,' said the man.

'Oh, I think there is,' said Megan, her feet squelching into pools of water.

When she jumped off the last step, she pointed at the unconscious body on the floor. 'Who's that?'

'Someone who asked too many questions. Turn around.'

Megan took a breath and did as she was told.

If anything, the man looked even worse than when she'd first seen him outside the cell. It was like thick dark grooves had been cut under his eyes, and his white hair straggled its way down his back.

She cocked her head at him, staring so intently it was like she was X-raying his soul.

There's something familiar about him, she thought.

It's his eyes.

'You're the boy in the film. The second one. You're Elias.'

'I'm impressed,' said Elias.

'Educated guess,' said Megan. 'What happened to you? After the film ended?'

'Until recently, I couldn't remember. Then I was shown the evidence. You saw some of it on that film.'

'There's more?

'Lots more. A lot of it featuring your grandfather.'

'Everyone seems to know that man but me,' said Megan.

'I knew him all right.'

'Meaning what?'

'Meaning I killed him,' said Elias. 'Him and all those like him.'

Megan swallowed. 'You're the one I heard about on the news.'

'Am I?' said Elias.

'Even gave you some fancy title. Generation Murderer or something like that.'

'It's Generation *Killer*,' said Elias, 'and it's a gaudy title that cheapens the authenticity of my message.'

He took a step towards her.

'Who do you think I am exactly?' said Megan.

'I think you're the granddaughter of Stanley Veins. A man who deserves to go down in history as a monster, every bit as bad as Mengele or any of the other Nazi butchers.'

'Getting sick of saying this, but I never knew my grandfather. How can you hold me responsible for what he's done? What have I ever done to you?'

'You? Nothing,' said Elias. 'You're a victim, just like me.'

'So you'll let me go?'

'Of course. After all, we're virtually related.'

Megan looked at him uncertainly. 'I don't know you.'

'No, but we have something in common. The mark on your hand.'

She covered the barcode-shaped smudge out of habit.

'My own went when my arm did,' said Elias, nodding to his empty sleeve, 'but I bore the same mark. All of us do. Tell me, what do you remember of your childhood?'

'Not much,' said Megan. 'The stuff I do remember, I try my best to forget.'

'Lucky girl. I assume then that the Gift Protocol means nothing to you?'

'Not a damn thing.'

He nodded his head. 'I envy you.'

'I don't get that a lot,' said Megan.

'Have you ever questioned why you can see the dead?'

'Those sorts of questions always have answers you don't want to hear.'

'It was bred into you,' said Elias. 'In a room very like this one. The men and women I euthanised were part of an initiative that manipulated the DNA of children at birth. The Gift, they called it. I was treated like diseased meat, poked around with, experimented with.'

He took a step towards Megan. 'So were you.'

'Bullshit,' said Megan. 'I was given up for adoption.'

'You can see the dead,' said Elias, 'because of the disease that lies within you.'

'That's not true. There's nothing wrong with me.'

Elias smiled. 'Do you know what my parents told me about my condition? They said my cancer was a gift from God, one that allowed me to see and care for those souls who couldn't care for themselves. And I believed them. My disease was a blessing that allowed me to do God's work.'

'And what?' asked Megan. 'They were lying?'

Elias pointed at the empty sleeve of his coat. 'Of course they were lying. The cancer was given to me and to Walter, my brother. Walter didn't survive it. I did, but I have no memories of the programme. All I remember is the Pen, and its mission. *This* is where that mission, and my service to it, has got me. I'm nothing but a sack of skin to these people, sent to care for those who have already died. Who will care for me? Care for you, when the cancer shows itself in your system?'

'This is all bullshit,' said Megan. 'I can barely ever remember having a cold.'

'It was like that for me,' said Elias. 'Then it wasn't.' His smile turned sad. 'Not remembering is what the likes of me and you do. I don't imagine you remember anything of your childhood, do you?'

She swallowed. 'That doesn't mean I have a disease inside me.'

'It means exactly that. I thought showing you the tapes would release your repressed memories, but it didn't. Perhaps it was because you weren't co-opted into the service of the Pen. When the programme ended, your grandfather smuggled you away to keep you safe, giving you the chance of a normal life. I wasn't so lucky.'

He took another step towards her. 'When you leave here, I want you to take our story to the world. Mine and Walter's.'

'I don't believe what you're telling me,' said Megan, 'so how do you expect the world to? It's insane. *You're* insane. It's too big. Too crazy.'

Elias smiled coldly. 'The media were quick enough to christen me the Generation Killer. They'll lap the story up.'

'What if I say no?' said Megan.

He cocked the revolver's hammer back. 'I don't want to shoot you. The truth will be better coming from you, but if I have to, I will. It won't change the power of the proof.'

He nodded towards the metal gurney. 'Get on there.'

Megan looked warily at the syringe dangling over it.

'Oh, don't worry about that,' said Elias fondly. 'Its bark's worse than its bite.'

This reassurance did little to move Megan, who stood deadly still.

Elias raised the gun slightly, then fired.

She screamed in surprise as the gunshot pinged off the tiled brickwork above her head.

Elias gestured at the table.

Megan moved towards it.

Megan had seen the spirit on the mezzanine. She was praying that Elias hadn't.

He glimmered, but there was something different about that glimmer. It was better defined, like he was being beamed in via a stronger signal than any spirit she'd seen before.

She prayed he was here to help her, but ultimately she knew better. When had a spirit ever helped her before?

When had anyone?

'Lic down,' said Elias.

'What are you going to do to me?'

'Shoot you, if you don't lie down.'

Megan risked a look upwards. The man spirit raised a finger to his lips.

387

I hope you know what you're doing, ghostie.

She did what Elias asked.

'The papers got it wrong, you know,' he said, pointing the gun at the straps lying limply by her legs. 'When they said I'd murdered the young ones I took.'

Megan began to reluctantly tighten the straps around her legs. 'I heard that you gave them radiation poisoning. Sounds like murder to me.'

'I saved them from a lifetime of agony,' said Elias. 'They died in days rather than pain-filled years.' He shrugged the stump of his arm. 'I released them. I don't expect thanks for such a deed, merely understanding.'

'Just one thing wrong with that,' said Megan. 'The way you "released" them. It's no quick, merciful death. It's cruel. It's twisted. It's out-and-out fucking evil.'

Yeah, it is, thought Joe. That's evil fucks for you, though: they're always ready with a bullshit excuse.

Taking a deep breath, he dropped down from the mezzanine, containing the grunt upon impact as best he could. Elias at least didn't seem to have noticed; he was fastening the second leather strap over Megan's chest.

Joe could easily get the jump on him . . .

He paused for a second, suddenly unsure.

Will it mean I break the laws, fighting Elias? Will it raise the Xylophone Man?

Memories of Daisy-May being swallowed whole assaulted him. He shook them from his head.

This is what I was brought back from the Pit for. Moments like this. Elias's motivations for committing these crimes don't mean a fucking thing compared to saving the life of an innocent woman. I'm the only one who can rescue Megan, so that's what I'm going to do – or die trying. Again.

Maybe that'll be enough to stay out of hell.

Guess I'll find out.

He sprinted towards Elias, gobbling up the space between them. A mere five feet away, his foot connected with a piece of masonry, the noise enough to make Elias turn but not to prevent Joe's shoulder from meeting his face. Elias screamed in pain as his nose exploded, both men landing on the floor in a sprawl.

Joe swung a fist at Elias's face, trying to add to the damage, a jolt going through his body, unused as it was to physical contact.

'I might be dead,' he panted, raining down blows, 'but I can still take a deranged prick like you.'

Elias raised his elbow, blocking a right hook, then drove his knee upwards into Joe's crotch, causing him to yelp in pain. The one-armed missionary squirmed out from under him, bucking him off then pushing himself away on his backside and scrambling to his feet.

They stood a foot apart, neither moving, both of them looking for an opening.

'You found the machine,' said Elias, glaring at him. 'How do you like being solid again? Does it make you feel alive?'

'What happened to your mission?' said Joe. 'What happened to your pledge to the Duchess?'

Elias smiled. 'Why on earth would I care about a pledge to that old cunt?'

Despite the knowledge of Elias's other crimes, the venom of this still stung Joe.

'The Duchess and her predecessors founded and continued the Gift Protocol,' Elias continued. 'No one has ever deserved to pay for a crime more than her.'

'You made a difference with your work,' said Joe, noticing out of the corner of his eye that Bits had begun to stir.

'You made a difference to *me*. That's a fact, whether you want to believe it or not.'

'I made no difference to anyone,' spat Elias. 'No one living, anyway. And I would have died in ignorance if not for Lucia. She opened her heart to me, as well as my eyes. She brought me the evidence. Showed me the truth.'

'Who's Lucia?' asked Joe.

'A blonde angel in a world of devils.'

Joe risked a look at Megan. She was strapped to the table, but safe for now.

Bits had got to his feet. He was in play.

'You ever stop to ask yourself why this blonde angel gave you the information?' said Joe. 'Question that perhaps she had an ulterior motive?'

'My life has been for nothing,' said Elias, and Joe couldn't work out whether he hadn't heard his question or whether he was simply ignoring it. 'Nothing.'

'I'm sorry for what's been done to you.' Joe took a half-step forward, noticing that Bits had moved closer to Elias, 'but it doesn't excuse the things you've done in return. And I don't understand *why* you've done those things.'

Then he looked into Elias's eyes, and he did understand.

There was a wildness there, a loss of focus and of reason he'd seen many times before as a living, breathing copper. They were the eyes of someone whose sanity had stretched, then broken completely, and people like that didn't indulge in logic, or compassion, or decency. They lashed out, desperate to lance the boil of their pain by spreading it. They murdered the youngest and oldest members of a family in a futile, despotic desire to wipe out an entire line, in the same way their own line had been wiped out.

And I have to stop him, because that madness makes him dangerous, and it makes him crafty, too. He's already proved he can run rings around me. He's been doing it since I first set foot in Manchester.

Joe took another step forward.

Elias grasped the oversized hypodermic needle and nudged it down towards Megan's neck. She stilled.

'You don't have to do this, Elias,' Joe said. 'You're better than this.'

'Stay back.'

Joe exchanged a look with Bits.

It was one that said *get in position, and make it snappy.*

'You know, there's something I still don't understand,' he said, playing for time as Bits did just that. 'The wendigo bullshit you fed us. Why?'

Elias chuckled drily. 'A misdirect. One I thought might scare you off. Couldn't have Stanley's ghost revealing who I was, so I wiped him from the earth and led you on a wendigo chase. I was hoping a corrupt policeman like you would be dissuaded from rescuing Megan if you thought something might eat what was left of your putrid little soul. But you kept coming. I was mainly worried about you recognising the boy.'

Joe frowned. He *knew* there'd been something familiar about the boy.

'I could never work out where I knew him from.'

'You brought him to me,' said Elias. 'Or at least you told me where to find him. At the school, back in Lincolnshire. When you were still hunting yourself down like an idiot. His face was covered in vines when you first met him. I retrieved him. Gave him Lucia's memory serum. Made him my pet. A pet, regrettably, I had to put down.'

Fuck, thought Joe. *I should have recognised the uniform. Did recognise it, just couldn't piece it together.*

Some detective I am.

'You didn't need to kill him,' he said. 'You didn't need to kill those poor bastards at the shelter, either.' He shook his head. 'Why did you?'

'I couldn't allow anyone to stop me before my work was complete.'

'You call this work? It's cold-blooded murder. And I say that's bollocks: you *enjoyed* killing those spirits.'

Elias bared his teeth. Joe was of the opinion he'd never seen someone quite so broken.

'Why shouldn't I enjoy it? I've given my lives for those freaks. Where's it got me? Soon enough I'll be one of them.'

'Why not just release Megan with the information?' said Joe. 'Why pump her full of radiation?'

'Because *I* was pumped full of radiation. It's *justice*.'

'It makes you just as bad as them,' said Joe. 'Surely you can see that?'

'My method of attracting attention is vicious,' said Elias, 'but vicious is the only thing the world understands.' He sneered at Joe. 'You were remarkably easy to manipulate, you know. You're not much of an investigator, Lazarus.'

'You've got me there,' said Joe, noting that Bits had silently worked his way round so he was directly behind Elias. 'But you should cut me some slack. I'm new to the good-guy game.'

'Enough talk,' said Elias, lowering the needle until its tip grazed Megan's neck. 'It's time to end this.'

'Fucking *right* it is.'

Bits hooked an arm around Elias's neck, wrestling him away from the syringe as Joe lurched forward, jumping onto the operating table and pushing the needle up and away from Megan.

Elias lashed out, catching Bits in the throat; the Mancunian spluttered, grabbing his neck and releasing his hold. Elias shoved him, then turned on his heel and ran for the entrance.

'You all right?' said Joe, jumping off the table.

'In enough pain . . . not to be dead,' gasped Bits. 'You need to . . . get after him.'

'We need to get Megan out of here,' said Joe.

'Go,' said Bits, feeling his throat. 'She's safe . . . with me. Can't let that fucker . . . get away.'

Joe helped him to his feet.

'Met cunts . . . like him before,' said Bits. 'Keep you around . . . 'cos they want you to see . . . how clever they are.'

'Lucky for you,' said Joe. 'You'd be dead otherwise.'

'Sorry . . . I stropped off in a piss . . .' said Bits.

'Sorry I gave you cause to,' said Joe.

Bits stuck out a hand. Joe took it.

'Now go get that *prick*.'

Joe knew Elias couldn't have gone far, but that didn't change the fact that the storm drain was empty. Water flowed over his feet and the roof overhead curved inwards, as if it were a tiled blanket God had thrown protectively over him.

He would have preferred something more bulletproof.

The lighting was different here too; the red of the previous room had been replaced by sickly yellow, slivers of light pumping out a dim, watery hue. A telephone was fixed to the wall, ancient if not yet retired. Because this place is still used, thought Joe. Maybe not in the last few years – it'd be impossible for the set-up downstairs to exist if that was the case – but recently enough for the rust and rats not to have taken it yet.

The tunnel dipped slightly and he spotted the fleeing form of Elias.

He kicked off, water firing from his feet as he ran, eating up the hundred or so yards to his quarry.

Elias turned.

Joe saw the gun in his hand.

A blink of orange light and a whisper of fire scorched the air as he threw himself to the floor. Drain water came up to meet him as another bolt cracked over his head.

'A present from Lucia,' Elias called. 'One blast will send you to the hell you deserve.'

'If I go there,' Joe replied, 'I'll be taking you with me.'

Elias fired again.

And missed again.

The water in front of Joe sizzled, birthing a wall of steam.

He set off at a sprint, using the steam as cover, his quarry's one hand working in his favour as Elias's aim lurched between wayward and appalling, bolt after bolt fired and missing, a tsunami erupting in the tunnel as a result. Elias roared in frustration just as Joe launched himself forward in pure save-the-world determination, hooking his quarry around the knees and bringing him crashing down to the ground. Both men landed hard, the inches of storm water doing little to soften the hard concrete beneath.

Think I preferred the old passing-through-everything thing, Joe thought, coughing up water. It was a lot less painful.

He reached for Elias just as the fallen missionary emptied the contents of an aerosol can into his face.

Joe screamed, his hands going automatically to his face, his eyes bleached and useless.

'A crude weapon,' said Elias, his words containing a smile, 'but an effective one. 'Pure soil atmosphere, weaponised.''

Joe heard him take several steps backwards, his footsteps echoing. Keep talking, he thought, because while you're talking, I can tell where you are, even if I can't see where you are.

A painful blur signalled his returning vision. He heard the whine of a gun.

He tried to open his eyes, but whatever Elias had sprayed him with prevented him from doing so. His back met the tiled wall, and he realised there was nowhere else to go.

The gun whined.

Joe waited for the end.

It didn't come.

Elias swore in frustration at his misfiring weapon.

Lucky, thought Joe.

Cold steel struck his forehead and he felt less so. He slumped to the ground.

The blow had loosened up his vision, though. As it returned, he saw that he was at the edge of the drain, a deluge of water flowing around and over him before it pitched itself over a sheer drop into even greater depths.

'You think you're a hero,' said Elias, grinding the gun barrel into Joe's forehead, 'when in fact you're just the second-rate pawn of the villain.'

'Last person to think of myself as a hero,' said Joe, the water below him demanding a blood sacrifice. 'Definitely the last person to call myself one. I've done plenty of wrong.'

'Who are you to dispense justice then?' said Elias. 'Who gives you the right?'

'Daisy-May Braithwaite, Warden of the Pen,' said Joe. '*She* gives me the right.'

He grabbed Elias by his pinned sleeve and yanked him forward, tumbling them both over the precipice, the water below thundering its approval, the men's arms bound around each other as they hurtled towards the churning depths.

The water hit hard.

It tried to spit Joe out. The current dragged him back under.

He bobbed to the surface. He couldn't see Elias.

The water dunked him again.

Then it took him for good.

Chapter Twenty-Five

Hatoyama was limping too badly to sneak quietly, and bleeding too badly to be anything but conspicuous. He was grateful, then, that the man sitting at the control desk was so engrossed in his work. He hadn't heard the shuffling, panting detective enter, and he didn't turn now as Hatoyama crouched down behind a desk.

Then he did turn, and Hatoyama had to choke down a whimper.

Sato. The missing nuclear technician. They hadn't found him at his apartment, but they'd found him now. He was *here*. At least part of him was. It seemed to Hatoyama that the man with the glazed eyes and drooling mouth was at war with himself. Like there were two barking Rottweilers inside him, tearing at each other for control.

He was unarmed, though, and as injured as Hatoyama was, Sato looked worse, like a sneeze of wind would knock him over.

And he doesn't know the bolt-cutter won't hurt him. To him, it'll look like a gun. At least I hope it will.

Hatoyama rose from his hiding place, his body sighing in pain.

'Hold it right there,' he said, training the bolt-cutter at Sato's midriff, 'and put your hands where I can see them.'

Sato smiled.

'Hands,' said Hatoyama, the arrow in his leg gnawing at him, confidence ebbing away. 'I won't ask again.'

'You won't need to,' said Sato, his voice prospected from hell.

With one fluid movement, he lifted the desk in front of him, raising it over his head and hurling it towards Hatoyama. The detective dived to the floor, the arrow taking the weight.

Blind with pain, he fired.

The air crackled.

Sato screamed. His body spasmed, a glowing blotch on his chest where he'd been hit. His skin hot-red, hands finding his face, fingers finding his mouth, he yanked his jaw open, choking on something foul and unseen.

Hatoyama stood there, the gun hanging limply from his right hand, helpless.

The head of something appeared in Sato's mouth.

Hatoyama forgot his pain. He looked on, disgusted, as a worm-like creature began to clamber out of Sato's gaping mouth. It withered and browned before his eyes, dropping onto the floor and curling in on itself like it couldn't take the shame.

Sato looked down at it, puzzled, as if seeing it for the first time.

Then he looked at Hatoyama and collapsed.

Hanna blinked, the connection with her possessed puppet Sato cut. The last thing she'd seen through his hollowed-out eyes was the paunchy detective who'd proved to be so troublesome.

She couldn't fail. Not when she was so close.

She turned to the followers on either side of her, then pointed at the Duchess.

No words were necessary. Her followers smiled and began to move towards their prey.

The Duchess smiled too.

Hatoyama dragged the barely conscious Sato into the control room, his dead-weight arm flung around the detective's neck.

I've got a hand that has no intention of stopping bleeding, a leg held together with an arrow and a prayer, and radiation so hot on my skin it's like I'm bathing in it. This is it. This is where I go out.

There was a table immediately in front of him, which was good, because it was thick, it was chunky, and it would conceal him if he shuffled behind its sight lines in the right way. The wrong way would reveal him to Hanna and her cohort.

He slumped down behind it, putting Sato into the recovery position. There looked to be nothing physically wrong with the man, but who knew what damage had been wrought on his mind.

Rising to his knees, he peered over the top of the table, bringing the bolt-cutter slowly up and resting its stubby barrel on the surface. He had a shot, but only of the Duchess's back.

For what that was worth. The bolt-cutter never seemed to run out of firepower (it had a self-perpetuating energy source, Mabel had told him once), but it had already proved to be unreliable.

Do what you're going to do or get out of my way, Duchess. I've got one shot at this, and that shot needs to hit Hanna the teenage witch, not the Duchess, former ruler of an afterlife realm.

He closed one eye, sharpening his line of sight, and waited for his moment of glory.

Hanna was right. The Duchess didn't want to admit it, but she *was* feeling better. Stronger than she'd felt in years, even when she'd still been Warden of the Pen.

That's because of the reactor, said Oma Jankie. *The reactor and the radiation it's vomiting out into the air. It's your lifeblood here, just like it is in the Pen.*

One thing at a time, thought the Duchess, as Hanna's followers rushed towards her. One thing at a time.

It was like something out of the movies, one of the glossy cyberpunk adventures his birth city seemed to specialise in, where machinery and magic and technology and body mutilation conspired in a neon-techno riot.

Hatoyama watched, gawping, as the Duchess stuck out a hand, raising the followers grouped around Hanna clean off their feet. She then whipped her hand to the left, sending the marionettes spinning through the air and crashing out of the window at the back.

'Try that on me,' said Hanna, and Hatoyama didn't like the way she said it. He liked her confident tone even less.

Get out of the way, he thought, staring down the gun barrel at the Duchess's back, waiting for an opening.

The Duchess could feel Hatoyama's eyes boring into her back, could feel too the hollow sensation inside that told her how little power she had left, radiation be damned.

Perhaps a little was enough if she played this right and trusted in the shot of a soil-breathing detective.

She pushed with her mind and everything she had left, stretching out her arms and her mind with them. Hanna was ready for it, but ready, apparently, didn't get the job done, at least not all the way; she was shoved backwards and sideways, taking the sting out of the mental blow but staggering nonetheless.

Fire, thought the Duchess, collapsing to the floor. Fire.

Hatoyama did, the bolt-cutter chugging and whining and

bucking in his hands, a slab of light and sulphur spitting from the barrel, a split second of surprise on Hanna's face, her hands rising in defence, a gesture as useless as it was understandable. The shot ripped one hand clean off, then struck her in the face. Hanna screamed, falling backwards, her remaining hand clawing at what was left of her features.

'Finish her,' said the Duchess. 'God forgive me, finish her.'

Hatoyama aimed the bolt-cutter, preparing to do just that.

'Wait, Detective.'

Hanna's voice was guttural. Scorched. There was clear, naked air where the left side of her face should have been. It made the smile she was attempting all the more hideous.

She rose unsteadily to her feet. 'Kill me and you won't find out the secret the Duchess is keeping from you.'

Hatoyama frowned, his eyes flicking from Hanna to the Duchess. 'What secret?'

'Don't listen to her,' the Duchess said. 'Kill her. End it.'

'There's nothing natural about the cancer you have,' Hanna said. 'It was engineered within you by scientists. It was called the Gift Protocol, and it was done at the behest of the Duchess. You can see the dead because of her. You're going to die because of her.'

Hatoyama flinched, then looked at the Duchess again. 'Is this true?'

She thought about lying, then decided lies had held the floor long enough.

Her shoulders sagged.

She nodded.

Hatoyama's gun arm began to tremble. 'I'm sick because of you?'

The Duchess nodded. 'I'm sorry.'

'She deserves to die for what she did,' said Hanna, her back against the window.

Hatoyama's whole body was shaking now, almost as if his inner turmoil was tearing him apart.

He began to move the gun away from Hanna, pointing it instead at the Duchess.

I could beg for forgiveness, she thought, but I don't deserve it.

He stood frozen, the gun in no-man's-land.

The Duchess watched him take a breath.

He trained the gun on Hanna once again. 'The Duchess may have done me wrong, but she never tried to nuke a city. I'm a cop. I take down the bad guys.'

God bless you, thought the Duchess.

He pulled the trigger.

Nothing happened.

An alarm started shrieking, demanding their attention.

A screaming grind began to sound from the reactor room behind them.

The Duchess looked to the observation window and the slowly revolving core behind it.

Hatoyama pulled the trigger again. Still nothing happened.

'You're too late.'

The Duchess turned back to Hanna. 'What have you done?'

She smiled her nightmare smile, then stepped backwards, passing clean through the back window and dropping out of sight.

'What's happening here?'

Sato, pale, drawn but conscious, looked past them at the main reactor.

'You tell me,' said Hatoyama. 'You're the nuclear technician.'

He limped to the control desk, his eyes never leaving the chugging, screeching reactor. He dropped onto a steel stool, his eyes switching finally to the screen in front of him. 'The reactor's back online.'

'That, we know,' said Hatoyama.

'It can't be back online,' said Sato. 'It would be disastrous.'

'Why disastrous?' asked the Duchess.

'Why disastrous?' parroted Hatoyama, a translator for words that couldn't be heard.

'Because there's no electrical power,' said Sato, 'and with no power, there's no way to regulate the water flow. No water flow, no way to cool the reactor. No way to cool the reactor, no way to stop an explosion. No way to stop an explosion, no way to prevent radiation gases being pumped into the sky. Hundreds of thousands will die. The lucky ones, instantly.'

Hatoyama stumbled, putting out a hand to steady himself.

He hasn't got much left, thought the Duchess, noting the detective's sagging frame. Not with the air like it is.

'How do we stop it?' he asked.

'We shouldn't need to,' said Sato, confused. 'It should have been shut down remotely the moment it came back online.'

Hatoyama and the Duchess exchanged a look.

Hatoyama turned back to Sato. 'A device called the Dog Catcher is blocking the signal.'

'Then we need to find this Dog Catcher and destroy it. If we do, the signal will get through and the remote team will be able to shut down the reactor.'

'It could be anywhere,' said Hatoyama. 'We'll never find it in time.'

Sato looked thoughtfully at the screaming reactor. 'There's another way.'

'Don't keep us in suspense,' said Hatoyama.

'Us?' said Sato, looking around the room, his eyes passing over the Duchess.

'Me,' said Hatoyama.

'There's a service ladder that takes you under the core. A failsafe was built under all of these 784 MWEs. If the reactor can't be shut down electronically, it can be done manually. You pull the switch, you flood the core. Problem is, with the amount of radiation now in the chamber, anyone who sets foot outside this room will be killed instantly.'

The Duchess and Hatoyama exchanged a look, if not a smile.

'Anyone living,' said the Duchess.

Hatoyama and the Duchess stood at the observation window. The alarm had become even more grating and insistent, if that was possible.

'My God,' said the Duchess.

Hatoyama said nothing, instead gaping at the reactor below. Forty of Hanna's followers stood in front of it, all of them looking up at the control booth, all of them ready, it seemed, to fight to their second death to protect it.

There are so many of them, thought the Duchess. And so few of me.

Hatoyama sighed in pain next to her.

'You look a little worse for wear,' said the Duchess.

'I've been exposed to what is likely to be a fatal amount of radiation,' said Hatoyama, 'and I've got an arrow sticking out of my leg. Luckily, it's you who has to fight your way through the zombie horde.'

'Just make sure you're still alive once I have. It's an awful lot of effort to go through for you to simply die.'

Hatoyama coughed, the force of it bending him double.

The Duchess felt a shift in her vision as the alarm continued to scream and Hanna's followers patiently waited for her down below, none of them moving an inch. 'There are so many of them,' she repeated out loud, each word fainter than the last.

'God doesn't knock two followers off every time you moan about it.'

'God,' said the Duchess wistfully. 'How I wish he'd get his hands dirty once in a while.'

'Even I know that's not the way he works,' said Hatoyama.

'I'm sorry for what was done to you,' said the Duchess. 'I'm sorry I lied about it, too.'

'Sorry won't change things,' said Hatoyama. 'Sorry won't stop the reactor and save the city. Fuck sorry.'

The Duchess smiled at him. 'Fuck sorry.'

She jumped.

The Duchess dropped to the reactor floor, the water at her feet just a trickle, the ugly core turning like it was being spun by a half-arsed toddler, and pondered Hatoyama's words about God. It wasn't how he worked, intervention. It was difficult to push the whole free-will angle, which was very much the Almighty's thing, if you stepped in every time a child of creation dropped a clanger. Alive or dead, he'd have to interfere with his unruly subjects' decisions constantly, course-correcting their hapless fuck-ups.

The Duchess got it, but that didn't mean she had to like it.

Because sometimes things are too big, she thought. Sometimes even the powerful need help. I need it now, God, if you're listening. I don't have much left in me, and the soil breathers aren't my responsibility, but retaining some basic sense of humanity, is. That's why I'm asking for just a little bit of help. I won't ask again. I almost certainly won't be around to ask again after this. I'll go to the Pit if that's what it takes. Just give me the strength to save this city. Please.

He's not listening, said Oma Jankie. *He never listens. I've always said that.*

You've always said a lot of things, the Duchess replied. Most of them are wrong. Some of them are downright evil. Every good thing I've ever done has been despite you rather than because of you.

She closed her eyes and began to draw on the reservoir of power within her. It wasn't the relatively wholesome power she had enjoyed in the Pen; this was different somehow. Tainted. Unclean, if intoxicating. The end destination might be the same, but the journey, she knew, was an unsafe one. The radiation here meant the potential death of innocent, living souls. She had no choice but to use it if she was going to save them, but it was going to come at a cost.

She just hoped the cost wouldn't be those innocent souls. Her own was already well past saving.

Hatoyama didn't know how she was doing it, only that she was.

The Duchess was in a trance. She stood swaying slightly, her arms outstretched as if conducting some unseen orchestra, and the air around her was speeding up, almost as if it were psyching itself for an assault.

A boutique tornado began to form in the centre of the room. It was as if God had gleefully unleashed a spinning top, a funnel of dust and wind making its way drunkenly towards Hanna's followers, who remained in their rigid formation but whose eyes found each other, their faith in their absent leader secure even if their faith in their own bravery had begun to waver.

A man and woman at the head of the formation were plucked from the floor, arms and legs thrashing powerlessly against the tunnel of wind, and now, Hatoyama saw, the formation did begin to break apart. Hanna's followers began to run, but to little effect; whatever the Duchess had created was seemingly hungry and wouldn't be sated until it devoured every last one of them.

How did I get here? he asked himself as the Duchess slowly

brought her hands together, an action that made the tornado, engorged with Hanna's followers, spin faster. I'm in the company of gods and madness. Perhaps that's what it means to be a god. Perhaps it turns them all mad in the end. The Duchess seems on the right side of it compared to her sister. At least I hope she is.

The tornado spun faster and faster until it was merely a blur of vector trails and limbs, and as the Duchess stretched out her arms, the wind tunnel began to rise towards the punctured roof. Hatoyama swore he could hear the screams as it passed through it into the darkening sky.

The Duchess dropped to her knees, her frail body trembling, her parched lungs breathing in the irradiated air. Sweat saddled her back, and her vision popped in and out of focus.

She'd done it. Hanna's followers were gone. Now all she had to do was stop a nuclear holocaust and she'd be able to put her feet up and have a slug of whisky.

She got to her feet, the alarm still celebrating the imminent reactor meltdown, and stumbled towards the grumbling, groaning cylindrical beast at the centre of the room. She didn't know what she was looking for specifically, only that it would be amongst the gubbins of the reactor itself. The proximity to such concentrated radiation would kill Hatoyama instantly – would already be killing him as he waited (no doubt impatiently) in the control room – but it would have little effect on her.

She stopped as she arrived at the reactor, because although it couldn't hurt her, that didn't mean that the thought of walking into a four-metre revolving metal slug laced with radiation didn't give her pause. Now that she was up close, she was struck by the intimidating nature of the machine. It was such an aberration, such a device of poison and wrongness, it felt to the Duchess like a graffiti artist had tagged the walls of heaven.

Deciding that philosophising would do the millions of Japanese residents facing the prospect of a nuclear winter little good, she walked through the slowly rotating wall of the reactor.

What's the plan here, little Rachel? asked the cawing voice of Oma Jankie. *You're no nuclear physicist. You didn't even graduate from high school.*

That's because you didn't let me go to high school, the Duchess replied. Now be quiet. The adults are working.

In truth, they weren't, they were more gazing in abject terror.

There was no water in the reactor.

Clouds of steam, water's estranged cousin, filled the core.

A dribble of water rested on the grated floor.

I'm too late, thought the Duchess.

Then she saw the lever. A chunk of red steel. If what Sato said was true, all she needed to do was reach out and pull it.

She crouched down in front of it, adrenaline and power coursing through her veins. She should be on her knees; that she wasn't made her believe in the Almighty, and his faith in her. He may not have been willing to interfere directly, but it was the Duchess's opinion that he wanted *her* to.

I won't let you down, she promised, reaching for the lever. I won't—

Hatoyama yelled out in fear as a blinding white cloud erupted from the reactor. The haze danced in front of his eyes, and for a second he wondered whether this was it, whether he'd died and ended up in heaven.

Then he blinked, and discovered he was still in the reactor's control room, and whether God was Old Testament or New

407

Testament, it was unlikely he'd have such a modest sense of style.

'She did it,' he said aloud. 'She actually—'

He never finished his sentence.

The world was too busy exploding to let him.

The Duchess had long known that the cliché of your life rushing before your eyes was nonsense. That was because despite the sometimes-contradictory evidence, the Almighty wasn't vindictive. Good or evil, right at the end he gave you the greatest hits. Or, more accurately, hit; the best moment of your life replayed one final time. Everyone deserved to go out on a high, that was how it had been described to her once. Even the truly evil, because after that high, eternity would come calling with the out-takes regardless.

When she'd died the first time, the Duchess had been rewarded with a memory from her childhood. It had been a particularly balmy New York summer's evening, when sunshine and night-time were in extended negotiations as to whose shift it was. She'd been with Hanna and Mabel, taking turns, along with the other neighbourhood children, gleefully running through a leaking fire hydrant. They hadn't talked to each other, the sisters. They hadn't needed to; there was just simple joy in running through the fountain of water. Joy too in sharing the moment with other children; it was a rare moment of collective glee.

Rainbows sprouted from the water as the last rays of sun hit it. That was one of her clearest memories. She'd enjoyed the peace of it, the feeling that at that precise second, nothing was expected of her, or of her sisters; that she could simply live in the moment and enjoy the miracle of creation and existence.

She was back there now. She wasn't in a desecrated exploding nuclear reactor. She was with her sisters in the sunshine, with nothing asked of her other than the simple requirement to enjoy life.

And it's been a wonderful life, she thought. Even when it's been terrible. I give thanks for it.

She was still on that sunny New York street when the world turned white for a final time.

Epilogue

Not everybody could see the film, but everybody talked about it.

It wasn't long, but it didn't need to be. It was a ninety-second call to arms that was also a veiled threat or implied promise, depending on your world view. That only half the people who clicked on it could see it only added to its legend and mystique, because those chosen ones embellished their descriptions for those less fortunate.

It began, inauspiciously, in an empty room. A chair sat in the centre of the frame. A teenage girl with a shock of white hair entered, walking calmly to the chair, then sat down. She looked straight down the barrel of the lens, and those who could see the video commented on her eyes. There was a coldness to them, an ancient wisdom that enraptured and unsettled in equal measure. *It's like they're looking into your soul*, that was what people said. *Looking, and judging.*

What the viewers couldn't decide on was the girl's voice. Many thought it high-pitched and verging on the hysterical, whereas others heard it as deceptively deep, grinding with bass and gravel. Some heard its seductiveness, if not the actual words themselves. Those people would have a role to play in the months to come.

For now, though, there was just this message, and to those who could see and hear it, it wasn't a hoax. To them, it was a miracle.

'My name is Hanna Jankie,' the girl began, 'and I died a very long time ago. Most of you watching this will dismiss that, and why wouldn't you? There are no such things as ghosts; it is one of the hard and fast certainties we know. And I agree with you: I'm no ghost, no wandering spirit striving for peace that's just out of reach. I'm a person, with hopes and dreams and ambitions, just like you. I've always been here, it's just that you've never been able to see me before. So, to answer a question that has troubled and enraptured the human race for a millennium: there is an afterlife. There is something afterwards. Take comfort in that, where you may.'

She leaned forward, placing her hands on her lap, looking every inch the dignified statesman.

'You're going to hear a lot about me in the days to come. I'll be called a variety of names, none of them very pleasant. A lot of people will claim I'm a hoax, or a bad-taste joke. I will understand this, even if it isn't true. Unfortunately for those people, I'm very real. As real as a nuclear reactor meltdown in Tokyo.'

She smiled sadly at this point, as if shouldering an immense burden. 'I'm sorry for the deaths I've caused. If I could have avoided it, I would have done. Those thousands of souls will always be on my conscience, but that's my burden to shoulder. To achieve great things, sacrifices must be made, and those souls have gone to a better place now. Why, the heavenly father wiped out a species because he saw what needed to be done. I've just killed a few thousand.

'You see, I'm a refugee, cast out from the afterlife, and there are millions like me, souls who are stranded here on the soil. The oxygen that granted them life acts as poison when they're dead, rotting away their memories and slowly killing them again. What gives us life – what renews us – is radiation. It's what we breathe in the afterlife. It's what keeps us us.'

She smiled again, this time as if she could see a future worth saving.

'I regret the loss to human life, but I don't regret what I've done. We needed a sanctuary, my people, and now we have one. All the dead are welcome here. There is room for everyone. The living, I would ask to stay away. The air will kill you, and I've left you the rest of the planet.

'Tokyo is ours.'

To the naked eye – certainly the naked eyes in the Zeppelin's cockpit – it almost looked as if they weren't moving. The soot-black clouds were endless, choking any sort of visibility.

They *were* moving, though, and quickly. Daisy-May's condition demanded it, even if her unconscious lips didn't.

'Is she going to die?' said Chestnut, sitting next to the lifeless body of the Warden. 'She don't look good.'

Mabel didn't turn to the girl, instead staring through the cockpit window at the sea of clouds ahead. 'Already dead, isn't she?'

'Yeah.'

'That sound to you like she can die, then?'

'Dead don't always mean dead,' said the girl. 'Not in the Pen.'

'Thanks, Confucius,' said Mabel. 'Your philosophical jabber's just what I need.'

She was right, though, the girl. Dead *didn't* always mean dead in the Pen. Sometimes that was a good thing, and sometimes it wasn't. Which of those things it was for Daisy-May, Mabel didn't know yet.

'You got a plan here?' said Chestnut, taking her place in the first mate's seat. 'Or are we just running?'

'Always got a plan,' said Mabel. 'Got four more if that plan doesn't work, too.'

She hadn't.

There was only one chance for Daisy-May, just one person who could repair the damage the Gloop had done to her, damage she'd exacerbated when defeating Uriel. The problem was, that one person would rather help the devil himself than Mabel.

The Zeppelin broke through the bed of cloud, and Chestnut placed her forehead against the window. 'So where are we going?'

Mabel pointed to the ground. 'Where no one's ever been before. Beyond the Pen wall.'

'What's there?'

'Person who's going to help Daisy-May. Beyond that?' Mabel swallowed, her throat dry. 'Beyond that, I don't know.'

In a world reeling from the nuclear disaster in Japan, the safe return of a missing woman called Megan Veins brought the lightest of relief.

A relief, though, it was, because the world needed good news, and Megan's return was that. That it was so mysterious was skirted over, at least initially. Like the other kidnap victims released by the Generation Killer, she claimed to have total amnesia. What she didn't have was a fatal dose of radiation poisoning. The experts pontificated on this, but Megan didn't, at least not publicly. She'd been through an unimaginable ordeal, the psychologists agreed, one that was bound to leave a few scars.

The truth, whatever that was, could wait.

413

And as far as the media was concerned, the killer was still out there. What was better for business than that?

'Don't like graveyards,' said Bits.

'No one likes graveyards,' said Megan, making him jump. 'They're graveyards.'

Bits still wasn't quite used to talking to the living. He had been unconscious when Elias had been spilling his guts, but Megan had filled him in on the juicy parts. If she could see the dead, that meant she'd been experimented on. Did that mean she'd develop cancer in the same way Elias had? Did she have it already?

'Least it's raining again,' said Bits, looking up fondly at the vertical downpour. 'Thought Manchester had sold out with all that fucking sun.'

They stood together, huddled against rain and wind one of them couldn't feel, the sky above them malevolent and coal black. A small funeral party stood a few yards away, watching as a coffin was lowered into the ground. Bits was annoyed to see that several of the mourners were wearing sunglasses.

'Raining, man. What do they need shades for? Always annoyed me in films, that. Fucking funeral, not a fashion parade.'

'You swear a lot,' said Megan.

'Yeah, I do,' said Bits. 'Sorry about that.'

'That's all right,' said Megan. 'You haven't kidnapped me yet. That's all that matters.'

'Low bar,' said Bits. 'My favourite height.' He turned to her. 'You recognise anyone here?'

She shook her head. 'They're just a bunch of strangers who knew a grandfather I didn't.'

Bits thought of his own grandfather. He hoped he'd made it to the Next Place. Wherever he was, at least he was free of the shackles of the soil.

'You're supposed to solve crimes, right?' said Megan.

'That's what they say.'

'Will you help me find out what happened to my family? Find out what they did to me?'

Bits stood there, considering. 'How much of that gas did Elias have left at the shelter? The shit that helps your memory rather than knocks you clean out?'

'Couple of tanks,' said Megan. 'Why?'

'Because if we're going to find out what happened to you, I'm going to need it. There's something else we need to do first, though.'

'What's that?' said Megan.

Bits looked away, determination on his face. 'We need to find Joe.'

'You still think he's out there?' said Megan.

'I know he is,' said Bits, 'and if we're going to find out what happened to your family – and you – we're going to need him. There's no better copper out there than Joe Lazarus.'

'You look upset, Remus.'

'An unfortunate side effect of disaster.'

Lucia smiled indulgently. 'The laboratory wall can be repaired.'

'I'm not talking about the wall,' said Remus, his face flickering and grimacing on the monitor in front of her. 'I'm talking about the Warden who shouldn't be. The ceremony wasn't completed. I have no legal right to the title.'

Lucia leaned back in her chair. 'You set too much store by precedent in the ancient laws. This is the afterlife, not a courtroom.'

'Thank you for your learned counsel. Whether you believe in it or not, certain procedures have to be followed, and until that girl pins the badge on me, I'll only ever be a dictator who carried out a coup.'

'There are worse things to be,' said Lucia. 'Dictators have the chance to rewrite history as they see fit.'

'I'll never be accepted unless it's by legitimate means,' said Remus. 'I have to find the girl, and if that means razing the Pen to the ground to do so, then so be it.'

'We'll find her,' said Lucia. 'She and that silly old sow Mabel can't hide for ever.'

'*We'll* do nothing of the sort,' said Remus. '*You* have work to do back there on the soil.'

'And I'm doing it,' said Lucia.

'The loss of Elias hasn't hampered you?'

She laughed. 'Hardly. My little Oswald served his purpose: he killed anyone who could jeopardise our operation.'

'In the most attention-seeking way possible. I still disapprove of that.'

'If you don't want the authorities to look at you, you create a big flashing distraction somewhere else,' said Lucia. 'The Generation Killer was that distraction. Bait and switch, Remus. Bait and switch.'

'What about Japan? You met with that homicidal maniac Hanna; you could have stopped her. She's essentially killed a city. Do you know how much attention that's going to draw?'

'Plenty,' said Lucia, 'but none to us. Besides, Hanna is something of a long-term side project of mine. Leave her to me.'

Remus grunted. 'And Lazarus's partner? Megan Veins? What about them?'

'Their escape was unfortunate, but of no real consequence. Who would believe her story?'

'And Lazarus himself?'

Lucia smirked. 'Joe Lazarus won't be a problem. You have my word on that.'

★

How quickly the extraordinary became ordinary.

Twenty years ago, the thought of video-calling somebody on your phone was the stuff of science fiction, but now, because of the strides they'd made, it was possible to speak to the dead. Not for very long, admittedly; ten minutes was the current record, and the picture would wave and wiggle disobediently for much of that time, but still, what a wonder. Remus would do well to remember that.

Lucia powered the monitor off, stood up, and picked absent-mindedly at the black barcode on her left hand. It was a bad habit she'd been unable to shake but really should; drawing attention to the mark was in no one's interest, least of all hers.

Slipping on her jacket, she headed for the door. He was waiting there for her, of course, her knight in shining armour. He clung to her like a child who'd lost their mother, but that was all right; children had their uses, particularly when they couldn't be seen or heard.

'Good evening,' she said, smiling at him. 'How are you?'

'I'm fine, ma'am,' her faithful bodyguard replied, nodding to her deferentially, his eyes glassy and unfocused. 'How was your day?'

'It was just peachy,' said Lucia. 'And I have a feeling this evening's going to be even better.'

Joe led the way to the lifts, and as Lucia followed, she smiled to herself. It was remarkable what you could find in Mancunian storm drains. Even more remarkable how useful those things could turn out to be.

Yes, she had plans for Joe Lazarus.

Big plans.

Acknowledgments

Firstly, it seems like a good opportunity to give special thanks to all the people that were instrumental in helping to pimp the first book after it was released.

Stuart Turton, Mike Craven, Adam Hamdy, James Oswald, Anna Stephens, Dave Wragg, David Fennell, Jonathan Whitelaw, Miranda Dickinson and Rob Parker are all actual real-life writers that were kind enough to read the book and say nice things. They were stamps of approval that meant a lot to me and helped legitimise Joe and the gang. Thanks guys.

There are several reviewers and bloggers who have been consistently generous with their praise and support – in particular Ania Kierczynska, Fiona Sharp and Rosie Talbot. A massive high-five to you all.

Harry Illingworth continues to be the best agent in the land, with the worst taste in football teams. Thanks for the support, mate – two books down, lots more to go. Team DHH is where it's at.

There wouldn't be a book without Gollancz. Editing it is always one of my favourite times of the year, and as well as Rachel Winterbottom's brilliant notes and funny comments, Brendan Durkin joined the gang this time, too. Thanks for your stellar work and pushing the whole thing up a level.

The Dying Squad series has a whole 'look' now, and that's thanks to Tomás Almeida – there's not a time when I don't look at the covers of these books and get a little chill. Appreciative sympathy to Jane Selley – for trying to repair my mangling of the English language. Honorary mentions to Will O'Mullane, Áine Feeney and Frankie Banks.

Several people gave me notes on a significantly worse version of the book you hold in your hands – hugs and kisses to James Briggs, Robin Simcox, Christa Larwood and Dan Woodall for your feedback and notes.

Thanks to the main beta reader in my life and still the coolest girl in school, Kirsty Eyre. Thanks for putting up with me, and for telling me when something in the books abjectly terrible. Thanks for the support. Thanks for being you.

And finally, thanks to you for reading. Stick around for book number three, I'll make it worth your while. It's a good 'un . . .

Credits

Adam Simcox and Gollancz would like to thank everyone at Orion who worked on the publication of *The Generation Killer* in the UK.

Editorial
Rachel Winterbottom
Áine Feeney
Brendan Durkin

Copy editor
Jane Selley

Proof reader
Patrick McConnell

Audio
Paul Stark
Jake Alderson

Editorial Management
Charlie Panayiotou
Jane Hughes

Contracts
Anne Goddard
Paul Bulos

Design
Lucie Stericker
Tomas Almeida
Joanna Ridley
Nick May

Finance
Jennifer Muchan
Jasdip Nandra
Elizabeth Beaumont
Sue Baker

Production
Paul Hussey

Marketing
Brittany Sankey

Operations
Jo Jacobs
Sharon Willis
Lisa Pryde
Lucy Brem

Sales
Jen Wilson
Esther Waters
Victoria Laws
Rachael Hum
Ellie Kyrke-Smith
Frances Doyle
Georgina Cutler

A sneak peak of the next installment in

The Dying Squad Series . . . The Ungrateful Dead.

Prologue

They came for us at night.

Not that night held any meaning any more. In our blackout bunker, time had ceased to justify itself as a concept. It was an elastic construct you knew existed, like air travel and elephants, but one you never personally experienced.

We were permitted one hour of light a day. This was a self-imposed diktat from my father, one my mother fought long and hard for. 'For the *texts*, my darling,' she would implore, her tone whispered, though no less urgent for it. 'Jacob must continue to learn the *texts*.'

'We know the texts by heart,' my father would always reply, jowls wobbling in fear as well as defeat. Finally, he relented, permitting a single flame for a single hour. We'd gather around it, my sister and I, her hair matted, her lips mute, making her mouldy bunny dance to the flame as I laid the book spine on my knees, my eyes squinting at the scratchy scrawl, my mouth whispering the words, my mother and father's eyes closed, their faces locked in rapture, their lips twitching soundlessly along as I read.

After an hour, my father would snuff out the flame between

finger, thumb and saliva and plunge us into darkness once more. He'd tell us of what was to come on the other side, the things we'd see and the glory that awaited us.

Then they came.

To begin with I thought it a dream, dead-float dozing as I was between waking and sleeping. Wood ruptured a few feet away from me, torchlight punching through a few seconds later. We shuffled backwards as a second beam of light invaded the room, painting belongings we hadn't seen properly for months in spiteful hues.

The men at the end of the light spluttered, spitting curses about the stench, and animals, and shit and piss. Their insults had not changed in the time we'd hidden away.

As they spilled into our sanctuary, I realised it had to be winter, such was the thickness of their coats. Torchlight slashed at us, barbed-wire beams lingering on our faces and groping our bodies.

'Is he there?' barked a voice.

Light blistered my eyes, my raised hand doing little to dissuade it.

'A man and woman,' another voice replied. 'A girl and boy.'

'Is he *there*?' the voice insisted.

I felt hands on me, prising my arms away from my face.

The smell of soured milk filled my nostrils. The musk of something curdled. A small grunt of satisfaction.

'He's there,' said the soldier.

Rough hands dragged me from a place I hated but that had until now sheltered us.

'Please,' said my father, '*please*. Let my son go. He's no good to you. Take us, but not him.'

What about Hennie? I wanted to say. *What about her? Is she not your daughter? Is she not your child?* It had always been like this.

I was the Crown Jewels of my father's eye, the justification for our existence. Earthly trifles were an indulgence. My sister was an indulgence.

My eyes fidgeted as we were dragged into the street, the black of the night a kaleidoscope of colours when set against what we'd been pulled from, the street lights crackling with aggression, poking at my skin, violating its pores, digging itself in.

A truck waited at the bottom of the street. The back of it bulged, flesh shapes pressing against its canvas hide. We all knew what it was for. We'd be together, at least. That meant something.

The soldiers yanked my family towards it, a hand on my back guiding me away.

'My son,' my father called out. 'Where are you taking him?'

A rifle butt answered. That was the way these men talked.

Hands spirited me away, firm but delicate, as if I were some sort of priceless antique the soldiers had liberated and didn't want to break.

'I want to go with my family,' I said to myself, to the soldiers, to God.

'No,' the soldier said. 'You don't.'

I asked where they were being taken, already knowing the answer. I wanted him to say it, though, this shaved warthog, this stumpy blob of flesh with a gun, wanted him to own the crime he was committing. Instead he said nothing, funnelling me towards an idling black Mercedes, its exhaust fumes warming themselves against the night air, a layer of frost caressing the vehicle's bonnet and roof.

A man stood on the car's running board. His trench coat was too well cut for him to be a soldier; it could have come from my father's own shop. Expensive-looking circular glasses perched themselves on his pointed, beak-like nose.

He smiled as we approached. No grimace was ever as terrifying.

'It's the one we seek?' he asked, looking past me.

Not him, 'it'.

The warthog soldier nodded, eager to please, or desperate not to displease. 'I've checked his papers. This is the boy.'

The man who wasn't a soldier nodded, reaching into his leather coat and withdrawing a silver cigarette case.

'Herr Himmler will be pleased.'

Minutes seemed like hours and days felt like decades. When we'd been hiding in our shelter, time had lost all meaning, but there had been tent poles to moor myself with. The hour of candle. A meal in the gloom. Habits. Traditions.

In the car, there was nothing. I would wake in a narcotic fog, permission slips of consciousness revealing the blur of a street lamp or the midday haze of fields rolling. I don't know how long we drove for. It could have been hours or days, but one thing was constant: the man in the back seat pressed himself against the window as if I were plague incarnate. The only time he moved was to inject me. I would feel the tip of the needle puncture my vein, narcotics flooding my system, dipping me under the haze.

Eventually the injections became less regular and something like clarity began to return. Trees flanked us, street lamps deserted us. Concrete absconded. *Where are you taking me?* I would ask, my speech slurred, my face dope-slack. The man simply looked away, as if such a question was nonsensical and not worthy of his time or mine.

Then it appeared.

The castle was a scar on the horizon's canvas. Three towers stood guard, the walls that kept them at arm's lengths so mighty it was as if concrete had been poured onto the sky to form them. Its appearance seemed to energise my travelling companion. He sat up straight, his left leg jiggling, pitched on the edge of his seat. 'How fortunate you are, boy. Wewelsburg is a place for the chosen few, not the filthy Jew. That a street rat like you should come here is perverse.'

It wasn't, though. Not when you considered what Wewelsburg was, what it represented, and who I was. When you considered that, Castle Wewelsburg and I were made for each other.

As we pulled up to the courtyard, the car juddering over the castle's blistered cobbles, a man stood waiting for us. He wore the uniform of Nazi royalty but not the bearing. There was a slovenly air to him. Receding greying hair stood up in clumps, and his untucked shirt climbed out from his pressed black britches. His face looked like it was squabbling with itself.

He opened the door, yanking me out without so much as a word of greeting. His gloved hands cupped my face, his shark-black eyes staring hungrily into mine. His leathery fingers creaked as he examined my skull, prodding and poking at it.

'Enough, Wiligut.'

A voice from behind my examiner rang around the courtyard, high-pitched and shrill. The man called Wiligut gave my head a final tap, as if trying to ascertain its hollowness, then stepped reluctantly aside.

My parents had sheltered my sister and myself from the worst of the Nazis' crimes, but there was no shielding a Jew from the likes of Heinrich Himmler. He loomed over everything, a pencil-moustached bogeyman whose existence demanded the end of ours. Hitler was reviled, but Himmler was feared; he was seen as the substance behind the Führer's bilious poison cloud. I never expected to meet him in real life, but real life, it seemed, intended for me to meet him.

He had a parched head, anorexic spectacles resting on a nose of skinny gristle, his face shorn of everything but the barest of features, like they were a luxury his genius didn't have time for. As he stood there waiting for me, the black castle loomed over him like it had been moulded to his exact specifications. I would later learn that it had.

Wiligut shoved me and I stumbled, my legs unconvinced, unpractised as they had become at walking.

Himmler frowned, reaching out a hand and taking my arm, preventing me from falling. 'Your manners do you few favours, Wiligut. Is that any way to treat a guest?'

'I prefer to think of him as a false prophet,' Wiligut replied. 'And will treat him as such.'

Himmler placed an arm around my shoulders, and my stomach lurched in response. 'You'll treat him well, because that's what I order.'

Wiligut trembled slightly, like his disgust was trying to escape.

Himmler crouched down in front of me, his mouth smiling, his eyes not. 'Your name is Jacob Block, is it not?'

I nodded. I saw little point in denying it. 'What do you want from me?'

He smiled.

'Everything.'

They watched as I ate. The act seemed like a betrayal of my family, but my body disagreed; it had received no sustenance for hours (days?), so when the casserole was placed in front of me, my hands moved of their own accord. I had devoured three mouthfuls before looking up to seek permission. Himmler smiled indulgently. Wiligut didn't try to hide his contempt.

'Do you know what we do here, Jacob?'

I shook my head.

430

'Perhaps you would like to explain it?' said Himmler, looking to the older man. 'Karl Wiligut here is the spiritual conscience of our movement. So much of what we've achieved – what you will help us to go on to achieve – is down to him.'

Wiligut peered into his glass of wine, a small smile on his lips. 'The credit belongs to you, Heinrich. My beliefs were there to be embraced by all – only you saw the truth of them.'

Himmler nodded towards me. 'Why don't you tell our young friend here the true history of the Fatherland? It is important, I think, for what comes next.'

Wiligut drank deeply, then replaced the glass on the table. He considered me with his coal-black eyes. 'What do you know of Atlantis?'

I knew little. I told him less.

'German culture – to which your Kike tribe has contributed precisely nothing – can be traced back to 228,000 BC,' he said. 'This was a time when the earth had three suns, and giants walked the sun-blasted earth. I myself am descended from the line of kings who ruled these lands.'

I chanced a look at Himmler, who was staring rapt at his apparent mentor.

'These lands were settled by the survivors of Atlantis, and my people were the best of these survivors, sages who were eventually driven into the wilderness by jealous rivals. In much the same way that your tribe seeks to drive out the true holders of the flame in our blessed country. I can read your mind, you see, little Jacob. It is a fetid, depraved thing, submerged in subterfuge and dishonesty.'

He's insane, I thought. He's either kidding me along, having a joke at my expense, or he's completely insane.

Himmler, though, hung on Wiligut's every word. I had no doubt he'd heard the diatribe on many occasions, but the expression on his face made it seem like he was hearing it for the first time. It was then, as Wiligut continued to rant about dwarves and dragons and telepathy, that I grew truly afraid. Not because I believed what he was saying, but because *he* believed it. And if he – and more importantly, Himmler – believed such ravings, then they would believe what was said about me.

Believe who I was, and what I was destined to become.

On the third day, they took me to the laboratory.

I'd been confined to my room, meals brought to me first thing in the morning and last thing at night, heaps of meat slopped onto plates of exquisite china, each meal feeling like my last. The helpings were so gargantuan when compared to the scraps I'd been used to in the shelter, I felt like a prize pig fattened for the cull. That a soldier sat with me, watching me devour every morsel, only strengthened that feeling.

There wasn't so much as a notebook in the room, so for hours I stared out at the castle's rolling grounds, a barrier of mist lingering at the perimeter, almost as if it were afraid of it. The world I'd left behind was unimaginable, the fate that was to befall my family unthinkable.

'They'll come for us eventually,' my father had said to me the evening before we locked down and hid away. 'It's inevitable. They'll come for us and they'll take us away, but if I can buy us a few weeks, then I will. Why, though, Jacob, will you not be scared when the jackboots finally sound?'

'Because of who I am,' I replied, 'and because of what I will go on to become when I die.'

'Quite right,' said my father, ruffling my hair despite his general distrust of affection. 'Your mother and I would prefer that you live a long and fruitful life before that blessed day, but if the Nazis have other plans, then so be it.'

He pressed a pill into my hand, closing my fist around it. 'I

432

want you to promise me something, if we're taken. Swallow this tablet. Don't hesitate. Don't think about it. It will be painless. It will be quick. It will not be suicide, which would be punishable by the Almighty, but escape. Within five minutes you'll slip away, and paradise will await. Promise me, Jacob.'

I did. It's easy to say yes when no doesn't present itself as an option.

I turned the tablet over so many times, I knew every groove in it, every last grain and indentation. It had been easy to conceal from my captors, and it would be easier still to let it slip down my gullet on a flume of water. It was what my father wanted. What he'd ordered me to do.

I want you to smile when you take that tablet, boy. It will liberate you in a way the living world never will.

I sat on the bed, looking at the tablet, wondering whether that sort of liberation was what I truly wanted.

Then the door was rapped sharply, the handle turned, and my hand made the decision for me, stuffing the pill into the pocket of my trousers.

Himmler stood there, a suit bag in his hand and a leering grin on his face. 'I thought I'd bring you a uniform more appropriate. Your new life starts today, Jacob.'

He slid down the bag's zip, revealing what was inside.

'I won't wear it,' I said, the words out of my mouth before my brain could quarantine them.

The smile on Himmler's face slipped its leash. 'Yes,' he said, 'you will.'

He took a step towards me.

I swallowed, wishing it was to wash the suicide pill down.

Several moments later, I studied myself in the mirror.

I'd seen the uniform of the Hitler Youth before, of course. What had started as a niche concern quickly became aggressively mainstream, members strolling around the school yard like they owned the place, which they did. The star I was forced to wear on my breast made me the juiciest of targets for these thugs. The teachers stepped in to begin with, then didn't. When we were banned from attending school, it was a relief. Certainly, it was to my mother and father. They felt school interfered with my real studies.

What would they say now, if they could see me in my Youth uniform? Thick brown shirt, tie around my neck, swastika wrapped around my arm like a tourniquet?

Endure, is what they'd say. *This life is merely the prelude, an indulgence before your real life truly begins. Wear the uniform. Raise your arm and salute false gods. Take whatever name they give you.*

Tell them nothing.

Protect the Pen.

Chapter 1

Poor but sexy. That was how Ella's dad described Berlin.

Ella wasn't convinced. As far as she could see, poor had sold out long ago, and sexy had always been in the eye of the beholder.

Certainly there wasn't much sex appeal in front of her. SO36 was an embalmed vision of punk rock past. Real effort had gone into making the club look as run-down as possible; it was like an interior designer had asked Alexa to show them weaponised nostalgia, then followed the AI's designs to the letter.

Not that Ella cared particularly. Punk rock had always been her dad's thing (her grandad's too, if the old man's stories were to be believed), and she'd never begrudged him teasing the little hair he'd had left into a blue mohawk. She'd even refrained from taking the piss when he'd bought a new leather jacket then spent the best part of a week making it look like a frayed life partner. Just like everyone else here, he hadn't so much tried to recapture his East German youth as chloroform it.

No one really seemed to be old in society any more; there were kids like her, and there were old-timers in retirement homes waiting to die. Everyone else took a hammer to middle age and pounded it into a smear of youthful mush.

The support band finished their set and the crowd dispersed, making their way towards her vantage point at the bar. She drew a few curious glances, as she'd known she would; she was the youngest person here by about thirty years. It wasn't just her age, though. She was the spitting image of her dad, and half the people here would have known him. Liked him, too, because he'd been that sort of guy. Even his enemies still loved her papa.

Ella shivered, taking a slug of water and noting, not for the first time, the slightly odd atmosphere in the place, the distrustful glances exchanged between the old punks. 'When a city's gutted down the middle like Berlin was, the stitches sewing it back together don't always take,' her dad had told her. 'If elephants never forgot, old punks stubbornly refuse to; defections and perceived betrayals throb still in the city's veins.'

What she'd give to see him again.

That was what tonight was about. The chance to make that crazy dream a reality.

'I knew you'd come.'

She turned to see a punk slouching against the bar. She hadn't noticed him approach, but then in his game she supposed that was a virtue. Certainly it was impressive when you considered his size and general appearance. Green trench coat, a straggling apology of spiked hair. Just another ageing punk in a room full of them.

The difference was Klaus Weber's profession.

'How did you know I'd come?' Ella replied. '*I* didn't know I'd come.'

'Because you loved your dad. Because today would have been his birthday, and there was nowhere he loved more than this place.'

She looked around and shook her head. 'It's like a punk crypt. A fucking rock-and-roll theme park.'

Klaus laughed. 'So cynical. You're a punk, Ella. It's in your blood.'

She took another slug of water. 'Do you have them?'

He clasped his hands together. 'I have one. That's more than enough, believe me.'

'I'm no lightweight,' said Ella.

'This isn't coke or ket. This is a medical-grade drug that doesn't officially exist.'

'For something that doesn't exist, an awful lot of people seem to know about it.'

'An awful lot of people talk shit,' said Klaus. 'I'm the only supplier in the city. You wouldn't have a chance of buying from me if it wasn't for your dad.'

'Will it work? Will I see him?'

'It'll work all right. Whether you'll see him depends on whether he's here or not.'

'If he's going to be anywhere, he's going to be here,' said Ella. 'It was his favourite place in the world. How much?'

Klaus told her. Ella considered the amount daylight robbery.

She was bathed in the light of night, though, so she paid the money and took delivery of the bright pink pill.

She threw it down her throat, chasing it with a slug of water.

Now all she had to do was wait.

It was called Spook and if it was a party pill, the Day of the Dead festival was its spiritual home.

The rumours about it had started a couple of months ago. About how taking it allowed you to see the dead. You didn't split it, and you didn't take more than one. Ella had been cynical – since that girl blew up Tokyo, *everyone* claimed they could see the dead – but ultimately, curiosity had drowned her cynicism.

Desperation, too. It was a year to the day since her dad had died, which meant it was a year to the day that a big part of her had died, too. If this drug was legit, it meant she could see him again. Talk to him. Let him know how much she missed him. When she'd discovered his favourite band were playing at his favourite club on what would have been his sixtieth birthday, well, she'd seen it as a sign.

A murmur went up from the crowd, one that hinted that within minutes the lights would dip, the band would come on stage and the real world would be forgotten for a while. That appealed to Ella. The real world hadn't been working out so well for her lately. Her school grades were in the toilet, and her mum was constantly on her case. It was like her mum didn't miss her dad at all. Like all she could do was sweat the unimportant stuff.

She looked around the club. Everyone here was old, but they were pretty visibly not dead. They were supposed to glimmer, ghosts. That was what people who'd dropped Spook said online, anyway. Not much glimmer here, just manufactured dirt and grime.

The track pumping over the venue's speakers came to an end.

The lights dimmed.

Here we fucking go.

The band took the stage.

Colonel, the frontman and lead guitarist, stood, arms aloft, a returning general soaking up the acclaim of his grateful subjects. Ella could never quite make her mind up about Colonel – he was either the coolest dude around or one you wanted to beat to death – but her dad always said that was the point of a good frontman. You didn't want them to be like you. *You* were boring, and you came to gigs to escape boring.

Ella swallowed. Nothing doing with the pill, yet.

'We are the people!' Colonel bellowed into the microphone. 'We are the power!'

The chant was taken up by the crowd, who pressed in closer to the stage.

A techie handed Colonel a guitar. Feedback rang around the room.

The first chords were struck in fury.

Then it began to happen.

It was like Ella had something in the corner of her eye. A shimmering blur of light, just outside her range of sight. The more she squinted, the blurrier it got. Then it solidified a little.

There was someone on stage with the band who wasn't the band.

She could tell that by the way they glimmered. Couldn't tell much besides that, at least not yet, but it was like there was a hologram up there on stage. A glitchy-as-fuck one.

Ella's throat was dry. She lifted her bottle of beer, frowning when she realised it was empty. She needed another drink. That would settle her down a bit.

She backwards-shuffled towards the bar, her eyes fixed on the stage. The figure on it was gaining clarity by the second. Whoever it was, they were short.

No.

Could it be him? It was what the rumours always said, of course, but she'd never really believed them. She just liked the fact they were there to believe.

Where was her dad? She'd been so sure he'd be here. Instead, she'd got an urban myth.

She called out her dad's name, more in desperation than expectation.

People were looking at her strangely.

'What are you drinking?'

Ella turned reluctantly away from the stage, realising she'd backed all the way up to the bar.

She blinked.

This couldn't be real.

A man was standing behind the bar. He had an old Stones T-shirt on, a pair of beaten-looking grey jeans and a shock of flame-coloured hair teased into a blizzard of spikes. So far so punk, but he also glimmered. And that was where the horror began, not ended: his face was covered with green vines. One had popped clean through his eyeball. Others wound their way out of his mouth.

'What are you drinking?' the flame-coloured vine man asked again.

Ella staggered away, knocking into the gig-goers around her, drawing looks of irritation she didn't notice.

Her throat got drier. Felt like it was tightening, too.

She stumbled, her knees going, the floor coming. She smacked against it, hard. A mosh pit had formed in front of her. Most people hadn't noticed her fall, but a couple had. They had the same vines as the man at the bar. A woman with a mane of them flowing down her back. A man with them wound tightly round his fists like a boxing glove.

Half the man's face seemed to be missing.

Ella began to scream, and found that once she'd started, it was difficult to stop.